'This is an outstanding novel, made
status. I loved it, from the first page to the end. Finely textured, deftly
woven, it evokes – with confidence and a rare beauty – late eighteenth
century England and France. The scene-setting is perfect, and laced
with rich, juicy details. The dialogue is period-convincing, and spoken
by meaty, believable characters: Cook and Derrien to name but two.
Hazzard is a tortured hero par excellence, a mixture of conscience,
courage and martial skill, a man who can fall victim to arrogance and
even cruelty.

'Better than Sharpe, gripping and intense, *Napoleon's Run* deserves
to be a runaway success'

Ben Kane, *Sunday Times* bestselling author of *Lionheart*

'*Hornblower* meets *Mission: Impossible*. A thrilling, page-turning debut
packed with rousing, rip-roaring action'

J. D. Davies, author of the Matthew Quinton Journals

'This book has it all. Combines great action with really good history,
and an engaging and original character in Marine officer William
Hazzard, who adds a satisfying dash of the swashbuckling Bombay
Buccaneers to some solid scholarship. In many ways this captures the
true – and surprisingly subversive nature – of early British imperialism'

Seth Hunter, author of the Nathan Peake novels

'A strong, fast-moving story by an author with a deep knowledge of
the period and the narrative skill of a fine story-teller'

Andrew Swanston, author of *Waterloo*

'This book has a rich cast of characters who will delight, enthral and
keep you turning the pages to the very end. A brilliant, thrilling read,
with a new – and very believable – hero. This is my favourite historical
novel of the year so far'

Michael Jecks, author of the Last Templar Mysteries

'Hugely atmospheric, *Napoleon's Run* by Jonathan Spencer offers a fascinating evocation of the sights, sounds and smells of the Napoleonic Wars. Thanks to an extraordinary attention to detail and accuracy, it paints a vivid and realistic picture of life on board ship, striking the perfect balance between a thoroughly absorbing history lesson and a thumping good read.

'Packed to the gunwales with action, this fast-paced story is also a very thoughtful thriller filled with intrigue and suspense. Leading a crew of wonderfully-drawn characters, Hazzard is not only a convincing action hero, but also one who offers a timeless insight into loyalty, trust and honesty'

Chris Lloyd, author of *The Unwanted Dead*

'A great read! Well-tempered and well-researched, with well-drawn, well-conceived characters who will, I am sure, be with us for a while'

Rob Low, author of *The Lion Wakes*

Hazzard's Convoy

Jonathan Spencer is from south-east London, the great-grandson of a clipper-ship captain who brought tea from China. He served in the Canadian army, studied ancient and modern history, and has lectured at universities and private associations on the subject of Napoleonic Egypt. He writes historical non-fiction under the name Jonathan Downs, his major work a revised account of the British acquisition of the Rosetta Stone, *Discovery at Rosetta*, (London 2008; Cairo 2020). He speaks several languages, has trained with the former Russian National fencing coach, and has lived and worked abroad all his life. He currently lives in the Western Cape in South Africa.

Also by Jonathan Spencer

The William John Hazzard series

JONATHAN SPENCER

HAZZARD'S CONVOY

CANELO

First published in the United Kingdom in 2024 by

Canelo
Unit 9, 5th Floor
Cargo Works, 1–2 Hatfields
London SE1 9PG
United Kingdom

A CIP catalogue record for this book is available from the British Library.

Print ISBN 978 1 80436 145 0
Ebook ISBN 978 1 80436 144 3

Cover design by kid-ethic

Cover images © Shutterstock; Istock

Look for more great books at www.canelo.co

Printed and bound in Great Britain by Clays Ltd, Elcograf S.p.A.

1

For R.F.

'The army is at half its strength… disease is prevalent, and the soldiers are in rags…When Bonaparte sailed, he did not leave a penny in the till, nor any cash equivalent. On the contrary, he left a deficit of almost 10 million… The soldiers' pay in arrears accounts for 4 million alone. […] He saw the fatal crisis approaching.'

Général en chef Jean-Baptiste Kléber
to French Directory Government
Venémiaire, An VIII
October 1799

Prologue

The saddle hammered beneath him, the thud of the galloping hooves beating in his chest as they charged through the scrub, the Arabian dodging the straggling boughs of desiccated trees, leafless limbs so many skeletal fingers snagging at his flying cloak. His two aides Leclerc and Duval leading an escort of dragoon guards just behind, *Général de division* Jean-Baptiste Kléber roared in anger, '*Vite, vite!*' Faster!

Far ahead he could see the lights of Rosetta, riverboats sliding downstream, trading *djerms* and *feluccas* drifting in the cooling breeze, lanterns swaying. Heavy with stars, the warm black skies faded to indigo as they touched the deep, darker seas of Odysseus and Poseidon beyond, somehow more ominous and threatening to Kléber tonight than ever before.

Kléber had heard the rumour: of the late-night gathering in the palace grounds in Cairo; of carriages and notables, and that Fourès girl once again dressed as a damned Hussar to escape notice – *Would he take his blasted mistress as well?* – of Monge and Berthollet and their hasty withdrawal from a lecture at the *Institut d'Égypte*, all to join Bonaparte as he plotted to slip into the night. The anger drove him onwards to his rendezvous with the great conqueror: how would Bonaparte explain himself? *How?* And part of him relished the confrontation to come.

He saw the firelight of a checkpoint ahead and shouted over his shoulder, '*To me!*' The escort of dragoons swept in tightly behind him, the dust rising with the staccato tattoo of their hoofbeats on the hard road, Captain Leclerc calling loud and clear, *Kléber! Make way for the general! Make way!* The guardsmen stumbled from a wooden hut, scrambling to drag the makeshift gate to one side, *Le général! Le général!*

Their sweating faces waxen in the flicker of burning braziers, Kléber and his escort clattered past, up the road to the centre of the port. The horses' hooves echoing among the darkened houses, they shot along the torchlit promenade by the Nile beneath a line of tall palms, sentries saluting, Aboukir Bay spread out beside them, leading out to the dark Mediterranean stretching to an endless black horizon.

They reached the *Quartier général* HQ, sentries calling out, soldiers scattering to clear a path. Even as he slowed, Kléber cast an eye about for Bonaparte's horses, his carriages – *None* – and was filled with a darkening rage. Jean-Baptiste Kléber was every soldier's ideal warrior: tall, broad-shouldered, fearless and brilliant, with a booming voice that could carry across a battlefield in the midst of an apocalyptic barrage. He leapt from the saddle, a trooper taking the bridle, his aides beside him as they strode across the quad of the old *maison de maître*. '*Where?*' he shouted. 'Where is the *général en chef?*'

Torchlight flickering in the onshore winds, guardsmen crashed to attention and slammed back the main doors for his thunderous entry. He threw off his cloak for an orderly sergeant to catch and called out, 'Well! Where is he!'

They passed lamplit offices, adjutant clerks and NCOs looking up, agog, getting to their feet, fearful Mamluk administrators standing in the doorways, bowing deeply as Kléber roared by: although Sultan *al-Kebir* was gone, here was the true Sultan of Fire. A young *sous-lieutenant* clerical officer appeared hesitantly at the end of the white-washed corridor, the all-pervasive smells of wax polish and sweet, steaming date and tomato couscous hanging in the stale air. The boy snapped a bow, his heels clacking together. '*Mon général.*' He held out his hand to indicate a glazed door opposite. Kléber stopped and looked. It was an office, a lamp glowing inside. 'Well? Where is he?'

'Answer the general!' snapped Captain Leclerc. The young subaltern swallowed nervously but said nothing, his hand wavering, his eyes closing briefly in apprehension. Kléber snatched at the scrolled brass door handle and looked inside. Beneath a suspended lantern casting a dull glow, he found only a single chair and a table – bare but for a thick leather-bound dossier.

'The *général en chef*,' stammered the subaltern. 'He said... to leave this, *mon général.*'

Kléber entered and looked down at the dossier, the *sous-lieutenant* backing away. '*Excusez-moi,*' he said, and disappeared behind Leclerc and Duval. Duval turned. 'Wait,' he called. 'Where is the *Général en chef* Bonaparte? What— *Zut alors...*' But the clerk had gone.

Kléber opened the dossier. The top sheet was a letter, addressed to him – and signed at the bottom simply '*Bonaparte*'. He could not believe his eyes.

> 'My dear General... Cambyses, Xerxes, Alexander the Great, Amr, and Selim I entered Egypt through the Gaza Desert as did we... The plague is one of the army's most redoubtable foes... remember that Mecca is the centre of Islam and do not lose sight of the fact that Alexandria must eventually become the capital of Egypt... I shall remain with you in spirit and in heart... I shall regard as ill-spent every day in my life that I do not do something for the army which I leave in your comm—'

Kléber threw back his head and roared. The glazing in the doors rattled and the men in the offices beyond shrank back in alarm. Kléber stared at the page, the paper shaking. '*By God!* That *bugger* leaves us,' he rasped, turning to Leclerc and Duval, waving the page at them. 'He leaves us with his breeches full of *shit!*' He slammed his fist into the table and it jumped. 'We'll go back to Europe *and rub them in his bloody face!*'

'Leave us...?' Leclerc did not understand. 'The *général en chef*?' He took the letter from Kléber.

They turned at the clop of stamping hooves coming to a halt in the quad, steel-shod boots running, and a call rising, *Out of the way, make way there!* Kléber stormed out of the office to see a breathless despatch rider hurrying through the main door. 'General... Major Dupuy, 2nd Cavalry – news from Aboukir. The *général en chef* ...' he began, then threw his arms out in despair. 'He is *gone.*'

'Gone? But... where?' demanded Duval, glancing at them.

Crushed, incredulous, Leclerc handed Duval the note.

'Run home!' exclaimed Kléber, forcing the words through clenched teeth. 'Back to France! He has abandoned *every* man in the army...' He looked at the rider. 'When? Where?'

'I heard from the command post at the fort not above an hour ago, *mon général*. Boats went out from a beach near Alex. There was shouting, some said there were shots – they sent a detachment to investigate, but reports were confused – local Arabs spoke of Milord Mamluk trying to stop him, but—'

'The Englishman? *Here?*' said Duval. 'He lives?'

Major Dupuy removed his shako and put a hand through his damp hair. 'They say General Marmont and Menou knew about it. Even that fool, that… that Institute *poet* Grandmaison splashed into the water, calling after the last boat to get aboard, the *savants*, the chiefs…' He shook his head. 'They have all left us, *mon général.*'

There was silence in the room. Then Duval turned to Kléber. 'What was it for – *what?* Mount Tabor, Acre! Jaffa! Thousands *dead…*'

Kléber moved past the rider, looking out through the main doors into the darkness, the Mamluk clerks ducking behind their office doors to avoid the sultan's anger. Kléber saw none of them, but stared far out to the lights of Aboukir, perhaps as if to see the ship that had taken Bonaparte. The smoke of battle on Aboukir beach had barely cleared from a month earlier, when he had driven his men down to crush the Turks, crowded on a defenceless beachhead – Bonaparte's tactics brilliant, General Murat charged into the tent of Mustafa Pasha and captured him at the point of the sword. Kléber had hugged the diminutive conqueror in exultation. *But now?*

That petty, private, selfish man.

He felt the tremors in his fists, of their first landings, of Nelson, of the loss of the fleet, the marches, the battles. 'What do you say then, *mes braves…?*' he murmured, men of the guard gathering in the front quad, looking in, disturbed, anxious. 'Perhaps he has gone home to save us, to make them see what we have done, hm?'

They looked to one another hopefully, and Kléber knew this was what he would face among the thousands he now commanded.

'Very well.' He strode down the corridor towards them. 'We have won too much honour here,' he shouted, 'torn a path through the pages of history – made even Alexander the Great a mere *ghost* of this damnable desert! While those who were here will remember *our* days, and speak of *us. And no man more shall suffer!*'

The men in the door stepped back, coming to attention, and he burst into the quad through the ranks as they called, *Vive le général, vive le général*, a cry once meant for Bonaparte, but no more, for this was Kléber, victor of the Holy Land, saviour of the army: the Man of Iron. He called to Leclerc and Duval, 'Where is *Chef* Caron? Where are the Alphas?'

Leclerc shook his head. 'We have heard nothing – he was to do thirty days, after Acre, by order of the *général en chef*, but…' He looked

4

at Duval, aghast. 'I have seen no release – could he be there still? After all this time?'

Kléber stared down at him, his anger rendered to a whisper. '*Where?*'

Leclerc looked out to the water beyond, and Rosetta's half-built fortress commanding the mouth of the Nile, then remembered. '*Merde alors…*' He mounted his horse, gathering the rein. 'Over there, *mon général*, the *sapeurs* took men on field punishment to construct Fort Jullien – under Menou's orders…'

Kléber looked out at the torchlit structure. '*Menou* again. *Ma foi*, the best bloody men digging damned holes,' cursed Kléber, turning his mount. 'I want them out *now*. On me.'

–

The crumbling medieval tower of the *Burj al-Rashid* lay now in heaps of dusty yellow stone, some of it sorted into piles of rubble and reclaimed blocks of masonry, much of it already incorporated into the modern, four-cornered, slab-sided fortress now standing in its place. Its low sloping ramparts rose to a patrolled parapet running the perimeter of the walls; behind and just below this was a sheltered inner walkway, joining the bastion corners, a large central square forming the fortress within. Vaulted eight-foot-high round-arched niches lined the walk, some packed with stores, others with arms, munitions or building tools – these served two arrowhead bastion corners and two round turrets, one of them as yet unfinished, the works delayed by the *savant* archaeologists.

Inside the cavernous interior of the large unfinished corner turret, among the debris and straw fodder stalls intended for pack animals, were some sixty soldiers, petty criminals, drunkards, brawlers: some were true *misérables*, wretched army labourers on some greater charge from France, obliged to dig for their sins – but most were unruly troops on field punishment duty, in tatters of uniform, some barefoot, all lying among mouldering straw in open pens.

On the arched doorway into the turret room was an improvised set of barred gates, to the old soldiers inside their only reminder they were in gaol. A central brazier still glowed from its use for dinner, its heat dissipating to the open skies above, for there was not yet a roof: the soaring twenty-foot-high turret walls reached upwards, open joist ports far above dark with the night, ready for the new floors and ceilings in the days to come. It was summer, and although the night brought a cooling breeze, it was still warm enough that men could look up at the stars above, and not feel the inclement chill of captivity.

Pleiny, a short, fat *caporal-chef* of the 9th *demi*, waddled past the gates and rattled his keyring as he did every morning before dawn. 'Hey hey, *Chef*, psst, you asleep, *hein*? Today you are mine again, eh, eh?' He laughed, a dry hiss, so much hot air escaping a bladder.

Sergent-chef Achille Caron, *chef-major* of the 75th Invincibles, veteran of the Indies and Americas, of Lodi and the Adige, saviour of Bonaparte at Arcole Bridge in Italy, opened a dark and drowsy eye and peered round slowly from his comfortable bed of straw. Little did the well-fed Corporal Pleiny understand, old Caron was quite happy in his stall, a reminder of his long-forgotten farm in Aix-en-Provence, which he had left thirty-five years earlier, musket in hand, to fight for his king.

Beside him, the best of the *Alpha-Oméga*, the dread *chasseurs à pied* skirmish platoon, 'the First the enemy sees and the Last' – so named by an Austrian officer in Italy after a handful of them had put an entire company to flight. The grubby and rarely shaven Gaston Rossy, the bespectacled long-shot St Michel with his prized Austrian rifle, and the scarred young Antonnais, survivors of battles untold, looked back at Pleiny as well. A hump among the straw shifted, as if there were an earthquake, and the giant Pigalle rolled over, an enormous boot pushing the paddock rail of the stall till it leaned away from his bulk with a groan. Pleiny and the guards had heard Pigalle could break a Charleville 1777 musket in two with his bare hands. His smile faded.

'Perhaps, Pleiny,' whispered Rossy, 'this morning you will have that terrible fall I predicted some weeks ago, hm? The one where *M'sieur* le Pig here does not catch you and instead puts a block of stone upon your head, *oui*?'

Pleiny gulped. He puffed out his chest. 'You are on the *péloton*! Lucky, you are, hm? *Lucky*. They said it was murder at Acre – and you should have been *shot*.' His courage began to fail him as Rossy looked back at him. 'You do as *I* command now, *m-m'sieur*…' but his heart clearly was not in it.

'Just bring me a little breakfast at eight,' sighed Rossy, pursing his lips with a slight frown. 'The boiled egg, I think – no, first the ham, then the Turkish curry, ah *putain*, what do they call it, *delicious*, you agree, *Chef*?'

Caron nodded indulgently, as he always was with Rossy. 'But of course.'

'And do not burn those little rolls with the butter baked inside, hm?'

Pleiny stiffened. 'You mock me – I know, you *mock* me. I am *not* stupid,' he stated slowly. 'But you shall see... You'll see I shall not be spoken to in—'

The crash of marching boots from the torchlit passages beyond and protesting voices reached Chief Corporal Pleiny. He turned to see a formation of officers marching down the north walk towards him, the equally fat Sergeant Poignard sweatily trying to catch them up, his fat cheeks puffing with the effort. When Pleiny recognised Kléber storming towards him he gave a look of stark terror, then threw himself to attention, staggering backwards and banging into the stone pillar by the gate hinge. Caron looked round and sat up.

'Open up, you fool!' shouted Captain Leclerc as they approached. 'Get those men out of there at once! By order of the *général en chef*!'

Pleiny looked from one to the other as the stone-faced dragoons descended upon him. 'B–but I... I do not underst—'

Poignard caught up, fumbling with his keys. 'Open the gate for the general, Pleiny!'

Kléber was now within twenty feet. '*Now!*'

Rossy picked up a stray sliver of wood from the floor and snapped it. At once, Pigalle was awake, the old alert-signal rousing him instantly, snorting awake, one huge hand reaching automatically for the musket that was not there. 'Rossy...?' Antonnais woke St Michel and they watched the barred gate as Pleiny rattled at the lock with his keys, Kléber looming.

'Achille!' boomed Kléber. 'What by God are you lazing in there for?'

Caron struggled to his feet. 'Orders, *mon général*, for letting Citizen Derrien be killed.' He shrugged. 'A small price to pay for the soul of the world.'

Pleiny's key unlocked the gate and Kléber shoved him through it, the little corporal staggering and falling back against the wall as the towering general marched in, Leclerc and Duval behind shouting at the erstwhile gaoler, 'On your feet, oaf! Name? Rank? Report!' Sergeant Poignard nearly fainted beside Pleiny.

A *chef de bataillon* hurried in from behind, dragged from his bed, hastily buttoning his tunic. 'But, General, the papers, Citizen Peraud, on orders from the *Bureau d'information*—'

Kléber wheeled on him. '*Who?*'

The Adam's apple of the *chef de bataillon* bobbed and quavered. 'In-in lieu of the *conseil militaire*…' He held out a sheet of paper. 'Acts of… of… of *treason*, of the fraternising and aiding the enemy in the field… Allowing enemies of the state to escape—'

'Enemies! *Putain de merde,*' swore Rossy. 'They were *peasants*, escaping our guns, and the *merde* grenadiers, *con stupide*…'

The *chef de bataillon* gawked with effrontery and looked to Kléber for support, but the general glared at him thunderously. He then looked about, at the walls, up at the ceiling. 'This,' he asked him, 'to pay for the swine Derrien?'

The *chef de bataillon* gulped. Caron shrugged. 'Château d'If was worse.'

Kléber turned to their gaolers, Poignard, Pleiny and all. 'They are hereby released. Is that clear?'

But the *chef de bataillon* was adamant. 'Th-they are my labourers! T-to build the fort! As attested by the *conseil militaire*, by—'

Kléber turned as if to seize him by his tunic front and lift him bodily from the ground. 'Have you *any* idea, Major, who these men are? These are the Alpha-Omega, of the 75th *Invincibles*. You *fool*. Consider the Citizen's prosecution overturned. *Expunged. Is that understood.*'

Pigalle at last rose to full height in the glow of the brazier, Rossy before him, arms folded, waiting. The *chef de bataillon* blinked and looked at Pigalle, then nodded vehemently. 'Y-yes, of course, *mon général*, I…' He backed away as Caron and the others moved. '*Chef* Caron, you are released… W-we shall send the papers to…'

Kléber ignored him and began to march off, Caron at his side, Leclerc and Duval bringing up the rear behind the other Alphas, leaving Poignard, Pleiny and the *chef de bataillon* at the open gates, grateful for their departure. Within moments, the *chef de bataillon* began shouting at Poignard, and Poignard at Pleiny.

They marched down the walkways of the fort, heels echoing. 'How many are you now, *Tartuf*?' said Kléber.

It was the old nickname Kléber always used for him – 'truffle' – from the day Caron had saved his wounded officer from a barrage by

8

digging a hole in an autumn wood and covering him with his body. Caron nodded. 'Not many. These are my best anyway.'

Kléber did not mince words. 'He left us, Achille. Went home, ran away… the little *shit*.'

Caron took a slow, deep breath. 'We heard the stories…' Caron had his own views on Napoléon Bonaparte, but did not want to argue with the big man. 'What do we do, General?'

'I want the men out of here.' Kléber knew Caron would understand. He looked down at the stocky old sergeant-major as they marched side by side. 'We're going home, Achille.'

Caron took a moment, then nodded. '*Eh bien*,' he said with a sigh. He had been in such a situation several times: in the Americas, on the Rhine, in Italy. 'We shall need an officer *parliamentaire*,' said Caron, 'to represent our interests to the English.'

The balmy air sizzling with the tang of flaming torches, Kléber reached the end of the passage and paused while a sentry opened a wooden gate. The general let Caron go through first. 'After Acre, I can think of only one.'

They filed through and went outside, Pigalle glowering at the sentry, who shrank back into the shadows. The fresh air of Rosetta washing over him, Caron looked out to sea at the British ships on patrol, distant lanterns on heavily armed broadsides, possibly scenting blood in the water: there was only one man he would trust. '*Oui, mon général. L'anglais.*'

Caron would have to find William John Hazzard.

Capture

The sands glowed cold in the pre-dawn darkness, a freshening sea breeze blowing in from the shores of nearby Marabout, the desert beyond reflecting a dull gleam of white starlight. The shredded leaves of palms high above thrashed and hissed in the wind, disturbing the silence.

Two sentries of the 3rd battalion of the 86th *demi-brigade de bataille* stood before a rough gateway in a dilapidated paddock-rail fence, the posts and lower rails half-submerged in drifting sand. Torchlight cast their deep, dancing shadows down an old roadway cleared between the low humped dunes, leading away into the darkness, now softened into drifts. From time to time the guards looked out, watching the movement of the sloping sand, hissing and sighing in the wind. Their voices were low, bored; there was little to see at this unused gate. The camp spread out far behind them, reaching almost to the shore, so many rudimentary huts built onto a handful of shattered adobe cottages, bleached army tents in neat rows between, horses stamping behind rough-hewn rails far to one side.

One of the men blew into his hands for want of something to do. He looked back at the hut behind them, at the light of the two tall torches, perhaps wishing they were inside, with drink, with cards. When he looked back out to the desert, it seemed different, but the undulating dunes remained blank, impassive. The buckles on his musket sling clinking loud in the silence, the other produced a pouch of tobacco, his special *hashish* mix to fight the boredom. But his eyes flicked to the lonely lane leading into the glowing desert, into the endless nothing. Something was out there.

They both flinched at the sound of a sharp slap and a crash from within the hut behind them, a muffled shout. They exchanged glances, one of them sniggering. The hut they were guarding was originally a clerical office for logging supplies received and supplies transported; it had grown, with additions, into a broad *Bedu* structure supported by struts, hanging rugs, curtains and canvas, offering separate chambers.

In one of these chambers, beyond the curtains to keep out the flies and blowing sand, was Citizen Juan-José Peraud of the *Bureau d'information*. Born of a Spanish mother, so he had been told, he had sought all his life to assert his Gallic heritage, and had changed his names to Jean-Joseph. More even than his previous superior Jules-Yves Derrien, Peraud had learned how to burrow secretly under his enemies and bring them down. By so doing he had neatly avoided the Syrian campaign of the previous year and remained behind, in Derrien's place in Cairo, and fortified his own authority. It had been a wise choice. Both Derrien and his erstwhile deputy Blais had not returned. Peraud had not mourned, and became the new Collector and Chief of Counter-Intelligence.

Wiping flecks of saliva from the corner of his mouth, he put his hands on a rickety table and leaned over a frail, shivering and bloodied figure being helped back into his chair by two unhappy and exhausted soldiers in stained shirtsleeves, one of them wiping his hands, seeing blood on his breeches, cursing, '*Ah putain, alors...*'

'*What of the Ottoman fleet?*' screamed Peraud persistently. 'Where is it *gone*? Where does it *combine*? Chios, Samos? Marathounda, Marmorice? Where, where, *where*?'

The civilian, in sodden twisted collar, torn coat and cravat, tufts of white hair at his temples matted and dishevelled, his bruised and cut cheeks marked with blood from back-handed blows, shook his head, trembling. 'I am... clerk, *m-m'sieur*... I... I only go... *Athinai*... Athens...'

'Lies! Lies, lies, *lies*.' Peraud slammed his fist on the aged table and it shook. He stood back, getting his breath. Short of torture, it was the simplest of interrogation techniques: constant repetitive contradiction, forcing the victim to bow to pressure from their own desire to tell the truth. It worked with the weaker mind. If it did not succeed, the only conclusions were either that the victim was indeed telling the truth, or that they were stronger than supposed. Torture would then begin – and everyone cracked, knew Peraud. Derrien had taught him so.

Peraud had admired Derrien, the late Citizen *Croquemort* – the 'Mortician' – he had known him for only some months. He had been a legend in Paris, and Derrien had inspired him to pursue duty and self-preservation only in the interests of the Revolution and the People.

Derrien's semantics had allowed Peraud a clear conscience, regardless of his brutality. He had adopted Derrien's severe style: the black frock-coat, the black cocked hat and cockade. However, he had adopted more than this from the dread Citizen *Croquemort*.

'A *clerk*,' he spat. 'Then you *write*?'

The little man shrank in the chair, confused. 'Wh-what? I... Y-yes...!'

Peraud surged forward, seizing his wrist. 'Which hand?'

'Wh-what!'

'*Which hand?* Left? Or right? *Aristera i dexia?*' he screamed in rough Greek. He leaned over him and shouted, '*Left or right, damn you?*'

'I... I do not understand—'

Peraud screamed at the two soldiers, 'Take his hands! Take them both!'

At first the soldiers did not understand, but one of them had been detailed to such duties before and took a deep steadying breath. '*Ah, merde alors...*' He grasped the clerk's shaking right hand, his comrade the other.

'On the *table*,' demanded Peraud, turning to stoop by a chair. '*Now!*'

Reluctantly, they pressed the man's hands flat on the tabletop. They heard the scrape of steel in a scabbard and Peraud turned, bringing down a short heavy Turkish *kilij* sword onto the table with a crash, mere inches from the outstretched fingers. '*Cyprus!*' He brought it down again. '*Naxos!*' Again. '*Rhodos!*' Again, the table flying with splinters, the blade embedded deep enough that he needed to wrench it free with enraged frustration, the soldiers struggling to keep the gibbering clerk still, the blade coming down again. '*Crete!*'

The old man cried out and managed to pull his hands through the soldiers' perspiring grip. 'I know nothing of ships!' he wept. 'I... I am clerk! For court in Athens... is all!' Mixed with Greek, his French was broken but comprehensible to them.

One of the soldiers shrugged to Peraud. '*M'sieur*... He is little, what can he—'

'I am not *monsieur, damn you!*' raged Peraud. 'I am *Citizen* Peraud! We have only *Citizens* in the Republic! Do as I command! Out here,' he cried, '*I AM the Republic!*'

The soldiers stiffened at this. Only one man had ever said that in their hearing. Citizen Peraud was truly the *Croquemort* reborn.

At the front of the tent, the sentries stopped chewing, their eyes on the undulating dunes. Nothing had changed, yet, still, *something* had. Perhaps it was the knowledge of Peraud and his brutality behind them, or the *hashish*-fuelled depths of the desert before them. Something on the cleared road had somehow changed. They stared. They were not wrong. The sands began to shift.

A small flare of firelight leapt in the distance. They peered into the dark: a fizzing ball of sparks shot along the length of the cleared road towards them, hissing and spitting through the sand. A low hump in the cleared path began to swell, followed by two others, one either side. They grew larger, the sparking fuse still speeding towards them. One of the sentries began to gasp, his mouth opening, but he had little time.

The three expanding masses of sand burst in clouds, to reveal three men: in the centre, in dark *Bedu* turban and *shemagh*, sleeveless scarlet jerkin open at the throat, a band of four dull white chevrons strapped round his bare arm, was Marine Sergeant Jory Cook, his face striped black and yellow with chalk and soot. On his left, the hulking shoulders of London boxer Arthur Napier, and on the right, the scarred, bearded figure of Sergeant Jeremiah Underhill. His voice gave a dry dusty chuckle.

'*Evenin*', lads.'

The low dunes erupted behind him, more men exploding into view, as two *Bedu* arrows whistled from the desert and buried themselves deep in the sentries, catching one in the throat, the other in the chest. Eyes bulging, mouth still full of chewing tobacco, the first collapsed choking, clawing at his neck, his back arched, the second man snatching at the arrow shaft in his breast as if for support, his knees buckling, and fell, staring out at the night, arms stiff. The fuse fizzed and snapped past the bodies and parted in three directions, fanning out and streaking to the distant quarters of the camp.

Tariq of the al-Kalbi and Marine Private Hesse, dressed in his *galabeyyah* and *Bedu* boots, sprinted for the bodies, stooped, broke off the arrow shafts, and dragged them away to the broken fence, concealing them in the sand. That completed, Hesse gave a nod to Cook and hissed '*Psst!*' The remaining marines followed them on their run into the camp. It was then that a French soldier staggered half-drunk from the hut.

Tugging at the buttons on his falls, the soldier turned to relieve himself in the sand – and saw Cook, Underhill and Napier. He stopped dead, his eyes wide, breeches dropping to his knees.

'*Ah, shite,*' muttered Cook.

As one, Cook, Napier and Underhill put their heads down and charged the man at the entrance. The combined weight of the three biggest men of the Special Landing Squadron crashed into the soldier and carried him through the fabric wall, snapping the guy-ropes, sending struts flying, the hides and rugs collapsing all about them as they ploughed through the debris – just as the three burning quick-match fuses found their targets, and the charges exploded.

The earth shook with a heavy *whump*, then again, and again. The newly landed and sorted powder stores went up in a towering white cloud, musket cartridges banging, kegs bursting, one explosion after the other, as smoke belched from the burning animal fodder and grain store. Men poured from the tent-lines, their clothes and hair alight, their screams mingling with shouts for order, the corralled horses whinnying with fright and stampeding over meagre wattle barriers.

Peraud spun away just as the flimsy hide-and-strut wall flew to pieces, the two French soldiers of the 86th *demi* launched backwards as Cook and Napier crashed straight through the partition, Underhill behind. Cook took the head of the first of Peraud's infantrymen, wrenching left, then right, and dropped him dead. Napier's broad hands reached for Peraud. Peraud scrabbled his way out from under the demolition, his hand seeking the slim smallsword at his waist, the heavy hides and rugs of the ceiling and back walls collapsing upon them all, the sounds of mayhem and of exploding powder barrels ringing in his ears. He ran for his life, Napier hard on his heels. '*Hoi…! Come 'ere, you!*'

Underhill snatched up the unconscious clerk and threw him over his shoulders. '*Got him, Cookie!*'

Cook bellowed to Napier, '*Arthur! Out!*'

Napier burst into the cool night, the remains of the tent collapsing behind him. The camp was in chaos, the black sky leaping with fiery clouds from two separate powder stores on the far left and right, tinder-dry trees and palisades burning fiercely. A red-faced French soldier in pale blue came running, stopped before them, frightened eyes wide, his musket levelled. Napier seized the long Charleville by the barrel and yanked it upwards. '*Give us that 'ere, you!*' It fired harmlessly into the air, and Napier smacked the butt into the soldier's head with a crack.

Cook staggered out from under the fallen tent roof, holding open an exit for Underhill. '*Arthur! Leave it, Christ almighty, boy!*'

Underhill ran out, the dazed Athenian clerk a silent deadweight. '*Don't think he's with us no more, Cookie...!*'

'*Just give us yer ruddy lock, 'Miah!*'

Underhill tossed him his sawn-off musket – one under each arm, Cook cocked the pair, and they began to run.

Three lines of white tents stretched down to the rising shoreline dunes shielding them from the beach beyond, clumps of palm and thickets of foliage once dark in the night now lit with garish colour by the flames of the camp. Bedouin horsemen rode down the lanes, slashing guy-ropes and riding down running men, the burning tents collapsing, trapping the French inside, the powder stores roaring in a hurricane of fire in the onshore breeze.

Cook leading the way, they charged down the sloping camp in tight formation through the French, none stopping to guess who they were, the remainder of the marines running along the sides, firing one after the other, a constant crack of muskets adding to the confusion, stray French troopers twisting, dropping. Cornishman Corporal Pettifer ran straight for a squad of French and levelled his brass-barrelled Navy blunderbuss – '*Have that!*' – the resulting blast scattering six of them screaming into the dark, two flying off their feet, dead before they struck the ground.

A dozen cavalry troopers had mounted horses and charged after the *Bedu* of the Beni Qassim and Awlad 'Ali – but the Bedouin galloped off into the darkness of the desert, the French left turning, searching, in disarray, their horses shying from the fires and the barracking bursts of musket cartridges and powder-kegs. They spurred their mounts and charged back into the camp, and saw the marines, '*La plage! Ils courent vers la plage!*' The beach! They're running to the beach!

At the bottom of the slope of the camp was a low ridge of scrub and grassy dunes, in the middle, a single passage to the beach beyond, wide enough for two pack-horses. Warnock and Kite raced to the gap and threw themselves against the sand wall of the dune, the others soon joining them: Pettifer, De Lisle, Porter, Hesse, Tariq and Cochrane. '*All present?*' Aye!

They knelt in ranks, giving staggered covering fire, the buck-and-ball loads bringing down two, three men with each discharge. When he saw Cook and the others, Pettifer stepped out. '*C'mon, ye old codger,*' he shouted, and fired another packed barrel from the blunderbuss into the French.

'*Out with ye!*' shouted Cook and charged through the gap, the rest following to the palm-lined shore beyond.

They charged down a short incline to the beach, the shore stretching out before them, littered with shattered casks, discarded sacks and broken carts, the ruts worn deep where they had been taking their supplies over the months, unnoticed by the blockade fleet. Fifty yards away lay a line of spear-bladed thickets and leaning palm trees, beaten by the winds, the ebbing surf visible just beyond, dragging rhythmically at a moonlit slope of dark, packed sand. Without breaking stride they ran straight for it, aiming for the deep cover of the thicket.

Underhill passed the sagging Greek clerk to Napier – *Go on boy* – who slung him like a sack over one shoulder and ran, his legs pumping at full speed, the marines behind. A cry rose as the mounted French troopers in pursuit erupted from a distant corner of the dunes.

Their number swelling to over a dozen, the French cavalrymen spurred their horses, falling in behind a leader riding bareback in his shirtsleeves, sword in hand. After a quick look over his shoulder, Kite shouted out, '*Customers! Time to scarper!*'

Cook, Underhill and Napier at the front, the marines raced across the scrub in twin files, none looking back, leaping the tussocks of grass and undergrowth as one, dodging left, dodging right, broken boughs and palm-fronds, detritus washed up by the tide strewn across their path, their boots thumping hollow in the dense brush, the thud of the troopers' hooves close behind, Underhill roaring, '*Get a move on, you ruddy heroes!*'

Charging through the dark thicket, they reached the expanse of the beach. Two flaming torches awaited, jammed in the sand and shingle. Bringing up the rear, Warnock and Kite slowed, dropped, rolled, came up on one knee and brought their muskets up to the shoulder and fired a second blast of buck and ball. Warnock tore at another cartridge, grating through clenched teeth, '*Where the bloody 'ell is he, Mickey!*'

Kite fired at the approaching horsemen, one of them twisting away, his mount's forelegs rearing, its rider tumbling. '*Keep yer ruddy hair on, Knocky! He's comin'!*'

16

The French cavalry sighted them and charged, silhouetted against the light of the burning camp, the smoke and stench of the fires wafting across the stinking shore, the bareback leader not twenty yards off when the first shot boomed out from behind them. Their rearmost rider was flung forward against his horse's neck, crashing heavily to the ground. Kite shouted out, '*He's 'ere!*'

From the direction of the camp behind the French cavalry, came six *Bedu* horsemen: at the front, the tassels of his tack flying from an ornate bridle and snaffle-bit, came a Mamluk, black *shemagh* on his head, long sleeveless *binish* robes flapping behind, a heavy 40-bore pistol in one hand, firing another round impossibly fast after the first.

The French charge faltering, Warnock pulled the snap-fuse of a dark cloth bundle in his hands, '*Bag o'tricks, Mick! Down!*' He hurled it with all his strength.

They threw themselves flat as the dark shape spun through the air, the burning quickmatch flaring and spitting just before it exploded far in front of the approaching French, a blinding white flash of magnesium and flying shrapnel, the horses screaming, turning away amid the thrashing hooves all around.

Another man fell, shot from behind; the rear troop of the French cavalry turned. In the light it was clear, the Mamluk bore the unmistakable scarlet sleeves of a British officer.

'*C'est lui! C'est l'anglais!*' cried one of them.

It's him. It's the Englishman.

The troop leader turned about to face them, sword high, and charged, the heavy blade reaching for his quarry closing at speed in an impromptu joust. Reins tied on the saddle-bow, William John Hazzard fired the Lorenzoni repeater again – but the flint fell with a hollow click. Warnock and Kite were still too close, and they had not yet tempted the French away sufficiently. Hazzard thrust the heavy handgun into its holster and drew his scimitar as he closed with the Frenchman. The *Bedu* either side of him in their turbans and *shemagh* held their scimitars out, whirling in slow preparation for the kill, and Hazzard urged the horse on, '*Hat hat hat!*' The horse dropped its head lower and accelerated, and they collided at full gallop.

The Frenchman's Turkoman horse reared in fright, Hazzard's Arabian shouldering into him at full speed, the leader's blade reaching, extended like a lance as if to unseat him or make him lean away. Hazzard's scimitar beat it aside in a looping parry, the steel shrieking and sparking, the surprise expanding on the Frenchman's face as the blade slid down his arm, over his sword-guard and across his neck as Hazzard charged past.

The Bedouins ploughed into the French horses – '*Yallah…!*' – the *Bedu* style unfamiliar to their victims: low and fast, riding through to the other side, never stopping. Spinning his horse about, Hazzard wrenched round to see Warnock and Kite still running in the distance, too exposed. He kicked his heels in and the horse leapt back into the melee; he fended off a clumsy overhead strike from a second horseman, the Frenchman's blade swatted away in *quinte* by Hazzard, the scimitar flicking over in riposte, taking the man's throat, a fountain of scarlet spraying as the horse galloped by, the rider slowly lying backwards and toppling to the ground.

Wide-eyed, the rearmost riders bore away back to the camp. In passing, a panicked chop came at Hazzard from the right, the attack caught by the gilt scimitar and parried, the trooper's sword flying off into the air behind him, the speed of the horse doing the rest, the body falling without an arm. Cries dulled as Hazzard pulled up sharp, the heat and chemical stench of the naphtha core of the smouldering bag o'tricks now harsh in his nostrils, the fleeing Frenchmen looking back over their shoulders.

Hazzard slowed his horse, his blood pounding, hands trembling. '*Hassanan,*' he whispered to the horse, patting its neck, and called to the *Bedu*, '*Hassanan…*' and to himself, '*Hassanan. All right… all right boy.*'

He saw Cook in the dark of the distant surf, angry as ever, one arm rising, turning, giving the signal: *come on.* Hazzard wiped the blade of the scimitar on his thigh, sheathed it and took the reins, nudging the panting horse forward. Muskets popped behind at the gap in the dunes as infantrymen met the horsemen and raised their muskets, giving a desultory fire.

Hazzard and the *Bedu* rode along the surf, the water spraying, the steaming horses cooling. They reached a clump of hanging palms touching the froth of the surf, the boat ready, bobbing, the marines waiting inside, muskets held at the ready, some drinking pints of water.

Hazzard dismounted and handed the reins to a waiting *Bedu* rider. Time was short, but he knew that the horsemen of the Beni Qassim would keep the French busy while they rowed out to sea. '*Shukran,*' he said: *thanks.* '*Ma'a salamati, ya Sheikh.*' *Go safely, Sheikh.*

They touched their hearts, lips and forehead to him. 'It was a good night, and brings much honour. *Wa aleikum as-salam, Hazar Pasha.' And unto you peace.* They rode off to intercept any French reinforcements, churning the surf into a foaming wake till they made the beach, the dark sand flying in clumps from their galloping hooves.

Cook and Hazzard shoved the boat off, the cool sea air a relief, insects clouding overhead, the great oak's forehead slick with perspiration. '*Took yer sweet ruddy time…*' muttered the old sergeant, pushing hard.

'I was busy.'

'Commandin' officer in the thick of it, choppin' at other ranks,' he muttered, shaking his head, stripping the four chevrons from his bare arms, the white of the stripes too bright in the darkness. 'By all that's holy in *bloody* Bristol…'

'Had no choice.'

'Too damn risky an' you knows it.'

Few but Cook would speak with Hazzard in such a fashion. But Cook had been with Hazzard for some ten years, since Hazzard had been a junior officer in the East India Company's Bombay Marine – and his back still bore the scars of a brute's lash, a hardened carapace of latticed tissue, a reminder of youthful hopes long since dead. In saving one Corporal Cook from the rope that day, Hazzard had sealed a bond that would never be broken – and Cook had taken good care of him ever since. But Hazzard was not in the mood.

'Will you get in the damned boat.'

Cook glowered at him, knowing he had made his point. 'Aye-aye. Sir.'

The boat floated free, the waves waist-deep, Hazzard's robes dragging in the tepid water as they both clambered in, finding their balance, the oarsmen heaving the craft through the pull of the surf and out to sea, the ebb carrying them away, the marines puffed from the run, but pleased with themselves. Hazzard looked at them all in turn. 'Wounds?'

'Petty's hurt his thumb, sir,' said Napier with deep concern. Some of them laughed, De Lisle giving Pettifer a shove, and all replied with a nod. Kite said, 'You was playin' that tight, sir. Thought it was me an' Knocky to take 'em all on our lonesome.'

Hazzard nodded: Private Mickey Kite, the quick-witted wag, with the Irish Cockney's winning smile, always enough to extricate him from most scrapes. Hazzard glanced at Warnock, the 'Burnt Man', missing an ear, the whites of his eyes bright in his dark scarred face, deepening as they pulled further from the distant firelight onshore, the pale moonshine from above casting their faces into shadow. Hazzard gave him a nod of acknowledgement. 'Well done.' It was as much as they would ever get, but it was enough.

Warnock nodded back. 'Aye, sir.'

Hazzard rose from the prow and stepped carefully back through the oarsmen and marines, nodding at each, and eventually sat beside Handley at the tiller, the only true seaman among the band of 9 Company. Handley passed him a telescope without Hazzard asking. Hazzard extended it, peering at the shore.

No one in pursuit, no lines of infantry forming on the beach to volley at them – they were too busy. He gave the scope back. 'What says the boat, Handley?' he asked quietly.

'Boat says can they do it all again, sir,' said Handley with a grin, shaved for the first time in a while, noticed Hazzard, not so much the tatty ginger scarecrow he usually was. They both chuckled. Handley had been with him at the Cape and HMS *America*, at the battle with Harry Race, and the beginning of Hazzard's fame – or notoriety. Hazzard looked to Underhill and the curious older civilian he had rescued. 'Well done, Sergeant. How is our passenger.'

'Sir. Doing well. Beat hard by a sturdy hand.' Jeremiah Underhill nodded, his ruddy dark face pocked and scarred, once across his bare upper lip, another cutting a thin gap in his Quakeresque beard. Even he too was looking his hard years – there were only a few to spare between Underhill and Cook. 'Mr Petrides, sir,' said Underhill with his odd parade-ground formality. Beside him, Porter dabbed at Petrides' cut cheek and forehead with a pad of liniment from his medical bag, the older man flinching slightly from the sting. 'Does the Turkish and the Greek, but hain't said much either ways, sir.'

Hazzard looked at him, and the other looked back, far harder than they might at first have imagined. '*Mials anglika?*' he asked, in Greek. *Do you speak English?*

The older man waggled his hand much as a Frenchman might: *comme ci, comme ça.* 'Little. But… *vous parlez français?*'

Hazzard nodded. '*Oui, d'accord.*' Hazzard was not surprised: the European voice heard most at the courts of the Sublime Porte in Constantinople was not English, but French. He had expected as much when they were assigned to retrieve him. Having had a French Huguenot mother, and been educated partly at Grenoble, Hazzard spoke like a native.

No longer the frightened creature beaten by Peraud, *Monsieur* Petrides rubbed one wrist. '*C'était un coup serré...*' *That was a close one.*

'Peraud...?' asked Hazzard, nodding at the wrist.

Petrides nodded. 'He nearly took my hand, with a sword.'

Underhill had grasped most of the gist. 'Aye sir, Peraud. Nasty type. Long streak o'piss-water in black, sir, just like that other creature Derrien from afore.' He grinned and looked at Napier. 'Till Arthur flattened him.'

Cochrane the Ulsterman slapped Napier playfully on the face. '*Yer a fackin' hero, big Art'ur,*' and some laughed quietly as the big boxer protested and blushed, '*Ere, gerroff, you lot*, his battered face twisting with both confusion and determination to get it right next time. 'Sorry sir. I just dunnos when's to stop.' They laughed all the more.

Hazzard nodded. 'That's good then, Private.'

'I made a grab for him,' said Cook, passing a wineskin of water, 'but 'Miah had Mr Petrides safe, so we got out.'

'What have you for us, *M'sieur* Petrides?' asked Hazzard.

'For your *capitaine*, the *Chevalier* Smith,' said Petrides. He tugged at his open collar, pulling at the stitching on one side, and withdrew a slip of paper. 'I am to give you this, from a source in Venice.' He handed it to Hazzard and watched his expression. 'We have word of a secret flotilla, bringing reinforcements.'

Hazzard took notice. The marines fell silent, watching the change in him.

'A source in Venice?' asked Hazzard. It seemed unlikely: the Adriatic was dominated by allied Russian and Ottoman ships.

'The Venetian fleet, yes, it was destroyed when Bonaparte took the city a year ago, *oui*? – but a French *Ordonnateur de Marine*, so they say, he saved a handful of ships, near to the Arsenal...' He tapped the note. 'This is a copy of the communiqué to London, as proof.'

The message was a series of triples and doubles – an Admiralty cipher beginning with 555-555, indicating it was from a director in the field, a consul possibly. He thought of Commander Charles Blake and Room 63, headquarters of Admiralty Intelligence. And with it came thoughts of Commodore Sir Rafe Lewis, the head of the serpent. It seemed so long ago. 'So this is reliable?'

Petrides continued, 'They repair enough ships under the eyes of the Austrians, out there, by the Venice Arsenal. Who can do this, I ask. These are no smugglers or businessmen, no *Ordonnateur de Marine* is here. We discover these are agents of the *Gendarmerie Extraordinaire*. They are the *Bureau de renseignements et information*.'

Hazzard felt a reaction from somewhere deep within. It was Derrien's *Bureau d'information*: the French intelligence service. 'Peraud again,' he said.

The boat bobbed and the oars dipped, the shoreline glowing in the light of the fires, smoke rising and drifting out to them. Petrides made a very French gesture with his hands.

'*Exactement*. The flotilla comes in secret down the Adriatic, so? With the Ottoman flags, yes? To miss the fortresses, of Ancona, of Brindisi, to hide in the coves of Vieste – instead of departing from Toulon, to avoid your navy in blockade of Malta.' He then added grimly, 'They will then combine, off Bari, and collect French and Republican troops in Puglia.'

Hazzard pictured the map and the heel of Italy, the Adriatic coast no longer friendly to the French. 'So close to Syracuse in Sicily, the Russian and Turkish ships... They would be mad.'

The marines watched and listened with half an ear; most had some French, enough to pass a guard post unnoticed, but some had turned to look out over the black waves. A shadow loomed: HMS *Tigre* awaited them, running dark, lamps out, sails reefed, the moon floating above, glowing through a gauze veil of cloud. She was a fortress, with her swivel-gun murderers, 36-pounder carronades, Long 18 bow-chasers, and spiked masts piercing a slate-grey sky. For now, it was home.

'*Oui, c'est possible*. But there is one thing more,' said Petrides quietly. 'There is word the flotilla is to meet an escort, *un vaisseau de bataille* – that is to say, a ship of the line – we believe somewhere in the Ionian Sea.' He looked at them. 'They say it could be of 74 or 80 guns.'

Cook understood enough and muttered an oath. '*By all that's holy*...'

'A French 80 out here?' murmured Underhill. 'Blockade's thin as ice...'

'She'd be a right ruddy bugger an' all,' agreed Cook.

Hazzard thought of their blockade, strung out along the coast of Egypt, ships so far apart they could rarely signal each other. A French 80 coming upon them could safeguard the landing of entire regiments for the outnumbered French *Armée d'Orient*. 'Do the Ottomans have anything they could put to sea to match her?' he asked Petrides.

Petrides shook his head. 'After the summer battle they regroup. The *Selim III* is at Rhodes with several smaller, the *Bedr-i Zafar* and others. But there are no plans to put to sea after the failure at Aboukir two months ago. New captains, they say. Even new admirals.' Petrides watched Hazzard's face. 'There was talk,' he added, 'after the siege of Corfu those months ago, of a French ship that painted her sails black, to escape.' The light played across the bruised face of the older man, his remaining hair glowing white in the hazy glow of the moon. 'I believe it is the *Généreux*.'

They all knew the name – *Généreux* was one of the two heavy ships in the rearguard of the French line that had escaped Nelson's guns at the Nile. For his own reasons, Hazzard would never forget that night over a year earlier: *had it been only so long?* He could feel Sarah in his arms in that packed, rocking boat, blood swirling at his feet in the scuppers, amid the deafening hush that followed *Orient's* ear-splitting destruction. None of them would ever forget.

'*Jaysus shite*,' murmured Cook. 'Looks like Navy rations for a while, lads.'

They looked up as the black hull of HMS *Tigre* drew ever closer, the marines silent, remembering, turning to watch him. Like Hazzard, they felt the welcome pull of the sea. 'Ready on your sea-legs,' he said. They all murmured *aye*, and prepared to go aboard.

–

They had arrived just after the second Dog Watch, and the galley chimney on the fo'c'sle brought the smells of Turkish spices, curry and roasting meat; Sir Sidney Smith was never one to let his crew go without, and certainly not while in the Levantine seas. Once the marines were settled in their messes, Hazzard moved astern with Cook and the *Tigre's* Marine Sgt Dickory, past the silent 24-pounder guns ranged along the tweendecks. A gunner's mate polished the gleaming black iron with more than workmanlike care, the moon casting angular shadows from the gratings and the boats above. An unseasonal warm wind had come in from the easterly fringes of Damietta: the *khamsin*, perhaps from Sinai. The planks had been doused with seawater, Hazzard saw, an old trick from the tropics – but here it had made a steam-bath of the place, wafting hot, damp air. He had slung his *binish* over one arm and pulled on his short-waisted old cotton and linen Bombay jacket, or what was left of it. As he walked, Hazzard clicked back the loading crank of the Lorenzoni, trying to look inside at the action to ascertain why it had failed.

'Misfire?' asked Cook.

'Mm. Priming powder not reaching the pan…'

'Ruddy liability, that clockwork thing.'

Hazzard pushed it back into its holster, and it bumped under his left arm in its sling, lumpen and heavy.

'Not sayin' he's cross or nothin', sir…' explained Dickory, breaking in on their thoughts. He pronounced it 'crorss', the way Smith might. 'But Sir Sidney don't like his senior officers settin' into the fray none too often.'

Hazzard liked Dickory. A short man, dark cropped hair, thick Limehouse accent by way of Kent and Chatham, one of Underhill's old cronies from bygone days, a stickler for the regulations but wise enough to know when to bend them. He had broken the Secret Mutiny on the *Tigre* and frogmarched half a dozen Navy Provost guards off the ship at Cyprus; he had also been on the Jaffa raid with 9 Company, and the ill-fated Acre raid, getting three boats out of a crossfire, escaping with musket and splinter wounds to the shoulders and chest. 'I'm not one of his regular senior officers, Sar'nt.'

Dickory allowed himself a brief laugh, blew out a breath and adjusted his black topper. 'No sir, you are decidedly not.'

They tramped up the steps to the quarterdeck and a marine at the rail slammed to attention at the sight of Hazzard. As he passed, Dickory gave the man's crooked beltplate a light smack. '*Full notch, full notch,*' he muttered under his breath. Hazzard looked past the eerie glow of the compass binnacle and helm to the passageway beyond: *Tigre* had relit the lamps now that her lost sheep were back in the fold. He heard the usual sounds of life aboard ship, and sensed that easy feeling of evening, of dinner, of regulated routine: raised voices and at times laughter from below decks, the sailors and the wives, the chorus of a song, or the clink of cutlery from the officers' gunroom just below – all things foreign to their life in the desert, on their own.

But the lookouts still tried to steal a glance at Hazzard and Cook, and it was this exposure he could not bear; it could make him long for the anonymity of the Sahara, the woollen silence, where a scuffle under a stone was as loud as Creation. The incongruity of the fellowship of the *Tigre* and his need to hide without restriction on his own terms left him ambivalent and morose, an odd malcontent wherever he was. However genial Captain Sir William Sidney Smith might be, the Royal Navy had caused the greatest losses in his life. The arrogance of their command, their intractability, their disregard for their own people, had cost his conscience the loss of innocents he could not rescue: of Sarah, of Jeanne, of the Lebanese and Palestinians at Acre, of Hugues Bartelmi and his family in Toulon – and the nation of Egypt itself. He still had nightmares, the forms of Sarah blurring into Delphine Lascelles, at once victim and saviour, firing the Lorenzoni in the hell of Jaffa. Alahum, cut down at Embabeh – *my fault*. Izzam, devoted to Hazzard, riding after him as he galloped through the fury of the 'Battle of the Pyramids – *my fault*.

But he was still *Hazar Pasha* to the *Bedu* of the Beni Qassim, to the Awlad 'Ali, who revered the names of their dead brethren, and those of Sharif Nazir, and Sheikh Ali Qarim, two more brothers fallen, whose gilt and ivory-handled *saif* scimitar hung now at his hip.

To the men below decks he was still 'Mad Billy-Jack', the man who had chased down his murderous commanding officer, Harry Race, and cut him to pieces; the man who had shouted down Nelson, damning him for allowing Napoleon Bonaparte to land his legions in Egypt. Nelson had failed to protect Egypt – but so had Hazzard, and it weighed heavily. Together they later condemned Bonaparte to wander among the fallen stone gods, to be lost in the dunes with the ghost of Cambyses, but it gave little satisfaction.

After Acre and the Holy Land, his world had changed. For reasons unknown, Commander Charles Blake RN, erstwhile friend yet perpetrator of Hazzard's initial misfortune, had extracted him and the men of 9 Company from the clutches of Sir Rafe Lewis and the Admiralty: they were now officially Home Office Intelligence operatives, controlled by William Wickham's Alien Office.

Now Hazzard set to his various tasks for Whitehall with a numb detachment and, he had to admit, a savage pleasure. Nine Company, the Special Landing Squadron of barely fifteen marines – the 'Oddfellows', as old Jervis had called them – had come in from the desert to Sidney Smith's HMS *Tigre*, the 'ship of spies', unofficial floating outpost of British Intelligence – and home.

As they moved past the helm, a call went up and the three of them turned at the sound of running feet, a lookout hailing to port, a light frigate coming in fast, dousing sail, the canvas glowing in the balmy darkness, signal flags rippling up to her masthead lanterns. Cook joined Hazzard at the shrouds, Dickory with him. 'It's the *Seahorse*,' rumbled Cook. 'Back from Sicily. Who lit a fire under 'er arse, then?'

Hazzard looked her over: no obvious damage, no warning flags hoisted. 'Message…?'

Dickory nodded beside him. 'She's a nippy hunter, sir, the *Sea'orse*. Sir Edward might've found a Frog creepin' round.'

A boat came rowing towards them even as the frigate reefed sail and dropped anchor alongside. Just astern of her in the near distance, Hazzard spotted the Spanish frigate *Volpone* standing off, waiting in the gloom. Her privateer commander, *Capitán* Cesár Domingo de la Vega, had been co-opted into service with letters of marque, and his lean 44-gun racer acted as a blockade frigate for the heavier 74s *Zealous*, *Goliath* and others as they came and went, between Egypt and Malta. Hazzard thought he spotted De la Vega on the distant deck, the man who had saved them all in a rough sea over a year ago: the flamboyant pale tailcoat, the gentleman's waistcoat and Cordovan suede boots – and jewelled Toledo rapier. He imagined the inevitable cheroot clamped between his teeth, and smiled to himself. It would be good to see him again. They stood for a moment or two at the portside rail, Hazzard thinking of Petrides' comments, about the threat of a flotilla, about the *Généreux*, and wondering if the *Seahorse* brought news.

'Cap'n Caesar's hangin' about,' noticed Cook in his Bristol rumble, and gave him a glance. 'Must be trouble.'

Hazzard agreed. 'As ever.'

Deckhands moved to receive the despatch-boat bobbing on the dark waves below. It drew alongside with a dissonant drum roll of hollow knocks and curses – '*Fend yer end, there, lad!*' – and soon a red-cheeked, breathless young midshipman sprang to the guidelines and up the boarding-steps. Gilray, the *Tigre's* Second Lieutenant, met the midshipman at the rail, took the proffered despatch, turned and bawled, '*Signals!*'

First Officer Lieutenant Wright and Marine Major Douglas appeared from behind, hurrying down the steps from the poopdeck, collapsing their telescopes, evidently having read the signals from *Seahorse*. 'Mr Hazzard,' said Wright. Douglas, in Marine scarlet mess dress, gave him a tight smile. 'Trouble again, William? What have you been up to this time, sir?'

Hazzard gave him a nod in reply, as Dickory touched his hat-brim. 'I'll hail the cap'n, sir.' He dashed off with two marines to alert Smith.

The midshipman watched as Wright tore open the despatch envelope. Hazzard and Cook joined them. 'News, sir?'

'No idea,' said Douglas. 'She came haring in from Damietta way, with Urgent splashed all over her masthead.'

Wright opened a stiff folded page bearing an embossed crest, and read through the note, just as Captain Sir William Sidney Smith appeared from the stern cabins, immaculate in braided Navy blue-jacket, dark curling hair blowing in the slight breeze, a broad-bladed Genoese sword clanking at his left side. 'Ah, Mr Hazzard. I should like a word with you about our Mr Petrides,' he said. 'With a rather splendid leg of lamb, I understand, and an excellent Chambertin.' He accepted the despatch from Wright and glanced over it, still speaking to Hazzard. 'I hear you put an entire squadron of cavalry to flight with merely an angry look.' Hazzard said nothing, but waited, Smith's wry grin changing to a mild frown. 'You are no use to anyone, William, dead in a ditch from a fruitless skirmish, tropical palms waving overhead romantically or not…' His words trailed off as he read the note. Then he read it again. 'Good God, John,' he said to Wright. He held it out for Hazzard and Douglas. 'From the French.'

A slow step came from behind as Commodore Sir Thomas Trou-bridge joined them from the Great Cabin. 'Sir Sidney?'

Tall, older than the others, but still the vigorous captain of HMS *Culloden*, and one of Nelson's most trusted, Troubridge was now commander of the blockade fleet, a duty he had taken on from Hood, and later Smith himself during the battle for Acre. Troubridge glanced at the paper, clearly suspecting the Alien Office at work. 'Cloaks or daggers, Sidney?'

'Apparently neither, Tom,' Smith replied, handing him the message. 'Rather unexpected, to say the least.'

Hazzard read the message with Troubridge. Though in French, it was open and unencrypted, intended for Smith personally. In a sloping hand it stated quite simply:

To the Chevalier Sidney Smith of the vessel *Tigre*, Jean-Baptiste Kléber, General-in-chief of the Army of the East, seeks an armistice to discuss terms of a peace accord. He awaits your officer parliamentary at your earliest convenience.

Kléber

Petrides stood by the darkened stern gallery windows in the Great Cabin, the captains still conferring across the polished dining table set with silverware and wineglasses, candelabra flickering, light winking from crystal decanters on small side tables, the low, worn leather chairs glowing from Turkish rugs on the whitewashed planks. With a crackling fire under a stone mantel, it might have been a luxurious gentlemen's club in London.

Wright waited with Major Douglas, Cook by the door, just as baffled as Hazzard: that peace could come from so simple a request was almost beyond reason. They had not yet engaged the French on land – ergo, the enemy had not yet been defeated: how then to proceed? After the weight of arms the French had brought to this corner of the world, simply to depart because Bonaparte himself had done so seemed incomprehensible.

'It must be a ruse,' said Troubridge, taken aback, thinking aloud. 'Sidney, you know these fellows, General Kléber and General Desaix. They are the finest they have, but can we *trust* him?' In the intervening months since Acre, Troubridge had changed: the revolution at Naples and the subsequent débâcle had changed them all. 'I will not oblige us to diplomacy yet again,' he insisted. 'Naples was enough for us. Enough for us all. And Nelson's health barely survived it.'

'Quite so, sir,' murmured Smith. 'I had Desaix's own officers in this very room not several months ago. I furnished them with those French newspapers—'

'It's stuff and nonsense. They could not be so ready to capitulate.'

'With Bonaparte back in France,' said Smith, 'possibly they see little point in remaining in Egypt.'

Troubridge moved to a decanter, Major Douglas helping him to a dry sherry, the crystal rims chiming a note in the stillness. 'It must be more than that,' continued Troubridge. 'They see the Grand Vizier, Yussuf Pasha, approaching the Sinai with a positive horde of Turks behind him.' He raised the glass briefly to all and took a sip. 'How many did they say?'

'Eighty thousand, sir,' confirmed Douglas, 'so it is claimed. At times this has reached one hundred thousand, depending on the local conscript levy. More reasonable figures suggest between forty and sixty. But the levy numbers fluctuate constantly with recruitment and desertion.'

'Good *God.*' Troubridge shook his head. 'My point precisely.' He glanced at Hazzard and sat in a button-backed leather chair, Smith seating himself at the head of the dining-table. 'Will, how many troops can Kléber muster to the field, would you say?'

Hazzard considered, with a glance at Petrides. 'They took thirteen thousand to Syria, sir, leaving ten or twelve in Egypt, including reserves and auxiliaries. They lost at least five or six thousand to enemy action and sickness... I should imagine they could put barely ten or twelve thousand in the field at once.' Hazzard repeated it in French for Petrides, who nodded his agreement at the figures. 'From what we have learned, sir,' Hazzard concluded, 'Kléber was no friend of Bonaparte's, and against the Egypt campaign from the start.'

Troubridge put a hand to his lined forehead, pained by the odds facing them. 'Good God above. Ten thousand against *eighty*. Even if exaggerated, and only forty or even thirty thousand, it is impossible. They must withdraw, for humanity's sake alone.' They all knew what the Turks would do if the French fell captive. After the Holy Land and the massacre at Jaffa, Hazzard could hardly blame them. 'After what we saw at Naples,' he said softly, 'my opinion of humanity has somewhat flagged, to say the least. Royalist, Republican... what we do to each other is beyond my understanding.' Absently, he stared into his sherry. 'And we captains all in the middle of it, judge and jury.' He drank, pinching his eyes shut.

'What news of the admiral, sir?' asked Hazzard of Nelson – but he glanced at Smith, who shook his head in quick warning. It was clearly not a subject to be discussed.

Troubridge was silent for a moment, lost in thought. 'Recuperating,' he said at length. 'Still recuperating... in that infernal palace, in Palermo.' He took a breath. 'So. We are the Mediterranean. We are the Levant, gentlemen. Ideas, if you please.'

'Kléber holds Mustafa Pasha captive, sir,' Wright reminded him, 'who led the landings on Aboukir in July. It is possible Kléber would use him to bargain. At least to gain some time.' Hazzard watched Wright, who forever proved he was far more than an acting naval lieutenant: he had been right-hand man to Smith for years and was undoubtedly an agent of considerable ability.

'That is precisely it, Mr Wright,' said Troubridge. 'This is not about going home with their tails between their legs. It's about gaining *time*.' He reconsidered the message and shook his head. 'Kléber is an honourable man, I am sure, but he is hard-pressed. This could be an attempt to halt the advance of Yussuf Pasha while we go through the very lengthy procedures of armistice and treaty, seeking and receiving Cabinet approval, Admiralty authority, everything. But what is he waiting for? Reinforcements to arrive to keep what few men they have in Egypt? It's madness.'

Major Douglas seemed doubtful. 'How could significant reinforcements get through, Sir Thomas? It would require half a dozen divisions at the least, another fifteen or twenty thousand men.'

'Kléber, of all of them, knows Bonaparte,' said Smith, 'knows he shan't send a soul to help, and the Directory government is virtually bankrupt. Kléber is the sort of commander who would want to save the lives of his men first and foremost.' He glanced at Hazzard. 'William, would you agree?'

Hazzard thought back to that night, standing in the surf, aiming the Lorenzoni at Napoleon Bonaparte, feeling the muskets trained on him as he challenged their god-general – demanding to understand, demanding to know *why*. 'Bonaparte does everything for himself. He will expect Kléber to do the same. If Bonaparte were here, he would find a way.' He thought of his own maxim to the marines of 9 Company: 'He would not stop. And never give up.'

'Major Hazzard is right, sir,' admitted Smith, glancing at the message lying between them on the gleaming mahogany, 'Kléber is alone…' He caught sight of Petrides, silent by the reflected candlelight glinting in the windows. '*M'sieur* Petrides.' Smith rose from his seat and bowed his head. '*Je m'excuse*, I apologise that we speak in English.' He then continued in French for his benefit, 'What then of this flotilla you describe? Is it large enough to bear significant reinforcements? Is this all that Kléber is doing? Buying time to bolster his forces?'

Petrides stepped forward into the gathering, staring pensively at the carpet underfoot. 'It is possible, *mon capitaine*. All that we know is that there is a flotilla, possibly of French-controlled Venetian ships, and it comes. *Eh bien*, were you France, would you not send reinforcements to succour your army, cut off in a foreign land?'

Smith nodded, looking to Troubridge. 'We cannot take the risk that it is not. We are spread too thin.'

'Yes,' agreed Troubridge, 'as are Malta and Cadiz...' He shook his head. 'We cannot go on like this.'

Hazzard watched the discussion, his mind ticking, weighing the possibilities. 'What of the *Généreux*, sir?' he asked.

Troubridge and Smith turned. Smith asked, 'The what?'

Hazzard looked to Petrides and spoke in French to Smith. 'Had you not yet debriefed Mr Petrides?'

'The *Seahorse* rather curtailed all that,' said Smith, 'before we could broach details with *M'sieur* Petrides.'

Petrides spoke. '*Alors*, apart from the flotilla, there was talk of a heavy ship of battle, of 74 or 80 guns, bringing the flotilla southward.' He glanced at the two captains. 'The source believes it could be the *Généreux*.'

Troubridge took a moment. It hit him rather hard. 'Now there's a thing.'

Major Douglas looked at Wright curiously, not sharing the Navy's bitterness. 'Was she... at the Nile?'

Wright nodded. All were aware Troubridge had been there, frustrated, run aground in the *Culloden* as the other ships engaged the French fleet at the Nile. Few, however, knew it had been Hazzard's young second in command, Lt Wayland and Ship's Master Handley who had ridden the heights of the Aboukir dunes and destroyed the offending shore battery, saving *Culloden* and her crew. '*Généreux* and the *Guillaume Tell* escaped,' said Wright. 'With two admirals, Villeneuve and Ganteaume.'

Douglas looked grim. 'The rearguard of their line.'

Smith kept one eye on Troubridge. 'Caught an offshore northeasterly and headed out to sea, past the reach of Nelson's guns.' The rivalry between Smith and Nelson was well known, though Smith bore the brunt of it far worse than England's hero. 'Contrary winds. Nothing Nelson could have done.'

'After the Ancona and Brindisi affair, I thought she had got back to Toulon,' said Wright, in perfect French to Petrides.

Petrides shrugged. 'Perhaps yes, perhaps no, or come back out for this purpose, we know not. Captain Lejoille, he was killed at Brindisi, yes, and the ship was taken by Troullet, the senior lieutenant. But to slip away from Corfu, and then slip past such once again…' He made the *comme-ci, comme-ça* waggle of the hand once again. 'It is the clever thing for a replacement captain, *n'est-ce pas?*'

Smith glanced at Troubridge. 'We can only hope that Russian or Turkish ships are as vigilant as ever, but even we allow some to sneak past.'

Hazzard looked at Smith. 'A flotilla with her in the van could break through our line just long enough to get men ashore in small boats – five thousand, eight thousand. It could be enough to tip the scales, prolong the blockade, drain us of resources. If she's for us, sir, we need to find her and stop her.'

Troubridge was clearly exhausted. He had been sailing between Egypt, Malta, Naples and Palermo in Sicily for weeks – this was one new problem too many. He sank into the chair. 'Admiral Bruix broke out of Brest, past the entire dashed Channel Fleet. Made his way past Cadiz *and* Gibraltar…' He shook his head. 'I can scarce believe it, but he did it with twenty-five sail of the line. After the antics of Naples, and the scolding of Foote, it's too bad, it really is.'

Naples had fallen to Revolutionary partisans a year earlier, just as Hazzard had warned the Neapolitan Prime Minister, Sir John Acton, in their furious argument in the study of Sir William Hamilton, the ambassador – but few could have imagined Nelson would have become so deeply involved in the rescue of the royal court. As the city tore itself apart, he ordered Troubridge and others to liaise between the Bay of Naples, Palermo and the Malta blockade. Captain Sir Edward Foote of the *Seahorse*, who had brought Hazzard and the marines in from Aboukir Bay with great care and pride, had been there, and accepted the partisans' surrender – yet this was countermanded directly by Nelson, to the fury of the Admiralty and Foreign Office.

Hazzard shared Smith's ambivalent respect and disapprobation of Nelson: the brunt of the consequences seemed to have fallen on Troubridge's shoulders – and now the Mediterranean Fleet was to be spread thinner still. 'It really is… just, too bad,' he repeated to himself, looking out of the stern gallery windows. The lanterns glinted off the black waves, hypnotic. 'No matter how we try to stop the world from falling asunder,' he murmured, 'it appears utterly *bent* on all manner of chaos and injustice.'

Smith looked to Hazzard. 'Any suggestions, William?'

'Yes sir,' he said. 'We go and get her.' Petrides met his eye and gave a single nod of affirmation.

But Troubridge shook his head. 'I cannot allow the *Tigre* to leave the blockade, Sidney, you're far too valuable here – especially now,' he said, 'with the possibility of peace talks.'

Wright cast a quick glance at Hazzard and suggested, 'What of our Spanish colleague, sir, Captain De la Vega and the *Volpone*? *Volpone* is faster than most, sir. If De la Vega finds *Généreux*, or whoever she is, he might take her by surprise, or at least disable her.' He gave a pointed glance at Smith, who now knew De la Vega well. 'He is, after all, an experienced pirate of sorts.'

'A man after my own heart,' said Smith with a wry grin.

Troubridge warmed to the thought. 'Yes, a noble brigand through and through. I like him. More than that, I trust him. Very well... *Volpone* to make a reconnaissance of the Ionian Sea in search of this... this rogue 74. And *Tigre* to remain and reinforce the blockade under your command, Sidney, to repel these transport flotilla reinforcements, should they get through.'

Hazzard and Cook came to attention. 'Sir.'

Smith stood and straightened his jacket. '*Généreux* must be approached with care, Mr Hazzard. She is not one to trifle with frigates or sloops—'

Something had cut Smith short, a look upon his face betraying knowledge of an unspoken deed, some dread event he only now seemed to recall. He closed his eyes and sighed, pained. 'Good God, William, my dear fellow,' he added softly, 'I must apologise...'

None spoke. Hazzard looked from Wright to Smith and frowned. 'Forgive me, sir, I don't believe I understand.'

'It was hearing her name,' Smith tried to explain. He shook his head, but it had gone too far. 'It was but a story, Will, that is all, of a despatch-runner, and *Généreux*...' He cleared his throat. 'And *Généreux* intercepting her. After the Battle of the Nile.'

Hazzard could not understand why, but he revisited that cold, dull room at the Admiralty, where Sir Rafe Lewis and Charles Blake had told him so very delicately of Sarah's disappearance, of her capture at the hands of Citizen Derrien. His heart began to pound, his pulse loud in his ears. 'I still do not understand.'

'There is no basis to the tale,' said Troubridge, defending Smith. 'None at all, Sir Sidney. I am sure Lt Tomlinson is conducting his duties at this very moment, and that *Valiant* is...'

Tomlinson: captain of HMS Valiant.

He had taken Sarah, taken her back to England, to her father in Suffolk – after Masoud and the Beni Qassim had read prayers, and covered her in pale blue Nile lilies, embalmed in *mumiya*, and floated her out to the waiting lugger – to HMS *Valiant*, and the care of the truest sailor Hazzard had met, Lt Tomlinson. He stared from one to the other, Troubridge's words lost to his ear.

Smith took a breath. 'My dear fellow, I thought you knew. It was but alehouse tittle-tattle, just before the campaign against Acre last year. *Généreux* had attacked various small ships, as you know, the chief being HMS *Leander* – but one of them was a fast lugger... carrying despatches.' He held his hands up in entreaty. 'God forfend it was the *Valiant*, as we have had no word about her since, neither good nor ill—'

'The *Généreux* intercepted the *Valiant*...?'

No.

Not again.

He could not lose her all over again.

'Has...?' Hazzard swallowed, his mouth dry, his tongue cloying, sticking. He had received no letter, sent no letter home to his uncle, to anyone, his mind cutting off all thought of England and safety, of home – he had been in the field too long, away from command and communication. 'Has Tomlinson *not reported*? After a year?'

Smith glanced at Troubridge. 'It was but a rumour, William, of the despatches, no more, and *Généreux* was feared to be the answer.' He glanced at Troubridge. 'I sent word to London. But, I have had nothing in reply so far,' he finished quietly.

Troubridge weighed in. 'I am sure Mr Tomlinson is patrolling the Channel reaches, fencibles, and round St Helens with *Valiant* as ever, Will, I am sure of it.' His voice softened with the evident sadness that had overtaken him. 'And that your lady is at rest, at her home, after such terrible sacrifice.'

Hazzard stared at them. 'But we do not know.'

'We damned well shall. Sir Sidney,' said Troubridge, 'we must request a search at once through Gib.'

34

Smith was already at his desk and dipping a pen. 'Yes, sir,' he replied. 'Sir Anthony at Admiralty House will have it.' He continued to write. 'Most urgent, for the *Seahorse* and Menorca.'

Their words felt muffled, as if he had no wish to hear them.

He had not confirmed landing. No one had.

Cook shifted behind Hazzard, ready to intervene. Douglas stood rooted to the spot; Wright looked to Smith, but none had suitable reply. Troubridge spoke with determination. 'Naples befouled everything, Will. We know only that Tomlinson missed a rendezvous with Hardy at Syracuse… and that Hardy waited, contrary to orders.'

Généreux.

Sarah.

With a shudder of rising awareness, awful in its overwhelming entirety, rolling from his very core, Hazzard realised: he had forgotten – *he had forgotten why he was there.* In his guilt, his endless shame, his underlying self-hatred, he saw now that he had been playing at being an officer for Smith, for Troubridge, even for Nelson, for too long – at Valletta, at Shubra Khit, Cairo, Jaffa and Acre – and Karnak, costing Wayland, his most devoted *protégé*, a severed hand.

Good God, what have I done. What have I been doing?

He had forgotten the truth, perhaps out of self-preservation: that he had come to rescue Sarah, to save her – and had failed. After this failure, for purely his own satisfaction, he had sought only to destroy. To destroy Derrien, destroy Bonaparte, destroy them all – *because it was their fault, their fault and their damned war, their fault and their damned greed, their slavering self-interest, their—*

But he knew this was not so. It was not them.

It was him.

My fault.

With the death of Sarah, and the death of Derrien, some part of him had lost his purpose. His blood had cooled. How might he have reacted a year ago, hearing that Tomlinson had not reported – he would have set the very seas aflame to find out.

Now that familiar evil stole upon him, the nerves singing, tautening – as the rage returned. His hands, limbs, weightless, tingling, as he felt the fire that had driven him to climb the broadside of *Orient* as she was being pounded to pieces by Nelson's ships, where he had found Sarah, caught her, and felt her in his arms for the last time.

He whispered, 'Jory…'

Cook stepped up close, ready, one eye on the gathered officers. 'Here, sir.'

'*Get us out of here…*'

'Sir.' Cook looked at Troubridge and Smith, then back at Hazzard. 'We'll get 'er for this, sir. For Miss Sarah. Not a man among us wouldn't do less.'

Hazzard's voice was scarcely more than a whisper. 'Nine Company, full kit, five minutes.'

Troubridge said something to Smith and Wright, and Wright threw open the door and called out, and soon Hazzard heard the thump of running feet as a boat was prepared. Hazzard stood staring, numb, unhearing, as Troubridge tried to reach him. '…*cannot be certain*, Will, but we shall find out, I promise. Just come back,' said Troubridge with a glance to Cook. 'Pirates and all.'

Cook nodded. 'Aye, sir.'

Coup

Delphine Lascelles left her office in Cairo's military hospital to begin her rounds. With October came still fresh fears of plague, an unwelcome guest returning annually for autumn and winter, afflicting high and low, stealing silently into the palaces of princes, and ravaging the poor and forgotten. Yet she had seen only isolated cases so far, at least within army ranks and, thanks to Private Millet the previous year, she knew how to treat it.

She closed the half-glazed door behind her and thought for a moment back to those days six months earlier, in Gaza, Jaffa and Acre – of Bonaparte striding into the plague hospitals, moving and tending the wounded, more out of arrogance than concern, she knew, to show them all, to snap them out of their fear.

And as she revisited these memories, she inevitably thought of Hazzard, driven by what demons she could never conceive, with the same disregard for consequence as Bonaparte – raising his gun at the immortal himself, then riding, *riding*, saving her, trying to save everyone. *How could he*, she wondered. *How?*

William.

But she had tried to put him from her mind, from her heart, though she knew she could never do so completely – it had cut deep. She stopped and closed her eyes, fighting the memory: while her countrymen suffered in the sands so near, she had rested with William John Hazzard and the English on Crete, and she felt guilt.

Yet these same countrymen of hers had wrought such hellish misery as she had never witnessed before. The devils of Acre far behind them, Derrien, Bonaparte, his siege, all vanquished, crushed by the victors who had then protected her: the invincible Sidney Smith, striding the gundecks and battlements, the gallant Spaniard pulling them from the beach – and Hazzard, so shot to ribbons she had been scarcely able to know where to start with her bandages, her eyes clouded with tears as she bound him in the boat, cannon-fire roaring overhead, blasting into the French grenadiers on the beach. *Stop*, she had cried as she worked, *stop*. But they did not. The shore, that empty 'No Man's Land' by the castle of Acre, had become a smouldering abattoir.

She breathed deeply, slowly, bidding the trembling in her limbs to fade, expelling the memories, thinking only of now, of how she clung to Réné – Réné Desgenettes, of how he had cared for her, of how she needed so very badly to work.

She moved with the slightest limp down the corridor and peered through the doorway to the main hall on her right, and saw the orderlies bringing new patients into the ward. One of them was being settled on a bed, still in uniform. She waved a hand and called gently to the attending nurse, 'No, no, Zeinab, first to *triage* and bathing, remember, then gown, *kaftan*, yes? Then to bed.'

Zeinab, in her white habit and *hijab*, bowed her head with a nervous look. '*Nahm, nahm, madame…*' *Yes, yes.* The girl hurried to it, and the two men supporting the soldier turned him about, his head lolling, and out through to the back.

How Delphine could bear the place any longer was beyond even her, the horrors it brought to mind, but she forced herself: it was *work*. She passed along the new wing – the integrated 'stables', as they had called it – and she passed the first stall, once fit only for horses but now for the wounded and injured, and saw where Colonel Laval of the cavalry had lain on the day he had murdered her nurses and friends.

Oddly, her heart calmed at his memory, and felt nothing: no dread, no regret for the way she had despatched Laval with caustic soda. Nothing. Now it was a young cavalry officer, his left leg taken off at the knee, the foot crushed by a horse, the infection having spread too far. He lay in a limbo of laudanum and *hashish*, safe and quiet for now. She moved on to the next – and the next, and the next, moving to the bedside on occasion, rearranging bedlinen, checking chamber-pots. She still did everything, could not stop, although she was Desgenettes' Chief Surgical Assistant.

When she emerged from the last stall she saw a familiar figure waiting at the end of the corridor: Maria, an uncompromising and dour Maltese, captured with her at Ramla by the Mamluk and held in the citadel of Jaffa. After Hazzard and the marines had rescued as many of the fleeing refugees from the harbour as they could, Maria had taken them on to Cyprus, and returned to Cairo that same summer to rejoin Delphine. *I have my duties*, she had said, and they had been together ever since.

'*Madame*,' she said urgently, approaching with her quick little steps, 'there is the man here for you.'

She hurried away to the main entrance, Delphine following. In the glowing heat of the tiled foyer they found an Egyptian in white *galabeyyah* and fine dark blue sleeveless *binish*, a white *shemagh* and black *iqal* circlet on his head – it was the Alexandrian interpreter, Masoud ibn Yussuf. He bowed deeply. '*As-salamu aleikum*,' he said. '*Bonjour*,' he continued in fluent French, with an earnest smile. 'It pleases me to see you well, *madame*.'

'Masoud,' she said, at first with delight, then with sudden apprehension added, 'It is not… news, is it… of…?'

Delphine knew that Masoud worked as local liaison at the *Quartier général* army HQ – but equally she knew that he was also a secret operative for Admiralty Intelligence, for Hazzard and Sidney Smith. Strangely, this created no conflict for her, her position being to treat all, regardless of nationality, and to get wounded men home safely – or indeed, to get everyone home.

'No, *madame*, the *Médecin en chef* Desgenettes awaits you.' He nodded at her outfit, and to Maria. 'You will need your medical bag, I am told, and perhaps an assistant. But we must be quick.'

'Is everything all right?'

Masoud nodded, but still looked apprehensive. 'We go to the citadel.'

Escorted by a troop of cavalry riding before and behind, the carriage rattled at a fast trot through the glowing heat of Cairo's broad thoroughfares, past the late morning trade of the busy stalls and open-fronted shops. It was a weekday, and the native Cairenes were out for business; what was not conducted in the shopfronts or in the streets, from goods in donkey-carts, was discussed at tables over the inevitable coffee and sweet mint tea.

It might have been easier to have taken a boat upstream, but nevertheless the cavalry troopers forced a path through the crowded lanes towards the southwest and the distant rise of the Mokattam Hills. Soon the rough stonework of the old aqueduct rose before them, its tall

Romanesque arches leading from a single square tower on the Nile. Much of it seemed dilapidated, the tower flanked by the white tents of the French garrison who had turned it into a fort. 'Originally, that was the water intake tower,' said Masoud, pointing. 'Fresh water rises there and was carried only to the citadel,' he said, 'over there.'

The hot air gusted in through the open window of the carriage, and Delphine squinted against the blowing dust. Shielding her eyes from the glowing sky, she peered along the line of stonework. A moment later she glimpsed the great slab-fronted walls of the sprawling citadel, brightly painted Ottoman minarets puncturing the sky. She leaned out of the open window into the heat, the carriage bouncing on its rough springs, the iron wheel-rims rattling on the loose stones of the road. 'I had not seen how broad it was,' she called to Masoud.

'They call it the Citadel of Saladin,' said Masoud, leaning out beside her. '*Al-Qalah'at Salah ad-Din*.'

As he spoke, the vast castle came fully into view: squat, round towers, some with decorative machicolated crowns reminiscent of Moorish Spain, bulging along the façade, streams of people passing between them through the massive tower gatehouses. The high walls were perforated at intervals by arrow-slit embrasures and firing loop-holes; domes of mosques slowly came into view, partially hidden beyond the crenellated battlements, promising palaces within palaces. Crafted by the legendary nemesis of Richard the Lionheart, it was an incongruous stone keep set in the dusty land of Pharaoh, the work of a medieval Ramesses. Now overrun by France, infantry wheeling through the gates, past huts, lines of tents and squadrons of cavalry, Saladin had been at last unseated by his oldest enemies. Delphine shuddered at its military posture, a mailed fist perched on these low foothills overlooking the Nile.

'We shall pass through this gate here,' said Masoud, 'through the *Bab al-Azab*, and meet Lieutenant Orléans *effendi*.'

The cavalry escort bellowed down orders to sentries, and soldiers stepped aside, the great twin towers looming above, then engulfing them as they passed under the high arches, the shade suddenly cooling, the sound of the horses' hooves clopping loud against the stone vaults above, the shouts of men echoing.

They emerged into the sun once again and dust-covered corporals with shining gorgets at their throats shouted at the straggling merchants filling the road with their wares – *clear a path there, putain d'la merde* – hauling back a vast iron gate. Then they were inside.

It was another town within the city of Cairo. They clattered along a narrow lane between high, flat walls, rows of small rectangular windows set far above, turning right, turning left, past ruins, past another gatehouse, until they reached the inner bailey walls and the Mokattam Tower. Soon Masoud ushered Delphine through a set of guarded double doors and into the cathedral cool of a broad, dark foyer of gleaming polished stone. Pillars reached up to vaulted ceilings, men stationed at every doorway beyond, light bouncing from every surface from distant corridors and high windows. To their left, a young officer rose from behind a wide desk, putting down a pen. '*M'sieur* Masoud, at last. This way, if you please.'

'Orlanns *effendi*,' said Masoud with a bow, deliberately employing a clumsy accent and mispronouncing his name; it was basic fieldcraft to him now, never revealing the extent of his knowledge. Delphine caught his eye, but he merely smiled and ushered her forward.

Orléans marched off down a wide corridor to a second broad chamber. They entered a great hall, skylights round a gilded dome soaring high above, every inch marked with pale blue and golden geometric patterns. Just ahead, a figure appeared in beams of floating dust caught by the sunlight, the Chief Surgeon, Desgenettes. Delphine rushed to him. '*Réné.*'

'*Mon cher*,' he said. They embraced and he kissed her hand – it was only then that she noticed the small entourage gathered nearby: four officers of varying seniority, and Dr Antoine, a young *savant* doctor with Desgenettes' medical bag. '*Madame* Lascelles, Chief Surgical Assistant, the military hospital,' said Desgenettes, introducing her to the straight-backed and elegant General Belliard, commander of the Cairo garrison. He stood upright and patrician, in a dark blue linen coat, his decorations and orders standing bright even in shadow; behind him came the tall General Damas of the cavalry and their staff. Delphine noted that there was something of the conspiracy about the group. They were shifting about, looking down, as if nervous or uncertain.

'You are sure of this, Surgeon-General?' asked Belliard quietly, his voice smooth, low, confident. 'We have no wish to lose him.'

Desgenettes was certain. 'It is gangrene, General.'

'Réné,' asked Delphine, 'what is all this…?'

Belliard took a breath and looked at Damas, then Desgenettes, and finally Delphine herself. 'We have heard a great deal of your heroism, *madame.* We have a patient here in need of urgent assistance – but some question whether we should provide it. In the absence of the *Général en chef* Bonaparte, this has become a matter of vital importance. It could help us bring an honourable peace. However, there are those who wish for nothing of the sort, and would bleed every man dry into the sands around us.' He glowered at her for a moment, challenging her to disagree, then looked to Desgenettes. 'General Kléber says to proceed?'

Desgenettes nodded. 'The general has determined we must do our utmost. But you are *commandant* in Cairo, General. The final decision is yours.'

Belliard clapped his hands behind his back with finality and glanced at Damas. 'To think the *général en chef* would have executed him.'

'The *général en chef*,' Damas reminded him pointedly, 'has run away home.'

Belliard acknowledged his own disappointment, and nodded with resignation. 'Quite so.' He jerked his head at the group. 'Let us be about it.'

Their heels echoing, the group descended a rough stone staircase into the still cooler depths of the castle, Masoud carrying Delphine's medical bag, the officers coughing and murmuring at the back. They came to a service landing, a barred door leading off to a closed quad, and still more battered stone steps. They continued their descent, the chill air growing rank, thick and stale.

At the bottom, two hulking guardsmen and a burly Provost-Sergeant waited. The sergeant nodded to Belliard, coming to attention. He then recognised Desgenettes. 'Surgeon-General. An honour.'

Desgenettes seemed unprepared for the salute. 'Likewise, Sergeant.'

'If you would follow me, *mon général.*'

The sergeant led them along a dripping stone passage, Delphine shivering, the staff officers muttering behind Belliard: '*Nom de dieu, they've put him in a damned dungeon.*'

The sergeant drew close to Desgenettes. 'We heard of the plan at Acre,' he said, his iron-shod boots grinding on the paving stones, 'to poison our boys who had the plague, to put them down, like dogs. And that you refused.'

From a barred window high above to their right, a flat square of light was projected down into the passage, the broad-backed sergeant's grey and white uniform glowing momentarily bright, then obscured by deep shadow on the other side as he continued. He glanced back over his shoulder at Desgenettes from the darkness. 'If I may, that was courage, *mon général*.'

Delphine looked at Desgenettes, shocked. He had said nothing of this to her. Desgenettes cleared his throat, uncomfortable with the praise. 'It was a difficult time.'

Eventually they came to a halt at an iron gate. The sergeant produced an ornate key from a ring and opened the antique Ottoman lock. 'Just to say… we know who we can trust.' The sergeant swung the gate open. 'General, the prisoner is yours. We shall remain here.'

Desgenettes nodded formally, and the sergeant ushered them in. Belliard and Damas moved in behind, clearly never having seen such accommodations before. More than a cell, they entered a narrow passageway with several gates and locked doors leading off, possibly storerooms, before it opened into a large chamber – rough stone walls met a high vaulted ceiling. A barred window far up the wall to one side, possibly at ground level, gave the only daylight.

In the shadows they saw a figure swaddled in dark robes and turban, sitting on the floor, leaning against the wall. His wrists and ankles were shackled to chains bolted into the stone behind him. Possibly sixty, he had a thick moustache and beard, his bare feet black with grime.

'*Mon dieu*,' hissed Belliard. 'Who is responsible for… for this… *this degradation*? It is beyond dishonour.'

Damas was unmoved. 'I hear it is more than our consuls have in the Seven Towers in Constantinople.'

Despite this, the man sat relaxed, one hand upon his knee, as if resting on a fine divan among silk cushions and wafting curtains.

'It is disgraceful,' agreed Desgenettes, removing his coat. 'But, General, perhaps we can have him moved for recovery to the infirmary above. Dr Antoine, *Madame* Lascelles, come. Let us to our task quickly now, lest we are discovered.'

'Discovered be damned,' grated Belliard. 'I will have the officer responsible moved down here in his stead.'

'Discovered?' asked Delphine.

She helped Desgenettes pull a smock over his head. 'There are those who would wish him dead rather than treated, Delphine.'

'But who is he?' she persisted. 'You can tell me that at least.'

Masoud bowed to the figure. '*As-salamu aleikum, ya Pasha al-Kebir*.'

Desgenettes and the generals watched and listened: the prisoner looked up, his demeanour alert, ironic, unfazed by his privation. He raised a hand and nodded in polite acknowledgement. '*Wa aleikum as-salam.*'

Masoud looked at them. 'This, I must tell you, is the great Mustafa Pasha, grand commander of the Ottoman armies, victor of the Russians, who once fought the valiant Prince Potemkin.' He looked about. 'What does he do in this dread place?'

Belliard confirmed Masoud's discovery. 'He was captured at Aboukir Bay by General Murat, Masoud *effendi*, who chopped off several of his fingers in single combat.'

'Which is why he has gangrene,' added Desgenettes, going through his bag, 'and why I have with me my best battlefield surgical assistant.'

Mustafa looked up at them with a level stare.

'By removing his hand,' explained Belliard quietly, 'we save his life. In saving his life, we may yet have a chance to guarantee a peace accord with the Ottomans.'

In the passage behind they heard shouts growing louder, peremptory orders – '*You will cease at once!*' – and the replies of the guard: '*We are the general commandant, and take no order! Who goes there?*'

The sergeant stepped away from the gate and, with a quick movement, locked them inside. 'General – we shall stand firm,' he called, and threw Desgenettes the heavy key – just as Citizen Peraud burst into the passageway with two deputies. Peraud banged on the barred gate.

'What goes on here? Who gave you this authority! You will unhand this prisoner of the State!'

Belliard ignored him and commanded Desgenettes, 'You will continue, Doctor.' He turned and advanced on the gate. 'So. *Citizen* Peraud. It is *you* to blame for this ill-treatment of an enemy, brought down in honourable combat and paroled under the Law of Arms.'

Twisted by burns and bruises inflicted by Cook and Underhill, Peraud's face shone with sweat and outrage, his knuckles whitening as he clenched the iron bars. 'He is *mine*, Belliard! You have no authority beyond the *général en chef*! You shall unhand him at once!'

Desgenettes stepped forward. 'The *Général en chef* Kléber has given his authority. You shall not let this man die.'

In his fury, Peraud heaved and rattled at the iron bars. 'Open this gate! Open it, damn you!' Stepping back, he tugged a small, screw-barrelled pistol from his coat pocket and Delphine gasped. She had seen it before. It was Derrien's. Derrien had once nearly executed her with it.

But before Peraud could try to raise it, the Provost-Sergeant shoved one of the deputies aside and put a dragoon blunderbuss pistol to the back of Peraud's head. 'One move more, Citizen, and I avenge the dead of Acre.'

Peraud froze. His stare flicked from the sergeant to Desgenettes and Belliard. 'Do you truly believe, General, *do you*, that if you save him, you can barter for terms? To what end? To surrender the garrison? The *colony*?' Belliard glanced at Damas – Peraud was raising the very uncertainties that had dogged their minds. 'If you attempt *that*,' spat Peraud, 'you are very much *mistaken*. You will return to France nothing but *traitors*.' The sergeant's gun pushed his forehead hard against the bars. 'And there shall be a reckoning for all those who betray the great *général en chef*!'

'The *général en chef* has abandoned us all, Citizen,' declared Belliard. 'All we have left are monuments to the dead.'

For a moment they stood in silence, Mustafa Pasha watching the play before him. The sergeant pulled back the cock on the pistol to its final ratchet, and Peraud clenched his eyes in anger. 'Sergeant. *You will pay for this*.'

The Provost scoffed. 'Achille Caron is right. We have already paid, *m'sieur le diable*.'

Delphine broke the spell, turning away to lay out Desgenettes' instruments on the white cloth on the floor, the metal clinking, her hands shaking, her face flushed with fear, with anger – until Desgenettes took the tourniquet from her hands. He glanced at Mustafa.

'Masoud,' said Desgenettes. 'Tell him, for surgery, we still follow the principles of the great Ibn Sina.'

Masoud nodded and translated into Turkish for the Ottoman lord.

Mustafa gave a tight smile, his lined, unshaven face worn by many such decisions, unmoved, and spoke. 'Then,' said Masoud, translating his reply, 'carry on, wise doctor.'

The pasha proffered his rotting hand with a rattle of chain, as if it were nothing – a tool for which he now had no use. The *savant* Dr Antoine undid the old dressing round the darkened stubs of the three dead phalanges. He held a small key, glanced at Desgenettes who nodded, then inserted the key into the wrist manacle and released the limb. The iron ring dropped with a dull clank to the straw on the stone floor.

Giving him a cushion for his head, they laid him flat, elevating the limb, and Delphine applied the tourniquet to the wrist, her cool, slender hands appearing so very alien on the Turk's dark, powerful forearm. From the gate, Peraud shot his last bolt.

'Be *very* careful, Surgeon-General! The *général en chef* will return and demand a reckoning!' He positively smiled at the thought. 'If you slip and he dies, he will be of no use to you and your schemes, and you shall have the blame!'

Kneeling beside the reclining Mustafa, Desgenettes looked back at Peraud. 'Let others use him,' he said. 'But let us save him.'

Delphine handed Desgenettes the first cutter. Mustafa Pasha met her eye, then looked away as Masoud intoned a prayer.

-

The fine Château de St-Cloud in Paris was in uproar. Thanks to the efforts of Lucien Bonaparte, both the upper house Council of Ancients and the lower house, the Council of Five Hundred, had agreed to evacuate the assembly rooms in the Tuileries Palace for fear of a Jacobin revolt, and had repaired to the magnificent château just west of the city. Now the splendid baroque corridors were blocked by outraged councillors and deputies in periwigs and top hats, all wild with talk of Jacobins, rebellion and a possible *coup d'état*.

Pushing their way through the arguing mob of politicians, former member of the Directory Emmanuel Joseph Sieyès led a tight group of luminaries marching in heavy step, headed by his greatest trump card: Napoléon Bonaparte. As they strode through the château, Sieyès talked animatedly all the while over his shoulder to him, of 'true Republicanism', 'national conscience' and 'the people' without taking a breath, meeting only Bonaparte's alert yet untroubled expression.

'...when I replaced your enemy Rewbell as one of the Directors last May,' assured Sieyès, 'I knew at once, General, that you were the man we needed,' he insisted, pushing past a knot of bewigged civil servants. '*Mon dieu*, let us through! It is of national importance!' He looked back to ensure Bonaparte was still with him, perhaps aware of his tenuous grip on the invincible hero. 'We shall see what has happened with your brother the president, and the Five Hundred—'

'We shall,' agreed Bonaparte, catching the eye of General Joachim Murat marching beside him: another hero of Egypt, and one at least he knew he could trust.

They turned a corner into a broad hallway, the panelled and painted ceiling of the great château rising far above, tall windows to their left looking out onto the grand quad filled with carriages and files of troops. Bonaparte watched the figures of the *Anciens* of the upper house silhouetted against the bright glass, the vista of manicured gardens and fountains stretching behind them down to the distant banks of the Seine, the November leaves blowing from the trees with the onset of sharp winter winds. More of the angry *Anciens* burst from the Galerie d'Apollon as they concluded their meeting, still in heated argument.

Bonaparte gave a slow look around him, aware that all eyes were on him and Murat and the marching escort of grenadier officers. There was no doubt they were a threat: hardened conquerors returned from afar, dark-skinned from the desert sun, fresh from battle, fresh from victory. Some of the onlookers pointed, calling his name, proud – until the crowd could resist no longer and burst with cheers. *Vive! Vive le général! Vive le général!*

Bonaparte raised a hand to wave, touching his hat brim, acknowledging his supporters. It reminded him of his return to Toulon just a month earlier, as he stepped down the gangplank of the frigate *Muiron*. His departure not two weeks earlier had not been marred in the least by the unfortunate incident on the beach. On the contrary, he decided: when he heard the people cheer on the quaysides, his confrontation with Hazzard had focussed his mind. Even here he thought of Hazzard, the captured scholar on Malta, discussing Caesar with him in a fragrant garden, and thanked him for demanding answers, for demanding to know the *goal*: yes, he was returning to save France. And so he would, through Sieyès.

In Toulon, Bonaparte had stopped on the gangplank, one hand on the guy-rope handrail, looking at the crowded dockside, hearing their cheers. He had been unprepared for this, part of him imagining he should return in secret, a surprise to Barras and the fools at the Tuileries in Paris.

But here he had been shown something different. They loved him. He had looked up at the banners waving on the surrounding cliffs, his long hair blowing and, for a moment, lowered his head, as if humbled

– then snatched off his cocked hat and thrust it to the air. Even the saluting guns of Toulon and the bands playing the 'Marseillaise' were drowned by the roar from the crowd, troops, merchants, women, children, all – the *people*. All of it – Malta, Egypt, Gaza, Jaffa, Acre – it had all been, he concluded, for the *people*.

Marching now through the flustered secretaries and officials, buffeted by elbows from all sides, they reached the sanctuary of an office, the Council deputies wrangling with the *Anciens*, coming to blows by the windows, Bonaparte and the army the threat to some, Bonaparte the answer to others. But Bonaparte ignored it all; Sieyès threw open the tall doors and they marched inside, as if Sieyès were a detective thwarting a great crime.

Inside was an elegant reception room of bergère chairs, Aubusson carpet, gilt and black-lacquered table with ornate oil lamps, a bronze of a winged Mercury on a plinth before windows looking out to the Orangery walk and fountain. Before the desk stood a very portly and worried Paul Nicolas Barras, one of the five Directors of the French government. His jowled face brightened at once with relief. 'Ah! Napoléon,' he said with a desperate laugh, coming forward to grasp the hand of his most famous *protégé*, leaning to tower over him. He spoke in a stage whisper, as if in secret. 'I am so very pleased, so grateful you have come – perhaps you can put an end to this, er...'

But Bonaparte withdrew his hand. 'How could you?' he said, stepping back. 'How could you, Paul?'

The giant of the Republic was taken aback. 'I... I do not understand...?'

Bonaparte was merciless. 'Understand? *Ma foi!* Draining our coffers dry, enriching yourselves all the while! And not a ship, not a single brigade or ducat sent to aid me in Egypt while I send jewels of conquest home!'

Barras looked round at them all, shrinking back. 'B-but that is not so! We... we—'

'How many golden baubles, how many silken gowns or silver buckles more for your mistresses must I buy with the blood of my armies?' shouted Bonaparte. 'You have lost us *everything*.'

Barras retreated, putting a hand out to the desk, stammering, 'N-no, I... I... That is not—'

Sieyès slapped a sheet of paper on the gilt-edged table. 'You will resign, Citizen Barras! You are relieved of your situation!'

Barras stared at Sieyès, then at Bonaparte. 'B–but surely, Napoléon, it is I…! I, who threw the general's baton to you on the 13th *Vendémiaire*! Is it not I who—'

'*Enough*,' called Sieyès. 'It was you who called himself King of France in the debauched salons of this city,' he accused, 'while others such as the general here were abroad fighting for our Republic! I have resigned, as has Ducos in sympathy, and Gohier and Moulin have been *arrested*. The Directory,' he declared, 'is *finished*. We bring a new era!'

Bonaparte approached Barras at the table. 'Has Talleyrand spoken with you? Explained our situation?'

Barras blinked and cleared his throat, then nodded. 'He has.'

Bonaparte held his gaze. 'Then we are as one.'

Sieyès watched them closely. Barras regarded Bonaparte with awe, his scarred, sun-browned features, no longer the pale boy he had once guided through the treachery of the Revolution. Here was power, returned from Egypt, greater than ever before. Barras had seen the writing in the sands, long before Bonaparte had set sail. 'Then, for you, Napoléon,' he said, 'I comply. For I believe in you.'

He paid not so much as a glance to Sieyès, who evidently felt himself in charge. Barras picked up the pen from the desk and dipped the nib. With a moment's hesitation, he looked at the young general. 'I hereby relinquish my post as a Director of France.'

Bonaparte gave a scarcely perceptible nod. In that moment between them passed five years of civil war, revolt, alliance, denial and desperation, Joséphine at the salon, Barras watching their first dance, battle in Italy, and a climb to victory – all now paid in full through their silent accord. The pen of Paul Nicolas Barras scratched on the page, and it was done.

Sieyès snatched it out from under Barras and waved it dry, holding it aloft triumphantly for the gathering to see. 'At last, the king is dead…' he said, '…and long live the Republic.' He looked about. 'With this, the Directory is put to an end.'

There was a banging at the door and the grenadier sergeant opened it, his men turning, muskets in hand, ready. It was Lucien, Bonaparte's brother, President of the Council of Five Hundred, his cheeks red and puffed, apparently having come at the run. 'Napoléon, they are debating at this very moment. They know *everything*.'

'So they should!' Sieyès held out Barras's resignation for Lucien to see. 'Our path is clear, Citizen President.'

Lucien flicked a glance at Bonaparte, who straightened his tunic, adjusted his sword and faced the door. The grenadiers looked to the general and formed up beside him. Bonaparte glanced at Sieyès, and indicated the door. In this moment of unlikely generosity, Bonaparte said, 'A man of the cloth should perhaps go before a show of arms, Citizen.'

Citizen Sieyès took the moment with pride. 'And for this service I shall thank you, General. Citizen President,' he said with a nod, 'let us sway the motion, and win the vote.'

Sieyès led the way out and Lucien followed, the general giving his brother the same closed face he gave everyone. 'The *Anciens* may have been difficult yesterday,' Lucien confided quietly, 'but the Five Hundred are adamant – they say the forced resignations are illegal, and Barras must stay. However,' he added, as they headed into the crowded hall, 'some deputies have somehow spread the rumour there might be an armed Jacobin uprising from within their ranks.'

'Really?' said Bonaparte. 'How alarming. Luckily, we are on hand.'

'Indeed,' murmured Lucien.

Sieyès leading the way, the generals and escort marched through the hall into the opulent foyer, and into the midst of the angry *Anciens* and Council deputies. '*Let this day*,' proclaimed Sieyès from the front, addressing the pressing mob, '*be forever remembered. That on 19 Brumaire, the people took back the Republic…!*'

There were cheers mingling with boos of *Jacobins, Jacobins*, the chants vying with each other. *Vive! Vive le général!*

Within ten minutes they found the angry crowd at the entrance to the Orangery behind the main building, the uproar of the assembled Council within echoing loud. Grenadier guards just inside the doors banged to attention as they saw Bonaparte and Lucien push their way into the bright conservatory, the grenadiers' tall mitre caps and muskets threatening, pushing back the resisting deputies, as Sieyès tried to shout the joyous news. '*The Directory is finished! Resigned! We shall have a new constitution!*'

They had set out benches around the walls, against the tall elegant windows, and some climbed up to see over the mob, calling from the back with anonymous impunity, screaming at Sieyès and the group. A hand rose in the midst of them, a voice calling to declare Bonaparte outlaw, bringing a new surge of conflict. General Murat and the grenadiers looked on, Murat's hand tight on his sword. 'General, we would not tolerate this in Egypt.'

Unfazed, Bonaparte moved in among them, the grenadiers following, seizing men by the neck and shoving them aside to make way, more voices rising.

Lucien helped Bonaparte onto a low raised platform. '*So, here!*' cried Bonaparte. '*I am he! I am Bonaparte.*' The mob stilled a moment to listen. '*I am he who brought you victory and safeguarded this nation. You dare cite the constitution? You yourselves have destroyed it!*' The shouts resumed. 'You violated it on 18 Fructidor – you violated it on 22 Floréal – you violated it on 30 Prairial! It lies *trodden* beneath your shoddy *corrupt* feet! *Beneath your contempt!*' He looked round them all: the black and brown frock-coats, the wigs, the bleary, weary and angry faces, the crowd of councillors filling the great length of the Orangery, watching him – and few watching the grenadiers. Bonaparte sealed the moment for them. '*And here is the truth! The Revolution,*' he shouted, '*is over!*'

The dam burst. The outraged Council deputies surged forward to seize Lucien, knocking Bonaparte backwards from the dais, the grenadiers calling out, *Protect the general.* They ported arms with fixed bayonets, and hauled him from the floor to Murat and his officers. Bonaparte staggered against them, trying to draw his sword. '*Lucien! Général Murat! Disperse them! Defend the Republic!*'

For the grenadiers, the blood on Bonaparte's face was enough, but Lucien Bonaparte drew his own sword and shouted to them, 'I would plunge this blade into my own brother's heart, if I believed he meant the Republic harm! *I command the Council be dispersed.*'

As one, Murat's company of grenadiers charged their bayonets and advanced into the crush of deputies. Somewhere a pistol cracked, and they fled for the exits as the grenadiers marched through the entrance, Lucien's voice calling out, '*Jacobins! Jacobins! After them!*'

Fleeing deputies poured through the fine glazed side doors of the Orangery into the gardens, stumbling, running onto the fountain walk, the grenadiers chanting as they advanced into the dissipating mob, *Vive le général, vive vive vive!* Bleeding from a cut to his face, Bonaparte marched behind them with Murat in the steadily clearing hall, the grenadiers chasing the councillors out into the cold November air, some staggering backwards on their heels, hands out to the grenadiers' bayonets, trying to reason, then breaking and tearing into the gardens beyond for their lives, the last cries fading to nothing but the patter of their running feet.

The Orangery quietened, its splayed blossom and fruit trees bearing mute witness to the end of the Revolution. A bruise to his forehead, Sieyès lay slumped and wide-eyed in the arms of two soldiers by the splintered dais, murmuring, 'I do not understand, I do not...'

Beside him, Lucien Bonaparte watched as the last stragglers ran helter-skelter down the steps of the broad walk to the distant ornamental gardens, some tumbling over the decorative hedges and plunging into the shrubbery for safety.

The grenadiers gathered from the side doors and the far exit. There was a handful of injured, trampled in the rush of the crowd, some of them older members. Incredulous *Anciens* entered to help, looking about with surprise at the sight of others limping to benches and seats in the lee of fine overhanging orange trees, their turning leaves reaching out to the glazed autumnal sky overhead.

Bonaparte stood in the centre, hands behind his back, as composed as he had been when he inspected the rubble of the Al-Azhar Mosque, or the slaughter of El-'Arish, or Jaffa, and the plague-pits of Acre. He turned to survey this latest triumph, sword in hand, so that all might recognise him: here was the master of ruin, the conqueror of storms. He looked out at the gardens, the Seine beyond, then the Orangery itself – its fine mouldings, its intricate leaded windows and the pale glimmers of sunshine – as if nothing would ever look quite the same again to him, as indeed it would not.

He looked round for Sieyès, saw him, and made his way towards him slowly, his heels ringing crisp on the cold stone floors. 'So. The Rubicon is crossed,' he said, surveying the scene, 'and Pompey is fallen.' None replied, the grenadiers gazing upon him with devotion. He looked down upon Sieyès. 'To overthrow the Directory, Citizen, you begged the Archduke Charles of Austria to rule France. And he refused you. You yet begged that Prussian dog, Brunswick, our hated enemy. And he refused you. But you thought, "No, this... this *Bonaparte*, yes, he will be useful."' He advanced on him with menace. 'All this, I see, Citizen, was born of patriotism, for love of the Republic,' he grated with loathing. 'Am I not correct?'

Sieyès nodded. 'Y-yes, yes of course, *mon général*... I... I have a completely new constitution, ready, waiting, for the *people*—'

Bonaparte cut him off. 'The Jacobin Councils are done. I shall amend your new constitution,' he told Sieyès. 'I drafted a constitution for Malta. In ten days. I did so again in Egypt. I do so for all peoples. And you and your' – he sought the appropriate words – '*esteemed* colleagues will attest to it, Citizen Sieyès. And France shall flourish.'

The grenadiers formed up behind Bonaparte and came to attention. There could be no doubt that coup of Citizen Sieyès had been poached from within by the master tactician himself. Sieyès looked up at him, for the first time evidently afraid of the erstwhile puppet whom he had sought to control. 'Y-yes of course… *mon général.*'

Satisfied, Bonaparte turned to Murat, to the grenadier officers and nodded. 'Joachim, we shall secure the château from further unrest.' He passed his eye over the discarded Sieyès, uninterested, and nodded to his brother. 'Come, Lucien. We go.'

As they strode out of the Orangery, Bonaparte muttered to Murat, 'Now, let us retrieve my army.'

Killer

The *Volpone* made Crete within five days; most ships would have taken ten. They had caught a timely Levant from the east and were blown northward by the last hot breaths of the Libyan *khamsin* and headed northwest to the Ionian Sea. They had spotted traders making for the southern tip of Italy, Leuca, or to Taormina in Sicily and beyond. Others headed north to Puglia and into the Adriatic, or eastwards to the Aegean islands and on to Piraeus – but the *Volpone* sought the hunting-ground of the *Généreux*.

When De la Vega heard the news of Tomlinson and the *Valiant*, he did not hesitate. He had risked everything for Hazzard to find and save Sarah, from Corsica to Naples, to Malta and into the inferno of Aboukir Bay at the Battle of the Nile – that *Généreux* might have interfered with Sarah's return home, especially in the sacrosanct state of death, had rekindled his outrage against his hated enemy, the French.

Just as with the chase to Malta, the *Volpone* set full sail, from her extended mainyards and stunsails to topgallants and flying jibs: staysails cracked and billowed fore and aft of the mainmast. The frigate sliced across the waves like a racing schooner, heeling with the wind, nose up, her copper bows flashing with spray as she ploughed the bright blue, beneath towering clouds under an endless heaven.

On some days *Capitán* Don Cesár Domingo de la Vega joined Hazzard in the cramped high foremast tops, just above the foretopyard, scanning the horizon through a fully extended telescope. It was a good position, the topgallant creaking above, affording an uninterrupted forward view across the prow, the jibs lofting just before them. The world was a dazzle of sail and sea, the knotted reefing lines rapping sharp staccato tattoos as they rattled against the taut canvas. The horizon stretched round them in a haze of blue, the dun shapes of distant Greek islands almost invisible against the sky.

The wind tugged at De la Vega's tail of dark oiled hair, curls of smoke blowing from a Virginian cigarillo clamped between his lips:

in his dark Moroccan leather coat, pale breeches and Cordovan boots, and with his fine royal court moustaches, he looked every inch the Spanish Don –the Toledo rapier at his hip, Venetian dagger sheathed in the small of his back, and London pistol rammed in his belt completed the picture. A privateer from Barcelona with official letters of marque, now also from King George, De la Vega considered this personal alliance to England his duty to Spain, by helping Sir Sidney Smith defeat Bonaparte in the Mediterranean – he would never comply with a flimsy treaty with duplicitous France. In truth, he did it for William John Hazzard, and he would do so to his dying breath.

Many of the two hundred crew were De la Vega's family – sons, nephews, nieces and adoptive cousins. They all took the same risks their father did, for him, and for each other. Alfonso, the first officer, was De la Vega's eldest son, a dark, quiet young man who had taken some time to accept their English guests the year earlier, but had struck up a nodding friendship with Wayland; Carlos the bo'sun was De la Vega's nephew. Topmen and riggers such as Rodrigo, Juan and Lluis, carpenters or gunners, had been born into the tribe or adopted – like the dark-eyed Elena, Alfonso's 'sister', with her scarred face, potions, talismans and shock of Moorish black curls, who had nursed Hazzard to health after the *Volpone* had rescued him and the marines from howling storm and battle with the French.

The Genoese-built 44-gun *Volpone* had been refined by Catalan shipbuilders for speed and combat, with all the hallmarks of Italian and Spanish craftsmanship, from Brazilian hardwood masts to elaborately carved finishes. She had a sharp prow and an unusually deep keel allowing for a thick-planked hull as strong as the famed USS *Constitution*, and the ability to perform tight turns while heeling heavily in a high wind, with the finest coppered hull in the Mediterranean – and was the fastest frigate most had ever seen. She carried thirty 18- and 24-pounder guns ranged along her gundecks, but unlike the average frigate, she had a raised fo'c'sle foredeck and a raised poop over the quarterdeck, providing three fighting platforms like a 74. It was on these that De la Vega had massed *Volpone*'s deadliest armament: 36-pounder carronades with explosive incendiary shells, Long 18s on her bows and stern, and a myriad of swivel-gun murderers. She was a fitting mate to Sidney Smith's *Tigre*, and a deadly adversary.

'This *puta Francesa*...' cursed De la Vega in a murmur, peering steadily through the eyeglass. 'She could hide in the little islands, *amigo mio*, waiting for her rendezvous...' He scoffed. 'She could be anywhere. Pah! But *Volpone* shall find her.'

They had plotted their course carefully, to think like the captain of the *Généreux* – to avoid Ottoman coastal forts and naval harbours, just as he would have done – then to enter the interior to prowl for undefended traders among the islands. De la Vega had let them all crowd round the Spanish chart spread across a table near the binnacle and wheel, and tapped a finger at the edge of Crete, following a fine contour line up to the western coast of the Peloponnese.

'This,' he had said, in his thickly accented English for the marines, 'is the edge of the Aegean, *el mar Egéo, sí*? They say the waters of the Greeks go down, *mil brazas, sí*? More than a *thousand* fathoms...' He indicated a point in the Ionian Sea. 'But I pray we meet her here, where this blue of the sea, this Aegean blue, it grows dark, *señores*, dark as wine, for *el fondo marino* – the floor of the sea, hm? – here she goes down, down to *el inferno del diablo*. These, so my *amigos* fishermen say...' He looked to Hazzard. 'How do we say, "*los profundidades*"?'

Hazzard understood. 'Deeps.'

'Mm,' nodded the Spaniard. 'They call this, *amigos*, the Deeps of Hades.'

De la Vega drew on a pungent cheroot, blowing a cloud of smoke as the onlookers stared down at the chart. Hazzard understood his vivid description – the clear azure blue of the Aegean did indeed darken, as if beyond the Aegean shelf, as it merged with the Mediterranean. Was this where Odysseus had been enchanted by Calypso, he wondered, in mythic waters. Captains might well have inscribed their charts, *Here are dragons*, he thought.

'We'll need plenty o'spots to hide, I'd say, sir,' said Underhill. 'Avoidin' awkward questions, I mean. Some high cliffs would be handy...'

'Y'auld sea-dog, 'Miah,' rumbled Cook, and they laughed quietly – but Hazzard knew he was right and nodded.

'Yes. Some of the islands have rock formations tall enough to conceal a topmast.' He looked about. 'So we can duck in if need be.'

Underhill gave his hideous half-grin, his broken teeth only partly hidden. 'Well... then so's can the Frog, eh sir?'

'Best eyes on the glasses, Sar'nt,' said Hazzard, looking to Carlos the bo'sun. '*Solo el mejor. Sí, Señor Carlos?*'

He put his finger to his brow in sharp salute. '*Si señor el Mayor. Como las águilas.*' *Like eagles.*

Warnock peered at the chart, studying it. 'I 'eard tell of these waters, sir,' he said. 'Back in Syracuse. Queer things. Mists out o'nowhere, boilin' seas and the like...' He looked round at their sceptical faces. 'Iss true, though, innit? That's what they said—'

'Ye're a right barrel o'laughs, Knocky,' replied Kite.

'Just sayin' we got to watch out, mate.'

They hooted with laughter – *An' the seas they did boileth* – De Lisle wiggling his fingers at Warnock and saying *boo* – and dispelled those misgivings which would nevertheless creep in. Afterwards, as the crew dispersed, De la Vega joined Hazzard at the starboard shrouds and looked out. 'A thousand fathoms...' He glanced at him. 'You say this still, yes?'

'Yes. Height of a man.'

De la Vega nodded. 'The height of a man.' He looked out at the waters sliding by, the cooling spray misting in the air as the evening crept in. 'A thousand men standing one on the other... What heights we could reach,' he mused, then flicked a glance at the blackness beneath. '*A qué profundidades nos hundimos...*'

To what depths we sink.

'A Spanish poet?'

'I thought it could be Cervantes,' said De la Vega equably, 'but it was only me.'

As they moved further north, they avoided a Turkish squadron on the horizon, shadowed a trio of small merchantmen in the hope it would draw out an attacker, but did not. Eventually they moved round the Greek coast to the entrance to the Aegean. Several of the crew and marines peered over the side in silence, watching the magical blue below, as if for gods or creatures that might rise up and swallow them whole.

In their search, De la Vega applied his smuggler's skills: for days they kept a shortened sail and prowled carefully past a warren of rocky coves, sniffing round Kythera and the small island chain stretching from the extended fingers of the Peloponnese, the gateway to the Cyclades, but with no result.

Hazzard went aloft with the lookouts, fore, main and mizzenmast tops, all. But in his more solemn moments, he spent much of his time as he had on the *Valiant* in pursuit of Sarah: brooding alone at the bows or fo'c'sle rail, one hand on the creaking shrouds of the foremast as the spray burst around him.

The marines kept a protective eye on him, the crew concerned, some crossing themselves, Christina in her black Moorish habit sensing something of his will, as if Hazzard himself were warding off the evil eye, daring it to block their path. Carlos the bo'sun had taken her away, little Elena refusing to go some evenings, sitting huddled at the base of the foremast with her small hands round her knees, watching him as she clutched her crucifix, intoning spells.

Underhill had caught a snatch of conversation between the men and noticed Warnock join Pettifer on the short steps up to the foredeck, as if guarding Hazzard, taking up their station like faithful hounds. Cook had seen it as well.

'Changed 'is tune from long past, eh, Jory boy?' hissed Underhill, working the bowl of his long clay pipe, nodding at Warnock.

'Aye,' said Cook, scarce able to believe it: Warnock, the Burnt Man, scarred, angry, facing up to Hazzard on that first day so long ago, resisting every order until Wayland took a bullet on Malta and put him to shame. 'He's good now,' rumbled Cook. 'All of 'em are. Best I ever had, 'Miah. The best.'

His stringy dark hair blowing, Underhill had drawn on his pipe. 'It was wrong of Sir Sid to tell the major as he did. Wrong.'

'How so?'

'Some things a man don't need to know. Till it be true and he can face it. But this – that the Frogs have taken even our dead from us… Jory, boy, naah, it's too much.' He drew on the pipe and applied a glowing match from the gangway lamp, clouds of smoke rising. He shook his head and gave a crooked smile, the dead and pocked flesh of his bare upper lip stretching with the strain of it. 'So now,' he concluded, 'Gawd help the bastards when we find 'em.'

Handley and Carlos had watched Hazzard at times, seen Cook drape a cloak over him as night had drawn in, for he would not come down till exhausted, falling into a cot in one of the small cabins, wrapped in his own disturbed dreams. Elena sometimes watched over him as he slept, on occasions embracing him to her soft warmth. But Handley knew him well, from near five years earlier, back at the Cape, and knew his ways. 'He won't come down till he's done, Charlie,' he had told Carlos. 'Mark my words. He never stops.' He had told him of the fight with Harry Race at the Cape. 'Never does.'

Carlos had shaken his head, his rough half-shaven beard untended in the long hours of their voyage, his dark skin glowing. He wiped his forehead with a patterned red bandanna. '*Madre de dios...* There is magic with us.'

'Good magic, Charlie,' assured Handley. 'Just you see.'

Up in the mizzen tops with staring bleary eyes, Hazzard now scanned the outcrops of distant islands far to the starboard quarter, knowing that every headland could conceal a haven for a raider. He hunted for the telltale spikes of masts or protruding yards, but saw nothing.

Généreux.

But where.

The *Généreux* was a heavy three-masted 74-gun French ship of the line, capable of battle with 100-gun First-Rates such as HMS *Victory* or the *Ville de Paris*. If Petrides were right, *Généreux* was a menace and had to be stopped. The idea that she could jeopardise the possibility of peace in Egypt was secondary to Hazzard, in thrall of his desire to know: *did Généreux stop Sarah getting home?*

'She could be safe, in Toulon,' De la Vega had kept saying. 'And we never find the *Généreux*. Never *know*.' They had discussed nothing else for nearly two weeks.

'And what if she put to sea months ago,' Hazzard countered. 'Got past Nelson, as they all did? She's here. I can feel it.'

De la Vega knew more than to argue with Hazzard's fixations – his last words had been an ominous reminder: 'You have purged the black blood for your lady, *amigo*. That dog Derrien, he is dead – *muerte*. Beware the blood does not take you once more.'

Hazzard peered through the blurring scope, his thoughts rambling, his weakened eyes blinking, the lashes obscuring the eyepiece. Of course the experienced De la Vega was right: *lack of sleep, lack of food, own bloody fault, fool*. But *Généreux* symbolised something else: Hazzard had left the tethered goats in Aboukir Bay for Nelson's tigers, and the captains had come, wreaking havoc upon Brueys' fleet, moored so neatly in line, so hopelessly trapped. Brueys, Blanquet, Du Petit-Thouars, all fighting like demigods, and all fallen. But the *Guillaume Tell* and the *Généreux* had slipped away quietly.

Sarah had died for that battle, died bringing England to the shores of Egypt, to rain fire upon the French, and England had come. But, *then*, he repeated to himself bitterly, then to lie helpless in the *Valiant*, a lugger despatch-runner, at the mercy of a shamed brute of a 74, now bereft of honour – it was too much for him to bear. No, Hazzard would not leave the task of lookout to others – if they stood watch, so would he, and for longer.

Tomlinson, Sarah – gone. It cannot be.

Hazzard knew there was little hope of stumbling upon their prey – or, still more unlikely, to approach her unawares in broad daylight. Hazzard gazed out at the world, the tilted boom of the aft lateen sail creaking just below him, a great pointer to the aft horizon, the frothing wake dissipating on the waves behind. The Aegean wind was fine and clean, gaining a wintry edge at times but otherwise warm, and he breathed it in to dislodge his fears. He raised the scope to his eye once more.

The marines were well integrated with *Volpone*'s crew, Handley aloft acting as rigging mate, learning from the privateers: taking a line and running the mainyard, dashing across barefoot. The nimble Maria-Luisa was best at this, and could swing outboard over the foaming spray just for a game. On several occasions Hazzard saw Handley swooping down with a howl, having tumbled, suspended from a lifeline, the Spaniards roaring with laughter, Maria-Luisa swinging down to dangle next to him – *Handeleh* – hauling him in, making him chase her into the tops, then nipping out and descending to the deck like an acrobat. 'I'll get 'er one day, sir,' he confided, Hazzard replying, 'I'm sure that's just what she wants.'

At nights, music often floated up from the gundeck below; there were near twenty wives and *cuchillas* – 'knife-women' – among the privateers, as battle-hardened as the men, the Moorish Spaniards like Halawa and Sofia from Algeciras and Ayamonte the most fierce. Hazzard had heard castanets and the percussive clapping of the dance. He had even sat on the midships step, looking on as they attempted one of Kite's lewd songs, interrupted by Cook at just the right moment.

'Our Polly would shave her fore*castle*,' Kite began thoughtfully:

'And stick her bum up, for young Jack to *rascal*;
He'd dive on her with passion,
(In much the French fashion),
And his nose would go right up her— Oh 'ello Sarge, want another
    beer then?'

'I'll be a-watchin' o'you, boy,' rumbled the big man, moving on, doing well to stifle a grin as the chorus struck up behind him.

Ohhhh, I'm Jolly Jack, I'm Jolly Jack, I'm master of the fleet!
An' if you're lurkin' round the 'eads,
I'll 'ave yer arse, me sweet, hoi!

The marines tried to translate, and Hazzard left as the gathering dissolved into yowls of laughter.

Underhill could often be found at the midships rail with Carlos or Garcia, one of the helmsmen, looking out silently, pipes glowing against a slate sky, puffs of blue smoke swirling about them, each to their long memories of a lifetime at sea. The remainder of the marines lent a hand where they could, repairing lines, cleaning blocks, sewing buck-and-ball cartridges for their sawn-off Charlevilles, and stitching bags of grape for the 18- and 24-pounders and 36-pounder carronades with workmanlike focus. With his apothecary's skills, Porter made sticky compounds for better matches and adapted their bag o'tricks snap-igniters with the *Volpone*'s chief gunner, Ezau, proud of his newly acquired Turkish arsenal of Greek Fire and incendiaries.

Once, Hazzard had found Warnock on the fo'c'sle steps, cleaning the hooked axehead of his Huron tomahawk.

'Was that from an enemy?' he had asked him.

'Yes, sir.' After a moment he added, 'Hurons were employed by the Frogs. I mean, the French, sir. We had the Mohawks. Mohawks made war on them.' He handed it to Hazzard to examine.

Hazzard hefted it. It was heavier than he had thought, but had supreme balance, as fine as any Runkel sword blade. 'What did you do before the marines, Warnock?'

Warnock looked puzzled, as if unable to remember. 'Farrier, sir,' with surprise, with sudden recall. 'In Horncastle. Joined the 69th Lincs and went to Canada.'

Hazzard wondered what he had seen. 'Was it bad?'

Warnock did not look up. He gave a small nod. Hazzard waited. After some time, Warnock said, 'Hurons, sir.' He blinked. 'Irukwa and Mohawk didn't like 'em none. An' I didn't, neither. Like me an' the Frogs, sir.'

Hazzard handed back the tomahawk. 'Why in particular?'

'Would chop up anything. Woman, child, newborn.' Warnock looked at the tomahawk, his gaze intense. 'Frog prisoners said it was Hurons. Said it, but it weren't. We could tell. Boot prints, bayonet wounds. Whole family. Even Sal, the daughter. My sweet'eart, she was. Used to gimme a sumac tea if we passed, with maple sugar. And I once got a kiss...' He wiped it slowly, feeling its edge, remembering. 'Them Frogs was my first scalps. Still alive when I did it, screamin'. Did it for Sal. Did it for hate.'

Hazzard's darkness often seeped through the planks below decks, and between the lighter moments the brutal reality of their task hung heavy in the air. At these times the rare sound below was the slow grinding of a blade on a whetstone, De Lisle, Tariq and Hesse masters of their trade, or the clicking ratchets of oiled firelocks. Even Napier and Kite would quieten, taken by Hazzard's grim medicine. They all watched, and waited.

–

Hazzard and Cook were at the taffrail of the poopdeck when it happened. Hazzard lowered his scope as he felt a chill brush his cheek. He looked over at Cook, his sleeveless marine jerkin suddenly bright against a grey and purple sky, his faded denim shirtsleeves almost luminous in the half-light. 'Jory.'

Cook turned, the big man nodding. 'Aye. It's coming.'

Electric storms flashed far in the distance, grey curtains of rain moving across a misty horizon, lightning bolts blazing silently in heavy air, the crew dead still, drumrolls of thunder muffled, sometimes not reaching their ears for minutes after. Hazzard heard a footfall behind him and turned to see Elena, her wide, black eyes watching him, the gusts of cold and hot wind blowing her wild dark curls about her face.

'*Solo un tormenta*,' he said softly to her, to reassure. *Just a storm*. He had once wondered what horrors had been perpetrated upon this small, gentle creature – but he knew the answer, as De la Vega had told him when they had first met: there was black magic in those deep eyes, and men had been fearful of her powers.

Elena took Hazzard's arm and clung to him, murmuring softly in her half-Catalan attempt to speak his name, '*Guilliamo.*' She rested her head on his shoulder. He could feel the heat of her, and he remembered those nights heading to Naples, racked by nightmare and demon, her warmth and witchcraft warding off the evils within him.

The distant rumbles in the skies faded, leaving behind an ominous silence. Elena tensed at his side and he looked out, raising the scope. '*Que està?*' he asked her. *What is it.*

'I not know…'

The wind had stopped whistling, and with it, even the sound of the sea. 'Jory? Anything?'

Cook scanned the horizon off to port, then starboard, but saw nothing. Too often they had seen it before in the Indian Ocean, all eyes ahead or looking out amidships, but none astern, to see if the hunter had become the hunted: he imagined *Généreux* stealing up into their wake, laying off at twice their range and loosing a few 36-pounder round-shots at them, enough to smash *Volpone* and send her foundering. But there was nothing.

The Catalans at the rails around them now stood still and looked forward, sensing the approach of something unnatural. Cook moved next to Hazzard. 'Can't see a ruddy thing,' he murmured. 'But I can feel it in me bones, sure as Bristol.'

Hazzard agreed. The hairs on the nape of his neck stood on end: *something was out there.*

De Lisle looked out from the midships rail when he turned, and Hazzard knew that whatever it was, they had found it. '*Jaysus shite an' all!*' He pointed.

Hazzard heard it before he saw it: a distant roar like a waterfall, as the cries came fast, from Handley, from the Spanish – *Dead ahead! Todo derecha!* Cook saw it just as Kite spun about on the fo'c'sle foredeck, his mouth forming the words just as the lookouts began to call, *Get yer ruddy 'eads down!*

Cook stared. '*By all that's holy in Bristol…*' It was all he could say.

Two hundred yards off the starboard bow, the cloud base had been blown open as if by a giant's bellows: bursting from the surface rose a twisting, spinning pillar of frothing seawater twice the height of the mainmast, raging with the thunder of a thousand galloping hoofbeats.

Hazzard stared. 'Good God… A waterspout.'

Spray whipping at their faces, the crew cried out, pointing, seizing their fellows, some falling to their knees in prayer, calling to their gods, Carlos barking his orders in Catalan and Castilian – '*A les tevas estacions! A tus estaciones, herminos!*' To your stations, brothers – his words lost in the pandemonium. The spattering rain lashed them in gusts, blasted by the freakish winds around the roaring funnel of water. De la Vega looked out from the quarterdeck with Hazzard, his eyes fixed on the indomitable power displayed before them.

'*Dios mio…*' he said. 'It is the edge of the world.'

Hazzard had seen smaller spouts erupting from the Indian Ocean – but nothing like this, certainly not that such a thing might reach up to the sky. He craned his neck to look upwards, beyond the masthead, beyond the cloud, as if he might find De la Vega's thousand men standing upon one another's shoulders, holding up the heavens. The twisting column thundered and began to move. '*Cesár… it will create a maelstrom at its core! Un torbelino…*'

De la Vega shouted down the decks. '*Todas velas! Timor a babor.*' *All sail, helm to port.*

They veered off to port, the yards swinging as Carlos braced to give the diabolic miracle a wide berth. The clouds lowered and the skies darkened, the murmurs of men at prayer all around Hazzard. *Where have we come to, Father, where?*

Hazzard gripped the rail tightly, in no doubt which was the greater power before them. '*Marines to the sheets and halyards! Lay a hand to larboard!*'

The twisting waterspout had drawn them closer and flexed, a great serpent, and had come to within a hundred yards, the wind vicious, the current dragging them towards it, the *Volpone* heeling hard to port, the wake from the bows streaming into a vast whirlpool as it slewed away from the ship.

Volpone heeled away from the destroyer in their path, the masts leaning to twenty degrees, fighting the vacuum of the twisting funnel. Carlos raised a fist at the beast towering above them and called out in Catalan and Spanish, '*Lluitem contra las vents! Luchamos los vientos! Viva, viva el capitán!*'

We fight the winds, we fight the winds! Long live the captain!

'*Viva! Visca el capità!*' came the call from the Catalans.

They hauled on the lines for their lives, the frigate fighting the wind and the waves, the rain whipping at them. Alfonso abseiled down a line from the mainmast tops and dropped beside him and De la Vega. '*Funcionando! Funcionando, padre!*' *It's working.*

The *Volpone* shuddered with the strain to port, the funnel sliding away to the starboard quarter as they rounded it, the helm tied fast by Garcia and his two mates, and the crew cheered.

As they bore off, the funnel seemed to dwindle among the sinking cloud, consumed, its sound muffled, the rain dying to spatters, the sky lightening. Hazzard felt Cook at his shoulder, the big man murmuring his own sacred oath, '*By all that's holy in ruddy Bristol…*' Elena clung to De la Vega, her crucifix tight in hand, and the four of them looked out from the quarterdeck rail, wondering indeed where they had come – but De la Vega seemed to know.

'So, *amigos*,' he said, 'these, I believe, are the Deeps of Hades.'

Hazzard watched the cloud sink around the dwindling geyser of water, its airborne spray wafting on the winds, falling upon them now like a mist, though it were born of De la Vega's *inferno del diablo*. Here, perhaps, were dragons after all.

A call echoed down from the masthead lookout. Far above the topsails, Hazzard saw the waving arm and trained his eyeglass. Abruptly, Alfonso hurried from his post at the fo'c'sle foredeck and sprang up to the foremast tops, climbing the ratlines like a cat. After a moment he called down. '*Niebla…! Todo derecha!*'

Fog – dead ahead.

The ill omens too much for her, Elena followed Hazzard past the mizzenmast and down the steps to the quarterdeck. De le Vega climbed out onto the broad footboard of the portside shrouds chainwale, focussing his scope in frustration. '*Madre…*' He looked back at Hazzard almost with accusation. 'Is this where she hides? In the mouth of this inferno? Or does she now send this to stop us, hm? *Dios mio…*'

The fighting airstreams around the waterspout had either been born of its creation or had caused it. What had seemed merely a misty horizon materialised now into a thick and heavy fog, a grey blanket rising fast before them. Hazzard used the eyeglass and surveyed it from bottom to top. The fogbank was higher than the mainmast. 'Jory…!' called Hazzard. '*Marines stand-to!*' The decks began to vibrate with running boots and bare feet.

'*Carlos, rocas!*' called De la Vega.

Rocks.

Carlos called from the foredeck, '*Sí, capitán!*'

Everyone listened; the crash of breaking waves would tell all: a submerged or sunken promontory or island, too small for the charts, passing unnoticed. But there was silence, only the slightest hiss of the rigging and the creak of the sails above. The fogbank grew gradually thicker and taller, the quelled sea darkening as it was consumed at the edge of the world.

The air grew cold and damp. De la Vega peered through his scope, unmoving. 'I like this not, *amigo*,' he whispered. 'There comes upon me the bad feeling...'

A call came down, first from Pau and Handley at the masthead, then from Alfonso and the foremast lookout. '*No, señor! No hay rocas!*' He looked down with some apprehension. '*Solo el mar.*'

No rocks. Only the sea.

Hazzard called up the mainmast. 'Handley! Range? Depth?'

There was a moment's silence, then came the reply. '*Range five hundred yards, comin' in fast, sir,*' he called, his voice distant yet all around them. '*Depth another thousand easy. Must be land in there somewheres – Pau and the lads can smell it.*'

They stared from the quarterdeck rail at the woollen blanket of silver-grey. It moved steadily towards them, an unstoppable wall. Elena pulled her shawl round her more tightly and shivered with fear.

'Wind'll go in a minute...' mumbled Cook.

As if compelled by his words, the sails rippled and fluttered at their edges as the wind slackened, briefly changed direction, then died. They began to feel the faint breeze of the cooler air in their faces, the source of the fog's power. De la Vega nodded, still peering through his scope. After a moment he gave the inevitable command. '*Carlos,*' he said, '*todas manos. Listos para la acción.*'

All hands. Prepare for action.

The air was punctuated by whistles, the hands leaping to their tasks, and within minutes the sails were reefed and the yards squared away. Hazzard could hear the cabin bulkheads being folded and stowed away, opening the main gundeck below; the 24-pounders rumbling on the planks, the crews coming to the quarterdeck carronades, cutting and lighting their linstocks, ready. The gun-crews buckled on their personal weapons – short swords, pistols – and loaded the murderers with bagged grape-shot: they knew their business, and *Volpone* was soon primed for action.

A moment later Handley called down to Hazzard, '*Smoke, sir! Gunsmoke on the air!*'

They watched as the fogbank slowly but steadily enveloped first the bowsprit, the fo'c'sle and foremast, and rolled inexorably astern, covering the tweendeck, the quarterdeck and mizzenmast, a sprinkling of clammy mist floating about them, halos of light dancing in the grey, high around the masts. Within moments, it had swallowed them whole.

Hazzard looked up but could barely see beyond the mainyards; the world had gone grey and thick, baffled, smothered. He could hear his own breathing, and the sharp clink of metal on metal as men moved slowly, lest they disturb the eerie quiet. Cook moved to the portside rail between two of the guns. 'Ye can't even hear the sea,' he murmured.

De la Vega strode down the main deck, his heels loud in the thick silence. '*Rocas, rocas, niños mios,*' he murmured. *Rocks, rocks, my children.*

The pale Christina, the healer, emerged from the passage to the aft cabins. She murmured behind Hazzard, sweeping the long trail of her black *hijab* over one shoulder, her hands held up, one eye closed, intoning a prayer to the spirits. Warnock and Kite on the starboard midships rail saw her, and Kite crossed himself. 'Summink bad out there, Knocky,' he mumbled.

Tariq clung to the shrouds, his eyes narrowed in his lined inscrutable face, his greying moustaches glistening, the Bedouin very much out of place, yet, like the seamen about him, familiar with the brutality of nature. Napier towered over him. 'Don't worry y'self, mate,' he said cautiously, staring wide-eyed and fearful. 'Worse things 'appen at sea, eh?'

'We are at sea, Art'ur,' Cochrane pointed out as he wound a line into a neat coil.

Napier continued to gaze upwards. 'Yeh… well, just an expression, ain't it?'

'Aye,' said Cochrane, handing Napier his musket, looking ahead, making the sign of the cross before them in benediction, the sling buckles clanking low and sharp in the hush. '*And yea, the Leviathan come out from the deep and did swallow Jonah whole…*'

Napier looked at him, worried, frowning. 'Don't say that, Cocky, mate… Don't,' he said. 'Scarifyin', that is.'

De la Vega strode back to the chart spread out across the binnacle by the wheel. The last fix had been at noon. Despite the suffocating grey, the helmsman corrected for drift, feeling the current, his eye ever on the ghostly mainyard and her slackened braces, watching for the merest twitch of direction from the wind. There was none. '*Madre,*' cursed De la Vega; he tried to calculate their position according to the soundings, but lost patience. '*Diez o quinze milles… quarente o cinquente! Que está estos?*' Ten or fifteen miles – forty or fifty. What is this? The tops vanished into the fog, then briefly reappeared, enshrouded, glowing, then disappearing.

Hazzard joined him and cast an eye over the chart. 'Could we be drawing near to Kythera?'

De la Vega shook his head and pointed at the compass. The needle swung to and fro, as if searching for direction as they were. 'Only if we sail to the backwards. North,' he said, 'she is gone.'

The current had already swept them some distance, but Hazzard reasoned he was right – not that far back upon themselves. The first islands they believed they would encounter on their present heading were the minor Strofades, and later the Zakynthos chain. 'We shall hear them before we see them,' said Hazzard.

'If we follow the sea,' said De la Vega, 'we can be caught in the *Giro del Jónico o Pelopes*, the ring flow, *sí*? Ionian or Pelops, and go first to west, to south, to east and north, and go mad.'

'The boats? The marines can man the oars.'

The boats could tow *Volpone* into the fringe of the Ionian current, or 'Gyre' as De la Vega had called it, where they might be lucky enough to be driven to the mouth of the Adriatic and intercept the reinforcement flotilla coming south. Other than the Strofades and major Ionian islands, there were no other landmasses before them but De la Vega was unsettled.

'And out there, *amigo*, in the breath of *el draco*,' he said. 'A thing from the deep.' He spat out the butt of a cheroot and put a new unlit cigarillo between his teeth. 'We shall see if *Volpone* can scent the wind. *Vámanos*, Garcia, Paco,' he murmured to the second helmsman, a bald Moorish blacksmith from Valencia. 'But with care, *sí*?'

'*Sí, mí capitán*,' nodded Paco without demur, his broad, bare arms holding the wheel rock-steady, Garcia on the ropes, slackening, ready to tighten at a moment's notice.

The rigging hung slack, the crew passing the lines and sheets slowly through their hands, then holding, alert, hoping to feel movement, even the slightest tremor of wind. Carlos watched them, murmuring his commands in a steady tone to ease their fears. They could hear the water against the hull. The gun-crews were tense, watching the sea, ready for their worst mariners' nightmares to come upon them. The air seemed to thicken, and all sound died. '*Dios mio*,' gasped one voice along the tweendecks, and they hissed, *silencio...* and waited, sifting the silence for clues, for fear of making a noise themselves.

Then it hit them: a primordial scream, the creature striking Carlos hard, out of nowhere, four feet across, a flurry of flashing white, a raucous screech splitting the silence, and he cried out, '*Diablo, diablo!*' and staggered backwards, crashing into the coiled lines around the mainmast water-butt, cursing as a large herring gull flapped down to the portside midships rail, its huge grey-topped wings clattering like musket-fire. '*Hijo de puta...*'

They stared at the beast, wide-eyed, and it screeched back at them, its dead eyes reminiscent of a vulture's. Hazzard let out a breath, *Christ*. It had as great an impact as an 18-pound round-shot. Carlos began to laugh at the crew and swore at them as they joined in, but others regarded the bird warily, a messenger of doom. Someone cursed it and threw something, a tinderbox tin, the clang on the wood loud as the bird squawked aggressively and lifted off, the fog swirling about its beating wings.

The *Volpone* floated free, the only movement the light swell slapping her copper-clad hull, the water steaming under swirling pockets of warm and cool air. Hazzard exchanged glances with Cook. Either there was land nearby or, worse, there was none; at sea they knew what gulls would feed upon. 'Eyes to yer watches, lads...' rumbled the big man, looking out, looking over the side.

Within moments Handley called down and the other lookouts joined him, their voices muffled by the fog above. '*Wreckage off the port bow, range thirty yards—*'

They clustered on the portside rail as the first debris drifted slowly into sight. Armed with boathooks, several deckhands clambered over the side on lines, down the boarding steps, to catch some of the debris approaching in the fog: splintered planks, a broken handrail, a cask bobbing gently. A section of broken topmast and ragged canvas floated past, tangled with its lines round a shattered lateen yard, a hook reaching out to take it in. Other more personal objects appeared: a length of torn fabric, a shirt, a shredded mattress with sodden straw spilling – and the macabre explanation for the seagull's presence. Underhill spotted it first.

'Man in the water. Look to survivors...'

He floated face down, his bare back pocked with powder-blasts, burnt flesh stripped from white ribs by sharp beaks, bare feet protruding from sunbleached trousers. Smaller gulls screeched as they flapped down and away, one tugging at the carrion, then ducking away as one of the crew threw something at it, splashing nearby. Another body drifted slowly into view, and another, some hanging just below the surface as if standing, long hair blossoming around them like weed, arms outstretched in the clear water.

'Poor buggers,' muttered Cook beside Hazzard at the rail. 'What ship was she, though? One o'theirs or ours?'

'Clothes could be Turkish,' said Hazzard. 'Or could be one of ours from Cyprus.'

De la Vega ordered a boat to be lowered, and soon it splashed into the waves amid the flotsam. They took the bodies aboard. Pettifer, Napier, Cochrane and Porter joined Hazzard as they looked down, watching. His long hair hanging in lank trails either side of his face, Cochrane looked gloomier than ever. 'Prayers for lost souls gone six fathom deep,' he said in his mournful Belfast twang. 'Yea, enter His gates with thanksgiving…'

He was answered by a low chorus from some of the others: …*and unto His house with praise. Amen.*

Hazzard watched the dead, noting the condition of the bodies. They had not been in the water long; there was little sign of bloat or putrefaction, merely the marks of carrion birds. He remembered floating beneath the battle in Aboukir Bay and wondered how many more floated there, unseen. He called to the starboard side where Warnock, Kite and De Lisle stood looking down. 'Lil? Anything?'

Still peering over the edge, De Lisle shook his head. 'No sir… small oddments, but—'

Handley's call came down again. '*Boat! Boat off the starboard bow—*' Hazzard looked up, the tops still invisible in the swirling fog. '*Three survivors, sir, flag unknown.*'

As he spoke they began to hear muffled cries, and De la Vega ordered the boat forward. 'Carlos… *Adelante… y listos.*' *Forward – and be ready.*

On the fo'c'sle, Alfonso fed a lifeline to a deckhand who clambered from the heads and weatherdeck onto the bowsprit stays, hanging low over the water, paying it out to Carlos at the tiller of the small boat. The boat's oars dipped quietly as it made its way into the fog. In a few minutes it disappeared, swallowed up by the cloud.

Hazzard joined De la Vega and Alfonso on the foredeck. 'Can you smell it?'

De la Vega nodded. 'The fire, *amigo… de cañones.*'

Gunsmoke.

Hazzard could taste it – cordite from spent shot and the sharp tang of charred wood and burnt pitch hung in the dead air, trapped, the fog bringing the metallic smack of iron to the tongue. The wreckage around them felt like the work not of man, but of some demonic creature, like the waterspout. Hazzard's mind ran to tales of Scylla and Charybdis, of monsters and perils of the deep.

Soon they heard the rhythmic splash of oars once again, and the deckhand on the bowsprit began to climb back from the stays, gathering the slackening line as he came, calling to Alfonso, the rope dipping into the waves just ahead of the *Volpone*'s bows.

The prow of the boat reappeared from the fog, materialising as if from another world. They were towing a half-sinking gig, two survivors inside, bare-chested and soaking, one trying to heft up the other, lying still. The deckhands leapt to the hawsers as the boat came in, and soon the wounded man was lifted out. Once his mate was laid on the deck, the other collapsed, exhausted. Marine Private Porter knelt beside his unmoving shipmate with his doctor's bag.

'He looks right gradely,' murmured Porter in his quiet Yorkshire, the fog leaving beads of moisture on his spectacles. He lifted the man's eyelids. 'But he's still at home and hearth, so to speak, sir, as me gran would say.'

The unconscious man was a dark-skinned Levantine, full-bearded, but with carefully trimmed moustache, barefoot, and wearing the elaborate patterned baggy *shalvar* trousers of the Turks. Porter brought out a vial of smelling salts and held it beneath the man's nose. His head lolled as if dead, but he coughed and spluttered, seawater spewing from his mouth, and there was a general murmur of approval from the gathering. Carlos and Pettifer carried him down to the cockpit behind De la Vega's own healers, Elena and Christina.

The other man took water and a cloak from Hazzard with shaking hands. 'Gawd bless ye, sir…'

Hazzard was surprised. 'You're English.'

The shipwrecked straggler took hold of Hazzard's hand, the scarred leathery grip of the weathered sailor still cold and wet from the sea. 'Sir, she's still out there…'

'Who is, seaman?'

'There's a devil on the sea…' His wide eyes blinked, frightened but hard. 'Was a Venetian, sir, frigate… who did fer us…'

'A Venetian?'

Carlos and the others took him forward to the fo'c'sle mess for food and water, De la Vega watching over Hazzard's shoulder. '*Un pirata veneciano, amigo*. They sail these waters, hiding, in the Macedon coast, in the islands… Murderous dogs.'

'A *pirate*? How do you know?'

'I know,' he said, heading for the fo'c'sle after them, 'for they leave only two survivors, *compadre*.' He called to Alfonso. '*Todos cañones listos.*' *All guns ready*.

Alfonso looked darkly at the gang carrying the sailor away, then out at the fog. '*Sí, capitán.*' He nodded at Hazzard. '*Pirata*. We find him.'

—

Seated in the fo'c'sle on a bench in patched and frayed breeches, a cloak round his thin, ageing shoulders, a flagon of rum in shaking hands, the English sailor was surrounded by the marines, devouring segments of melon, orange and lemon hungrily.

He was older than most, missing several teeth, gaunt with a lined, weather-beaten face, long, lank, greying hair hanging in wet, matted tresses past an unshaven silver-stubbled jaw. He was nearer sixty than fifty, thought Hazzard, creased eyes worn by endless years at sea – a ragged man, bereft of care. Then Hazzard saw it on his right arm: a tattoo of a ship rolling on the sea in full sail, and the name, HMS *Leander*.

'Who are you, seaman?' asked Hazzard.

The sailor fought to stand up, but Hazzard put a light hand to his shoulder and he settled again. 'Many thanks, your honour, Able Seaman Shepherd, sir, the *Leander*, foretopman, as was.'

Underhill glanced at Hazzard and De la Vega, and said in a low voice, 'HMS *Leander* was at the Nile, sir. We saw her come in with *Swiftsure*. Only a 50-gunner, but she went straight into the French line after Nelson.' He hesitated, knowing what memories the tale would bring back. 'They was two keels ahead of us on *Orient*, sir. Hit *Franklin* and *Purple Soovereen*. Sorry, sir, the *Peuple Souverain*.' He nodded sagely. 'Gave 'em hell on earth, she did.'

72

Shepherd watched the exchange with wide ingenuous eyes, chewing another giant segment of Seville orange. 'We did, sir,' he confirmed. 'Raked them big buggers, down the gullet o'the one, and up the arse o'tuther – beggin' your pardon, sir.'

Hazzard felt the pricking of Sidney Smith's words just before they left the *Tigre* – that what had happened to *Leander* might have happened to *Valiant*. 'What brought you to this, Shepherd?'

Shepherd swallowed and looked up, blinking his red-rimmed eyes, dark with fatigue. 'Captured, sir, by the Frenchies, last year it was. Left in a Corfu cell till the Russkis come and got the Frogs. A few of us was took by a good Turkey merchant cap'n who can tell a good man o'the sea, sir. They got us out, me an' my mates, the last left.'

'What about the Venetian frigate?'

Shepherd shook his head, his voice dropping, his eyes narrowing as he looked into memories. 'Come out o'nowheres, sir, waved us in, like they was sufferin', and when we got close enough, bang, dismasted us, boarded us, swarmin' all over, chopping up the lads, takin' cargo – then set us alight and fired their guns. Dropped one right down our holds… Blew us apart… Only me an' Rafiki got away.'

De la Vega nodded at Hazzard, blowing smoke as he relit a cheroot from a lantern candle. '*Venecianas. Hijos de perras…*' He pinched his fingers together for emphasis. 'No *respect*, you see? *Piratas*. The privateer, *amigo*, he wants the ship and the cargo, to sell. He even does so for his country and king. But not *el pirata*.'

But Shepherd had not finished. 'But that's not all sir. A Frog 74 come behind her, like they was together. Fat, bulgin' bows, guns like I never seen…'

Hazzard kept very still. 'Did you see her name?'

'No, sir. But she weren't no regular 74.' Shepherd shook his head, adamant. '*Leander* was took by the *Jenny Rooks* last year, sir— Er… beggin' your pardon, sir, the *Généreux*. And I'll ne'er forget her. Back then, she was ridin' heavy, tops all wrong, sailed like a brick… Guns slow to come out…' He shook his head again, the damp twisted tangles of hair spinning round his grizzled jaw. 'No, sir, this one was… well, like an 80- or a 90-gunner. She weren't lyin' skew-whiff, nor rollin' with slack braces. No, sir, her tops were tight, and not a stray line in sight.' He looked at Hazzard, warning in his eyes. 'She was packing a whole row of smashers, sir, extras, if y'ask me, big enough to stow away in, half-door ports to the mid-deck for 24s and giant doors to

73

the lower, big as *Victory*'s.' He blinked round at them. 'She were a right monster.'

For Hazzard, the frustration was maddening, that here was a survivor of the *Leander* and *Généreux* before him, yet still no certainty she was back in these waters.

Napier put a tentative hand in the air, to ask a question. 'What happened with *Leander* and the *Jenny Rooks*, sir?'

Handley answered. 'I heard *Leander* carried the victory despatches from the Battle o'the Nile to Naples,' he said, glancing at Shepherd. 'But I thought it was the *Gwillam Tell* that got you, not the *Généreux*.'

Shepherd shook his head. 'Nay, matey. It was the *Jenny*. Should ha'seen us, lads,' he affirmed with pride. 'We dashed round her, we did, brace to starboard, brace to larboard, bring her about, back and forth, led her a merry dance good an' proper in our little *Leander*. Mr Berry an' Cap'n Tom got us to fire like we was old Jarvie at Cape Vincent himself. Knocked her from stem to stern, we did, and still she couldn't take us none...' He shook his head, remembering. 'She was fallin' off the wind an' losin' her trim, the lot. Till she shot away our mainmast, and they hit the starboard rail. Three gun-crews gone... young'uns and all. Including little Jerrer. Only ten years, he was.' He nodded in the ensuing silence, staring into nothing. Although they understood only through the translation by De la Vega, the Spanish listened gravely. 'We had no sail left. Cap'n Tom had to strike the colours to save us. Had to. Cap'n Berry, who'd been under 'is lordship on *Vanguard* at the Nile, he concurred, he did, and so it was. *Jenny Rooks* was a-smoulder, every ball of ours found its mark, mates, we got 'er well good, we did. They killed one score and five of us, four young officers an' all, even Downie – while we counted for near *three hundred* o'their lot.' He nodded his head emphatically. 'An' that's a fact.' Hands patted his shoulders, and he raised his flagon and drank.

'I got it,' said Napier, a little behind everyone else. 'That oke, Bannister!' He looked at Hazzard and De la Vega in appeal. 'No, sir, it's true. All round the blockade I 'eard – when he was took by the Frogs, they said on the *Zealous* that ol'Bannister, he stood up to the Frog cap'n, he did, and told him where to put hisself, he did!'

De la Vega translated for the crew. There was general approval and Shepherd shook his head, his face clouded with smiles and remnants of anger. 'Aye, that's true, cock. Cap'n Le Jolly he was, with his big hat and his big boots, and sword he never used. They couldn't come and board us as we'd blowed all their boats up – and they ours. But when they finally did, some were lootin' of our personals – our possessions, mates, and that's 'gainst the rules. Some others wanted the doings of our mast construction, I swears, but neither the chippy nor his Mate said a word, and they were beat for it.' He looked up at Hazzard. 'Cap'n Tom and Cap'n Berry protested, they did, but some say they was knocked about, too. I didn't see, but they said as much. Bad blood it was, sir. They took us off to Corfu on the *Jenny*, and tried to get us to sign on in the Frog navy! That lot couldn't tie a bowline on dry land, let alone aloft in a gale. I mean, I asks you.'

Unable to restrain himself, Napier prompted him. 'So Bannister cries out to the cap'n, "Hoi! Give us our ship back," he does!'

'He did, when told to sign on as Frogs,' Shepherd confirmed. '*Never, ye damn' French bugger, give us our little ship back and we'll fights till we sinks!*'

There was laughter from the marines. Hazzard translated for De la Vega and the Spaniards, and the crew applauded, *bravo, bravo*. Shepherd looked down, embarrassed at Hazzard and added, 'Sorry, sir, he might of said rascal, not the other.'

'I'm sure he did, Shepherd,' said Hazzard.

'Did us no good. We was all shipped, officers paroled 'omewards, but some of us was slung in a stinkin' clink in that fort on Corfu.' He took a swig of his rum ration. 'I heard, not a few weeks later, sir,' he continued, 'that Le Jolly had painted her sails black as Lucifer, and slipped out from under the nose o'the Russkies… and the Turkey, too. Skinny was, she got shelled off Brindisi, and Le Jolly killed, they said.' He nodded, grim. 'Justice for our kiddies and our little ship.' He shook his head and looked up at them, trying to understand. 'I owes the *Jenny* a bloody nose, sir.'

Hazzard knew the feeling. So did the marines, it seemed.

Généreux.

'We'll have 'er, laddie, mark my words,' grated Underhill.

But Shepherd wanted to warn them. 'But she's devilish crafty now, sir. Last I heard, there's a new cap'n, they say – a Renard, or Renward, someone said.'

Hazzard felt a stray memory return. 'Was it Renaudin?'

Shepherd's face lit up. 'That's it, sir. That's him. Like Renard the fox, they said, but not quite.'

Hazzard had heard the name only once before: an older Captain Renaudin, from the Battle of Ushant five years earlier – talk of disgrace, confusion over an abandoned crew. But the younger Renaudin cousin had stayed with his men: the young officer who later fought off a ship of the line and four Spanish frigates all on his own – a fighting captain.

Renaudin. Now in command of the Généreux.

De la Vega glanced at Hazzard. They both knew. Hazzard did the calculations: *Ninety guns – not seventy-four.*

Assume the worst: 42-pounder cannons or Long 36s to lower deck, 24-pounders to upper, 18s, not 12s, at the quarterdeck rails, bow- and stern-chasers – and 60-pounder obusier carronades with explosive shells on the fo'c'sle and poopdeck.

Hazzard detected within himself a peculiar mixture of determination and a primal fear. He had felt this way once before, in India, in the jungles of Karnataka, and he felt it now: this was a tiger-hunt – and their quarry had apparently become a man-eater.

'Had you heard anything else?' he asked Shepherd. 'Whether she had sunk or captured *avisos* in the area, last year, before *Leander* was taken...?' He tried to keep the hope and reluctance from his voice. 'Had you heard anything of the *Généreux* and HMS *Valiant*?'

Shepherd looked thoughtful for a moment. 'No, sir, and I knows *Valiant*. A lugger I saw at the Tagus in Porto, she was, when I was on blockade years back. But no, I ain't heard of the likes of her in the Med since, sir.'

It was no answer for Hazzard. But the uncertainty was gnawing at his nerves. De la Vega watched him, knowing what was going through his mind. 'Not yes, not no. *Muy bien*, we get her.'

'Whoever she is.'

De la Vega looked determined. 'Some have told me of the *sesenta*, this... this 60-pound French *cañón*. It is slow, hm? But...' He wagged his head. 'But *peligroso*, dangerous, *sí*? We can play the *snic and snac*, in and out, back and forth, *sí*, but... the guns they often win the test.' He dragged on his cheroot and exhaled, the smoke blooming to the ceiling joists just above. 'And I want that *Veneciano*, *amigo*.'

Hazzard cast a glance at De la Vega, then looked at Underhill, Pettifer and De Lisle. 'Ninety guns. We'll lure them in,' he said, 'and give them both a shock.' He waited for the others. 'What says the boat?'

With his customary dusty laugh, Underhill's gravel tones came quiet but certain. 'Oh, boat says let's bloody get 'em, sir.'

The marines murmured *aye* in approval and De la Vega shrugged ironically. '*Muy bien.* Ninety, it is only two times as much as us.'

Carlos called, *Sí*, but the Spaniards chorused in their best English, *Aye*. The door opened to the tweendecks, and Elena stood in the light, a whittled crucifix in her small hands, looking to Hazzard, in fear of dark omens.

De la Vega blew out another lungful of smoke. 'Then, *compadres*, let us set the trap. We have the big fish to catch.'

Traitor

South of Karnak the temperature was an autumnal thirty degrees on the Réaumur scale. The sand felt as sharp as the sun, the air a heavy viscous heat that had to be inhaled with conscious effort. Some had said it had cooled from a month earlier, and they felt a strange relief. But *Sergent-chef-major* Achille Caron of the 75th Invincibles knew that a hundred metres to the east, away from the Nile breeze, the temperature would climb to forty. The *Alpha-Oméga* trudged slowly through the silence, their camp some distance behind now as they headed into the broiling rocky foothills of the eastern mountains.

'Why did we not come at night, *Chef*?' puffed Rossy wearily, his words coming with some effort. 'Though I do enjoy seeing the majestic landscape, I could perhaps have preferred the stars at night.'

Caron agreed. 'Orders are orders, *mon enfant*, and trouble is trouble, no matter how hot she comes for us.'

They moved step by step, the dust kicking up at the toes of their worn boots, clouding behind them at their heels, each track an ephemeral mark in the eternal sands, soon to be erased. They had new *chasseurs* join them to make up the numbers, and the newcomers kept pace with Antonnais and St Michel, who would look back on occasion to find them still there. The pair were irritated they had been promoted to corporal and a measure of responsibility – life had been so much easier before.

After another hour Caron stopped and took a longer rest. He examined the rock formation ahead: a sandy gully between two rising red rock faces. They were close. When he saw the trail before him, he was not surprised when young Antonnais went on ahead, stopped and looked back.

'Horses, *Chef*.'

'*Très bien*, Anton.'

They climbed the rise in the sandy trail and stopped in a V cleft between the radiating heat of the sloping rock either side. Caron dropped his pack and took out an eyeglass. He looked down to a flat clearing of sand below, roughly fifty yards wide. After scrutinising the area, he slid the scope shut and tucked it in a pocket.

'*Alors*,' he said. 'We have arrived.'

He pulled out his long white silk scarf, and Antonnais fixed a bayonet to his Charleville with a loud grating 'click', and held the weapon out, ready. Caron tied the scarf to the dulled bayonet blade, checked the priming-pan of the pistol in his belt and the holster pistol hanging down his right thigh. Both were loaded. He took a mouthful from his water-skin and slung it over his shoulder.

Big Pigalle stared down at the clearing, unhappy. It was surrounded by the rising rocks, numerous trails of drifted sand between, some trodden, some unmarked. 'I like this not, *Chef*. It is a bowl.'

'I know, *enfant*,' said Caron, taking the improvised flag of truce from Antonnais. 'But you stay here.'

The white scarf catching the hot wind and flapping overhead, Caron walked out into the sand, the musket held high, an unlikely Moses with Aaron's rod – hoping to be seen, hoping not to be shot at.

Rossy and the others took up positions among the high points in the red crags, the heat from the iron rock burning their hands and knees. They soon settled, the wind whistling gently, the fall of sand a hissing serpent, the ratchets clicking loud as they cocked their firelocks. Rossy sighted Caron, now small below in the clearing of sand, standing still, waiting, the white flag blowing. Rossy settled down to watch, resting his bristling chin on his hands, eyes alert for any movement. He did not have to wait long.

Within minutes, Bedouins appeared as if by magic in every gap of the rocks, on every trail, some on horses. Nestled in the shade of a crevice not ten yards from Rossy, St Michel lowered his head and sighed, easing the lock of his Austrian rifle-musket: upwind from behind them both had come two riders, Mamluks. He made the usual *hsst* sound to Rossy and pointed in resignation over his shoulder. They had been outmanoeuvred.

Rossy turned and saw them, and shielded his eyes. 'Ah, *bonjour*,' he said – then, with a polite nod of the head. 'Two coffees and one of those little *poğaça* pastries, if you please.'

The sky behind them was a blinding blue: one rider was all in white, a Moorish turban around a spiked helm, chainmail hanging past an elegant bearded jaw, a long spear resting on the stirrup, a long bent-angled Turkish *yataghan* sword at the hip, each ready for use in a heartbeat. Rossy got reluctantly to his feet and heard Pigalle rustle from his post.

'They are better even than us,' murmured the big man.

Rossy agreed. 'Mm. But never tell them that, *M'sieur* le Pig. It is bad for their pride.'

The second rider, in a dark *keffiyah* headdress and golden *iqal* circlet, could resist no longer and began to laugh, undoing the dark *shemagh* to reveal a smooth, caramel skin, an ornate jewelled diadem on the brow, meeting in hanging teardrops of pearl down the bridge of a delicate nose. She smiled and said in French, 'I should not find you so amusing, *M'sieur* Rossy, but I fear I do.'

It was Shajar al-Durr, leader of the Tarabin *Bedu* and one-time ally of Caron at Acre. They had not forgotten her charge across the No Man's Land of the Damned Tower into the French grenadiers, shielding them with a whirlwind of dust.

Rossy bowed graciously. '*Madame*, at your service.'

Pigalle rose slowly to his full height and bowed. 'Lady.'

'*M'sieur le géant*,' she replied to Pigalle, 'saviour of innocents. We are far from Acre. But we owe the debt of honour. Such memories persist in these deserts. It is all we have. Already you have grown in the tales of the *Bedu* to become Samson, slaying hundreds with the jawbone of an ass.'

Pigalle considered the idea. 'I have not tried such a thing.'

She smiled. 'It is in your Bible, *mon petit*.'

Caron returned, followed by another two on horses. '*Madame* Shajar,' he said in salute.

'*M'sieur le sergent*,' she acknowledged. 'You have found your army again.'

Caron sensed it was a fond rebuke. At Acre he had torn the badges of rank from his shoulders and arms, and lost all respect for his general – and been shot for his pains by Derrien. Shajar had seen too much of his plight, too much of his anguish among the dead at Acre. She had seen him laid so bare, she deserved nothing but the truth.

'I have my duty,' he replied, 'to my children here. And to the *anglais*.'

She considered his words, then bowed her head in accord. 'As do we all.'

'Bonaparte has gone home to France,' he said. 'You have triumphed.'

Speaking for the first time, the Mamluk in white spat at the ground. '*Ha!*'

Shajar ignored it. 'You knew him well.'

Caron looked out at the glowing desert, his chest working hard to breathe, his words coming with a weary sigh. 'So perhaps we all thought. I will await to hear the judgement of wiser men. Acre,' he said, 'brought out the best and worst in all of us.'

Rossy watched them and looked up at her. 'But here we do the good thing, *madame*.'

Shajar turned her stately gaze on him, a Madonna in robes and pearls, and for a moment he closed his eyes, savouring the blessing of her presence. 'We do.'

'And the *anglais*?' asked Caron. 'We need him.'

Shajar stiffened. 'I cannot reveal him to you, *m'sieur le sergent*. For fear of your army.'

Caron understood. He knew she would never be able to trust them with such intelligence – though perhaps after today she might. He thought of Derrien, at Acre, falling dead in the surf; Caron had recognised the elaborate sword at his side, the same sword Caron had taken from Hazzard at Malta: the *espada ropera*. He wanted to return it, as a point of honour. He looked off into the heat. 'I have something of his… and more, to thank him for the *enfants* here about me.'

She shook her head. 'I cannot say,' she admitted, 'for I know not where he is.'

With a sigh, Caron nodded. 'I understand, *madame* Sheikh.' He gathered up his pack. 'Anton, St Michel, off you go with the *madame*.'

Shajar gathered up her rein. 'As we agreed,' she said.

'As agreed,' replied Caron.

The silent Mamluk turned his mount brusquely, and the pair of Alphas followed, heading back along the way they had come, descending the track to the cooler sands below. Shajar and the others watched.

'Are we now the hostages, *Chef*?' asked Rossy quietly, with a glance to Shajar.

Caron hefted his pack. 'Ah, no, *mon fils*. We are only the servants to new masters.' He looked up at Shajar al-Durr. '*Insha'allah*,' he said. *God willing*.

'After you. *Je vous en prie*,' she replied in her fluent French.

They headed down to the sandy clearing, where now a stream of men and women were already at work, pulling packs from mules, laying out the stand of a large pavilion. By the time they reached the bottom, the escort caravan of the great Murad Bey and his Mamluk cavalry *sanjaqs* had arrived.

–

An hour later, Caron, Rossy and Pigalle stood waiting in the shade of the erected Mamluk tent. It was open on three sides, hanging rugs raised for air, and large enough to accommodate thirty on Turkish *kilim*. Inside were ranged a dozen tense escort officers of the 2nd Dragoons and 1st Horse Artillery, dusty and tired from the journey. Reclining before them, against thick embroidered bolster cushions, were Murad Bey and his *sanjaq* lords – a number of amirs and sheikhs, including Sheikh al-Mansur, his men behind him, watching the French.

Beside him, on separate *Bedu* blankets and rugs, sat Shajar al-Durr and her closest Tarabin escort – men, women, none armed but for the curved *khanjar* or *jambiya* daggers in their belts. Of them all, Caron watched her most closely.

Opposite, with his aides De Savary and Rapp, sat the scourge of Murad Bey for over a year, *Général de division* Louis Antoine Desaix. Murad beheld them all with a ferocious aspect, but Desaix wore his usual placid, serene expression, which spoke of a genuine care and concern for all those under him. It had earned him the title of *Sultan al-Adillu* – 'the Just Sultan'. To be called to parley with Desaix would be a matter of some mutual import.

They had drunk the minted tea, shared coffee and refreshments. The gathering quietened and Desaix spoke. 'I take it that the great Murad Bey has heard that Bonaparte Sultan *al-Kebir* has returned to France.'

The Mamluk interpreter leaned over Murad's shoulder and whispered. Murad nodded irritably, as if it were common knowledge. '*Nahm, nahm.*' *Yes, yes.* He then barked a question back at Desaix and the interpreter looked apologetic.

'My lord Murad says, what is it that you work here, alone, that you call your enemy to take tea with you, and we sit like two old fools?'

Desaix smiled and nodded at the other officers, who chuckled and nodded. 'Hopefully not like fools.' He tilted his head, looking at Murad, his free hand resting on one knee, relaxed in his power, but with no posturing or pose. He sighed, as if in appeal to Murad, 'We approach yet another month and yet another year, Murad Bey, of fruitless pursuit, and greater foolishness in the desert mountains, where we each lose lives and gain nothing.' The interpreters translated, murmuring in the Mamluks' ears. 'As you see, we have horse, foot and artillery. It is a sad truth that we can continue this forevermore.'

Murad snatched angry glances outside: at the French cavalry beside his Mamluks; at the display of four field-guns from the brigade ranged beyond the clearing, with the remainder of his Mamluk horsemen in uncomfortable détente.

'But that is not why I have come here.' Desaix frowned for a moment, then said, 'I seek the advice of Murad Bey.' The interpreters hesitated, then translated.

'Ha!' snorted Murad, and his amirs laughed with him.

Undaunted, Desaix continued. 'How would he advise an enemy in a superior position, who wishes to come to terms and make peace with him?'

The tent fell silent as the French watched the Mamluks, who were equally surprised. Caron watched the staff officers. They looked to one another. Some shrugged, nodding; some kept a closed face, cards close to their chests.

Desaix consulted a despatch, as if checking notes, his eye glancing at its contents. 'For I believe he knows the great Yussuf Pasha brings an army of eighty thousand across the Sinai,' he said quietly. 'To take Egypt. And keep it.' He smiled lightly. 'But not for the Mamluk. For the Ottoman Turks.'

Murad was no diplomat: he had all the skills of evasion and deception, but blew hot and cold for all to see. 'Eighty thousand!' He roared at his advisers, his questions cracking like whipcord in the hot, electrified air, each side ready to reach for their weapons. 'Yussuf! He is mad! Another fool!' spat Murad. 'He has twenty or thirty thousand, if so many.'

Desaix nodded. 'I feel this is not to Egypt's benefit,' he suggested. 'Or to the lord Murad.'

Al-Mansur looked to Shajar al-Durr. She sat like stone, watching, her Tarabin women still. Eventually Murad heaved a sigh, unable to argue further. The interpreter's hushed voice broke the silence.

'My lord Murad suggests Dessay no longer wishes to dance. He is tired.'

Desaix gave a philosophical tilt of his head once again. 'A man can dance with but one partner at a time.'

Murad fumed. 'Then which partner must I choose! I stand for Egypt, not for Ottomans!'

Desaix looked pained. 'It is not I who must choose, but Murad Bey. For Yussuf, he comes upon Egypt, as they did long ago under the first Selim sultan. Now comes the third Selim.'

Murad stared at him, then slowly his great bearded face creased into a smile, his thunderous eyes crinkling at the edges. 'Ah…' He nodded, looking at the amirs either side. He leaned forward, tossing a date into his mouth, chewing thoughtfully. 'Then what does Dessay propose?'

Shajar snapped a sharp word across the heads of the amirs at Murad, startling Caron. 'Has Murad grown so old he would give his advantage to his enemy?'

Murad winced and mimed a duck: '*Nyat nyat nyat!* I hear a woman quacking at me.' There was laughter. 'Enough! We are not married, Shajar al-Durr, that you may insult me in public like a poor husband!'

Al-Mansur tensed, his men behind reaching slowly for their daggers, but he shook his head. Shajar trembled with anger. 'The French are outnumbered by Yussuf. They cannot fight you as well. Of course he asks for peace!'

Murad raised his arms. 'Begone with your Bedouin beggars! Your tramps and sheep-stealers! You know nothing of what we do here!'

Desaix addressed Shajar. 'Would the *madame* Shajar Sheikh not agree that Yussuf is a threat even to her own brave Al-Tarabin?'

Shajar cursed, red-faced. 'Of course he is, *m'sieur le général*,' she replied in fluent French. Murad frowned, unable to understand until his interpreter came to his aid. 'But I can see your ploy, and it is a good one for the ears of fools.'

Desaix was quite earnest. 'I beg you, *madame*, you will see no ploy.' He looked plainly at the pair of them, and addressed the assembled *sanjaqs* as well. 'Good people, our great general, Bonaparte Sultan, has gone home. He will not return.'

There was silence.

'But we have no wish to let the Turk destroy Egypt or the Mamluk,' said Desaix carefully, his audience watching with suspicion. 'We can stand against Selim Sultan, hold him back, even were he the tide of a great sea – but only if we can come to terms here.'

Rossy murmured to Caron, '*Putain d'la merde*, *Chef*, is this what we do now...?'

'It is, *mon garçon*. Peace requires fewer principles than war.'

Caron watched, aware of the slow, grinding approach of that same monstrous machine that had swept them all along to Egypt so many lifetimes and battles ago. It was not the threat of war he saw before them; it was the threat of peace – just as deadly, it would brook no interference, and its injustices were to be accepted. Negotiations had begun.

'Giza will be acceptable,' said Desaix, 'if the Mamluks come no closer before our withdrawal. And we shall march out to Sinai to bring Yussuf to a halt.' He added plainly, 'Armistice shall bring Yussuf to a halt. And our English enemy will help us to ensure it is so.'

Murad leaned back, threw an angry glance at Shajar, then at Caron, 'Hingleesh! Again! You now rely upon your enemy for assistance. Pah!' He gave a nasty grin and shook his head. 'I know of an Hingleesh you will never own.'

Someone shouted from the back, '*Al-Aafrit al-ahmar! Al-Aafrit al-ahmar!*'

The Red Devil.

At the thought of him, at the sounding of his name, Caron looked round, half-expecting a dozen ghostly *Bedu* of the Beni Qassim to come riding through them, at the forefront, Hazzard, the red-coated *anglais*. Caron remembered Murad – the turban, the robes, the sword they said that could behead an ox in a single blow – leading his Mamluks to raise the wall of dust with Shajar, to help Hazzard and Caron get the Turkish civilians out from the clutches of Derrien.

Murad caught sight of Caron, his angry eyes fixed on him in a moment of recognition, and he tossed his head in a nod – they both had thought the same thing. But Hazzard was not there.

Hazzard.

Caron remembered Kléber's words – *we need the anglais* – and all Caron could think of was his failure to find him. He felt light-headed, as he had when first he saw ancient Jaffa, and knew, *knew*, that his countrymen would betray God and Man both, and comport themselves like beasts in that holy place, where once Elijah had trod.

'As do you, Murad Bey,' continued Desaix reasonably. 'As should we all. For God abhors any disturbance of peace, does he not?' The Qur'anic quote was not lost on the assembly and many bowed, intoning a prayer. 'For which I pray He will forgive us all.'

The Mamluks watched Desaix – his ease, his beneficent demeanour – as if Desaix were a holy man himself. But Shajar got to her feet, having none of it, her Tarabin retinue rising along with her.

'Murad Bey betrays those who fought Sultan *al-Kebir*, all those who died. In the revolt, in Acre, at Aboukir.'

'Never!' retorted Murad. 'I warned Mustafa at Aboukir – *warned* him of the castles of men, of Banaparteh Sultan, but he would not listen! And his army was blown away as the dust, as I foretold!'

'And then you fled once more to the tombs of the dead!' She turned to Caron. 'And you, *m'sieur le sergent*, have used my forgiveness as a tool for your general, made me an instrument of this… this *deception*.'

Desaix interjected, 'The Ottomans come, dear lady, regardless of our fears. And they come in their tens of thousands.'

'Then Murad will fortify himself, and fight Ibrahim Bey once again, as he did years ago at the expense of all.'

'Lies!' boomed Murad. 'Ibrahim! Ha! *Al Caliph min al'adami!* He is a fat man on Ottoman cushions!' His retinue laughed, repeating his words, *the Caliph of Nowhere*.

Shajar looked to Caron, his face waxen, the sweat pouring off him. 'And what is it that you want then, *m'sieur le sergent*? Peace? Or more destruction when at last you go?'

Caron had no answer, but stood his ground, his voice a dry gasp. 'I need the *anglais*,' he said. 'We need d'Azzard. Only he can stop the Turk.'

She stared at him, wide-eyed, shaking. 'You shall never hear tell of him from me! Who then is the traitor here? You, *m'sieur le général*, treating with an enemy as your wicked soldiers die in the sands, so many wasted souls, devoured by the pagan gods of this land?' She turned her accusatory gaze upon Murad. 'Or Murad Bey, who would sign with a new master! Sheikh al-Mansur *al-Hakim*,' she said to Al-Mansur, 'you should choose your friends more wisely.'

She gathered herself and her escort as Desaix and his staff rose to their feet, her eyes flicking briefly to Caron and the Alphas. 'When next we meet, *m'sieur*, shall we be enemies again?'

Shajar al-Durr stormed out, and Caron watched her go, a sense of something dying within: a recognition that she had been the only true hope for her people, for the *misérables*. Desaix and a cadre of officers stood before him.

'So, *Tartuf*, are we in danger when we ride out from here?'

Caron was uncertain. 'Shajar gave her word for the day, *mon général*, and I trust her. But she will defend her tribe from any threat, regardless of cost.' He looked at Murad. 'Murad has the foresight of the politician.'

Desaix looked across at the Mamluks. 'It seems the politician's time has come,' he said. He glanced at Caron sadly. 'And we shall be put out to pasture.'

He turned to head back to the negotiation when Caron asked, '*Mon général*, can you and the *général en chef* get us back home?'

Desaix looked wistful. 'He is my dearest friend, as you know,' he said, but his serene gaze hardened, 'but I will not allow us to be dishonoured, to be sent home in defeat to the general, having failed him in our duty.' He regarded Caron thoughtfully. 'To survive, we, too, must become politicians.'

'Then I shall be the officer parliamentary, *mon général*. I shall treat with the Turks – Al-Mansur, Murad, Shajar, all rode with me at Acre when I defied Citizen Derrien and his corruption. They can use me as hostage.'

Desaix took a long breath. 'You have done too much here, *Tartuf*. I would not throw you away so easily. But if it comes to it,' he said, 'then so it shall be, as you wish.' He gave a thin smile. '*Insha'allah*.'

Caron watched him turn away to his staff, but felt the presence of Al-Mansur at his elbow. 'Murad Bey,' began the sheikh, 'is wiser than many believe.' He handed Caron a rolled leather loop, threaded through a dull bronze coin. 'This is the mark of Murad. Hazar Pasha has one likewise,' he said, 'making you both holders of Murad's favour. Should you go to Yussuf Pasha, this will guarantee your safety.'

Caron looked at it. It was the size of an old Louis sovereign, but he knew its value was far greater.

'Farewell, *m'sieur le sergent*,' added Al-Mansur. 'You carry many hopes. Murad knows you will prevail. You know, he calls you *al-Asad qadim* – the old lion.'

'Hm,' muttered Caron. 'Too old, this lion.'

Al-Mansur bowed and made a gesture of prayer to him. '*Rabbena ma'ak, effendi.' God be with you.*

Caron watched him go as Rossy approached. 'What was that, *Chef*?'

'Trouble,' he said. 'She has a new disguise. She looks like honour.'

'No,' said Rossy. 'We have not seen this disguise in some time, *Chef*.'

Caron thought of Hazzard: the *anglais*, he suspected, knew all this would come. Caron would find him, somehow, eventually. But if not, he decided, this old lion would throw himself down as an offering to Babylon.

—

It was a quiet afternoon at the Admiralty, the November rain easing along Whitehall, leaving the fresh cold air heavy and sweet with the rich loamy smells of horses and freshly turned earth from carriages in the street. A junior despatch officer in white wig and bluejacket hurried up the broad stone steps of the central staircase. Red-cheeked and puffing, young Midshipman Selby reached the first floor and turned left along the oaken corridor towards Room 63, but paused when he saw the one-armed Major Carteret of 35 Company, Marines, complete with red coat and shining steel gorget.

'Hullo, Jim,' said Carteret. 'Something in?'

'Yes, sir – is Mr Pryce about, sir?'

Lieutenant Pryce was the duty Signals officer – among other things, in charge of the giant semaphore Shutter Line on the roof. Carteret took the despatch and gave it a quick glance. 'Has C and C done with it? Where is their stamp?'

Codes and Cyphers was the first stage for despatches. 'No, sir. Signed and stamped received, but it's for Sir Rafe direct otherwise. Mr Samson said.'

Carteret read the reference number, saw 34'18'89 at the top, and knew at once what it could contain. He looked along the dark-panelled corridor to the end rooms: the chart room, the briefing room, the backstairs, dimly lit from above by its leaking skylight, and opposite, the unremarkable door of Room 63 – the office suites of Sir Rafe Lewis and the HQ of Admiralty Intelligence. 'Sorry, Jim,' said Carteret, 'but Lt Pryce is in with Sir Rafe at the First Lord's apartments.' He flipped to the second page, seeing French but no ciphers. 'Marked urgent?'

'No, sir.'

'Well, you know what to do,' he said, and flapped it back to the boy. 'Pop it in the lock-box for when he gets back.'

Selby smiled with relief. 'Thank you, sir. Hate to barge in on bigwigs.'

'Wise man. Come on.'

Pulling various other folded pages from his inside pocket with his remaining left hand – mostly receipts for stabling and fodder – Carteret marched him to the door bearing the small tarnished oval brass plate numbered '63'. He fished out his key, turned the lock and they went in.

The front room, as some of them called it, was fairly bare and had the unlived-in feel of a redundant dining room, its polished table, chairs and cold grate neither welcoming nor foreboding, saying nothing – as was the custom in Room 63.

'Duty!' called Carteret, glancing at the papers in his hand, distracted.

After a few minutes there was a distant clatter and the far door opened. A young officer of Marines put his head round – a new boy, Carteret did not know him well – an Honourable heir to someone, he had heard. 'G-good morning, sir.'

'Morning, Lieutenant. By hand,' said Carteret to Selby. The boy handed over the despatch to Carteret, who then passed it to the embarrassed Marine subaltern, who succeeded in scattering them all to the floor – along with Carteret's other notes as well. 'Oh for heaven's sake, I've got them,' grumbled Carteret and scooped them up with his one hand, the Marine officer red-faced with apology, too uncertain to assist the one-armed veteran, the younger Selby biting back his smiles.

'I... I do beg your pardon, sir, it's—'

'My fault, lad, my fault.' Carteret examined each, one by one, as he slapped them on the table. 'Yours... ah... mine, yes, yours, right... Ah, there we are. Into the lockbox for Sir Rafe, cleared from C and C.'

'A-aye-aye, sir,' said the marine, closing the despatch box.

'There you are, Jim,' said Carteret to Selby. 'Off to your break, lad, while there's still a hot grog for you.'

'Thank you, sir!' said Selby, and dashed off.

Carteret nodded brusquely to the Marine officer. 'As you were, Lieutenant. Always ready, what?'

The boy nodded. 'A-always, sir, yes. Good day, sir.'

'Jolly good.' Carteret shut the door behind him and headed down the backstairs, tucking the new despatch into his inside pocket – aware it contained details regarding Egypt, because its reference number bore the cipher identity of William John Hazzard. Further, that because of his enmity to Hazzard, he knew Sir Rafe Lewis could not be trusted. He hurried to collect his cloak and headed out through the back door.

–

An hour later, Commander Charles Blake, RN, in civilian clothes as befitting his secondment from Admiralty Intelligence to the Secret Service of the Alien Office, picked his way through the riverside collections of old crates, broken casks and beached boats, in a mournful drizzle along a deserted stretch of the Thames Embankment, the rain dripping from the brim of his hat. He turned through a stone arch leading to The Wharf, an unremarkable public house, frequented by watermen and passing bargees – and ideal for clandestine meetings. He saw his regular darkened corner, and the cloaked shape of what he presumed was Marine Major Carteret, waiting.

Blake ducked under the low beams and hanging pewter tankards by the dead and damp smouldering fire in the soot-stained stone hearth. He caught the eye of the landlady, Mrs Nelly Lunn, a stout-armed naval widow – and now a trusted Admiralty informant. Pulling a deep golden bitter at the tap, she gave Blake a brief nod as he slipped into the high-backed oak cubicle and joined Carteret.

'James,' Blake said quietly.

Blake was a calming, soft-spoken influence on most of his colleagues, both peers and senior officers, his steady, bland gaze like that of a trusted manservant, concealing a mind that could conceive actions several moves ahead of others. Carteret sat back, relieved at his arrival.

'Charles.'

'I received your note. I presume all is…?'

Carteret waited as a glass of dry sherry was put before Blake. 'Thank you, Nell,' he said, and Nelly moved off swiftly. Carteret raised his own glass. 'From Cadiz, they tell me. Your health.'

They toasted and drank. Carteret passed the despatch across the table with a practised hand. 'From General Kléber to the Directory government. Its effect on the peace could be disastrous.'

Blake unfolded the page. It was a personal letter, to the five Directors. Blake cast his eye over the page. 'And when did this come in...?'

'The Mid Watch – a French brig, caught off Toulon. They tried to sink their despatches, but the ball slipped out of the handkerchief or some such nonsense, and our fellows spotted the letters floating.' He flicked a glance at Blake's reaction as he examined the contents. 'Sir Rafe has yet to see it. He would certainly never have passed it to you or Wickham at the Home Office.'

Blake knew full well Carteret was right: inter-service rivalry was nowhere more acute than with Intelligence. Although currently with William Wickham's Alien Office, Blake had worked with Commodore Sir Rafe Lewis in Admiralty Intelligence for nearly five years – he knew Sir Rafe was a law unto himself.

Carteret wanted to explain. 'With the possibility of peace from Kléber's contact with Sidney, Hazzard and Smith will need to know about this at once. It could ruin everything.' The one-armed major was clearly disturbed. 'This is how it ends for all of us,' he said. 'Left behind, forgotten. Even the French. It's too bad, it really is.'

Blake read through the letter, translating by sight. '*My dear Citizen Director...* Barras, presumably, or Ducos perhaps... *The army is reduced to half its strength... disease is prevalent, and the soldiers in rags...*' He looked up. 'Hazzard's reports suggested as much, but...' He carried on reading then stopped. 'Deficit of almost ten million...?' He frowned. 'I think we calculated eight, but... *the soldiers' pay accounts for four million... and such is the situation that I inherited from General Bonaparte ...*' He scanned the rest. 'Frank, bordering on direct. This will be exaggerated, for government consumption, of course...'

Carteret leaned forward and hissed urgently, 'They are *done*, Charles, *finished*.' He was a formal man, Blake knew, but he was seeing something different from the stiff *major d'omo* of Room 63. 'And as you can see, Kléber has no idea that Bonaparte has seized power.'

'Quite. We have endeavoured to keep it that way.'

What had happened in Paris after Bonaparte's triumphant return had been discussed among the French Committee of the Alien Office. Blake had heard a whisper from their man in Alexandria of the general escaping, of Hazzard aiming a pistol at Napoleon Bonaparte. Knowing Hazzard as he did, without question Blake believed it true.

'From what I've gleaned in 63,' said Carteret, 'Smith is already gaining their confidence and might well have begun to parley by now.

We could have them out in months, Charles.' He tapped the letter with his finger. 'But if the Cabinet see this, they would want to *finish* the French – no honourable armistice, no marching out under arms, but outright capitulation.' Carteret sat stiff-backed with a compacted outrage. He looked out at the window and the grey light of the river, a coal barge sliding slowly past. 'And how could we? We have not defeated them in the field. They are not a defeated army clamouring for surrender.'

'Mr Hazzard would do his utmost to get them out.'

Carteret took heart. 'Then Hazzard is still active? Have you heard anything?'

The expression 'active' or 'inactive' had become new code for alive or dead. Blake took another sip of his sherry. 'Yes, Sir Sidney confirms he is still very active.' He hesitated, then fulfilled the *quid pro quo*. 'This letter explains my news. To complicate matters, we have had word of a French reinforcement flotilla. From Venice.'

Carteret stared. 'Sir Rafe has said nothing. Was it confirmed?'

'Mm. Captain Day, consul in Turin. He saw the chits for supply ships and transports which were then certainly laden in Venice and Ancona, but direct sight was later lost by the Watchers.'

Carteret knew Day was in the top echelon. Then Blake lowered the boom, his voice low. 'What is difficult is that between forty and eighty thousand Turks are soon to descend upon Kléber.'

Carteret considered the news. 'The Grand Vizier, Yussuf Pasha?'

'Yes.'

'Eighty thousand?'

'Yes. The levy at one point raised it to one hundred thousand.' He cleared his throat. 'The real question, James, is whether we want this peace requested by Kléber.'

Carteret stared at him. 'Of course we do. Expelling the French is the Levant desk's first priority.'

Blake let him consider for a moment. 'Our alliance with the Ottomans seems fairly robust, but could easily be broken.'

'How?'

'Imagine Yussuf Pasha coming to terms with Kléber.'

'The French would be evacuated – in our ships, I would say, and the Ottomans would move in.'

'Precisely.'

Carteret frowned. 'But…'

'How quickly could we mount an expeditionary force after the Texel operation in Holland?'

Carteret failed to understand. 'How quickly?'

'What,' asked Blake, taking a different tack, 'have you heard of the French engineers' reports of the Suez canal exploration?'

Carteret did not understand the sudden change of subject. 'It was declared an utter botch, wasn't it, but the Committee doubted their figures were…' Something dawned on his face. 'Good God.'

Blake looked back at him, waiting.

'All of this,' said Carteret, 'so that we might seize *the Suez canal, once it's dug out by the French?* Good *God.*'

'It is far simpler to allow the French to build it – all they would require is a re-examination of the data and works could begin. Once complete, we could then stage our counter-invasion and bargain with the Ottomans. But we have no army *present* to enforce this peace,' said Blake. 'We are not *ready*, James.'

Carteret hissed across at him, '*You cannot be serious, Charles…* Let all those men die out there in the damned desert? Because we are not ready to treat with the Ottomans? French or not, it's bloody *barbaric.*'

Blake sipped from his sherry. He looked across at the polished bar; a few watermen were coming in, greeting Nelly. He waited for Carteret to consider the options.

'The Ottomans would return to their old alliance with France,' assured Blake. 'Our men in Constantinople have seen the danger. It is very real.'

Carteret stared blankly into the pub interior. 'And we would be left with nothing.'

'Nothing but a hostile Ottoman Empire.'

The old marine swallowed his indignation and nodded. 'Very well. Peace, we say then. But just not yet.'

'What would happen,' he suggested in a low voice, 'if Admiral Lord Keith were to get wind of this letter?'

Carteret spoke in a dulled voice, not quite yet resigned to the plan before him. 'If Cabinet had it as well, he would abandon Sidney, discredit him,' he admitted. 'Sink the peace talks.'

Admiral Lord Keith had taken over from Jervis as the new commander of the Mediterranean Fleet, and was no friend to Smith, or Hazzard; he was the same Admiral George Elphinstone who had taken the Cape in 1795 and had been party to the scandal of the murderous Marine Captain Harry Race – as had Blake, as well. That Race had been Hazzard's childhood companion had meant nothing to Keith, and he had ordered Blake to send in Hazzard regardless, 'to interdict, overpower, or otherwise eradicate' the threat Race and his marines had posed to negotiations with the Dutch. Hazzard had certainly done so, and more. Hazzard had hated Keith ever since – and hated Blake for being complicit.

Carteret sat back, looking at his old colleague. 'You would let that happen, Charles?'

Blake accepted that what he was proposing was doubtless what Sir Rafe Lewis might have done – and part of him regretted it, but he could see no alternative.

Carteret was saddened, disappointed. 'When I lost this,' he said, indicating his empty sleeve, 'I thought I could continue to serve, to help the chaps in the ranks. To keep them safe, even without being there.'

'And so you have, James,' said Blake. 'For years.'

Carteret stared at the tabletop miserably. 'But not today.'

Blake remembered a similar moment of realisation with William John Hazzard, in a rowing boat at the Cape, and Blake recognised that he admired such men, with such honest hope. 'We cannot do it every day,' he said, as much to himself as to Carteret, 'but only that we might be able to do it tomorrow.'

–

The sun beating down, but cooled by a westerly wind, Citizen Poussielgue was received at the portside rail of HMS *Tigre* with no less warmth than any other gentleman – but Marine Sergeant Dickory took one look at him and wanted to put him back in the sea. 'As you were, matey,' he muttered to a marine who came to attention.

Lieutenant Wright stepped forward, bowed his head, and spoke in halting French, as if it were a struggle, though he was fluent. Citizen Poussielgue should never discover, if he did not know already, that he was aboard the Ship of Spies. '*M'sieur*, may I to introduce... er... to you, the Captain Smith, Knight of the Order of the Sword, and Commodore of the British fleet of blockade.'

Citizen Poussielgue, in linen frock-coat, white waistcoat and cravat, responded with an effusive manner not usually found in the officers of

Foreign Minister Talleyrand, and bowed with a flourish. 'An honour to make your acquaintance, *m'sieur le grand chevalier*. There are few who have not heard of your exploits.'

Smith seemed charmed, and replied in French. 'You are too kind, *m'sieur. Enchanté.*'

'*Pas de tout*. We are all but tokens on the board, are we not? Pawns to our nations, *m'sieur le commodore*, and you outplayed our greatest commanders at Acre. You have our most sincere compliments.'

Smith had played this polite parlour game many times, but could not help but be swayed by the diplomat's unexpected courtesy. He bowed once again. 'As doubtless your soldiers would agree, *m'sieur*, luck is the most capricious of allies, and the most dreadful of foes.'

'Truly, a *bon mot* worthy of our own great *général en chef* himself,' Poussielgue replied.

'Will you take a sherry? It was intended for the Spanish Dons, so I can guarantee its quality.'

'But of course. However,' he said, looking at the coterie of officers around him on the quarterdeck, 'I was hoping to meet the Colonel Douglas, whose gallantry at Acre so moved our General Berthier. Is he not with us?'

Smith was pleased to tell him. 'The letter from General Kléber made it all the more expedient for us to send Major Douglas on a mission to convince the Grand Vizier that we all might come to an accord without bloodshed.' He paused, wishing to remind Poussielgue of their true purpose. 'Lest lives be lost unnecessarily.'

Poussielgue shrugged in a gesture of informality. 'I trust we can come to such an accommodation, among friends.'

Smith afforded him a tight smile. 'Indeed, I must reiterate that whatsoever we might agree here must further be ratified not only by my government in London, but by both the sultan and Czar of the Russias, as members of our alliance. Alas, we cannot put the world to rights alone.'

'But perhaps we might try,' insisted Poussielgue. 'Such is the honest hope of the *Général en chef* Kléber.'

'My deepest wish as well, Your Excellency.'

Dickory watched them as they moved off past the helm to the Great Cabin, but came suddenly stiff to attention as the sun-darkened *Général de division* Louis Antoine Desaix quietly appeared at the rail, still to mount the final boarding step. His long hair had been tied back into a tail, but it still blew about his neck in the breeze as he paused, casting an assessing eye about him, his gaze finally alighting upon Dickory. Dickory stiffened and barked, '*M'rines...!* General sa-*lute*! Atten–*shun*!'

The decks of the *Tigre* reverberated to the synchronised crash of boots as the marines stamped to attention for Desaix and ported arms. The bo'sun piped him aboard, Marine Lieutenant Yolland giving the salute. Smith looked round – and for a moment might have thought it were Bonaparte himself, in indigo linen coat, the sun catching the Revolutionary orders pinned to his breast, the gold of his epaulettes and sword. With him had come the desert war, the pursuit of Murad across endless miles of sand and dust – yet none of it betrayed by the general's placid demeanour.

The pipe stopped, and Desaix bowed his head in acknowledge-ment. He looked about – at the ship, the crew, the gleaming guns, the masts and rigging soaring far above – finding the evident discipline of the British Navy disturbing: it forewarned of a foe they had yet to face in Egypt, and one as sophisticated as themselves. One of his staff officers murmured to the other, '*At least the anglais are civilised... to a point.*'

Quietly Desaix asked Yolland, 'Is your *M'sieur* d'Azzard with us?'

Yolland replied discreetly in French, 'No, sir. Mr Hazzard is on... other duties.'

'Mm.' Desaix nodded slowly, looking about again, at Dickory, at the marines. 'Do you know,' he said, 'the *Général en chef* Bonaparte has... a *numen*, a spirit, of power. All can feel when he is near. One can see him in the face of every French soldier... because he dwells in their hearts.' Desaix followed Yolland to meet Smith on the quarterdeck, his eye wandering over the marines, as if he were trying to pick out Hazzard. 'Just as *M'sieur* d'Azzard is in theirs,' he said. 'Though he is not here, I see him all around.' He looked over the ranks, the round-hat brims lowered over the eyes, the muskets held taut and unwavering, the intent. He was at once impressed and saddened. 'All around.'

Yolland held out a hand, indicating they should join Smith. 'Perhaps today we can reunite your troops with their *général en chef*, sir. And bring everyone home. With honour.'

Desaix looked at him, considering Yolland's words. 'If they wish it. Yussuf Pasha, *m'sieur*,' he said, with a nod at the marines, 'is not the only threat.'

Tiger

The sea smouldering with vapour, the *Volpone* followed the fog as it rolled westwards through the night towards Leuca and the heel of Italy, and took them out into the swirl of the Ionian Gyre. The sails fluttering with a faint breeze, Paco felt the movement of the wheel in his hands for hours, head down, eyes closed, feeling the tug of the current, testing for wind. Shepherd went aloft with Handley and Pau, and within a short time they smelt bitter smoke and spotted the cloudy red glow of fire in the fog – it was the remains of Shepherd's Turkish merchantman.

Wreathed in tendrils of what De la Vega called the dragon's breath, the *Volpone* crept forward, approaching the floating wreckage, the pitch-painted timbers still burning fitfully. A column of black, oily smoke twisted through the blanketing fog, drifting among the fumes of Neptune's demons.

The *Volpone* was well disguised in her old role of defenceless Levantine merchantman, lamps lit, her tarred jolly-boats slung along her stern broadsides, ready to drop and bumble smartly to the next waiting client; the rails just above them were festooned with lines and cargo nets swagged from her upper deck rails – concealing her gun-ports. From the galley chimney came the aromas of fenugreek and sandalwood, the exotic scents filling the air with the promise of priceless pepper and spice – and the sweet odour of opium. To any eye she looked a fat, lazy merchantman stealing through the fog to avoid customs men, plump with the luxuries of the Orient.

Cook and Hazzard stood with De la Vega and Alfonso on the fo'c'sle foredeck. De la Vega had quietened, as if the Venetian responsible for this were something of a personal matter for him, as much as the *Valiant* was for Hazzard.

'We shall find them, *amigo*,' he said softly in his Castilian Spanish. 'We shall find them both.' He turned to Carlos waiting behind. 'Follow the smoke, *hermano mio*, and find the wind. We go where she goes…'

Carlos touched a finger to his forehead, his expression grim. He knew what was to come. '*Sí, mi capitán.*'

Maria-Luisa and the mainmast hands moved along the mainyard with Pau, barefoot, checking the reefing knots; the mainsail was dropped but shortened in the infernal air, the canvas glowing red with the smouldering fire wafting about them. Maria wanted to be ready when the call came. Her spiked hair cropped short to keep it free of fouling in lines and tackles, her feline eyes gave her an implike Puckish air. She looked up at Handley above in the tops to smile or give courage, but he did not see, watching through his eyeglass. The topsails breathed gently with the merest signs of life, and *Volpone* moved forward through the smoke and fog, leaving the fire behind, a creeping animal in a dense jungle.

The marines looked out from the guns, crouching behind the straw mattresses ranged along the rails on either side, clothes dark, blades dark, their faces smudged with soot and painted stripes, some wearing the black *shemagh* once again on their heads, for all the world the Ismaili assassins they had been at Jaffa and Acre – and Hazzard knew they were hungry for action.

Among the *Volpone*'s guns De la Vega had also revealed to Hazzard and Cook a locker on the poopdeck, taken by Hazzard to be no more than signal flags given him by the Royal Navy. Instead, inside were yard-long wooden poles fitted with dull gleaming conical warheads of beaten copper, at their end a steel tube and thick fuse. Hazzard recognised them – his ship had come under fire from them under Hyder Ali. They were Indian rockets, from Mysore.

'By all that's holy in ruddy Bristol,' murmured Cook.

'*Sí, sergente.* Straight to *el diablo*. When I buy the Greek fire from the Turk at Crete, he sells me these as well.' He puffed on his cheroot. 'Better, he said, than from Sriringapatna.'

Seringapatam had been Tipu and Hyder's fortress arsenal in Mysore, overrun six months earlier by Baird, Wellessley and the Highlanders. Hazzard knew what the rockets could do. De la Vega was playing his part of tethered goat well – and no ordinary goat at that.

Hours passed. Pau joined Handley up in the maintops. Neither had been able to determine the extent of the great fogbank, now slowly breaking up around them. The wind freshened, but only just enough to stir *Volpone*'s sails. Hazzard heard a hiss from his right and looked out over the dark water. The air was suddenly cold, the fog precipitating into a dampening mist. De la Vega stood at the starboard foremast shrouds, leaning into the lines, scope fully extended, watching. Hazzard and Cook on the portside shrouds just behind, trying to pierce the dense veil. Alfonso waved a hand to Carlos.

'*De nuevo.*'

Carlos nodded to Ezau, the chief gunner. He touched a glowing linstock to the tail of a swivel-mounted 3-pounder murderer. The sudden bark of the unshotted cartridge echoed, then dropped, dead against the muffling fog all around, the smoke twisting and merging with the mist.

'Making a ruddy row, bloody place lit up like Vauxhall Illuminations,' rumbled Cook beside him unhappily, reading his thoughts.

'We're the bait. The goat.'

'Aye…'

Hazzard raised his eyeglass – the fog reflected their lamplight, transforming it into an opaque barrier, blinding them. He felt helpless.

De la Vega stiffened. '*Attenda.*'

Wait.

Hazzard felt it: the wind shifted, and he felt its breath against his neck. Cook glanced at him and they both knew the fog would not last long. Carlos called to trim the topyard braces, and the yards swivelled gently, the canvas filling. Hazzard saw Shepherd up above, the old foretopman feeling the wind, looking out, ever looking.

'*Amigo,*' whispered De la Vega, his hand out, beckoning, as he looked through the glass. 'Watch there.'

Hazzard joined him and stood at his elbow, the foretopsail sending its unwilling air down at them, warm, then cold. His fear was they could be drifting towards shore: not even the priceless naval chronometer on *Volpone* could help much, the stars blotted out by the fog, allowing no positive fix for nearly two days. They were all relying on De la Vega's instinct.

Then he looked through a gap in the fog, and saw through it.

Lights.

'Jory.'

'Aye.'

The mist began to thin before them; a light wind blew gently into his face, then died. The wind was shifting again, but with it came something Hazzard could not pinpoint. He shivered with nerves, felt his jaw clench tight.

'Pass the word. Make ready,' he warned Cook, his voice low.

Cook leaned back and whispered to Cochrane. The marines checked their belts and cartridge bags, pistols, blades – the Catalan gunners beside them crouched low as well, one man in each team gently swinging the wick of a glowing linstock slowmatch, each looking into the darkness.

De la Vega strained forward through the shrouds. '*Amigo – mira…*' Look.

Hazzard saw them again –lights – and what he had feared:

Land.

Through the fog they could at last see the night sky, stars appearing and vanishing with the parallax effect of their movement and the mist. Lamps glowed on a distant shore, black hills humped against the night.

'*Watch…*' murmured De la Vega, staring through the eyeglass, a cheroot clenched in his teeth. '*Carefully… Alfonso – linternas…*' Somewhere behind Hazzard, Alfonso snapped his fingers. One by one, the lamps and lanterns of *Volpone* were closed and darkened. The night swallowed them whole, gathering them into the fog of the black sea. De la Vega hissed his commands to Carlos and Hazzard heard him: *Guns, full sail. Stand by.*

The bare feet of the crew thrummed softly across the decks as they ran to their stations, every eye on the swirling dark dead ahead. They wanted to be ready for action, but also had to maintain station, as bait – for the tiger. The coastline faded with mist, then reappeared, revealing their course towards an unknown shore. The breeze picked up, the topsails filling, and the fog began to disperse. De la Vega whispered to Hazzard, 'Watch the lights…'

'*There,*' came a hiss from the foggy heights above. It was Handley's voice. He called down to Hazzard in a hoarse disembodied whisper. '*Dead ahead sir, Sheppy spotted something…*'

The coastal lights blinked – on, then off, with no particular pattern, then again, until once again they vanished, then reappeared, the mist swirling. Having evaded coastal patrols most of their days, the smugglers of *Volpone* knew very well what this meant: something was passing between *Volpone* and the coast, blotting out the lights. There was only one thing large enough to do that.

De la Vega shouted out, '*A estribor! Todas velas!*' Hard a-starboard, full sail.

Alfonso turned and bellowed across the decks, '*Todas velas! Cañones de babor listos! Rápido! Rápido…!*' *Larboard guns ready, quickly.*

The screen of fog and mist to port burst with light. Lanterns suddenly dazzling in the dark, bells clanging, the prow of a low-slung frigate emerged from the fog in full sail not fifty yards off the port bow, turning hard a-port to intercept *Volpone*'s course. She was old-fashioned, low amidships with a high sterncastle like an antique caravel, two giant lateen jibs running from her bowsprit to her fore-mast, her yards swinging as she spun her wheel, the crew calling madly from the deck and rigging, waving swords, ready for what they thought would be an easy kill of yet another Levantine trader. It was the Venetian pirate.

There was a bright flash, the air thudding with twin percussions as the Venetian fired a brace of warning shots from her bow-chasers, the 9-pound rounds howling through the air, only to crash into the waves just ahead of the *Volpone*. But De la Vega was waiting. '*Cañones listos!*' *Guns ready!*

The Venetian was close-hauled on a curving collision course, heeling round to cut off the *Volpone* and attempt a rake of her bows, but was too slow, even in the freshening wind, and found herself running alongside – just as Alfonso gave the order: '*Despejen las portillas!*' *Clear gun-ports.*

Cook shouted along the gundeck, '*Marines stand to,*' and Underhill bellowed, '*Buck an' ball, steady on yer guns and waits for the command!*'

The marines rose with their Charlevilles from behind the concealed 18-pounders on the exposed upper deck as *Volpone* swung back towards the Venetian into the attack: the crew dropped the loose cargo nets and opened her main gundeck ports, baring her teeth. The Toledo rapier bouncing at his hip, De la Vega leapt to the portside shrouds on the quarterdeck. '*Fuego en cuatro!*'

Fire in fours.

Warnock curled his lip and whispered, '*Knock knock, twats…*'

The calls from the Venetian crew changed to cries of alarm as the first volley of the marines' musket-shot peppered the railings and rigging, a dozen men whirling away, struck by buckshot and heavy .65 calibre ball. *Volpone*'s main-deck 24-pounders fired in groups of four, belching orange and yellow clouds of flaming wadding, followed by four double-shotted 18s from the upper decks. The pattern repeated all along the broadside in clusters of fire in an almost perpetual thunder, pounding the Venetian's starboard bows and midships incessantly as she tried to turn.

The Venetian's ageing hull flew to pieces, slabs of cracked oak shattering, her rails and gun positions disintegrating in clouds of splinters, the crew swept away as incendiary shells exploded against the fo'c'sle and foremast. De la Vega was not trying to take the Venetian as a prize, but aiming for the guns and the hull: he was trying to kill as many of them as possible, and sink her.

The *Volpone* took hits, none effective, but a stray round crashed into the tweendeck rail, hitting an 18-pounder gun-carriage. Two of the crew were thrown against the main hatch and water butt, and the Moroccan gunner, Rampa, was struck by the slewing gun-carriage, caught under the wheel, crushing his left leg. Hazzard ran along the portside guns. '*Warnock, to me!*'

Their black *binish* flapping like bats' wings, Warnock and Kite hurried round, slinging their muskets as Hazzard knelt by the wounded gunner, Rampa's dark-skinned leg bright with blood. '*Lift that bloody carriage!*'

Ezra shouting behind – *Fuego, fuego!* – the other guns continued to batter the Venetian, the air roaring with the blasts. Two of the wives, Halawa and Sofia, bustled forward, pushing Kite aside. '*Si, si, pequeño, lo tenemos!*' *Yes, little one, we have him!* Warnock got in beside the larger of them, Halawa, in her voluminous black skirts, and took a grip beside her under the rear trucks as she counted, '*Uno, dos, tres!*'

Warnock heaved with her and the carriage lifted, Halawa crying, '*Tengolo, tengolo!*' *I have him!* Hazzard dragged Rampa back to the mainmast, Porter skidding down beside them, dropping his bag. The Venetian slewed round and fired its starboard guns, the rounds whistling overhead, some thudding into the hull below, most missing. Warnock and the crew hauled the carriage round on its tackles. '*Come on, Mickey, give it some!*' Halawa and Sofia cursed at the ship, waving their fists. '*Hijos de putas! Ti mataremos! Ti mataremos!*' *Sons of whores. We'll kill you.*

Shouting at the top of her lungs, Halawa picked up the remaining incendiary-packed shell from the rack with one hand and thrust it down the muzzle. Kite rammed it and the crew ran out the gun. '*Right Knocky!*' Warnock sighting along the gun from the side. '*Clear, hombres!*'

They replied, '*Clara!*'

Warnock waited a beat as the Venetian gun-crew opposite drifted across the gun muzzle. '*Knock-knock…*' he muttered, and shouted, '*Fuego!*'

Halawa put the linstock to the touchhole herself – '*Bastardos italianos!*' – swearing foul oaths at them, *Comeme el culo, mierdas!*

The gun boomed, the shell igniting in the cannon's mouth and spun in flames, a whirling Catherine wheel, crashing through the Venetian gun-crew – it exploded against the base of the mainmast, just over the midships gratings, Warnock roaring, '*Have that eh, eh! How's bloody that?*'

The Venetian heeled away, its rigging collapsing, flames spreading as Volpone maintained fire all along its broadside. Screaming figures emerged from below decks, their clothes alight, leaping overboard, Halawa spitting and cursing at them all the while.

Porter bound Rampa's fractured leg. '*It's nowt,*' he called to him over the roar of the guns, '*but it'll get tha' to surgeon, lad.*'

Hazzard helped him pull Rampa to his crewmates as *Vopone* turned to port and brought the fo'c'sle into action, Cook bellowing, '*Smashers, make ready!*'

The heavy carronades were packed four in a line at the rail, Napier dragging a fifth carriage over to the portside, the Catalans trying to keep up with the big boxer – '*Move it, mateys!*' Alfonso was calling the order: the short snub-nosed 36-pounders gave a low *whump* with every shot. One after the other, the heavy rounds crashed into the Venetian frigate, carrying away the fore and mainmast shrouds, the spritsailyard whirling off into the dark, the bowsprit collapsing, a flaming jibsail floating down to the deck, dragging over the side and into the water. The foremast began to tilt astern, her forestays gone, and the mainmast toppled in flames, the stress to port too great; it fell with a crash, the crew of the *Volpone* cheering.

The Venetian crew abandoned ship, some falling into the sea, some leaping from the dropping taffrail. The frigate began to settle and sink, her top deck planking bursting under the pressure, a gun and carriage lurching forward, leaning out of its burning gun-port, the fires sweeping up the rigging and into the sterncastle. Underhill called the reload once again, but Hazzard put up a hand. '*Nine Company, hold your fire!*'

The remains of a boat swung from a torn hawser, the retaining painter alight, eventually snapping, the splintered carcass turning over as it fell into the water with a splash, men swimming towards it, calling out, Cook's voice calling, '*Men in the water! Ready a boat!*'

But there came little chance to effect a rescue: with all eyes on the flaming Venetian frigate, few heard the calls from Handley, Pau and Shepherd aloft. '*Enemy sail to larboard!*'

Hazzard turned at the sound of his voice. As the call came, the first rounds from a dark sea beyond the opaque dazzle of the mist, smoke and flames howled overhead.

'*Get down!*'

Hazzard threw himself flat with the marines and gunners as 18-pound balls rushed through the rigging, one crashing through the foremast shrouds, splitting the ratlines. Holding a hand up to cover the glare of the fire, Hazzard lurched to the fo'c'sle steps and ran up to the rail to look out: somehow another ship had crept in behind the flames and fired from the far side of the burning Venetian; the captain was using the flaming corpse of the Italian pirate as a shield. Moments later, Hazzard saw it.

Her sails flaring ghostly bright with a hellish firelight, muzzle-flashes sparkling along her upper fighting decks, she emerged from behind the smoke and flame of the burning wreck and Hazzard saw her whole. It was a heavy ship of the line, heeling round to starboard to come into the attack, her giant French tricolour ensign flapping astern, garish in the orange light. She fired again, impatient to be rid of the screening Venetian, heavy carronade rounds crashing through the hapless sinking frigate, the Frenchman pounding her into the sea. It was utterly merciless.

Good God, thought Hazzard. *All to get a better shot.*

Cook's voice boomed across the decks: '*Frog man o'war off the larboard bow…! Nine Company, stand to and spend 'em dear!*'

Hazzard stared, his gaze taking her in – she seemed another deck taller than the Venetian pirate, half-shutters to her middle deck gunports, closed around gaping 24-pounders, her lower deck ports shut tight, easily four feet across, big enough to take Long 36s or even the 42-pounders he had imagined, her upper decks crowded with massive *obusier* carronades. There could be little doubt that this was Shepherd's mystery leviathan. In the blaze of fire, her name appeared in tarnished gold across her broad, flat hindquarters, confirming his fears:

Généreux.

There came a deep, sonorous boom, muffled among the clouds of fog. Howling overhead came the unmistakable whistling rush of whirling chain-shot. Hazzard saw the twin iron rounds parting the mist, a smoking, spinning diabolus. It tore through the Venetian wreck, spent, but striking a glancing blow to the *Volpone*'s foremast crosstree, just below the joint with the topgallant mast. There was a cry from above and a figure fell. Hazzard heard Handley calling out, '*Maria!*'

The foremast and yard sagged to starboard, swaying from its fore and aft stays, the yard tipping. In the clinging mists above, Maria-Luisa swung helpless on her lifeline, one hand grasping for a stay, for anything, one bare foot catching the topyard footropes, a torn shard of canvas flapping and lashing at her. The rigging hands scrambled from their posts, calling to her, but the crosstree began to shatter at the joint, and she cried out, '*Handeleh…!*'

Alfonso sprang up the foremast, Carlos running to join him, Hazzard looking up. '*Handley! Can you reach her?*' He felt impotent, wanting to climb after Alfonso – when there came another blast from port and a cloud of splinters. Porter seized him – '*Sir!*' – and dragged him down heavily to the deck, the debris rattling around them.

The guns roared behind them – a burst to the hull planking, part of the bower anchor cable flying off into the night, splinters rattling around them – and Hazzard cursed Renaudin, cursed at the carnage of the Venetian – *God, Christ, you bloody, bloody bastard* – as if calling him names would somehow diminish an enemy who had been *so very, very bloody clever*. He called to De la Vega as in a dream, the words lost as the gunners replied to the Frenchman. '*Cesár…*'

Above their heads, Shepherd leapt into space to reach Maria-Luisa, catching a line from the foremast fighting tops, now straining under pressure from the starboard shrouds. He reached the breaking crosstree just as another salvo from the *Généreux* came hurtling up to them. Maria-Luisa stretched out as the whirling iron chain-shot crashed through the topgallant stay. Shepherd was swept away with a scream, almost cut in half, Maria calling, '*Seppi!*'

Maria-Luisa dropped, swinging from her lifeline, but Shepherd fell free, his thin arms windmilling as the gaunt old foretopman spun down to the deck, a falling leaf, a hand snagging a loose line, jerking him round. He struck the starboard midships rail with a crack of bone, hit a gun-carriage, and landed on the deck. In moments he was surrounded by the deckhands, Porter rushing in – but Shepherd gazed with wide unblinking eyes at the stars he knew so well.

The crosstree began to splinter and collapse. The mast toppled, the rigging catching much of it, but the topgallant yard broke free, swung vertically, striking Maria-Luisa violently. She was jerked on her lifeline like a ragdoll and flung astern as the yard crashed outboard, momentarily suspended in the rigging. Elena's scream pierced the gunfire as she watched her sister. Handley leapt from the mainmast tops. '*Diego! Be ready!*' His arms outstretched, his lifeline snaked out behind him. He caught her lifeline long enough to jerk her back to the mainmast fighting tops – but he swung into the foremast backstay, spinning viciously, calling out after her as she struck the platform railing. The topmen lunged for her, caught the line, and grabbed her as Handley swung back. '*La tenemos! We have her, señor!*'

Underhill and Alfonso ran to Shepherd, but Napier went berserk. Roaring, he and Cochrane swung a carronade back, thrusting a 36-pound shell down the muzzle. '*Ram it, ram it! Más rápido! Rotten Frog bugger'll pay fer that! Pay fer our Sheppy!*' Cochrane rammed the muzzle with wadding and grape. '*Rammed, bae Gawd, Art'ur! Give 'em a kiss from Lucifer!*' The Frenchman swung within range: the enemy crew cheering, fists in the air at the crash of the crosstree. Napier crouched to the side of the carronade. '*Knock-ruddy-Knock, matey. This is fer Sheppy, from Arfur...*'

The powder flared at the touchhole and the carronade erupted, the trucks leaping back, the snub-nosed barrel jumping as the flaming load belched a trail of smoke, arcing into the darkness. The whirling iron smashed through the *Généreux*'s fo'c'sle rail, sweeping two guns aside. Men at the rail were cut in two at the waist, others crushed by the gun-carriages, the base of the mast bursting with fragments as the shell exploded. The Spaniards roared, '*Guerillo guerillo!*'

Her bows flickering with muzzle-flashes, a salvo of 18-pounder round-shots hammered into the hull of *Volpone*, some bouncing off her heavy planks, one striking the copper plating at the waterline, shards of metal sparking bright and flying into the darkness, the floundering Venetian sailors crying out, trapped in the midst of the gunfire as the waves erupted among them. The Frenchman began to turn slowly to starboard – and in so doing, ran down the swimming survivors of the Venetian ship.

Arms waving, they went screaming under her bows as *Généreux* ground them into the sea, the fog too heavy for the lookouts to see, men pointing down at the bows, their calls going unheeded. Hazzard could hear Cook shouting red-faced over the rail. '*Bastard! Ye bastard! Men in the water! Hommes dans l'eau! Men in the bloody water!*'

Hazzard called the next firing order down the port midships tween-decks, then shouted down the main hatch, '*Pettifer, keep those damn pumps running and sight your larboard quarter 24s on her rudder!*'

De la Vega saw him and called from the quarterdeck with a savage pleasure. '*Here is your tiger, amigo! Maldito a Dios y al diablo!*' he cried from the shrouds. *Damned to God and the devil.* '*Fuego! Fuego! Sangre por sangre!*' *Blood for blood.*

Hazzard pointed back at the foremast. '*We cannot take another hit like that, Cesár! We will lose the foremast!*'

'*Then we lose it, amigo! They will pay for this! Timón a estribor! Tirantes a babor!*' *Helm a-starboard, brace to port.*

Hazzard had never seen him like this: even as Carlos and the riggers reinforced the forestays to the foremast, De la Vega braced to port and swung his helm over, and *Volpone* leaned into the turn, pulling away from the lumbering *Généreux*, speeding ahead – then Paco spun the wheel back again and Alfonso cried out, '*Tirantes a estribor!*'

She swung back to port to cut across the Frenchman's bows, just as *Généreux* had tried to do to *Volpone*. *Généreux* sensed the threat and had already begun to turn away to port to bring her starboard broadside to bear once more, the fog rolling in burning clouds all about her as *Volpone* resumed fire.

Several of *Généreux*'s upper gun-ports burst with the impacts, a rail on the tweendeck gangway flying to pieces, the martingale supporting the bowsprit snapping and lashing out, a round crashing through the small sheet-anchor cable, men crying out as the yards twisted, the mainyard swinging on her braces as they tried to haul away. But De la Vega had the wind and spun to port after her, Ezau again giving the order on the 18-pounders on the exposed tweendeck, '*Fuego, fuego, fuego.*'

'*She's haulin' away fast!*' cried Cook, hurrying towards him. '*She's on the run!*'

Généreux turned away, but *Volpone* turned to engage. *Généreux* was ready. *Volpone*'s port bow erupted into splinters as a 60-pound *obusier* carronade carried away the bowsprit stays and shattered a section of midship rail, the cries of the Spaniards and marines reaching Hazzard as the weather deck and its tackles flew to pieces. *Généreux* came at them to cut off *Volpone*'s course. Hazzard watched it all in a muffled silence. It seemed only a matter of time, *Volpone* overtaking *Généreux*'s shuddering turn, *Généreux* trying likewise. It had become a race, each trying to cut off the other to attempt a rake from the bows.

It was then Hazzard remembered the full story of Renaudin. He ran to the portside fo'c'sle steps, snapped out his telescope and focussed on *Généreux*'s waterline.

Although a twin-decked *Téméraire*-class 74, she seemed as heavily armed as a First-Rate. And Jervis's old First-Rate *Ville de Paris* had reminded him: he saw them all along the lower deck gun-ports, some open, some closed.

Viewing-ports.

Pettifer and more marines came running up the main hatch ladder, calling, '*Pumps are strugglin', sir! We're takin' water!*'

Hazzard watched as *Généreux* fell behind and began to turn hard a-starboard, as if to collide with the *Volpone*. But he knew that was not the aim. Her yards swinging, her heavy bows came round as *Volpone* sped onwards: having let De la Vega gather speed, the Frenchman was deliberately dropping back now to attempt a rake from astern. Hazzard was out of time.

He slapped the scope shut and ran to the starboard quarterdeck steps, taking them two at a time, throwing off his *binish* as he went. '*Pettifer! De Lisle! Hesse, to me! Into the boat!*'

Cook was on him at once, calling from the portside gundeck rail. '*Sir! She's comin' round! We lost the boats!*'

Two of the three boats they had prepared were gone, blown to matchwood along with the tackles and booms that had suspended them, but one survived, slung from its davits on the poopdeck, on the unexposed starboard quarter. '*Got one left, Jory!*' Hazzard raced up the steps to the poopdeck as he called to the bo'sun, '*Carlos! Esto bote! Vamanos!*' This boat. Let's go.

Cook stared, looked back at *Généreux*, her portside bows swinging slowly towards *Volpone*'s stern, and got it. '*No, damn ye, sir!*'

Cook charged up the steps after him, past the mizzenmast as Hazzard scrambled up and around the shrouds onto the chainwale stepboard; the big sergeant managed to grab the sleeve of his Bombay scarlet, leaning out after him. '*Ye can't shove off while ye're open to fire, sir!*'

Hazzard jerked himself away and pointed out at *Généreux*. '*She's got 60-pounder obusiers on her foredeck and taff, Jory! You stay – the men can't afford to lose you!*'

Cook's brick-red forehead creased with anger. '*No, damn ye, boy! They can't afford to lose you! Sir!*'

As if to prove Hazzard's point, another brace of round-shots came howling through the air, followed by another, spouts rising, spray drenching them, Cook unflinching. Pettifer, De Lisle and Hesse clambered down the lines into the boat swaying ten feet below on the two tackle moorings. De la Vega leapt up the steps and caught his eye.

'*Go, amigo,*' he called to Hazzard. '*Go! We snic and snac, sí? I shall have him, this madlito asesino!*' *Damned murderer.*

'*Damnation.*' Cook cursed Hazzard. '*Ye'll push God hisself too far one day!*' His face cast in shadow from the mizzen lamps, his greying hair telling of long-forgotten campaigns, he knew he would have to relent. '*Throw your grapple to her bower cable whiles we keeps her busy!*' Cook turned and roared down the decks. '*One Section Marines, bag o'tricks and Greek fire-lamps if she closes! Two Section, below to the pumps! Move yerselves like Davy wants yer arse!*'

Underhill ran back along the line of guns, a mad ringmaster in an infernal circus, his hideous grin broad as he laughed through the gunfire. '*Let's be at 'em, me heroes! For Sheppy, the Leander and all the mad kings of Hispaniola!*'

The Spaniards chorused back at him, '*Viva! Viva! Viva Don Cesár!*'

Cook watched as Hazzard moved along the stepboard and jumped down into the swaying jolly-boat, landing on the forward bench seat, Pettifer and the others half-catching him, sending it swinging on its lines. Cook turned and bellowed, '*Carlos! Drop him!*'

The davits swung and the jolly-boat plunged on its lines to the waves and smacked onto the water. Hazzard tugged the hooked mooring block from the iron ring at the prow. '*Cast off astern!*' Pettifer shouted back, '*Clear aye!*' Hazzard clawed at the tarred paddle at his feet in the scuppers and drove it hard into the water. '*We want that starboard bow! Come on, dig!*'

The small jolly-boats had been packed for four crewmen, shot, cartridges and equipment, and there was barely room enough for their feet. Hazzard guessed they would have only moments before *Généreux* spotted them coming round from behind *Volpone*'s stern, just as he himself had spotted the small gunboats at Damietta, coming in to attack the *Tigre* the previous year. He hoped he could get to the *Généreux*'s bows, at least – and that De la Vega could outwit Renaudin for long enough; the *Volpone* could not take another engagement.

They paddled fast in tight unison, wheeling away from *Volpone*'s starboard quarter, tossing and pitching on the frothing wake propelling them even further, Hazzard driving them forward – straight towards the turning French battleship. '*De Lisle, bring us to larboard! Dig! Dig, Hesse! Schneller! Schneller!*' *Faster, faster.*

The little Austrian beside Pettifer dug deep into the spray – '*Jawohl, jawohl*' – as De Lisle pulled the tiller round hard and swung the prow on an interception course for the *Généreux*. Hazzard's pulse banged in his throat, the Bombay jacket tight on his shoulders, the spray bursting in his face as he convinced himself he was right – *must be* – and that Cook was wrong – *must be, must be* – because Hazzard had seen the weakness: he knew how to stop *Généreux*.

She has viewing-ports, he kept telling himself, *new First-Rate viewing-ports.*

The flash of firelight on the mist dazzling, the *Généreux* loomed large not fifty yards off, heading straight for them. Her portside guns blazed, geysers erupting around her, rounds crashing into her broadside in showers of spark and smoke, the yards pivoting, her great jaws turning to try to cross *Volpone*'s stern. The tactic had failed, and the *Volpone* dodged, coming about, sending whirling langrage shrieking into *Généreux*'s rigging, sodden lines snapping, a yard listing, men falling, one catching a line high above.

Volpone turned away to starboard as fast as a racer, as if trying to run, her yards swinging, squaring, ready to brace to port. Hazzard imagined Handley up aloft, lithe as a cat. *Go on, Handley, get her out of here.* Between the raging ships, the single jolly-boat paddled straight for the bows of the charging hunter. Hazzard did not look away from her, seeing Bonaparte's flagship *Orient* in Aboukir Bay, the *Tonnant* and *Alexander*, HMS *Orion* blazing at *Orient* as he had tried to climb her shuddering broadside. And now he was going to do it again. But he had to: to save *Volpone* and De la Vega – and send *Généreux* to the bottom.

'*Come on! Dig, Petty, dig!*'

Généreux heaved herself round in her turn to port, three great jibs flapping then billowing from bowsprit to foremast tops as they filled with the freshening wind, and she staggered round, an angered behemoth, ploughing through the swirls of mist parting before her, Hazzard paddling, hearing her great timbers groaning with the strain, his gaze fixed on her. '*Thirty yards...*'

A symphonic howl filled the air as *Généreux* fired a salvo of flaming round-shots from the quarterdeck and poopdeck carronades, tearing through the dark grey of the mist in a trail of blazing orange and black smoke. *Volpone* replied in kind, blasts thudding into the upper gundeck at the stern as she passed, leading her attention away from Hazzard and the boat at her bows, the *picador* luring and taunting his bull, her rounded stern spinning through the waves as *Généreux*'s round-shots sent geysers of water soaring.

Twenty yards.

Ideally, they wanted the starboard bow, to the lee of the gunfire, all eyes on the enemy to port, but if they went to port Hazzard cared little – he would do it anyway and damn them all. He threw down his paddle with a clatter, gathered up a coil of line and a grappling hook from under his seat, the bows bearing down on them, mist engulfing her tops, her lanterns swinging in the haze above, her guns thudding, the night sky glowing from the burning Venetian far behind.

As if in a blast of sunlight, the stern of the *Généreux* lit up in a sheet of white, men raising their arms to cover their eyes and look away. Adapted by De la Vega for smuggling and inshore operations, *Volpone* had a low, curved fairing of polished and carved wood rising by the forward rail of the foredeck, just forward of the foremast, like a binnacle. It housed a three-sided shutter lamp with magnifying lenses, taken from a small Barbary lighthouse. They called it the *faro*. De la Vega had thrown open the shutters. The blast of light cut through the darkness and caught the *Généreux* full on the port broadside in a bright dazzle, sufficient to distract, if not to blind.

In her eagerness for a chance at *Volpone*, *Généreux* had paid little heed to the small boat under her nose, much as she had run down the drowning men of her erstwhile ally.

'*Here she comes, sir!*' cried Pettifer from behind.

The boat rising and falling as it struck the waves, Hazzard looped the end of the coiled line round the hook on the prow and hefted the grapple in his right, waiting. '*Steady as she goes!*'

'*Helm aye!*' came the reply from De Lisle.

Généreux closed the distance: *ten yards.*

The boiling bow-wave rose to twice a man's height, the white spray mingling with the drifting mist, the roar of the water and the ship's mass filling Hazzard's senses. He had remembered Renaudin – the name, the scandal – and knew why only the upper deck guns had opened fire, the lower deck still shut tight – because he had remembered the *Vengeur du Peuple*, and knew that Renaudin would never forget it either.

Five yards.

Hazzard watched, focussed on the bows, the forward edge of the keel coming for them. The warship then adjusted several degrees, swinging away from them, and Hazzard cursed: it was too late now to cross her bows – their jolly-boat was now heading to the port side, and could be caught in the gunfire of the two duelling ships. The *faro* light was suddenly doused, and the frothing spray at the approaching bows glowed.

Yes, moving very fast now.

'*Ready…!*' called Hazzard, battered by a cataclysm of sound, dwarfed by the vast wooden castle looming into the fog above. '*As she passes, come about hard a-larboard!*'

'*Helm aye!*'

The bows of *Généreux* thundered past the jolly-boat's small blunt prow and De Lisle pulled her hard about, the boat skidding, slow to respond, the forces too strong, Pettifer and Hesse paddling deep, the craft spinning, matching the warship's course. Hazzard could hear himself shouting as the spray burst and the swell hit them with the power of a surfacing whale.

The boat yawing and pitching on the turbulent wake, Hazzard swung the grappling hook in a tight, fierce loop, and launched. Fashioned from three bound boathooks, the grapple looped up towards the ship's portside bow as it roared past, the guns blasting overhead. The steel claw bounced from the damaged bowsprit stays, hit the smashed weatherdeck rail and dropped, snagging the swinging iron cable and shaft of her 12-ton small bower anchor, held fast against the hull by the chainplates – just as Cook had wanted. It was enough. Immediately, Hazzard threw the coil of line into the water and dropped flat. '*Brace yourselves!*'

The line tautened and sprang from the water with a snap, and the boat was jerked forward. Spray flying from their bow, the boat flew alongside *Généreux*, the warship dragging them along at speed, their harpoon embedded in her thick hide. Barely three yards above them was their target: the *Généreux*'s lower-deck gun-ports.

Hazzard believed Renaudin would keep these ports shut unless absolutely necessary – because of the *Vengeur du Peuple*: raked by HMS *Ramillies*, battered and holed by four hours of fire and dismasted by HMS *Brunswick*, the *Vengeur* had listed and begun to founder, her lower gun-port lids smashed or torn away by collision and round-shot – the open ports had taken in huge volumes of water, the pumps overwhelmed, the scuppers swamped. His elder cousin, Captain Jean-François Renaudin, had taken to the first British rescue boat, leaving his crew behind, but the younger Lt Cyprien Renaudin had stayed with them till they were pulled to safety, the ship taking some 150 souls into the deep. Hazzard knew Cyprien Renaudin would remember that. And he had. But he had forgotten the small viewing-ports – most of which were standing open.

Blasted by spray, the jolly-boat pitched and rocked from beam to beam, knocking against the hull then shying away, roughly in line with the fourth lower gun-port. Pettifer hurled a second grappling hook upwards – it snatched at the foremast stays just fifteen feet above with a clang as it bit into the wood, chain and heavy knotted ropes of the shrouds. '*Ready, sir!*'

The *Genereux*'s lower gun-ports were over a yard wide, top-hung single doors levered up by chains from within. They were large enough to bear a viewing-port, a narrow side-hinged softwood hatch allowing for fresh air while keeping the ports closed. Each was roughly a foot wide, possibly six inches high.

The boat slewed, banging against the hull, torrents of water gushing fore and aft of them as the pumps worked – Renaudin was taking no chances as he heeled round. It would be a matter of moments before the grapple alerted men at the rail above to the presence of intruders below. Hazzard took hold of the rope – but just beneath the chainwale above, between the chains securing the shrouds to the hull, a row of heavy cannon rolled out of their open upper deck gun-ports, one after the other. They were not 18s, but 24-pounders.

'*Heads down!*'

The guns fired. They clapped their hands over their ears and bent forward, shouting with the roar, Hazzard recoiling from the percussion, the air hammering at his chest, flaming wadding flying from the muzzles, particles raining down among them. For a moment Hazzard could hear nothing, deafened, his ears whistling. Nauseous from the constant pitch and yaw of the boat, Hazzard turned and shouted to Pettifer and Hesse, '*Bag o'tricks!*'

Pettifer shouted back, '*No, sir! I should go!*'

'*Dammit, Petty!*'

The boat rocking back and forth, Hesse fell against him – '*Scheisse*' – they knew they had little time. Pettifer dived for the stores under his bench seat and pulled out an oilcloth satchel. He tugged out the fuse and its tight coils sprang out; he took hold of the glass-paper igniter. '*It's a one-minute match, sir!*'

Hazzard called to De Lisle, '*Lil, when I go, cut the painter and get out of here!*'

De Lisle shook his head, his gaunt, wet face showing wide eyes bright in the lamplight from above. '*Not leavin' you, sir!*'

'*At least twenty yards off! No argument!*' He looked at Pettifer. '*Light it!*'

Pettifer pulled the snap-igniter. The match hissed and spat, and Hazzard slung the satchel over one shoulder, the tar-coated fuse flaring behind him. The boat nearly tipping him over, he took the end of Pettifer's grappling line, pulled himself up onto the bench seat and jumped.

Leander.

Valiant.

Tomlinson – and Sarah. Are you with me still?

His boots slammed against the planks – *I'm on, damn you* – and he heard himself raving, *I'm on, I'm on, you bloody bastard!* He scrambled for a foothold as he walked the wall. Four 18-pounders on the fo'c'sle foredeck far above banged in quick succession, the air thudding with the percussion, the quickmatch hissing behind his right ear.

Fifty seconds.

He reached the lower gun-ports, hanging between the third and fourth, the satchel's oilcloth nearly slipping from his shoulder – *Christ* – knowing that if it went off, it would kill all three of them below as well as Hazzard himself – for it was no ordinary bag o'tricks.

The first shots came without Hazzard noticing, the flat reports drowned in the roar of the guns as *Volpone* replied, aiming for *Généreux*'s stern. He heard Pettifer's blunderbuss blast upwards from below and felt the rush of heat as fragments whipped past him, and he flattened himself against the broadside. Another burst from somewhere above and something shredded his jacket, tearing across his shoulder-blade, and he shouted in pain. He looked down. They had not cut the towing line. Above, men of the watch appeared at the rail, one pointing down.

'*Ennemi à bord!*'

Enemy aboard.

Limned in the dull lamplight from above, a figure moved along the tweendeck gangway and looked down: fringed epaulettes, broad cocked hat tipped forward over one eye – for a moment Hazzard thought it was Bonaparte.

Renaudin.

More musket-fire from above, its flat snapping almost unnoticed till the gunwale of the boat burst with a hit, musket-balls smacking the churning surface around them, the waves rising in tall spouts.

'*Canot! Canot an-bas! Les sabords! Les sabords!*'

Boat below. The gun-ports.

Pettifer fell forward in the boat, hit, fizzing shots splintering the bench-seats of the boat, the three marines firing upwards, and Hazzard knew De la Vega and Cook would be watching. *Come on, Jory, come on, Cesár, for God's—*

From far off, the wail of a banshee's scream filled the air, shocking every man in the ship above, as De la Vega fired his prize trophies: two copper-headed Indian rockets streaked overhead with the howl of a thousand demons. Hazzard saw the fire-trail, his mind transported to the jungles of Mysore. *Lord Jesus above…*

He tried to shield his face, tucking his head down by his elbows when the explosions came. One missile tore through the ratlines and running rigging to the mainmast, the explosive bursting high over the ship with the spread of a firework, and the other struck the stern quarterdeck guns with an ear-splitting crash and *whump* of powder. Hazzard took the moment.

His left shoulder roaring with pain, he swung himself sideways to the fourth gun-port door, its rectangular viewing-port pinned open, its dripping chains hanging with weed, alarmed voices inside echoing through the small rectangular hatch. Looping the line round his left wrist, he hung on, the pain from his back lancing through to his chest. His boots clawing at the hull planks and studs, he dragged the bag off his shoulder, the quickmatch almost burned down to the oiled canvas cloth, and thrust the satchel into the open viewing-port.

Twenty seconds.

It would not go in. The bag was too big.

'*God, Christ above, come on!*' He rammed at it over and over again, trying to crush the satchel into the aperture – *bloody fool, bloody bloody fool* – cursing himself, unable to see why it would not fit, counting the seconds. The reloaded 24-pounders under the chainwale board and shrouds just above rolled out once again. Then he saw the buckle clasp on the top of the satchel, catching on the small viewing-port frame. It would never go in. He looked up at the 24s just overhead, ready to fire.

Fifteen seconds.

He jerked the bag from the viewing-port, slung the hissing satchel onto his shoulder again, and hauled himself upwards on the line, a nauseating wave of vertigo flooding him. He flung his right hand out for the chains bolted to the hinged lower half of the gun-port shutter only a few feet further up – just as his line was cut. His weight thrown – *Oh, Christ* – his right hand snatched the chain of the shutter door and he swung forward, his boots scrabbling and slipping on the chains and edges of the large gun-port below. He swung himself back, his left hand hooking at the open gun-port frame, the satchel sliding from his right shoulder and down to his wrist, the yawning mouth of a 24-pounder sheeting water onto his forehead.

Five seconds.

With a shout, Hazzard heaved himself up by his left hand and with his right slung the heavy satchel overhand into the open gun-port, past the cannon's mouth, the quickmatch hissing, sparking bright in the gloom. The pack landed with a thud, Hazzard catching sight of the loader looking wide-eyed in the light of the flaring fuse. Part of Hazzard's awareness noted the lamplit interior, a glimpse of a faded blue-checked shirt, the painted beams low over their crouching heads – and he thought of a French seaman on *Orient* who had once saved his life. '*Baissez-vous! En bas!*' he called. '*Vite!*' Get down! Quickly!

Two seconds.

Possibly not enough.

The jolly-boat veering off, the towline finally cut, Hazzard tried to turn, hanging from the edge of the gun-port – *Get off get off* – lifted his knees, and pushed outwards from the hull.

Something hit him like a hammer in the left side, spinning him, and he gasped as he tumbled and struck the black waves, the breath rushing out of him as he went under, turning end over end in the frothing wake, just as the satchel-bomb detonated.

It had been packed with shrapnel and two improvised grenades with their usual magnesium and gunpowder core, each of some two pounds in weight – but the whole had been bound round a quart of liquid naphtha in an old rum bottle, courtesy of Jeremiah Underhill.

The gun-port exploded with a double report and a flash of white light, flame bursting from the open 24-pounder ports, a smashed half-shutter door whirling out into the night, its chains flailing through the air. The retention lines of the loaded 24-pounder snapped and the gun fired low, a waterspout erupting twenty yards to port, the loose cannon vanishing inside with the recoil as it bucked backwards into the interior of the crowded gundeck. Flames spouted from the other ports either side, leaping to the ceiling and across the planks. Powder lockers followed in a series of dense muffled bangs, the cries of the gun-crews swallowed up as Hazzard saw their faces again, the churning water throwing him up and dragging him down, the explosions now no more than baffled thuds.

In the distance, *Volpone* braced about to windward, hauled close and turned fast, De la Vega ready to pour fire down *Genereux*'s throat. But, bruised and burning, *Généreux* doused her lamps and moved off, smoke pouring from her upper gundeck ports, the clouds mingling with the last of the mist, angry shots from the fighting tops falling short as Hazzard burst through the surface for air.

He fell back into the water, submerging again, floating, the sky so close overhead as he spun gently in the slipstream of the warship, stars masked by a grey shroud of mist, the salt stinging, numbing his face, his shoulder, his back, and he thought of Cook. *Blood in the water, Jory...*

Dimly Hazzard watched the hindquarters of the smouldering ship as she ran southwest with the light wind until she was gradually enveloped in the mist, a figure at the taffrail looking back, unmoving. *Généreux* vanished, the golden name across her stern fading as she reached the rolling fogbank and disappeared.

Hazzard had little sense of victory or revenge. *Did you attack the Valiant? Did you?* he asked Renaudin, his mind slowly drowning in the skies, part of him beyond caring, wanting to be free of the pain, the waves welcoming.

Daylight.

The *Volpone* had opened the *faro* once again to find him, the sea bright, a moving silhouette not far off: the tarred jolly-boat approached, Hesse paddling slowly, a cloth wound round a bloody shoulder, Pettifer likewise, pointing, holding his ribs tight. '*You got 'im, Lil,*' and De Lisle's oath coming clear, '*Jaysus shite... I got 'im,*' paddling from the bows, waving. '*O'er 'ere, sir...*'

Bobbing gently to his left, the lights on the Italian shore burned clear and inviting in the distance as the mist moved on the wind, the only sound the splash of the little jolly-boat as it paddled towards him. *Blood in the water,* thought Hazzard, slowly spinning, drifting. *Always blood in the water.*

Gold

Delphine Lascelles led the mule and cart down a dark, narrow lane, then saw the large tarnished tin lantern glowing high over the tall latticework door halfway along. Moths fluttered around it, their wings flashing silver in the stultifying heat of a humid night. She brought the mule to a halt and murmured to Maria beside her on the bench-seat. 'This is it.'

They were more used to the pony and well-sprung trap for hospital rounds, usually complete with an armed escort – but the cart served as good camouflage on a late night in Cairo: Delphine had received a message, and knew she should come at once. Maria tied off the reins, collected Delphine's bag, and they climbed down into the filth of the packed dirt, riven by countless river floods.

The narrow lane smelt of dead fish, fetid with the trapped heat of the day by the muddy effluent banks and reeds of the Nile. Onlookers hung back in darkened doorways, veils across their faces, sweet smoke curling up from pipes and cigarillos: older women, girls, fallen *khawal* boy-dancers, made up as women in cheap gowns – whatever the customer might want, all was on offer. They watched the French-women with dull-eyed indifference, the numb stare of *hashish* or opium, bored, disconnected.

A figure approached from the thick, cloying darkness at the end of the lane. Delphine clutched at Maria's arm as the Maltese nurse reached for a dagger at her belt – since the Mamluk attack on the road to Ramla in the Holy Land, the pair would never hesitate again to defend themselves.

Delphine recognised Masoud and relaxed. '*C'est bien.*'

Maria eased her grip on the short *jambiya* dagger in her belt. Masoud drew closer and bowed. '*Madame* Delphine, *Madame* Maria.'

Delphine whispered, 'Masoud, what is this? What do we do here?'

He moved to the door and knocked. 'It is a matter that could be of some importance, and I needed your attention,' he said. 'The lady has been of some value in the past. It was I who sent for you.'

It was one of the older brothels in town. Maria looked at the signs posted on the doorway: symbols indicating the services offered, the price, an army declaration in French that soldiers must use only registered *femmes publiques* – 'public women' – or face the consequences of morbid infection and fatigue punishments. She had seen it all before – she had advised Desgenettes on the health warnings.

The door opened and they were beckoned in by a quiet boy in his late teens, eyes downcast, a misshapen harelip. '*Masa al-hayri*,' he said, with a curtsey to the European ladies, and Delphine replied, '*Bonsoir.*' Masoud put a hand to the boy's shoulder, speaking softly. 'Take us to Faiza, Nazrim.'

Nazrim led them through diaphanous multicoloured hanging fabrics into a foyer, the air thick with incense to mask the odours from both outside and in. Above, another tin lantern hung, illuminating a cramped staircase. Young women in veils and dancers' gowns, some even in the more exotic French corset and pantalettes, emerged from a room to the left – the brothel's makeshift *harem* quarters, as if the tenement were a make-believe palace. Some stood on the stairs, looking and assessing the newcomers. Delphine could hear the thud of boots upstairs, the cries of women in chambers above, muffled shrieks and laughter, music from beyond.

Nazrim led them to the right into a small salon, dim in the glow of smoking oil lamps, rich wooden furniture and *kelim* carpets – there was a desk and chair, paper, inks, brushes and pens for accounts paid and due, taxes and receipts. Seated on the floor, her back to a sofa, staring, blood on her temple and cheek, was a dark-skinned young girl of no more than twelve, thought Delphine. Her dishevelled black hair was cut in the fanciful Cleopatran bob, a thread of silver chain around her crown, a single cabochon gemstone on her forehead; her shoulders were bare, a jewelled bustier across her flat chest, her midriff bare to a broad tasselled and braided fabric belt, dark skirts blossoming about her on the floor, her dirty feet protruding, showing a bright anklet of beaten copper. Crouched beside her was Faiza, the madam of the establishment, looking up with relief.

'Ah, Masoud ibn Yussuf... and *madame, al handulillah.*' *God be praised*. She turned and spoke over her shoulder. 'Zumoa, show them.'

From the dark of the far corner emerged Zumoa, a broad-chested Nubian bodyguard of possibly thirty years, in sleeveless blue jerkin, broad *shalvar* trousers and turban. He pulled a set of curtains aside and revealed the unmoving body of a French soldier. He crossed his enormous bare arms and bowed his head, as if in disappointment with himself. '*Madem*,' he said to Delphine, watching the girl on the floor with concern. 'He is *morte*, Masoud *effendi*.'

Masoud moved quickly to the body, Delphine and Maria joining him. They rolled it over, the limbs stiff, the eyes wide, pupils black and unseeing. Masoud sighed deeply. 'There will be trouble…'

Maria put a finger to his throat, just to confirm. 'Dead.'

'*Morte*,' rumbled Zumoa.

Masoud sniffed at the body and looked at Faiza, then Delphine. 'Opium…?'

'Not mine!' cried Faiza. 'Ah, *not mine*. I care only for my little one here.'

Faiza was in her late forties, with greying henna-red hair that once might have been auburn, and the bright playful *kohl*-rimmed eyes of the Hawamdiya girl she had once been, her forearms tinkling with bracelets and bells, an ebbing beauty wearing her fortune about her neck, should business go awry. Delphine had paid visits to Faiza before, seeing to the women in need, often taking them back to the hospital. She also knew that Faiza was a useful source for Masoud.

'A new girl, *Madame* Delphine, from the east, as I told Masoud *effendi*,' Faiza protested in passable French. 'She takes something to drink, this oaf, this fool, hits her, hm, and falls down, *boum*. And I ask, who pays? Who? Then Zumoa cannot wake him for he is dead, and the girl speaks.'

Masoud watched her carefully, sifting the story, then asked Zumoa, 'Truly?'

Zumoa nodded his head slowly in assent in that strange new argot of Arabic and French. '*Nahm, papa.*' Yes. 'I guard secret.'

'Very well.' Masoud turned to Delphine. 'When the girl speaks, we must listen.'

Delphine looked at Masoud. They had not met since the business in the citadel. Masoud knew his trade: if he said it could be important, then Delphine would pay attention.

There was a crash upstairs and Maria looked back into the foyer and the stairwell, but only laughter followed. Zumoa bowed to Faiza to attend to the disturbance. 'Who pays?' he repeated in French, his frowning features glowing almost with threat at Faiza as he regarded the girl. 'Not she.' He went out and they heard his heavy tread on the stairs, possibly sufficient to instil a sense of order.

Faiza pulled Delphine closer. 'She is a child, *madame*, bare eleven years if I am right, but would not *go* from me, father dead, mother how you say, *disparu*, disappeared. I take her in and I say, who pays? A good question, I say!'

'*Eleven* years old, Faiza,' hissed Delphine. '*Répugnant!*' Disgusting.

'I was younger!' snapped Faiza, sulking. 'She was not here to lie with customers. She was *not*. I… I did not know she was with him…'

Maria made a pad of soft cotton lint as Delphine examined the girl's eyes, ears and mouth as Maria swabbed away the blood on her face. 'Pays for what, Faiza? Pays for her upkeep in a *bordel*?'

'We take her to the Swiss orphanage,' said Maria.

'No, no, *je vous en prie*,' insisted Faiza. 'She drinks or smokes the pipe, talks the nonsense and falls down, *boum*. Like the man, what can I do?'

'What did she say, Faiza?' asked Masoud.

'*Sacre…*' Angry, Delphine looked into the girl's pupils, wide with the transfixion of an opioid. She glanced at Maria. 'Laudanum?'

Maria shook her head. 'Opium smoke, what the soldier took.'

'I pay my taxes, I pay the Janissary!' Faiza protested. 'I get *hashish* for the pipes, he gets his money. We are careful!' She looked at them accusingly. 'It was Banaparteh Sultan who killed the four hundred! Not I! They took away Nour, you know, and she was *gaziya* – a dancer, special, who could dance the Saidi to music and wore the *telli*, a beauty! Not, how you say, a public woman – and the Janissaries *drowned her in a sack*.' She spat. 'A sack! Infected, say the French *physicien*, and the Janissaries *kill* her so. Who…? Who ordered it! Banaparteh!'

'That is nonsense,' muttered Delphine.

'It is not, it…'

Maria's cleaning of the wound revealed a contusion on the temple and a short cut – from a ring, most likely, thought Delphine. She dabbed it with spirit and the girl flinched, showing signs of life for the first time. Masoud looked into the girl's staring face. 'Now, my little one. What did you say?' He smoothed her hair gently, then cradled her soft chin. 'What was it now…?'

She blinked, then turned to look at Delphine, her breath coming suddenly in short gasps. '*Mima.*' Mother.

'Now,' hushed Faiza to them all. '*Listen.*'

The girl spoke in the rushed, breathless monotone of a child, the Arabic a mere whisper, Faiza translating. 'Her brother,' said Faiza. 'His friend has gold, lots of gold for them. He is… a grand servant now…'

Masoud flicked Faiza a glance. 'Do you know yet who is the friend or the brother?'

Faiza shook her head. 'No – shh, here she speaks…'

Delphine listened, the girl's whispering otherworldly, as if from beyond the grave.

'He comes for me, she says,' continued Faiza. 'The learned one…'

Maria scoffed, busying herself in the bag, preparing a dressing and wrap. 'Is this why you called us? *Aya.* We have patients all through the night…' They had modified a type of glue to hold the bandage in place, and she daubed this on the skin of the girl's temple as Faiza continued. 'He is servant of the pasha.'

There was a silence as Masoud looked at Delphine. 'Now it comes.' He asked the girl, 'Which pasha is that, my little?'

The girl did not turn her head but her mouth smiled slightly. 'Jehza.'

Masoud looked again at Delphine. They both knew the name.

Al-Djezzar.

The Butcher of Acre.

Delphine had heard all of the stories from Sir William Sidney Smith: Ahmed Pasha al-Djezzar, who immured men in his castle walls, whose victims' screams echoed in the quad of his citadel; Al-Djezzar, who had ceremonially strangled hundreds of Christians in a mass execution to spite Bonaparte, their gagging retches music to his delighted ears; Al-Djezzar, who had offered a bounty for each French soldier's head and who had sworn to 'throw Bonaparte into the fire'. William John Hazzard had met him, and called him a madman.

Masoud asked softly, 'What does he do for the pasha, this wise one?'

In an otherworldly trance from the opium, the girl turned her head, still staring, not seeing them. 'He comes to find the heart of Sultan *al-Kebir.*'

Delphine and Maria stopped. Faiza's eyes were wide and accusatory. 'You see? You *see*? I tell you so.'

Masoud asked, 'Your brother's friend will cover you in gold, hm?' But the girl was lost in a world where she was raised up to dwell in a land of palaces and princes.

'Apply the gauze,' Delphine said quietly to Maria, moving round to look into the girl's face so she might not be so afraid. 'Nefer,' she said – not necessarily her name, but a safe option, meaning 'beauty' – and the girl stared, nodding, while Delphine's heart hammered against her stays beneath her blouse. 'Nefer, why does your brother wish to find the heart of Sultan *al-Kebir*...?'

Masoud translated for the girl, his voice appealing, tender.

The girl answered breathily and Masoud looked at Delphine. 'To bring Sultan *al-Kebir* to an end.'

Delphine watched the girl, the eyes dark and blank. She looked at Masoud. 'It could mean anything.'

'No,' said Faiza, looking to Masoud for support, 'it does *not*. A man has received gold from a pasha to bring an end to Sultan *al-Kebir*. There. *Voilà*.'

Masoud looked at the dead soldier, pensive.

But Faiza went on, red with indignation that she would lose a valued asset. 'Gold that I should receive now. I had arranged the *zawag 'urfi*, the secret marriage, so that no law is broken, so that this girl is taken to husband, but now, when I say who will pay, she answers, a brother who has gold! He must pay, for I will lose money!'

Maria whispered, 'They called the *Général en chef* Sultan *al-Kebir*... the Great Sultan.'

Masoud spoke quickly. 'As we saw in attending Mustafa Pasha, the French army is divided, *madame*. There are those who would stay, for the honour of their *Général en chef* Bonaparte, and others who would go home, evacuate.'

She nodded. 'And the generals who wish to leave...?'

'They are in command. And even now would negotiate peace with Captain Smith. But if one of them is a target of assassins, a treaty could be broken and the Ottomans return in force – or the French defeat them, and stay in Egypt.'

Delphine looked at the girl. 'She is just a child.'

'Perhaps,' agreed Masoud, 'but we have part of a name or sobriquet, *al-hakim*, the wise, or learned, suggesting education, from Sidon, Acre or Syria, the land of Al-Djezzar. Perhaps the assassin is at the university in Baghdad,' he said. 'Or here already, in Cairo.'

'The Al-Azhar...?'

'Perhaps. One of my informants says an Ottoman Arnaut in Cairo, released after Jaffa, boasted that Sultan *al-Kebir* would be dead within the month – by men paid by the pasha.'

Delphine looked into his eyes, the intensity and urgency well concealed, simmering below a natural control. 'Does he mean Bonaparte? Do they know he is now gone to France?'

'If a French sultan is murdered, *madame*, Egypt could suffer a mutiny within the French army.'

Delphine had seen mutiny at first hand, in Jaffa, when the storming division had run riot with rapine and bloody murder on women, children and all. She could still remember the spring-pressure of the trigger beneath her finger even now, as she had fired Hazzard's Lorenzoni, again and again. She felt a wave of nausea – and thought of such terror coming to Cairo. 'What of Réné?' she asked faintly. 'He must be warned…'

Masoud tried to reassure her. 'Yes, of course, *madame*. The Dr Desgenettes would help if he could, I know this.' His eyes flickered to a new thought for her. 'But it would put him in the dangerous position, between the camps. Or, indeed,' he added, 'we could trust to one who would act without hindrance.'

Delphine understood, and would not repeat his name before Faiza or others.

Hazzard.

Maria watched her perceptively. 'You speak of him, don't you? Of Jaffa?'

Delphine nodded. 'Yes.' Desgenettes could wield influence, but… our friend would find an assassin – and stop him. *We must tell William.* 'To stop a civil war, or mutiny—'

Faiza interrupted. 'What is this? What is it you say between you? My reward?'

'I have taken steps,' said Masoud. 'But we must hurry. There is only one way.'

Delphine looked at Faiza, her anger rising. She dug out two old Louis sovereigns from her special pocket under the belt at her waist and gave them to her. 'Here. Take your payment, then,' she said.

Faiza looked at the coins. 'You see? I serve the good Sultan *al-Kebir*! I want no damage, no Mamluks or Bashi-Bazouki coming with the pashas. This is for my service!'

Masoud took her hand harshly. 'And for disposing of the soldier.'

Faiza snatched the coins away. 'Zumoa will do it.'

There was a sound of approaching hoofbeats in the street – a horse halting and walking. Faiza pulled back the floating red curtains and looked out through the window as Masoud flitted out.

Delphine closed up her bag, got to her feet and stooped to pull the girl to her feet. 'Maria…'

'*Oui madame*,' said the Maltese nurse without hesitation, and helped her up.

Faiza watched them. 'But what…? What do you—'

'The orphanage,' said Delphine. 'With us, with anyone, Faiza, but not with a *husband*, secret or otherwise.'

'This is not practical! I have saved the Sultan *al-Kebir*!' Desperate, she turned to a carved sandalwood box on the small table beside her. 'Look, look, *look* – she had this in her little bag, this paper! It proves it!'

She held out a crackling, browned sheet of stiff notepaper. It was covered in block-printed or stamped Persian Farsi characters with no identifiable word structures, perhaps in the hope that few in the western regions could read it easily. At the bottom was a stylised signature and indeciperable ink-stamp – but it was sufficient to prove its Ottoman origins from some sort of senior official, though not who.

'What is it?' asked Maria.

'Perhaps for the payment. This may be the proof we need.'

The door opened again and they felt the heat of the street waft in as Masoud returned. With him came a rider in dark blue and white *maghrib* headdress and robes, two cartridge bandoliers across his chest, a pistol in his belt, a sword at his hip: a Tarabin *Bedu*. '*Madame*,' said Masoud, 'we must go. At once.'

Noise burst from above with more laughter as a man fell down the stairs, women chasing him angrily, shouting at him as he fetched up against a small table in the foyer, snapping its legs as it collapsed with a crash, a copper jug clanging to the tiles and rolling.

A corporal of the 85th demi-brigade stood laughing on the stairs, pointing at his comrade being smacked by the women as Zumoa descended towards him slowly. The French soldier tried to stand, then lay still. Zumoa took him by the front of his tunic and the white belt at his waist, and hurled him through the open front door into the street, the corporal cackling fit to burst, the women hurling insults after him.

Zumoa looked into the salon. He saw Masoud and the Bedouin, Delphine, Maria, their packed bag – and the little girl's hand tight in Delphine's. His eye flicked from one to the other, and finally to Faiza, who sat on the floor, hiding her face, biting the back of her hand as if in grievous loss. Zumoa met Delphine's eye, and the little girl's, and bowed.

'*Madem*,' he said, and stepped aside.

Masoud and the Bedouin rider leading the way, they hurried out into the night.

–

Several hours before dawn, not a stone's throw from the dark streets of Faiza's private house of public women, a small crowd of locals had gathered behind a squad of soldiers in the darkness by the reeds on the banks of the Nile; the deep indigo sky shimmered on the glassy surface. Fishermen in their boats and punts passed by, the pinpricks of their lanterns bobbing on the black water, mingling with reflected stars and moonlight.

Some in the crowd murmured knowingly to each other, '*Crocodiles*,' as a soaked body was hauled up the banks and dropped unceremoniously onto the stinking mudflats – followed by another; although Nile crocodiles certainly prowled the reed beds and river's edge, they all knew a crocodile would have left little behind. Both were French soldiers.

Lantern in hand, the laughing corporal of the 85th knelt beside one of the bodies and bit off a vicious curse: '*Putain de merde.*' He moved to the next, his shoulders sagging with disappointed recognition – then exploded in sudden outrage. '*Ma foi... salauds de merde!*' He jumped to his feet and hurled the lantern at the spectators, who dodged, some running away.

He nodded to a waiting sergeant. 'It is Defosse.' It was the man who had fallen down the stairs and been thrown into the street.

'Name, unit?' demanded Citizen Peraud of the *Bureau d'information*. He looked down at the body as the corporal from the 85th *demi* stiffened to attention. They all knew of Citizen Derrien. They said this one was even worse.

'Defosse, Pierre Pydrovic, Citizen,' he replied formally. 'A Bohemian, 1st Battalion 85th *demi de bataille*. When I came out of the... the *bordel*, he was gone,' he protested. 'I thought, you know, *salaud*, he has gone to the barracks, but...'

Peraud looked at the exposed neck of the corpse. It was badly bruised, broken, from a single blow: a club or very strong hand. He leaned forward and sniffed. The sweet, sticky smell was all over the body. 'Opium.'

'A fight,' suggested the corporal in despair. 'Who knows… for opium, for a girl, for…' He glanced at one of the *khawal* boys and shrugged. 'For I know not what.'

Peraud looked at Zumoa. 'Explain. *Isri.* Quick.

The Nubian's eyes were bright in his black face, and they stared straight into Peraud without demur. 'He is *morte.*'

Peraud took a handkerchief and put it to his nose and mouth, just for the smell, and made a brief gesture to the corporal of the 85th. 'If you please, Corporal. And move these wretches back. They disgust me.' Then, as an afterthought, 'But take those there.'

Led by the outraged corporal, the squad of soldiers seized the nearest spectators – three men and a woman – and pushed them, shrieking in fright, to their knees before Peraud. He looked at them. 'What happened?'

They had been watching from the darkened doorways – two were the painted *khawal* dancing boys. They clasped their hands as if in Christian prayer, jabbering protests, clutching at his coat. '*Effendi, le, le, leh!*' *No.* Peraud smacked the hands aside angrily and drew from his pocket not the screw-barrelled pistol of Citizen Derrien, but a longer Turkish three-barrelled turnover pistol. He preferred it to Derrien's antique, which was, he had decided, not suited to his peculiar mounting-pressure technique of interrogation.

'*Eh bien.*'

The first *khawal* was no more than seventeen, his smooth, delicate face made up with rouge paint and *kohl* eyeliner; he had long braided hair, wore elaborate earrings, a cheap necklace of common gemstones, a loose turban with swathes of silks and a stained gown. He shook with terror, gibbering in his low street-argot to his older companion, then in French to Peraud. 'No no no, *m'sieur! J'vous enn pree!*' He tried to smile hopefully. 'I… I c-can give the *m'sieur* great pleasure, I—'

'Shh, yes, yes, I'm sure you can.' Peraud looked at the older *khawal* beside him, his lined jowls quaking, his long unkempt hair hanging now in damp sweaty tangles, his make-up smudged over a late-night stubble as he clutched the boy tightly to him.

'He is just boy! Is boy, *m'sieur!*'

'Do you understand me?' asked Peraud reasonably, his eyes locked on the older *khawal*, quite possibly the boy's pimp. 'Do you? Do you truly understand?' He tilted his head in mocking sympathy, put the pistol to the boy's forehead without looking and pulled the trigger.

The explosion made people jump and the boy's head snapped back with the impact, a dark cloud of blood blowing out from the back of his skull, the body dropping awkwardly to the road. 'There!' said Peraud happily. 'Now you see, *n'est-ce pas*?' His face contorted in rage. '*I am Citizen Peraud! Of the Bureau de renseignements et information! Tu crétin! Comprenez!* Understand? *Understand*?'

The older *khawal* dancer screamed, and was immediately smashed across the back of the head by a musket-butt – *Silence, vous idiot!* – and he began to sob and shake uncontrollably, his face collapsing in tears, his hands pulling his rose silk *shemagh* over his head as if to hide. The others began to moan and whimper, the small crowd growing, pushing against the French soldiers. Peraud looked at Zumoa, turned the bronzed barrels of his pistol on their spindle with a well-oiled click, locating a new loaded breech, cocked it, and pointed it at the weeping man.

Peraud had little interest in the dead troopers – yet another soldier, a brothel, drink, opium. He had seen this before; one soldier more, one less, who cared, he thought, as there were always more of them somewhere. What irritated him was that Zumoa was not forthcoming. Peraud waited. The heavyset Nubian looked down, his fingers writhing in indecision. 'You have taken money, Zumoa,' said Peraud. 'This means you owe me a service.'

Zumoa answered without hesitation. 'Yes, *effendi*.'

'What happened? I am now patient.'

'I do not know—'

'I am no longer patient.' While looking at Zumoa, Peraud pulled the trigger.

The old *khawal* collapsed and the spectators screamed, the soldiers beating at them as they ran back to the nearest houses and the dark streets, some running to the river, falling into the reeds, floundering along the riverbank, anything to get away, braving even the monsters of the Nile.

'It is he!' shouted the woman on her knees, pointing at Zumoa. 'He knows!'

The corporal of the 85th seized her by the hair. 'What? What did you say? *Matha qult'!* He was there?'

'I hear to him!' she stammered in broken French. 'Hear he say of the Sultan *al-Kebir*!'

Peraud faced Zumoa, then pointed the pistol at his temple. The big Nubian started to breathe heavily and mumbled, '*Lorr, l'or…* Gold… she say, for brother…'

Peraud raised an eyebrow, interested. 'Gold?'

'*Il sait!* He knows!' shouted the woman again, then gasped as the corporal yanked the handful of her thick hair and pulled her back into place.

Peraud looked at him, then pushed the pistol against his head with greater ferocity. '*Do not make me ask again.*'

Breathing hard, the air whistling audibly through his nose, Zumoa seemed to give in. He said between clenched teeth, his deep voice still steady, 'A girl, her brother comes, a wise one. The money, the promise, *gold*, for the life of a *sultan*… for Sultan *al-Kebir*.'

Peraud watched him for a moment. His mind ticked, the words flying into conjunction: *Sultan al-Kebir, gold, assassin.* But how, he thought; the only Sultan *al-Kebir* they had ever known was now far away, in…

A slow smile crept across his face.

Oh yes.

He had forgotten Egypt was now a new world. With new sultans.

'Where did the girl go, Zumoa?' Zumoa hesitated. Peraud pushed the gun harder against his head. 'Come along now…'

The big man cursed, his control possibly more to prevent his own desire to seize Peraud bodily, for the Frenchman would have stood little chance. 'Zumoa does not know… She departed… *partait, partait…*'

But Peraud knew the ways of night creatures. The lure of gold, of lust, of opium – it was all so very *base*. He knew the opium dealers, the smugglers, from the work of his own family, from the depths of his half-blooded soul he had tried to suppress, to forget: *Juan Peraud* – not Jean, but *Juan*. And once again their stench assailed his nostrils. 'Where did she go? Who went with her?'

For the first time in the face of Peraud's unblinking savagery, Zumoa grimaced in pain. For him, this was the worst: giving up his great secret.

'*Madem.*'

'*Where is she?*' demanded Peraud as he marched through the dark foyer of the military hospital, his men behind. But for the desultory glow of the few lanterns they carried, the place was thick with the sickness of night, their fearful eyes glancing at beds as they passed, the bandages, the blood of the young and the old. They filed through to the corridor leading to the administration block by the stables, and one of the soldiers kicked in the glazed door to Delphine's office, the small panes shattering as it banged against the wall, glass tinkling to the floor.

'Search it,' ordered Peraud. Holding their lanterns high, they began turning over the contents of the desk, emptying drawers onto the floor, while others charged onwards into the staff quarters.

Gamila, the night nurse, spotted the lights at the end of the corridor and heard the noise – she tried to run but they cornered her in the passage to the stables. '*She is not here, m'sieur!*' she cried. 'She go, to the victim, in the town…' she said in broken French.

Peraud pushed his way through to her. 'Then why is she not returned with her victim?' he shouted. 'Why?' The patients in the nearby stalls began to stir, orderlies hurrying to the main ward to calm them.

The corporal from the 85th emerged from behind a curtain at the end of the corridor, candlelight throwing a gleam on the whitewashed walls. 'The bed is empty, Citizen, not slept in.'

'But what has she done?' cried Gamila.

'Crimes against the state,' said Peraud, drawing his pistol yet again that night. 'Where is she?'

The smells of its oil and powder filling the air, the pistol hovered in the girl's face and she began to sob, hiding behind her hands. A night orderly rushed in, his arms outstretched. '*No, no, no, m'sieur, qu'est-ce qui est? What what what?*' He stood in front of Gamila in the darkness of the candlelit corridor, shielding her, and the soldiers cocked their firelocks, stepping back. 'I… I am Omar, the orderly,' he gasped. 'The *madame* is not here, *je vous le promis*. I swear it.'

From the rear of the stable block came a shout – *Who the hell is that?* – and Peraud turned. A fierce red-haired, red-bearded doctor strode down the passage, apparently roused from his bed, pulling a pale blue *binish* gown over his shirt and waistcoat, setting his spectacles on his forehead. A powerfully built man, grey temples stood out from a hard, sun–baked desert complexion; Peraud guessed at once that he had seen action and was likely not easily intimidated. 'Who in *hell* are you?' demanded the doctor.

A broad smile creased Peraud's face. 'Ah, *m'sieur le médecin*.'

'Yes I am the doctor, damn you, and what do you think you're doing frightening my staff and disturbing my hospital in the middle of the bloody night?'

Peraud stifled the urge to laugh. 'I do beg your pardon, Dr...?'

'De Bretagne. *Colonel* De Bretagne. And who in hell are you?'

Peraud ignored the question. 'Where is *Madame* Lascelles if you please.'

'I've no idea but you try this secret police nonsense with me and I'll have you dragged up before Chief Surgeon Desgenettes in the morning. Now get *out*, all of you.'

Peraud did not move a muscle. Instead, he pointed his pistol at Gamila and Omar again. 'Shall I ask again?'

'What in God's name——?'

'Doctor, where is *Madame* Lascelles?'

De Bretagne snarled at him, his voice low, contemptuous. 'You filthy little Dago shit. Too piss–poor a man, you have to scare little girls, eh? In the 9th *demi* we spat turds like you into the front trench as cannon fodder.' The soldiers tensed as De Bretagne slowly advanced on Peraud. 'Look at you. Half Porto or Spaniard pretending to be one of us. Shame you're not real Corsican or Italian, eh? Then you'd have got somewhere, like our noble hero the general. Oh, but he ran away, didn't he.'

At the mention of Bonaparte's heritage, Peraud's face tightened with hatred and he hissed, his breath scything through clenched teeth. 'You *dare*...'

'Oh I dare.' De Bretagne took a step forward. 'I was there when they scaled the walls of Gozo, took my wounds and helped them over the walls when they began to sing. And I sang with them.'

The corporal of the 85th put his own Boutet pistol under the colonel's chin.

But Omar burst forward, holding out his hands. 'No, no!' he cried to Peraud. 'She, the *madame*, she went perhaps to the *Quartier*, Citizen... She went with the Chief Administrator of Sultan *al-Kebir!*' He looked desperately from one face to the other. 'His Excellence Sharif Masoud *al-Hakim!*'

'Yes, that's right,' said De Bretagne quietly, flicking a look at the unwavering pistol held to his jaw. 'Masoud ibn Yussuf. Takes her to work for Command.' He looked at the corporal. 'Look down, very slowly, boy. And meet your splenic artery.'

The corporal frowned and blinked with incomprehension, then glanced down. In the colonel's right hand was a scalpel, its blade no more than two inches long, its tip touching the corporal's floating ribs.

'Eight to ten seconds, and you're dead while walking.' De Bretagne moved slightly, pushing the pistol harder under his chin, the scalpel closer. 'I say you'll make it five feet before you drop, *salaud de putain*.'

For a moment there was silence in the hospital. In the distance, a patient coughed. An empty bowl dropped to the floor with a metallic clatter. Peraud put up his pistol. The corporal likewise backed away, withdrawing his Boutet carefully, his eye on the scalpel, which remained rock-steady.

Gamila rushed to the colonel and he put his arms about her as she began to sob. They could all remember what had happened the previous year with Derrien – hospital staff put against walls and shot – and De Bretagne had vowed it would never happen again.

'Chief Administrator of Sultan *al-Kebir*...' repeated Peraud.

Omar nodded vigorously. '*Oui, oui, citoyen*.'

'They should have returned. Some hours ago. Why take a... what do you call them? A *victim*... to the *Quartier général*?'

De Bretagne dug in a pocket for his handkerchief. 'How should he know? He's just a damned orderly.'

Omar protested, 'Perhaps to *le grand Médécin* Desgenettes, *m-m'sieur*...'

Peraud turned away to think. Three names he had heard in conjunction now: Desgenettes. Masoud. And Sultan *al-Kebir*. He pocketed his pistol and turned to Omar. 'Tell me,' he said, as if testing a child, 'who is the Sultan *al-Kebir*?'

'*M-m'sieur*...?'

Holding tightly to Gamila, De Bretagne lost his temper. 'Oh for God's sake *get out*!'

Peraud turned away, the thoughts playing in his mind, ignoring De Bretagne, ignoring them all, calling out, '*Sous-lieutenant* Senlac! Send messengers to every gate, to every checkpoint, to every mooring-post on the Nile! She is not to escape the city!'

As they crossed the forecourt to the horses, Peraud said to the corporal of the 85th, 'What is your name?'

'Brentil, Citizen. Of six years' service.'

Peraud reached his horse, a trooper holding the reins ready for him. 'You are hereby relieved of your army duties, Citizen, and are now my new deputy in the *Bureau d'information.*'

Brentil's scarred face lit up. 'Yes, Citizen.'

Peraud flung his leg over the saddle and pulled on the rein. 'Follow and learn. I want the Lascelles woman.'

–

When he was sure the last of them had gone, De Bretagne led Gamila away to the stable stalls, trying to comfort her, but she broke and ran for the door up ahead, leading to a storeroom and the outer door to the rear quad. She threw herself inside and ran to Masoud, Maria and Delphine, flinging her arms round Delphine's neck and clinging to her. '*Oh, madame…*'

'There there, *Gamille,*' she said softly, tears coming. 'You were so very brave…' They had heard it all, Maria and Masoud insisting she stay quiet, saving them all.

Omar hurried in after. '*Madame*, they will take you if they find you—'

'This is madness,' said Delphine. 'We are not fugitives.'

'We are now,' replied Masoud.

'Did you not see?' said Maria, looking out of the glazed door to the rear quad where two horses stood ready. 'That dog Peraud has surely killed us, but the girl is safe, *madame*. She rests at the orphanage – but you must *go*.'

Masoud hefted the bags of supplies they had collected and glanced over the lines of shelving around them. '*Madame*, we can rely only upon the senior Command officers, and those who do not follow Peraud and the *Bureau d'information.*' He looked at Omar and Maria. 'Be careful. In a way, the mutiny has begun.'

De Bretagne stormed in, swinging the door shut. '*Merde aux yeux.* I shall have him and every one of those damned little wretches from the 85th – reserve battalion bastards, I'll warrant, fed up with real soldiering…' He brought down a medical test bottle from one of the high iron shelves, snatched out the cork and took a swig of contraband

Scotch whisky. 'I'll have them digging ditches at Damietta before next week.'

He tore open the door to the quad, marching them outside into the gleam of a flickering coaching-lamp, the smells of leather, manure and hay mingling with the cool damp of early morning. The lone Tarabin Bedouin emerged from the shadows, leading a third horse, a dappled bay, and he and Masoud secured the bags to the saddles. De Bretagne continued, 'He will throw up checkpoints on the main roads to the ports, armed, with a special day-word to which they will have a special reply. If incorrect, arrest, interrogation or summary execution, no excuses. I have seen it before.' He nodded to the Tarabin. '*Rabbena ma'ak.*' *God be with you.* He lowered his voice to Masoud. 'Sinai will be easier than the Delta now.'

Masoud nodded. 'Yes.'

'Masoud knows,' said Delphine.

Masoud bowed. 'As does our guide.'

'Then hurry.' De Bretagne gave him the half-emptied bottle of Scotch and embraced Delphine. '*Ma petite lionnesse.*'

'*Mon cher Colonel Max.*'

Maria took her hands. 'I will be with Réné,' she said forcibly, then attempted a thin smile. 'We have seen too much for this to defeat us, hm?'

'Yes, Maria.' Delphine tried to laugh, wiping away a tear, her heart battering at her ribs.

Masoud mounted and called down gently, '*Madame...*'

She turned to the horse and gathered the reins, De Bretagne helping her into the saddle. 'Ha!' he said, with a happy thought. 'I'll pin the theft of the horse on those *salauds de merde.*'

'Maximilien...'

They looked up at Delphine, the four who would be left behind, their words haunting in her ear. 'Get us all home,' said De Bretagne, his arms held out as they walked off, the horses' hooves thudding dully on the straw strewn across the cobbles, and into the black morning. Delphine looked back, the coachlamp casting a dim glow across them in the quad, until the hospital was swallowed up by dark corners and the shadows of palms.

The Tarabin said simply, '*Yallah.*'

Come on.

Bosphorus

It was a pleasantly warm afternoon for early December in Constantinople, and Special Envoy Thomas Marmaduke Wayland, Acting Captain of Marines, hurried as best he could through the winding streets from his lodgings in Fatih up towards the vast enclosing walls of the Topkapi Palace. Seabirds hung in the brisk cool wind from the Bosphorus, some wheeling above, bright white against the arc of blue, their cries bringing him memories of the sea, where he longed to return – and above all, to get back to Hazzard and the men of 9 Company once again.

However, he had paid his dues on active service, losing his left hand at the Battle of the Memnonium, and taking a leg wound on Malta, where he had set 9 Company and a ragtag corps of militiamen across a road to turn away six hundred enemy shock-troops. Taking another bullet in the chest at the Battle of the Nile, as he charged the shore batteries to protect Troubridge and HMS *Culloden*, had left him with no visible impairment apart from a healthy distrust of his fellow man – another lesson learned at the feet of William John Hazzard, if only Wayland had but listened.

He stumped up the ancient cobbles, the calf of his bad leg never healing properly, sore with the damp winter, his brass-tipped mahogany stick clacking on the stones as he passed familiar tradesmen calling to him – '*Marhaba Wayalandeh effendi!*' – calling to one another, arguing over goods in carts, goods slung over horses, over donkeys, much as he had seen in Cairo. Among the twisting streets and stone steps of Fatih, they had come from the overflowing *souk* nearby. Soon he was up and on the hill with its broad shade trees, grasses and gardens. The great dome of the *Ayasofia* cathedral rose before him.

He stopped and gazed, as he did every day, vestiges of his once youthful enthusiasm catching him up. *How ever did I get here?*

Still over a hundred yards off, the great central dome of the ancient Christian basilica was now surrounded by ornate Islamic minarets, the vast rambling cathedral of the Byzantines and crusaders now as Muslim as the Blue Mosque far to his left, over the gardens and parade ground of the Janissaries. He could have accepted quarters at the embassy in Timoni House, up in Pera, a somewhat aristocratic suburb, but it was not *here*, in the heart of the history of the world – and Sir Sidney Smith had wanted Wayland to be close to the Sublime Porte itself, and keep an ear open. As a clandestine operative of the Alien Office in London, it suited Wayland perfectly.

Fine horses trotted by on the road on the distant far side of the gardens, gentlemen of noble seat riding with aristocratic beys, and horsemen from the Caucasus with astrakhan hats, *shasqua* swords and fierce moustaches, all mixed with slow-moving omnibuses bearing evening workers homeward, and coaches disgorging civilian tourists, pointing at the sights before them, artists erecting easels to capture the scenes.

Though a serving officer, Wayland did not wear uniform most of the time, and kept a lower profile, in top hat, dark grey topcoat, pale waistcoat and breeches. It helped him move more easily through Constantinople, which was filled with a multiplicity of foreign colours: ranged beside the bright red of the elite *Nizam-i Djedid* troops and baggy *shalvar* and fez of the Albanian Janissaries, were the bluejackets of the British Royal Navy, the black of Prussian emissaries, and *jäger* greens and imperial blues of the Viennese and Russian courts. Among these were the faces of an empire stretching from the Danube to the Nile Cataracts: Somali and Sudanese notables, hair braided and jewelled; women in gold and black; Sufi and Shia, Kurd and Armenian, all plying their trade at the fulcrum of the world, the new Troy.

As Wayland watched the ever-changing spectacle, a figure up ahead in a dark coat gave a discreet nod and doffed his black top hat, as if to a passer-by. Wayland had seen him already some way off, and felt the rumblings of irritability. Young Stanford was a quick-witted assistant, bright, and usually brought irksome problems from Home Office despatches – but without question he was the best informed of the British Foreign Service in the Porte.

'Good afternoon, Stanford,' said Wayland stiffly as he stumped past, forcing his assistant to catch up to his deliberate increase of speed. 'Have we a meeting set?'

'Not precisely, sir,' apologised Stanford diffidently. 'More of a summons than a meeting.' He extended his stride to match Wayland's mild limp – they said Stanford had come straight from Balliol College, Oxford, and begun full service in the Diplomatic Corps at once. A gifted linguist, he seemed far more experienced than his years, and Wayland doubted he was as young and green as many believed. Having worked now for some while with Wickham's Aliens networks, Wayland also doubted he was ever told the full truth about anything: more than an aide, Stanford was something of an irritating guardian angel.

They passed the vast medieval buttresses of the crusader cathedral. 'When and where?' asked Wayland. 'Do we go to the *Bab-i-Ali* or Alemdar Street?'

The *Bab-i Ali* was literally the 'High Gate', otherwise known traditionally by the French expression 'Sublime Porte', of the Topkapi Palace just ahead; Alemdar Cardesi was the address of the second magnificent Sublime Porte palace built for the Grand Vizier, just to the west of the sprawling Topkapi harem grounds. It mattered because they would need more time to get there, to find a cab or sedan chair. A bearded trader in robes and coloured turban stopped them – '*Kahve, effendi?*' – pointing to a coffee stall some distance off. Wayland replied politely, '*Hayir, teshekir ederim.*' *No, thank you very much.*

'No, sir, it's an impromptu, at the Arch,' Stanford said, checking his fob-watch. 'In about five minutes' time.' The Arch was office-shorthand for a quiet place behind the great Hagia Sophia, or *Ayasofia* cathedral mosque. 'We shall be meeting Colonel Percy. He comes bearing instructions.' Stanford grinned. 'Apparently he might bring his… niece, is it?'

'Oh for God's sake. His mistress, more like.'

'Quite, sir.'

With the Grand Vizier Yussuf Pasha charging towards Egypt at the head of a ramshackle army of nearly a hundred thousand men, and the French staggering on their back foot after the departure of Bonaparte, Wayland wondered what more could this wretched Percy want. He was neither Admiralty, Alien Office or diplomat, but had been throwing his weight about with the embassy staff, demanding two military attachés for his own use, and had the reputation of a nasty depot martinet. Percy had some sort of clout, but nothing that Wayland knew about.

Stanford seemed to overhear Wayland's thoughts. 'All we know, sir, is that he is well placed, a personal acquaintance of his Lairdship and others.'

He meant the ambassador, the Scottish Lord Elgin. 'Lordship will do, Stanford,' said Wayland, growing more sour by the minute.

'Yes, sorry, sir. Some of the chaps call him Tom the Bruce. Och-aye the noo, and so forth.'

Wayland glanced at him. 'He is a descendant, you know.'

Stanford looked at him earnestly. 'So I understand, sir.'

'Then watch it. Or they'll lock you in the Tower for being a Jacobite in disguise.' To Wayland, Elgin looked a vigorous fellow, and had more than earned his posting, starting off as an officer in the field.

'Yes, sir. As to Mr Percy, he is, for the time being...' Stanford leafed through pages of notes produced from an inside pocket as he avoided people on the thoroughfare. 'On secondment from the 3rd Foot, the Scots Guards, on special assignment from the War House, stamps, seals, Lord Melville, et cetera.' War House was more civil service jargon for the War Office.

'To poke his bloody nose in,' finished Wayland, wondering who had given Percy his shilling: Old Jarvie would never have stood for it – and he hoped Jervis had been made First Sea Lord by now. 'Keep your ears open, Stanford. We have no idea whose side Percy is on.'

'Absolutely, sir. Hush-hush and mum's the word.'

As they reached the far end of the *Ayasofia* and the towering walls of the Topkapi, they held back as a company of Turkish troops marched past in perfect unison, in grey fitted coats and the familiar long trailing fez, immaculate, their boots striking the paving stones as one. It was the regular detachment for the changing of the guard, as impressive as Horse Guards, thought Wayland.

As they waited, he cast a glance at the emissaries attending at the great *Bab-i-Ali* gate, the 'Porte' itself. It loomed high over their heads, a gateway for giants and emperors. He felt a sudden pang – if Hazzard had been with him they would have mused about the ancients: of Troy; of Xerxes, Constantine and Romanus; that here once had stood Theodoric the Goth to marvel at the water-gardens, canals and colonnades: *Who could have built such wonders, for surely this is the work of gods.* Even after some months in the ancient city for Sir Sidney and the Aliens, Wayland still thought the same.

When the guard had dispersed, they passed the southeastern corner of the cathedral, occupied by the domed tombs of the sultans, Selim, Murad – names that still resonated within him, still calling him to the desert in Egypt. They descended a broad set of steps at the base of the giant minaret soaring high above them as the *muezzin* began the afternoon call to prayer, the wailing *adhan* echoing among the stonework, each phrase repeated in the near distance from the Blue Mosque. 'Best hurry, sir,' said Stanford. 'He hates the noise.'

Jacaranda and cherry blossom trees marked a passage behind the cathedral, bulging at this point with two- and three-storey towers and niches, known to the intelligence services generally as 'the Arch'. Wayland had little fondness for the Arch or its environs. It was tacitly recognised as neutral ground and a well-known place for clandestine meetings – between messengers, emissaries, and unofficial government parties – to the extent that complex negotiations could be achieved by secretaries hurrying between parties secreted along the lane; but Wayland hated the feeling of exposure. On departure, one could acquire a number of tails, often on a whim, merely following out of curiosity or even practice, and it was a tiresome chore to lose them in the outlying lanes.

They rounded the last corner of the lane and came to an archway leading to a shaded nook with a stone seat and an elaborate fretwork shutter, affording privacy to a secret tryst, be it among spies or lovers. Waiting inside were two figures: one was a British officer in red coat, gleaming boots and breeches. Beside him, in broad bonnet and parasol, was a lady, young enough to be his daughter – his 'niece', surmised Wayland.

His walking-stick clicking on the cobbles, Wayland went straight past, Stanford saying nothing as they continued onwards, checking: the nearby buttress niches were vacant but for a couple of sellers of baubles and fabric, reaching out and speaking their patter, their voices fading as Wayland stopped to examine the weave of a small prayer mat. He mumbled in Turkish, 'Anyone?'

'*Hayir, Waylandeh effendi.*' No.

Wayland waited for a moment as Stanford took a length of silk voile in hand, very interested, one eye on the path they had just taken, but no one was following.

'*Teshekir*, Faisal,' said Wayland, and smoothly put a coin on the trader's table, which Faisal discreetly swept away as he set out a stack of fabric.

Stanford glanced at him. 'Sir?'

Wayland nodded. 'Very well.'

They turned back, the other sellers looking away, busying themselves: Faisal had done his work. They reached the corner and entered the Arch. In the cool shade, the call of the *muezzin* seemed somehow muffled. Percy's face was as red as his coat.

'You again. You went straight past us, man,' he hissed in outrage. 'What the devil's wrong with you?'

This confirmed all Wayland needed to know. 'Colonel Percy, I presume.'

Stanford tucked his head down and whispered, '*Indeed, sir, 'tis he.*'

Percy was a broad-chested man who stood with his feet shoulder-width apart, hands behind his back and scowled at the world, displeased with what he saw. His close-shaven head revealed a balding pate, long sideboards and dark moustache, which served to make him look even more thunderous than he doubtless already was most of the time.

'Of course I damn well am. You're *late*,' he fired at them. 'I have things to do.'

Wayland bowed to the lady. 'As do we all.'

'Well? Are you Wayland, sir?' demanded Percy in exasperation, as if the answer might give rise to some sort of argument.

'I am.'

'*Lieutenant* Wayland?'

'Yes. Of a sort.'

'What? Then address a colonel in the Scots Guards as *sir*, dammit!' He looked Wayland up and down. 'Good *God*, look at you! Tassels, topcoat and sashes, probably curly-toed slippers somewhere. Have you gone completely native?' He waited. 'Well?'

Wayland was remarkably unmoved. 'Have you been in Turkey the full hour, sir, or just hopped off the boat for the tuppenny tour?'

Percy's eyes widened. 'How *dare* you! I've a good mind to report this impudence to your commanding officer!'

'By all means, do,' said Wayland. 'If you can find him. He's probably beyond Sidi ben Ali, or the Sinai, or Dendera.'

The lady tugged on Percy's arm. 'Uncle, apologise, *je vous en prie*,' she urged, in a lyrical French accent.

'Apologise? I am his superior officer!'

Stanford moved in, doffing his hat. 'If I may intrude, Colonel, may I present Acting Captain Wayland, His Majesty's Marine Forces, on secondment to the Foreign Office courtesy of personal request of

Commodore Sir William Sidney Smith, the First Sea Lord and His Imperial Majesty the Sultan of the Ottoman Empire.'

Going bright red, either with frustration or anger, Percy took a stumbling step back, his small blue eyes glittering, his voice returning. 'The *sultan*? By God, that damned Smith's been up to his tricks again...' He glanced for a moment at the missing left hand, the stick. 'It's *you*. I thought so. I've heard the tall tales – playing the wounded hero, are you? My God, you really are one of that... that Special damned Squadron of Jervis's, aren't you, with that insubordinate fellow Hazzard? Oh yes, I know all about *him*—'

'I do indeed doubt that,' said Wayland, with more than a note of warning,

Stanford folded his letters away, smiled, and doffed his hat to the lady. 'And ma'am, if I may, I am George Stanford, Principal Private Secretary to His Majesty's Naval Attaché, the Sublime Porte, at your service.'

The lady curtsied, and Percy stepped back a pace and cleared his throat. 'I do beg your pardon... *Madame* Celeste Dupuy de Crozes. My nephew was former liaison to the French Mission... but, since his death...' He hesitated; an uncomfortable note of warmth rose in his voice. 'She is now under my protection, as my niece, and an acquaintance of Lord Elgin.'

Wayland thought she could have been no more than twenty-five, a beauty in her pale cotton dress and linen jacket, a trailing cream scarf, bright against her dark hair, pulled back but coiffed to frame a gentle expression and delicate complexion – yet one that had certainly seen travel, and more of Constantinople than the tuppenny tour. She was, he thought, exquisite.

Two years before, Wayland might have blushed crimson and stammered, but with service in the desert, something inside, he knew not what, had broken. Perhaps, he thought, he had been around Hazzard for too long after all. He bowed. '*Enchanté, madame.*'

Her expression lit up with delight. '*Ah, vous parlez français, m'sieur le capitaine?*'

'*Mais bien sûr, madame. C'est la langue diplomatique du monde civilisé.*'

Stanford murmured behind his hand to Percy, 'The captain said it is the diplomatic language of the civilised world, sir.'

'I know what he said, dammit, boy!'

Stanford nodded blandly. 'But of course you did, sir.'

Wayland continued in English, 'May I offer my condolences for the loss of your husband, *Madame* Dupuy.'

Celeste curtsied again, nodding. '*Je vous remercie bien*... It is some years now, my Lucien.' She looked away for a moment. 'Lost to the Revolution, in Paris.'

'Very well, Mr Wayl – er, *Captain*, let us proceed...' Percy harrumphed, turning away to a leather case resting on the stone seat behind.

Stanford stepped forward and drew Celeste artfully away from the conversation to come. '*Madame*, I wonder if I might ask how you have been finding the *souk* here in Constantinople? I fear I have had little success, *aucune succés*, finding something for my dear aunt...'

Percy watched them go, then held out a sheaf of documents, his voice low and grating. 'There are rumours circulating that your damn-fool Commodore Sir Sidney Smith is effectively fraternising with the enemy, sir, negotiating some sort of private peace, holding talks with Kléber and Desaix and such like.'

Wayland kept his face still. 'I find that difficult to believe, Colonel.'

Percy glanced over his shoulder, as if for fear of being overheard, and fairly spat back in reply, 'It's true, damnation, and here's your proof.'

Wayland hung his stick from his left forearm and took the stiff blue folder with his right, resting it on the prosthetic wooden hand in its black glove, an action he had clearly done many times. Percy looked away, as if squeamish or out of some personal distaste.

Although reluctant to accept it, Wayland indeed thought it more than possible that the story was true – especially since the Alien Office was behind Smith. Their brief was simple: to expel the French from Egypt. No one, including the royal court, had specified how. Still, he deflected smoothly. 'As the duly designated ranking officer in lieu of Sir Thomas Troubridge, Sir Sidney is empowered to respond to all such overtures, Colonel, especially peace, if so entreated by an embattled enemy.'

Percy scoffed at this. 'Not to his own bloody benefit and at the expense of proper procedure, he's not.'

'Colonel, it is international naval custom that if your enemy strikes his colours to half-mast, it signifies he needs your assistance – and we give it without hesitation, even in battle, in the interests of ending hostilities and saving lives.'

'Nonsense, man! This isn't the Navy in some piffling storm at sea. He's playing cock o'the dungheap in exchange for a grand house on the Seine, or some such frippery – I'm no fool! And I tell you he is overstepping the mark and treating with the enemy without sanction. The War Office is up in arms, while Lord Keith tries to hold the Med against Bruix with one hand and control Nelson's whining interference in Naples with the other!'

Wayland looked up from the pages. '"Whining interference"?'

Percy seemed to have run out of hot air, and blinked. 'Well, his constant complaints, you know, surely, while he's up in the hills, diddling his mistress and cuckolding that old fool Hamilton. He's an embarrassment!'

Wayland looked at Percy. He had no fears of such men any longer. They were a bad gale that inevitably blew themselves out, and this one had no hold over him whatsoever.

'Come, sir, you know precisely what I mean,' blustered Percy. 'Nelson has blotted his copybook, plain and simple. Meddlesome, when he could have been patrolling the high seas.'

'Colonel, it is the view of this office that we enjoy our current state of naval supremacy thanks entirely to Lord Nelson,' said Wayland coolly, glancing at the top copy of the documents. 'And there are those, such as I, who would not be alive without his… *interference*.'

'Well, of course, I meant no—'

Wayland looked up from the papers. 'Most of these are in Turkish script.'

'Yes, I know,' Percy said, with an irritable wave of the hand. 'Translations are at the end. Despatches from Ottoman captains, pilots of vessels in and out of Alexandria and Damietta, witness to French prisoners being rowed ashore, generals going out to HMS *Tigre* for dinner and God knows what – wine and gala concerts, for all we know.' He stabbed a rigid finger at the page Wayland was reading. 'Evidence that this is not acceptable behaviour for a Royal Navy blockade.'

'And you would like me to stop it? From Constantinople?'

'Do what you have to do, sir. You're the… the 'cloak-and-sword' man, aren't you, or whatever it is. Send orders, get travel warrants stamped by His Imperial Mumbo-Jumbo in his palace here, I don't give a damn, but this must stop or there'll be hell to pay. If necessary, sir, you sail out to Johnny Gyppo-land and tell him yourself.' He turned away dismissively. 'I conclude my instructions to you, sir.'

Wayland closed the folder. 'Where in London did this rumour originate?'

Percy grew angry again. 'That is none of your damned affair, sir! Admiralty, perhaps, the Cabinet Office, who knows?'

The couple returned, Stanford leading Celeste by the arm. '...jolly interesting, madam, *je vous remercie bien aussi.*'

'Aha,' she trilled. '*Et moi aussi, enchantée.*'

Wayland bowed at her return. After a moment he asked, 'What think you, *madame*, of a peace accord for Britain and France?'

Percy gawped at him. 'Really, sir! That is indiscreet...'

She looked at him thoughtfully. 'Surely it is of the utmost importance, *m'sieur*. The utmost.'

'You seem very *au fait* with matters of state, *madame*,' said Wayland, ignoring Percy.

Celeste inclined her head, her eyes playful. 'I have the ear for certain matters, *m'sieur*, and not for others, such as of my uncle, which I find too trying to hear.'

Stanford bowed his head in salute. 'How very wise, madam.'

She smiled, as if mildly flustered by Wayland's attention, and asked, 'Will you be attending the embassy ball, *m'sieur*?'

'Ball?' Wayland looked to Stanford. 'Which ball is this?'

'Oh yes, sir. Eight o'clock, Timoni House. It was in your boxes last week, and I sent an RSVP that, yes, the office would attend.'

Celeste held Wayland's eyes for a moment longer than perhaps she should have. 'It would be wonderful if you could come,' she said.

Silently Wayland agreed that, yes, it would indeed be wonderful. 'Alas,' he said, indicating his walking-stick and the files, 'I am no dancer tonight, nor ever. I will be on duty.'

'Oh, with regards to that, sir,' said Stanford apologetically to Percy, 'I have a note from HE's office for you...' He delved into his inside pocket for the note from the ambassador's secretary. 'Apparently a Sir Wilfrid Blakeney will be arriving at the northern dock this evening. An acquaintance of yours, I understand, sir? He seems to expect to be greeted by you personally, Colonel.' He handed the note to Percy.

Percy glanced at it, cursing under his breath. 'Damn fellow. Been threatening to come for months...' He looked at Celeste. 'So, I shan't be able to attend this evening either, my dear.' He looked at Wayland.

Celeste positively beamed. 'Ah, perhaps the brave *m'sieur le capitaine* will be my chaperon instead.'

'I could square that with the duty officer, sir,' said Stanford, giving Wayland his most direct bland stare, which tended to signify its importance.

Wayland acquiesced, and bowed to Celeste. 'Then it would be remiss of me not to do so. I shall call upon you at half past seven, *madame*. Shan't I, Stanford?'

Stanford gave a single affirmative nod. 'Oh, absolutely, sir.'

–

Timoni House, to the chagrin of a string of British plenipotentiary ambassadors before, was rented from the wealthy Italian Timoni family, who had been quite happy letting it for a vast sum to the British government for decades. It was rumoured they had hardly ever been in it. All knew that one of the first things Lord Elgin had wanted to achieve in his new posting was an official embassy for Britain, without a landlord – and after the victory at the Nile, the sultan's court heaped blessings and fortune upon the English beyond their expectations; negotiations were soon underway, and plans were being drawn up.

In the meantime, the stately neoclassical house had served well, and was ideal for the annual Yuletide ball. Wayland and Celeste Dupuy rattled up the drive in their open coach and four, enjoying a balmy evening, the light glinting from the silver-threaded livery and jewelled feathered turbans of the Turkish driver and footman up front. The trees had been hung with lanterns, and music tinkled across the fine lawns and gardens before them.

After they had left Colonel Percy and Celeste at the Arch, Wayland and Stanford had marched off to Alemdar Cardesi, a good distance off, giving Wayland time to think. 'What in hell was that, Stanford? He virtually accused Sir Sidney of Conduct Unbecoming, for God's sake...'

'Whispers on the grapevine, sir. Were you surprised, sir?'

'Surprised? Utterly flabbergasted that they'd even found out about the talks, let alone that Sir Sidney was discussing terms.'

'It must be the Admiralty on the mutter, sir, rather than the War House. Sir Sidney has more enemies among his naval colleagues than he does in the army. But we can have you on the *Mebda-i Nusret* frigate tomorrow morning for Cyprus, and hope either for a British man o'war to be moored and waiting, or another Ottoman to take you straight to the *Tigre*.'

·'That serious?'

'After that little chit-chat with *madame*, yes, sir.'

Wayland understood. 'Hence attending the ball.'

Stanford shook his head. 'Apologies for dropping you in things like that, sir, but Celeste Dupuy she is not – and neither is she the colonel's niece, though this might be the story she has spun him.'

'What makes you think all that?' They sidestepped a man hauling a barrow, the old wooden wheels bumping along the uneven cobbles.

Stanford kept his voice low and fast. 'Because the real Celeste Dupuy de Crozes died of old age without heirs some years ago, according to one of Mr Wickham's French informants, who rolled up his sleeves and checked. Celeste Dupuy is a cover legend she has adopted.'

Wayland was by now accustomed to such revelations. 'Very well. What else?'

'I cannot say for certain, and it would be quite an opportunity if I were right, but her real name could be Madeleine du Pont-Clair, daughter of the *Comte* d'Ivry, who was jailed in '92 and later executed. She went to Corsica, where she became the governess-companion of one Paula Maria Bonaparte.'

Wayland stopped for a moment. 'Pauline *Bonaparte*?'

'Yes, sir, the general's favourite younger sister, apparently. When the family fled Corsica for the mainland, Madeleine du Pont-Clair went instead to Spain with an introduction to the royal court at Escorial, where it was suspected she played a role in secret meetings that led to the Franco-Spanish treaty of '96, effectively pushing us out of the Med.' He gave a quick smile. 'If I am correct, sir.'

Wayland stumped onwards. 'And she's here? With that idiot Percy?'

'Indeed, sir. The name rang a bell and she roughly fitted a physical description I had once read, so I took it upon myself to direct her attentions elsewhere as you spoke, and make my own gentle enquiries of her.'

'Well done.'

'She has been here a fortnight, and let slip a few titbits. She already seems to have knowledge of the Turkish fleet and our ships of the line in the harbour. It was rumoured she has a connection to the *Bureau de renseignements et information*, who have deployed her in missions throughout Italy and Switzerland, and even in Vienna, masquerading as an émigrée. But the Alien Office knows very little for certain.'

Wayland shuddered at the mention of the Bureau, for it led him to Derrien, and the man Masson on the heights overlooking Aboukir Bay that night: the man who had shot him. 'What sort of connection?'

'I believe she is the sister or cousin of one of the Bureau staff.'

'Then she could be useful.'

'Yes, sir. With luck, you can avoid the dance-floor altogether, sir, and keep it to the Small Library.'

Wayland understood his suggestion. The Small Library was used for various underhand purposes. 'All right. Have we Watchers in place?'

'Yes, sir. I sent a note with Fasial at the Arch for Crushers in the grounds, sir, to lend a hand to the regular Guards troop if necessary.' Stanford checked his watch again. 'I have one of the pool carriages booked to meet us in Fatih at seven, sir. That should allow time enough to swing past the colonel's billet in Pera to collect the lady by half past.'

'Us?'

'I'll hop out before the turn-off and trot along to Timoni to monitor the arrangements and meet you there, sir,' Stanford said. 'I suggest uniform for you, sir, in case we have to frighten the natives.'

He meant the embassy staff, and Wayland agreed, thinking of Percy. 'Quite so. Red coat and brass buttons it is.'

—

Later, in the welcoming grounds of Timoni House, their carriage slowed to a halt, the hoofbeats echoing against the low brick walls as they drew in behind a number of others, their passengers alighting up ahead. 'They say anyone and everyone will be here,' offered Celeste.

'That very nearly did not include me,' admitted Wayland. 'And I am fairly certain I am not anyone at all.'

She laughed and held his arm. He looked into her eyes and could see within them no guile, no secrets, only an intensity, a longing of some kind, a longing he wished he could fulfil. 'Perhaps,' she said wistfully, 'it is a joy merely to be part of something.' She looked across the lawns, distracted, as if she had given something away.

'Yes,' he agreed, ever the outsider looking in. 'Perhaps it is.'

She turned back to him, a quick smile, and put a silk-gloved hand on his left arm. She felt the joint of the severed wrist under its leather cowl and the prosthetic wooden hand in its glove. 'You have given enough to them already.' She looked down, as if lost in her thoughts. 'They take too much,' she said, and squeezed his arm.

Hazzard had once told him of Naples, of meeting Lady Hamilton, of her kindness, and something else – a warmth, he had said, a care – and had often fallen silent, saying no more. Wayland had now at last understood, in this bluff harshness all about them – of cannon, wood, iron, powder and steel – that to receive such kindness, this tender warmth, if only for the merest fraction of a moment, was enough to remind him of all that was good in the world, all that was pure. And he felt it now: Celeste's body against his, the pair clutching secretively at each other, clinging to some unknown rock on a storm-tossed shore.

The carriage slowed and stopped and a footman opened the door. Wayland stepped out, leaving the stick behind, to help Celeste down the step. She lifted the hem of a grey silk evening gown, revealing a matching slipper and delicate ankle as she searched for the step down. '*Oh la…!*' She laughed, stumbling, and he caught her. 'What a lucky landing,' she whispered.

'Careful,' he said, his smile inches from hers, 'lest I lose the other leg.'

He had come in his short-waisted 9 Company scarlet coat, dark blue breeches and turned-down Turkish boots, the tassels of his plain *shemagh* sash at his waist dangling over a curved *kilij* in a gold-mounted black leather scabbard swaying at his hip. Wayland ignored the stares at his bold Marine scarlet, like Hazzard's, scarred and stitched – though perhaps with more pride, each tear a memory of serving with him, and those feats he had done upon St Crispin's Day.

The eyes sized them up as he and Celeste ascended the steps, the light playing across the diadem of her tiara and the various orders pinned to Wayland's breast – round his collar and cravat a broad red-and-white-striped ribbon, suspending a jewelled crescent moon of gilded red enamel with gold sword; it had been presented by the Grand Vizier in the company of Sir Sidney Smith, an honour Wayland had fought off for weeks, demanding it be given to Hazzard or 9 Company as a unit. He had accepted it only after Smith revealed that Nelson himself had recommended it in his letter of promotion: *For Valour and Actions Unseen in Defence of His Majesty's Fleet at the Battle of the Nile.* Since he was in Constantinople, Smith insisted, he was obliged by diplomacy to wear it. But Wayland did so more as a reminder of Hazzard and sad memory of their losses, of Sarah, of Jeanne, in a victory which all still toasted – all but the men of 9 Company, who mourned. And Wayland was firmly one of them.

The front step was occupied by over a dozen guests in their varied habits and costume: gowns, turbans, and elegant Persian trews. To one side of the doorway, he spotted Stanford, who had managed to arrive before them. He nodded to Wayland and melted into the crowd in the foyer.

The house opened before them to reveal a broad foyer with a grand staircase curving up to a gallery, ornate plaster ceilings hung with chandeliers, a string quintet in the corner, strains of Vivaldi and Corelli filling the air. Wayland looked left and saw Stanford again, weaving his way through the crowd to the opulent ballroom, where the rest of the orchestra were warming up. He took Celeste through to make their introductions in the line.

Lieutenant-Colonel Thomas Bruce, the Earl of Elgin and Kincardine, His Majesty's Plenipotentiary Ambassador to the Sublime Porte, smiled patiently as the guests processed past him, bowing to the ladies, an easy smile bestowed to all comers. He was pale – perhaps unwell, thought Wayland – elegant, long-necked in an exuberant white cravat, his greying hair fluffed in the Pitt fashion, his grey-blue silken coat bright with orders and insignia.

'Oh, *mon dieu*, he is handsome, *n'est-ce pas?*' confided Celeste.

'If you say so,' allowed Wayland.

An elderly lady in front overheard and whispered over her shoulder in a thick Bohemian accent, 'They say, my dear, it is the Scot in him!'

'Only the luckiest English can claim Scots blood, ma'am,' confirmed Wayland.

They laughed and soon were shaking hands with the entourage, Lady Elgin the hostess ushering friends to particular places, and Elgin himself grateful for a familiar face from his own staff. 'Mr Wayland, my dear fellow... Showing the colours and looking grand tonight. Bravo,' he said, with the mildest Scots burr, then, with a glance at Celeste, '...But undoubtedly outshone by this enchanting creature...?'

'*Madame* Celeste Dupuy de Crozes,' Wayland said, stepping aside. 'Émigrée, my lord, with whom I believe you are briefly acquainted.'

'Yes, of course, from the mission. *Enchanté, madame,*' replied Elgin, kissing her hand, looking to an assistant beside him. 'Do you see,

Neville? I told you, the French lady is always the gem of the affair. Though not a word to the locals, mind.'

Somewhat older, his hair greying to white round his long whiskers, Sir Neville Chandler, in dark Guards uniform, bowed with a kindly smile. '*Bonsoir, madame*. A wager happily lost.'

Elgin leaned in to Wayland and murmured, 'We shan't be having any of your comicals tonight, shall we, Mr Wayland?'

'None to concern, no, sir.' It was Elgin's personal reference to espionage – the work of funny-men, as he called them.

But Sir Neville peered at Wayland and rumbled quietly, 'I believe the Small Library is worth a look this evening.'

Wayland bowed. 'What a good idea, Sir Neville. I'll make it part of the tour.'

But Sir Neville's voice bore a note of warning. 'There might be certain difficulties, Captain. Of a *Parsifalous* nature.'

Wayland met his eye, and bowed. 'I am obliged to you, sir.'

'Captain.'

Celeste whispered to him, 'What did he say?' She giggled. 'He is so *old* and magnificent…!'

Thrilling at the décor, the gowns, the exotic headdresses and fluttering fans, she followed Wayland through the ballroom, the orchestra wailing in its dissonant tuning, servants with trays delivering chilled Athiri, Chablis and Fiano, and fizzing herbal and lime concoctions.

Wayland introduced her to all, and she replied to the introductions in French, in English, in Italian. Wayland laughed, proud of her skills and social ease – until he saw the cause of Sir Neville's 'Parsifalous' warning: the sight of a distant red coat, and bright buttons of Colonel Hereward Percy. He was on the far side of the group under the grand arch, with several other senior officers.

At the same moment, Percy looked up and their eyes met, Percy's face a mixture of frustration, confusion and anger, his bull neck suffusing a deep red. Without taking his eyes off Wayland, he made a curt apology to his colleagues and stormed off, banging his glass down on a passing tray.

Wayland watched him, his heart hammering in his chest – *Where in hell's he going?* – fearing that Percy was now a loose cannon and could foul the entire evening. *Where are you, Stanford, for God's sake?* He could not take the risk of hunting down Stanford in public, and could hardly do it surreptitiously as they made their way through the crowd. He would simply have to hope Stanford was prepared for the bloody man. The thing now, he thought, was speed.

He bowed to the ladies about them and Celeste linked her arm in his. When at last they had made their way through the packed ballroom, the orchestra had begun playing a clutch of light dance and *divertimenti*. Beyond the dancers and onlookers was a set of richly decorated panelled doors, flanked by a pair of liveried staff beside two tall black and gilt torchère plinths, topped with lolling palm fronds. One of them bowed, opened the knurled latch and ushered Wayland and Celeste inside, closing the door after them.

'But what is this…?' she asked, fascinated, looking about in the comparative silence after the ballroom.

'Welcome,' said Wayland, 'to the Small Library. Sir Neville thought you might be intrigued.'

It was indeed a library, though by no means small, lined with bookshelves and furnished with elegant sofas and wicker-backed chairs, the centre occupied by a gleaming octagonal walnut table with a voluminous flower setting, all beneath a lofty painted Italianate ceiling hung with a fine crystal chandelier, bright with candles.

Across the room from the door were two French windows leading to the dark side-terrace. To the right were two further gilt-panelled mahogany doors leading into the interior salons and administrative offices. Wayland looked about curiously. 'I believe there are some fine rare books here…'

One of the doors to their right opened and Stanford entered, in bluejacket and white breeches, gold epaulettes, buckled shoes and smallsword, the uniform of a naval lieutenant. Celeste was delighted. 'Oh, *M'sieur* Stanford. You, too, are officer in the Navy?'

'*Bonsoir, madame.*' He half-laughed, 'Oh, absolutely, hurrah, heave-ho and so forth…' Apparently in a hurry, he reached into his inside pocket, somewhat flustered. 'I beg your pardon sir, at this late hour, but various despatches have come in, some very important.' He spilled some of them onto the octagonal table and fingered through them absently. 'Ah, yes, this, this, and er… this, for the attaché upstairs.' He stopped, held one up in particular and wagged it. 'Ah, but this one in particular he wished you to affix the AO seal, if you would be so kind, sir? It's just back here in the office, I believe…'

He bustled off back to the open door, leaving the other despatches on the table, obliging Wayland to follow. Wayland glanced at Celeste.

'Would you excuse me, my dear? I shall be just next door for only a moment, I'm sure.'

'I shall look at the books,' she replied happily.

The pair headed off, Stanford fussing over the despatch in question, holding the door open, evidently leading to a passage. 'This, sir, I do apologise, should not have got past the duty clerk or Codes and Ciphers.'

The passage stretched to the far end of the building, lined with muffling hessian and red felt fabric; halfway along was a set of carpeted steps up to a loft space. There was dim light at the far end, but no office. Stanford fell abruptly silent and shut the door behind them, leaving them in the dark.

They turned to two decorative foliate scroll mouldings on the door panels, and swung them upwards, revealing two spyholes. Stanford pulled two stools round for them.

'Heave-ho?' murmured Wayland as he sat. 'You forgot to say, "Ahoy, me shiverin' mateys". And your epaulettes are on back to front.'

'Can't be perfect when needs must, sir.' Stanford put his eye to one of the holes.

'Watchers?' asked Wayland, peering in.

'Two above, sir...' confirmed Stanford in a whisper.

Bordered by the shadowed ring of the peephole, to Wayland the image seemed akin to a magic lantern show: Celeste moved first to the far bookshelves, took down a book, then grew larger, wandering towards the door they had just passed through. She leafed through the volume in her hand. Wayland looked at her as she unwittingly approached: her gown, her necklace, the luminescent glow of her soft bosom. She then returned to the central table, but kept her back to them, obscuring much of their view.

'Dammit,' said Wayland. 'How many did you leave? Five?'

Stanford did not take his eye away, the light from the spyhole falling across his cheekbone. 'Seven, sir. She should feel safe enough.'

Wayland watched again. The theatrical scene they had played was key: designed to instil a sense of disorder, opportunity, and then pressure, it left her no doubt there was but one chance to seize the moment. In the past, they might have left five or nine despatches, the odd number to convey further disorder, yet the reassurance that missing items would likely not be noticed.

There were two sets of shuffling footsteps from the darkness behind, and Wayland detected the dull flicker of a candle. Stanford said, 'Here he comes, sir.'

Candlestick in hand, a liveried attendant lit the way down the passage for a perplexed Colonel Percy. He stopped when he saw Wayland. 'What the *devil* is going on?' he whispered. He marched towards them, the attendant departing. 'Sir Wilfrid, as you very well know, sir,' he complained, 'will not be leaving Palermo for *another month*. How in—'

Wayland gestured to him, the spyhole a bright dot of light in the gloom. '*Come.*'

Sensing something beyond his own outrage, Percy joined them, baffled. 'What on earth are you—?'

Stanford had not moved. 'I think this is it, sir.'

Percy looked from Stanford to Wayland. 'I... I do not underst—'

Wayland moved aside from his spyhole, his voice cold. 'Observe, Colonel.'

Percy sat on the stool and put his eye to the hole. Almost at once he leaned back, turning to Wayland, shocked. 'But... But that's... That's my—'

'Niece?' suggested Wayland.

Percy flushed, but said nothing. In the library, Celeste moved away from the table, arranging the abandoned despatches curiously. Percy looked back again, unable to tear himself away. 'But why are you...? I...' He then sat back and fell quiet. The full realisation seemed to descend upon him. He lowered his head. 'Damnation...'

'I believe she has acted, sir,' said Stanford.

Percy grimaced as if in pain, his face contorted with anger for his folly. '*Dammit, dammit.*' After a moment he looked at Wayland again, appealing to him. 'Sh-she said... that she...' he swallowed, evidently mortified, 'that she was fond of me.'

Wayland watched him and felt a modicum of sympathy: Percy had been passing her off as his widowed niece for so long, he had actually come to believe it, when in reality she was nothing more than his mistress. She would certainly have convinced Percy of her love and devotion for him – as much as Wayland had so far convinced her of his. Wayland moved to a third peephole above and looked in.

There were two knocks from the floorboards above – the signal from the Watchers in the loft with a bird's-eye view of the room below. Wayland took the decision and nodded to Stanford. 'Very well.'

'I agree, sir.' Stanford reached for an embroidered bell-pull beside the door and jerked it once.

'What are you doing now? What do we...?' asked Percy, glancing at the pair, then back to the spyhole. '*For God's sake...*'

'It is in hand, Colonel,' murmured Wayland, watching Celeste.

A few moments later, the door to the ballroom opened and a gentleman and lady were shown in, the lady greeting Celeste effusively, the gentleman bowing as the door closed behind them. Then it all happened very quickly: the French windows to the terrace beyond opened and two men appeared, dressed as groundsmen in labourers' coats and dark slouch hats, one with an empty jute sack over his shoulder. This distracted Celeste enough for the gentleman to take her arms from behind, and she fell back against him, dropping her silk purse to the floor, just as the lady clamped Celeste's mouth shut and waved a phial under her nose. Celeste shook her head violently back and forth to get away from the odour, but the ether salts worked quickly and she coughed, struggled for a moment, then sagged unconscious in the gentleman's arms. The larger of the gardeners pulled the jute sack over Celeste's head right down to her ankles, took her briskly from the gentleman, and slung her over his shoulder.

'*Good God...*' mumbled Percy as he stared.

The gardener carried the sack out to the terrace with his companion, who shut the French windows quietly behind them. The gentleman scooped up the purse and left it on the table, opened the door to the ballroom for the lady, bowed to her, and the pair went out. It had taken no more than thirty seconds.

Stanford straightened, reaching for the latch just above Percy's brow. 'If you'll pardon me, sir...'

He opened the door, the dark passage flooding with light, and they re-entered the Small Library. Percy strode to the terrace doors to look out, as Wayland headed straight for the octagonal table. In the cleverly rearranged pile there were now only five despatch letters. Celeste had assessed their value and taken two, to maintain the odd number. He could not help but admire her skill. 'She is a quick study.'

'I cannot believe it,' insisted Percy. 'She's just a *girl*, for God's sake—'

'But a somewhat dangerous one, sir,' said Stanford to Wayland as he opened the purse. He took out an unusual bright silver 80-bore pistol. 'A Kalthoff repeater,' he said with admiration. 'Hefty monster,

.38 calibre. Hollow stock for powder and ball, eight shots. A Swiss improvement, no less.'

Wayland considered all of those unspoken mutual feelings he had detected between them in the carriage – their magnetism, and how very alike they might have been, the two of them – but pushed them aside. He told himself that, had it come to it, Madeleine du Pont-Clair might well have trained that pistol on him, if only to survive. Despite this, he felt little but disappointment – not in her, but in himself.

Percy was speechless. Wayland delivered the *coûp de grace*. 'Colonel, we do not believe you were complicit. However, the interrogators will doubtless want a word.' The door to the ballroom opened and the music of the orchestra filled the room; one of the liveried men on guard waited discreetly. Percy was being dismissed. 'But,' added Wayland, relenting, some vestige of his old self still intact, 'Horse Guards and the War Office will learn only of your cooperation.' He looked away, as if embarrassed himself. 'At least, that is all they will hear from me on the matter. You have my word.'

Colonel Percy looked back at him, taking in his words. He stood quite still, booted heels together, his chin up, a proud man – but one who doubtless felt a fool. After a moment, he nodded, straightened his red coat, belt and sword hanger, finding difficulty with the admission, but evidently gracious in defeat. 'I am obliged, Captain Wayland,' he said formally, adding with apparent sincerity, 'You are... a gentleman.'

Wayland bowed. 'As are you, sir.'

Percy turned and stepped out into the ballroom. The guard closed the door behind him, the strains of a polonaise now muffled to their ear. Despite the Percy affair, Stanford seemed more than usually buoyant. 'The best plant-and-peep operation I have yet seen, sir.'

'Yes, Stanford, well done,' said Wayland, watching the closed door, knowing full well what Percy had truly become: that most dangerous of creatures – the vulnerable man. 'Though it has led to unpleasant repercussions.'

'At least the loose cannon has been secured, sir.'

Wayland looked at the scattered despatches on the octagonal table, unseeing, uncertain what regrets played at the edges of his mind. 'Authority has been granted for passage?'

'Yes, sir. The *Mebda-i Nusret* frigate,' confirmed Stanford. 'A fine cabin booked for the dawn tide for Cyprus, the captain paid in silver and awaiting our special cargo.' He concluded cheerfully, checking his watch, 'Which should still be sleeping peacefully, sir.'

Kingdom

A small single-masted Maltese tartane scooted out of Valletta's Grand Harbour, running with the wind, its twisting path marked by a frothing wake on the bright blue of the choppy water. It cut southwards across the nose of the vast Fort St Elmo and out of the harbour mouth, evading two French patrol boats, their bells clanging behind; dark figures of locals on the shoreline danced and waved, cheering the tartane onwards in its escape, as the captain tried to outwit the fortress guns behind him and reach the British blockade ships several hundred yards further out.

Fort St Elmo remained silent, a mute giant looming over the imprisoned ships at her quays, one of them just visible, the towering 100-gun *Guillaume Tell*. But a square-topped coastal fort on the southern corner of the harbour entrance opened fire, a trio of 12-pounder cannons barking angrily, their plumes of grey smoke snatched away by the wind. Geysers of water erupted all round the little trading ship as she heeled to port, then back to starboard, trying to haul her flapping lateen mainsail round to catch the winter northwesterly – just as a round-shot crashed through her stern quarter, the bows lifting as she tried to right her course.

A signal gun banged from a 16-gun blockade despatch-runner which sped in to the rescue, jibs billowing, her sleek lines cutting an arc across the waves, commands to the tartane echoing through a megaphone – *Come to larboard, this way, this way!* – her starboard guns and bow chasers loosing a rapid series of disruptive shots at the fort, peppering the stonework, bursting on the rocky shore at its base, the spray flying.

But it was not enough, and the fort fired once more on the Maltese trader, splintering her starboard midships rail. Some of the crew dived overboard, trying to swim to the safety of the closing British ship. It was too much for Lieutenant William Harrington, acting Captain of HMS *Alexander*, watching the affair off the north corner of the harbour mouth. Incensed, he strode to the quarterdeck rail and shouted down to the tweendecks, 'Mr Farleigh! Are there any Maltese militia left in those harbour forts?'

'*No sir, all manned by French,*' his First Lieutenant called back. '*Maltese pulled inland or expelled, sir!*'

'Then take us in and reduce that damned thing to rubble! I'm fed up with its nuisance!'

'*Aye, sir!*' and the order echoed down the decks: '*Forward firing positions starboard bow! Heads'ls and courses, Mr Covey! Fire as she comes to bear!*'

The heavy 74-gun *Alexander* swung her yards and the dazzling canvas bloomed aloft, the foaming spray flying from her bows as she turned inshore and ran out a battery of her starboard guns. The French patrol boats in the inlet turned as if to give fire, then thought wiser and dashed for the quays. Farleigh continued with his firing commands: '*Target off starboard bow, ranging shot if you please, Mr Ransen!*'

A single 18-pounder at the starboard bow boomed and a smoking iron ball streaked in a low trajectory over a hundred yards, crashing into the corner of the squat stone tower, Ransen's voice echoing from below, '*Fire as she comes to bear, 24s upper and lower.*' Two 24-pounders roared in succession, followed by another two, an unexpected thunder from a cloudless sky.

Each round found its mark and the fort flew to pieces, the medieval crenellations bursting into powder and rubble, tumbling onto the rocks and smashing into the breaking surf below. One of the gun embrasures cracked open, the walls collapsing, wooden beams tilting, splayed like broken limbs, two of the offending 12-pounder guns lurching through the resulting cavity and plunging to the sea below, carriages and all, men falling after them. A cheer went up from below decks and Harrington watched with satisfaction. 'Thank you, Mr Farleigh, compliments to Mr Ransen and a quarter tot for the gun-crews.'

The rescue sloop intercepted the crippled tartane, picking up the swimmers, escorting her to the line. There was a chorus from below decks – *Three cheers for Lord Willy* – and Harrington grinned, knowing his nickname all too well. He shrugged into his collar, the air cool. With two years' service on the *Alexander* in the Mediterranean, he knew his ship and the frustration of blockade duty; that little bit of action would help blow off some steam from the stoked foundry simmering below decks.

Farleigh hurried up the steps and joined him on the quarterdeck. 'Maltese picked up, sir, only five rounds spent, gunner and mate rather pleased with themselves.'

'As they should be.' But Harrington was still angry. 'Damned cheek – French blazing away at every poor little devil trying to make a break for it. Put me down for the powder.'

'And the tot, sir?'

Harrington glanced at him. 'Surely the QM can pay for something,' he grumbled. He looked out at the signals fluttering up the masthead of the *Northumberland*, another 74 in the offshore squadron further out, offering assistance – but a moment later she raised a postscript: BRAVO ONE FORT SUNK.

Farleigh chuckled, but sobered quickly. 'Any word from the captain, sir?'

Harrington stared out to sea. 'Food supplies still the problem, Neapolitan delegates running him ragged, he says.' Captain Ball had been dragooned into service as president of the Maltese Congress, trying to distribute food to the population, now expelled by the French from Valletta. 'He won't rest until he knows Naples is stable and reinforcements are coming to replace the Portuguese marines.'

'And from Palermo...?' He meant word of Nelson. The officers always did, when they asked.

Harrington shook his head. 'None yet.' It was a sore point with them all.

Just as Farleigh was about to reply, he spotted movement far out to sea. A moment later the cry came down: *Ship of sail to starboard beam*.

They raised their eyeglasses. In the circle of the eyepiece, Harrington saw the silhouette of an unknown frigate on the starboard tack. She was listing heavily, an array of colours flapping aloft: the Ottoman crescent moon, the coat of arms of the *Armada Reál* of Spain, and the giant British red ensign flying astern. They watched as the frigate shortened sail and slowed, bracing about and coming down to meet them. She drew nearer, her bows lifting in the swell, her copper plates bright, the bowsprit and tops showing signs of repair, her hull pocked with scorched, splintered impacts, gun-port lids missing, her boats gone. It was clear she had seen heavy action.

'Who is she?' wondered Farleigh, squinting through his scope into the bright sky. 'Neapolitan man of war...? Correction,' he added. 'Our marines at the bow, sir – red coats—'

'Red coats?' said Harrington. He focussed on a dark figure at the fo'c'sle rail; he stood unmoving, in faded scarlet, one sleeve gone, the exposed arm wrapped in bandage in a sling. Beside him was a taller, older man in ragged Marine scarlet jerkin and a loose robe, a sword-bayonet at his hip.

'Good God,' said Harrington. 'It's them. Douse sail and bring her alongside, Charles. Send for young Dawlish to pilot them to the Admiral...' After a moment, Harrington lowered his eyeglass thoughtfully. 'And ready the surgeon to receive wounded. Just in case.'

–

There had been more than blood in the water after De la Vega had pulled Hazzard and the others aboard. Some of the crew had been jubilant, reliving the view of Hazzard clinging to the hull of the French ship, the bomb parcel in hand, the explosion: *Ba-bouam, si!*

But others had not, rejoicing only that they had escaped, now filled with sorrow that some of their compatriots had not. Hazzard had knelt beside the lifeless form of Shepherd, and three other topmen who had come down during the battle, men he hardly knew, Esteban, Maraceno and Achino, stricken that he had not acted sooner. Elena slept at the bedside of her sister Maria-Luisa, her broken leg in splints, her fractured ribs strapped tight, stroking her long black hair, as she called endlessly for Handley.

They had laid them out one by one: the gunners from below decks, the wives and sweethearts who had once danced – among them Halawa, who had loaded and rammed with Warnock and their menfolk, and paid the same price, their bodies equally twisted and maimed, their remains dignified now only by white shrouds.

De la Vega stood like stone at the quarterdeck, looking out, his soot-blackened face streaked with tears he bore in silence. Part of Hazzard was angry with him, for not listening, for his desire for vengeance – but he knew the Frenchman would have caught even Nelson off guard. The only answer had been to face *Généreux* – and few could have done better than Cesár Domingo de la Vega. In all, they had lost twelve dead and thirty injured, ten severely – a tally the

Gentleman's Magazine in London would have dubbed 'negligible' – having sunk a 32-gun Venetian pirate and seen off a French 74.

But Hazzard felt otherwise, as did the marines. In their desert operations they took great care in their calculated risk. They had forgotten the arbitrary nature of battle at sea, and Hazzard was reminded of its agonies beyond any one man's control, the wind and the sea reigning supreme.

As the last of the mists had cleared, the stars looked down from the heavens, and 9 Company stood still and surveyed the dead, each downcast in his own thoughts, their faces drawn and as blackened as the charred wood and molten iron around them. Porter had struggled with the *Volpone's* surgeon, Ramirez, and felt his inevitable failure to save more; his head hung the lowest. They had buried the dead at sea, De la Vega presiding. Amid the lamentations, Cochrane led prayers to an Almighty who seemed at last to be looking down upon them in peace, and navigated them through winter squalls blowing south from Taranto and Sicily, fighting the hot southerly winds from Libya and Tunisia.

After making what repairs they could at sea, De la Vega laid down a course for Syracuse, tacking against the west and northwesterly winds, putting further strain on the foretopmast crosstree. Handley had stayed aloft for three watches straight, ensuring the braces held, then staring from the mainmast tops to the foremast, reliving Maria-Luisa's fall, his impotence. De la Vega joined him, the pair staying in the tops, De la Vega's voice a soft murmur, until eventually Handley knew it was time, and descended. On Christmas Eve, they lit the candles for *Nochebuena*, and Cochrane's Yuletide prayers for peace on Earth bit more deeply than usual: *Volpone* still suffered her losses and damage, listing to starboard, her pumps working hard.

In Syracuse they stopped for revictualling and makeshift repairs, news of the battle having already reached the port. As the casks and crates were swung inboard from a lighterman's barge, a hard-faced young midshipman, in dark boat-cloak, confirmed that Lord Nelson commanded the blockade of Malta, but that Lord Keith was his new Commander in Chief.

Hazzard read the message from the Castello Maniace, handed over by the boy, all of sixteen years of age. 'Good God...' he mumbled to Cook. 'Keith promoted above him, Smith given the Levant... Nelson must have had a fit.'

'I can feel it in me waters,' agreed Cook, looking at the cloudy grey sky. More winter rain was coming.

'If I may, sir,' said the midshipman, 'Lord Nelson scarce leaves Palermo nowadays. We see little of him.' The boy continued, and Hazzard felt the hope drain out of him: Nelson's help tracking *Généreux* was crucial. 'But Lord Keith might still be off Malta at Marsa Sirocco.' Hazzard knew he meant the port in the southeast of the island, near Marsaxlokk. 'With fair winds, you might catch him before he sails for Menorca, sir.'

Hazzard nodded. It was useful intelligence. 'And no word of *Généreux*?'

'None, sir. Not since New Year's Day, even from the Portos who go out that way from time to time. It was they who told us what happened,' he said with some pride. 'Seems you gave her what for, sir.'

Hazzard did not agree. 'Not enough.' He looked at Jory. 'She could have gone straight through to Toulon for repairs.'

'Or be lyin' doggo in some Sardinian bolt-hole, for all we know.'

'Maybe.' They both knew how fallible the blockade patrols were. There was only so much the Navy could do.

The midshipman hesitated, but asked, 'Are you... really Mr Hazzard? And Sergeant Cook? From the Bombay Marine, and Egypt?'

Hazzard had forgotten the world knew them – forgotten that feeling of exposure, though he had learned to fight it down over time. 'Yes. This is Sergeant-Major Cook.'

The boy looked at them both: at their scars, the torn and stitched red coat, Cook's *binish* robe and jerkin, the tasselled sword-hanger of the gold and white scimitar at Hazzard's hip. 'An honour to meet you, sir. My uncle was a marine.'

Hazzard nodded. 'His name?'

'Oldfield, sir. He fell at Acre.'

Hazzard remembered him. He saw them all, like ghosts: Oldfield, Douglas and Smith, conspiring by the light of lanterns in the Ward Room of the *Tigre*, bending over a map of the terrain of Acre. Then he could only imagine Oldfield, in the trenches beneath the Damned Tower, clearing the field like Ajax at the walls of Troy, sword in hand, taking French grenadiers down before he was overcome by fire. He had been told of it by Douglas and Reiz. 'I knew him, briefly. The French were moved by his bravery. They buried him with honours.'

The boy stood straighter, with a defiant pride. Hazzard turned away, but the boy stopped him.

'They say you met Bonaparte, sir.' The midshipman looked him in the eye, intent, not eager or zealous, but needing to know. 'Near killed him, say others.'

Hazzard stared back, his mind reeling to be hurled so suddenly into those occasions once again: bursting in on the god-general in the interrogation of Tillery, Derrien screaming, *Get down*, his pistol out – and all the while, the wide cold eyes recognising him, the clear voice: *Mr Hazzard*.

He gave no reply, but handed the message back to the midshipman. 'Thank you for the information.'

The midshipman watched him walk across the quarterdeck and into the cabins beyond. 'Is it true, Sergeant-Major?'

Cook looked thoughtful. 'And more. But ye'd never believe it, lad.'

–

That evening, there was some debate in De la Vega's cabin. Weighed in the balance against Lord Keith, Hazzard would rather they went direct to Nelson, and had no desire to meet Lord Keith at all. 'Palermo,' insisted Hazzard. 'Of all the Navy, Nelson should hear about *Généreux* first-hand.'

They stood over a chart in the Great Cabin, De la Vega's grand bed hidden by folding bulwarks, broken furniture now cleared. Alfonso, Carlos and Ezau joined them with the marines at the long carven table.

'We 'ave to report to C-in-C,' warned Cook in his basso rumble. 'He's either off Malta or Menorca, sir. That's what Sir Sid said, and that middie at Syracuse said likewise.'

Hazzard did not want to see Lord Keith ever again. Their history was too fraught. He looked at the walls of De la Vega's cabin, the light pouring in from the ornamental gallery of stern windows, odd shadows from the shattered panes now blocked out with dark wooden panels, the renewed restraint lines on the 18-pounders along the sides, the timbers reinforced; he looked down at the long, heavily carved table, where he had first sat that night so long ago, punctured with splinters as a rescued prisoner, with a similar sense of failure.

Cook would not let it drop. 'And C-in-C has to be told about Sir Sid's despatch from Kléber.'

'And what would Lord Keith do with that?' demanded Hazzard. 'He'd tell Kléber to go to hell and be damned. We know him.' He thought back to the Cape in 1795. 'He sat in conference promising the world to Colonel Gordon and the Dutch at Cape Town, but knew full well the fleet gun-ports were opening to blow Simon's Town and Muizenberg to Kingdom Come. *Knew* it,' he reminded them all. 'And damn near took us along with half the mountainside.'

Cook looked to Pettifer, Handley and De Lisle. They had been there and knew he was right. 'Got to report, sir,' apologised Cook. 'Even if we're Sir Sid's spies an' all.'

'We no longer report to Admiralty. We report to Wickham at Aliens or the Home Secretary alone.'

De la Vega frowned. 'Please, what is *spoiz*?'

'He means *spies*,' said Hazzard. '*Espías*.'

'Ah, *sí sí*.' He stubbed out a cigarillo and reached for a glass of sherry.

Hazzard glanced at the marines. 'What says the boat? Underhill?'

Pettifer looked to Underhill, who took a breath. 'Be most fine to get to Palermo and kick orf the old boots, sir, but Jory's right – 'is lordship Lord Keith is like Old Jarvie,' he said, almost apologetically, referring to John Jervis, Lord St Vincent, the former Mediterranean commander. 'A stickler for discipline. We might be with the Aliens, sir, but 'is lordship might not know it. Would seem a bit skip to the rest o'the fleet if a troop o'jollies didn't report, and he could hold us for insubordination or worse, just to spite Sir Sidney – Sar'nt Docky said they parted in very bad temper, sir, very bad temper. C-in-C would scupper Sir Sid first chance he got, with us in the middle. Sir Sidney would fix it, aye, but it would be a delay.' He looked around at them. 'And we all wants the *Généreux* now, sir, don't we. We got a score to settle.'

They murmured their *ayes* and Hazzard knew the old-timer sergeant was right. De la Vega drained his sherry with satisfaction, put the glass down and looked at Hazzard. 'Malta, *amigo*.'

–

South of Valletta, the *Alexander* and *Northumberland* passed them on through the thin blockade – ships barely visible to each other, gaps wide enough to force an armada through, thought Hazzard.

Eventually they passed the *Perseus*, a bomb craft, her low, flat deck occupied by giant mortars, deckhands at the rails, pointing, surveying the damage to the *Volpone*, the scars on her broadsides, the state of the men on the quarterdeck: Hazzard in shirtsleeves, one bandaged arm in a sling, his Bombay scarlet slung over one shoulder, the marines still and silent. A lieutenant doffed his hat among otherwise weary, silent onlookers. They encountered the 64-gun HMS *Lion*, but eventually found the *Queen Charlotte* riding at anchor round the jagged stony headlands, off the port of Marsa Sirocco, taking on a supply of fresh water, and passing over powder-kegs and guns in return. Hazzard clambered into the jolly-boat beside Cook, bracing himself for the visit to come.

Once aboard, they made their way past the cannons of the tween-decks, marching in step, wanting to get the matter over as quickly as they could. The half-light through the gratings and boats propped above cast stark shadows on them as they went, gunners stepping aside, carpenters stopping their work, looking, whispers shooting along the groups of men and women working. Hazzard had forced his bandaged arm into the split scarlet sleeve of his Bombay coat, the Lorenzoni holster slung at his left hip, the scimitar of Ali Qarim on the opposite. Cook had reattached his discoloured red sleeves with their four sergeant's stripes to his Marine jerkin, his *shemagh* sash round his waist, a short Turkish cutlass and a jewelled *khanjar* dagger at his front, baggy Turkish *shalvar* trousers tucked into boots. A barefoot gunner's mate held open the panelled door for them to the passage beyond.

Hazzard felt he had gone back in time, to his first visit to Jervis aboard the *Ville de Paris*. He thought of Wayland, of Sarah, of leaving Tomlinson and the *Valiant*. Like the *Ville*, HMS *Queen Charlotte* was a First-Rate 100-gun ship of the line, flying the Vice-Admiral's flag. The overall dimensions of the ship were grander and more spacious than the efficient 74 – reminiscent, thought Hazzard with irony, of Bonaparte's own flagship the *Orient*. Their boots clumped as they strode aft through the lower passage, past the plain carved stairs to the upper and lower gundecks, a pair of marines escorting them to the Admiral's Day Room at the stern. Two marine guards at the door stiffened to attention and ported arms. 'Mr 'Azzard, sir.'

Hazzard nodded at the compliment. 'And Sar'nt-Major Cook, 9 Company.'

They stared for a moment, looking from one to the other, Cook and Hazzard's faces dead, as dark as the panelling around them. The elder of the marines said, 'Hawkins, sir, posted from *Orion*. We was there at the Nile that night…' Hazzard knew he meant the Battle of the Nile. 'Told Cap'n Jim I spotted you on the *Orient*. He said he weren't surprised.'

Captain Sir James Saumarez: sank a frigate with a single broadside, then lumbered in to hammer the French line, his guns unleashing seven hundred pounds of flaming iron with every salvo.

'Was quite a night,' said Hazzard, glancing at Cook. 'I'm obliged, Hawkins.'

'Sir.' Pleased, the marine knocked. 'You bringin' us some trouble, sir?'

'We'll try.'

Hawkins' face split into a broad smile. 'We'll be there, sir, if you needs.' He opened the door, and they went in.

The white-painted, low-beamed ceiling made the room bright, revealing a Spartan ascetic style: no decanters, mahogany or Persian carpets here, only bare planks, a workmanlike table and low-backed chairs by whitewashed bulwarks, and the humped hindquarters of 24-pounder guns either side, the sharp tang of their black-lead polish cutting the air.

Behind a desk to the right, with a view of the doorway and the curved stern gallery windows opposite, sat George Elphinstone, now Vice-Admiral the Lord Keith, commander of the Mediterranean Fleet, writing, dipping his pen, the nib scratching. He did not look up, his Lowland Scots accent rolling across to them. 'I can give you ten minutes, Mr Hazzard, if that is sufficient.'

The two marine guards turned about smartly and left them, their eyes taking a last glance at their guests' peculiar costume with a strange pride.

'Sir,' said Hazzard. 'Nine Company to report.'

The pen stopped scratching. Lord Keith looked up with a frown. 'Report? My, my,' he said, looking more intrigued. 'One might suspect you were a serving officer, Mr Hazzard.' His eye swept the pair of them and he sighed. 'Which I must presume you are, despite all evidence to the contrary.'

He signed his page and blotted it, then stabbed the pen into its holder and sat back, his bagged eyes heavy with fatigue, his jowls pale, the grey curled periwig barely hiding his shock of white hair beneath.

Stickler for discipline and martinet though he might be, Hazzard knew Lord Keith worked first, played never, and rested rarely.

'Well, this should be interesting, sir,' said Keith. 'Sergeant Cook,' he added, with a nod. Hazzard noted he did not use 'sergeant-major' – it was not his confirmed rank, though Sir Sidney was happy to grant him the honour. Cook did not bat an eyelid. He had stood before the desk of far more dangerous officers than Keith.

Cook nodded. 'Milord.'

'Very well, proceed, Mr Hazzard.' He made a gesture at several sheets of paper before him. 'I have your written record. It makes fascinating reading…' The suggestion was clear: he was not pleased.

'The *Généreux*, sir. We engaged her, inflicting severe damage—'

'Severe?' asked Keith. 'Number of enemy guns destroyed? Crew killed or wounded? Masts broken? What severe damage precisely, sir? I need details.'

Hazzard took a step forward, but Cook held him back. 'A glance out of your window at Captain De la Vega's ship would confirm it. He lost twelve dead and thirty injured in a cause not entirely his own.'

Keith grumbled and sat forward. 'You will mind your temper with me, sir. I am not the Earl St Vincent,' he said. 'Nor the Lord Nelson. Or, what is he now…?' he mused. 'The Duke of Lilliput or Laputa, or some such Swiftian nonsense…'

'Then perhaps I should have gone to him first.'

Hazzard heard Cook mumble something – possibly *Jaysus, shite an' all* – but ignored him. Keith stared back, but Hazzard did not back down.

'What became of her, Major Hazzard? *Généreux*.'

'She escaped in fog, sir, running with the wind. If Petrides' intelligence is correct, she could be at the head of a reinforcement squadron, combining even now in the Ionian Sea, bound for Egypt.'

Keith listened, yet was still almost mocking. 'Egypt. Indeed?'

'Yes, sir. Kléber is suing for peace, but possibly without the sanction of his government. It is most likely he does so in the hope of delaying the advance of a large Ottoman land force until the arrival of reinforcements from France.'

'What then of Malta?' asked Keith. 'Are we wasting our time here? The French lie besieged before us. Might Malta not be the target of a relief convoy instead?'

'Bonaparte's army is stranded in Egypt, sir. He has near fifteen thousand men there, and but a handful here.'

'So… I *am* wasting my time at Malta. Their lordships and I are to be taken for fools.' He smacked his desk with the flat of his hand. 'For God's sake… is there no end to your arrogance?'

He rose, his coat swinging, the light catching its orders and badges, its old-fashioned great button-back cuffs glinting with gold braid as he clasped his hands behind his back to look out of the windows. 'And what, pray, has Captain Smith done about this magical turn of events, I wonder? Kléber suing for peace – the answer to our prayers.'

Hazzard hesitated. 'He will doubtless have replied to draw Kléber out.'

Keith turned, accusing. 'More than that, sir. He has done precisely what I feared he would do all along – taken centre stage in his own melodrama. He has *invited* peace talks. *Invited* them, and invited commissioners aboard one of His Majesty's ships for the purpose. Did you not know of this, sir?'

Hazzard looked back at him and replied bluntly, 'No. We have been in battle at sea with a former target of Lord Nelson.'

Keith narrowed his eyes. 'Do not cheek me, sir, by God.' He took an angry step to his desk and snatched up a sheet of paper. 'Here sir! It is all here – General Desaix and that Citizen Pussy-algae fellow, invited to discuss terms aboard HMS *Tigre*.'

Hazzard knew he meant Poussielgue, the diplomat, but said nothing. Keith smacked the page down again. 'He has had *no* Admiralty order, *no* corroboration from Cabinet, nothing conveyed through me. *Nothing.*'

'We are tasked with the expulsion of the French from Egypt, sir, by whichever means possible.'

'And we are tasked with the utter destruction of their military capability!' snapped Keith in reply. 'Not their damned salvation!' He paused. 'You set sail in early December?'

'Sir.'

'Then things have moved apace, rather faster than you might know,' continued Keith. 'It is not merely that Kléber has no sanction from his government, thus negating any document he might sign, but that he has no idea of what his government now constitutes.'

'How so, sir?'

'Because Bonaparte staged a *coúp d'état* in November. We learned this but three days ago and believe Kléber is still in the dark, and indeed that none of his letters or requests to Paris have been so much as looked at, let alone answered. Bonaparte is now effective leader of a triumvirate, sir. He is but one step from crowning himself *king*.'

Hazzard went cold. He heard Cook beside him let out a breath. '*Christ a'mighty.*'

He saw Bonaparte's face again, heard his voice:

Mr Hazzard.

And he had had him in his sights. Twice.

They say you met Bonaparte, sir. Nearly killed him, say others.

But did not.

'And Smith can have no idea of this either, until our runner arrives at his blockade.' Keith delivered it like an accusation. 'And meanwhile, he is wining and dining the enemy!'

'If this is true, sir...' considered Hazzard, playing for some time to think, until it hit him: '...then Bonaparte will be more determined than ever to secure Egypt, now that he has power. The entire expedition was virtually a government ruse to maroon him a thousand miles from Paris—'

'Well, here he is, back home safe and sound, a hero's welcome and First Consul, if you please, knees under the desk, his backside on the throne. And Vaubois' men down here are now *also* more determined than ever to hold on to Valletta.'

Keith fell silent for a moment, pensive, weary. 'Our task,' he said, 'is grown ever more difficult. And the men despise it. Sitting in blockade, idle, loading drills, endless maintenance. They gamble, brawl – and e'en in church parade, they pray not for God's forgiveness, but for danger and the Devil and a battle with anyone. It is against nature, against... all *sense*, dreaming of violence.' He looked at them both. 'Well, you both know, I dare say.'

'Aye, sir,' confirmed Cook sadly.

Keith took heart from this. He moved away, hands writhing with each other or bunched into fists behind his back, noticed Hazzard, as if he were fighting, too – and perhaps he was, thought Hazzard. Keith stood staring out at the sea and the sky, perhaps to escape it all himself, the shadow of the balcony above washing him grey, ashen. He looked down, bitter, then cast an eye at them both. 'And *Généreux*, to add further insult, now sits pretty in Toulon under repair.'

Cook swore under his breath again and Hazzard took the news like a blow: their chance to take *Généreux* was gone. 'When, sir?'

Keith's voice had dropped – no longer shouting, no longer angry with Smith or Hazzard, or Bonaparte, resignation following frustration. 'She's been there since some time,' he said, 'most likely after you gave her a taste of her own medicine.' He paused, rueful, awkward in acknowledgement. 'And a hearty dose at that it was too.'

It was almost a compliment, and he cleared his throat to cover the apparent lapse. 'She has a new captain, man called Renaudin...' Keith moved round his desk back to his chair. 'And your observations about her new armoury could be quite accurate. Cap'n Peard of the frigate *Success* is standing off Toulon, and he believes your reinforcement fleet is massing, though we have no clear evidence as yet. Perhaps your Mr Petrides had things wrong.'

Hazzard thought of Petrides. *Could it have been clever disinformation? To throw them off the scent? Was Petrides a French plant himself? Why?* 'And Lord Nelson, sir? He is not in the blockade?'

Keith looked up, almost startled, and his expression hardened with disapproval. 'No, sir, he is not,' he said. 'He sits at the feet of the salacious Neapolitan royal court nowadays,' he said, evidently disappointed for all of them. He gazed at the desk, at the limed planks beneath his feet. 'What is Palermo brought to now... A den of thieves. Forbidding trade to all and sundry, refusing grain to Malta, refusing revenue to their own people dying in the damned streets while they wassail and feast... and Nelson in the midst of it all, being lauded and lionised in the most repugnant way. We have all tried – Ball, Troubridge, his brother officers.' He added irritably, 'But Nelson will hear none of it, and denies the orders of a superior officer. I refuse to engage with him on the matter any further. I have said my piece.'

Nevertheless, he cast an eye once again through the gallery windows to the sea beyond, a strange sadness evident in his expression despite his bluff condemnation. A Portuguese ship of the line was lowering goods to a tender and taking troops aboard, possibly the marines they had heard about. Hazzard waited.

'That armistice of the summer in Naples, after their damned revolution, captured rebels and Jacobin prisoners, by God. It was appalling,' he said, and looked at him. 'Mocked-up trials, mass gibbets, beheadings, like the bloody Terror of Paris – all wrought by the king's courtiers. Nelson does not see it. Will not.' Keith said at last, 'He is not the man he once was.'

He looked through the papers on his desk, settling himself in his chair once again. 'Perhaps you will galvanise him, sir, where I have failed. You seem to have that effect. For better or for worse.' He found what he was looking for and held it out. 'A warrant. For resupply and refitting in Palermo, for Captain De la Vega and the *Volpone*. Paid for by the Royal Navy with my seal, and... some small compensation in coin,' he said, turning away again, '...for his losses.' He cleared his throat. 'Something, at the least, for the families. His crew not being salaried seamen of His Majesty.'

Hazzard took it. The old man was not as bad, perhaps, as he might pretend. 'I thank you, sir. They will be grateful.'

Keith regarded him for a moment. 'Report then to Lord Nelson, if you can but find him. Repair and refit. Take your rest. You had quite a time of it. Sar'-Major Cook, you should have known better. We look to sober heads to control our officers, or had you forgot?'

Raised to sergeant-major once again, Cook came to attention for the first time: Keith had proved himself. 'Aye, sir. Not for want of tryin', my lord.'

'Hm. I can imagine.' Keith picked up his pen once more and bent to his work, giving them a final admonishing glance. 'Mind your step about me, Mr Hazzard – we have clout in Whitehall as well as out here. I know of Mr Wickham and his rogues. And tell Smith to tread warily, for I will not risk further ships to sail to his rescue. You are dismissed.'

'Sir.'

They turned to go, but as they opened the door, Keith muttered as he continued to write once again, 'Never liked them,' he muttered, 'viewing-ports...' He perused a paper intently. 'People forever trying to put things through them. Or so I hear.'

Hazzard looked back at him. Lord Keith had heard the full story – which Hazzard had omitted from his written report, relating only the conduct of De la Vega and the *Volpone*.

Keith waved them away with his pen. 'Go harum-scarum back to the Devil where you clearly belong, Mr Hazzard,' then adding warmly, 'and Godspeed with it. Close the door on your way out.'

Hazzard watched him, but the admiral continued to write, the quill bobbing. No wonder some called him Uncle George.

'Sir.'

After days of tacking against the northwesterly under white-streaked skies, they rounded the Aegadian isles off Trapani on the western reaches of Sicily. They passed by the sunlit Gulf of Longuro and Castellamare in the Tyrrhenian Sea, and were waved on by the 74-gun HMS *Audacious*, a veteran of the Nile patrolling the sea-routes to Naples. Soon *Volpone* rounded the striated cliffs and towering crags of Capo San Vito, and finally Capo Gallo, the great gulf of Palermo opening before them, cradled in the rocky embrace of Monte Pellegrino, its great curving ridges reaching down to the sea. They ran the recognition signals up the masthead and headed into the harbour, and an uncertain reception.

The city clustered in the central basin against the foothills, the towers and cupolas of churches and grand civic buildings misty in the pale grey morning light. Fine streets and grand baroque façades yielded at the waterfront to manufactory sheds and warehouses on the wharves. Cranes and tenders served merchantmen and warships alike, some quays deserted, a few Sardinian and Ragusan ships in evidence, but not many. The British presence loomed large – HMS *Vanguard*, *Zealous* and *Foudroyant* at anchor, heavy 74s all – riding alongside bright-painted Neapolitan men-of-war in their royal red and white livery, Portuguese frigates and a grand royal Porto 80-gunner – even an Ottoman frigate, low and sleek as a dart with streamlined lateen sails, flying the imperial red ensign of the white crescent moon and star.

One foot on the rear truck of a quarterdeck gun-carriage, De la Vega surveyed the scene through an eyeglass with Cook and Hazzard at the mainmast shrouds, looking out, the crew doing likewise down the midship rails and fo'c'sle.

'Palermo, *amigos*,' said De la Vega. 'A good place for the *siesta*. A city of the ages.'

The morning was cool, though to Hazzard and doubtless all the other marines, it felt cold, barely a fraction of the warmth they were accustomed to in Egypt, De la Vega's elaborate cabin thermometer reading only 12 on the Réaumur scale. 'It's a new year...' said Hazzard with realisation. 'A new century.'

The previous year they had been roaming the desert near Karnak, near the temples of Ozymandias with the Tarabin of Shajar al-Durr –

and he had shared a night with her beauty under the painted stars of Ramesses' eternal blue heavens. With thoughts of her raven hair and velvet-black eyes came thoughts of Delphine Lascelles – just as fearless, selfless, dedicated, who seemed to need no one, certainly no man – and certainly not Hazzard. *Tell me, Sarah, have I abandoned her as well?*

'Missed New Year's Day,' mumbled Cook distantly. 'The Year of Our Lord Eighteen-'undred. By all that's holy in Bristol.' His brooding brows knitted heavily and he murmured, 'Never thought I'd see it.'

'Edith will thank you for the letter,' said Hazzard. They had left a bundle of them from a few of the men with the quartermaster of the *Queen Charlotte*. 'She won't thank me for keeping you so long.'

'Thank me for nuppence an' all,' replied Cook. 'Share money still in ruddy Barbados, most like.' Shares from prize money were notoriously slow to come through. Every camp they hit, every munitions dump or provisions wagon was noted and valued – though not technically captured, Smith said it would go down as 'stores/munitions, enemy deprived thereof'. Smith had also promised that Wickham would see their families received their salaries, or banked them with interest as they chose. 'Six shillin' a week should keep 'er sweet.'

De la Vega puffed smoke philosophically. 'We miss *la Epifania* also. More important. For the children, *sí*. But... ehh, *que pase lo que pase*.' *What happens, happens.* He handed the scope to Hazzard.

Hazzard surveyed the skyline, the winter sun coming through, a soft glow over the mountain, seabirds drifting in the foreground. Somewhere in there, he knew, was Nelson. His battleships rode at anchor, pennants flying, like so many medieval knights waiting in the camp of their king. He began to feel the power of the man – no wonder Lord Keith could not bring him to heel.

'*Aya*,' said De la Vega. 'We must bring in this new year, *compadres*, this new century, you say. It is not Napoli, but I know the good place here.'

Hazzard peered through the scope. 'Why am I not surprised.'

'*Un caballero*, a gentleman,' explained De la Vega to the ignorant, 'he knows such things.' He flicked the stub of a cheroot overboard and called for Alfonso to fire the required salute. 'And I need more of the *cigarros ligeros*, and Rioja, and all the things necessary.' Very shortly, *Volpone*'s guns boomed, and the answering signal came in reply, and a patrol sloop lowered a gig, sending a pilot to bring them in.

Through the scope Hazzard watched a red-coated platoon of British marines marching on the dockside, wheeling to form up with another unit in grey, possibly Portuguese, as they had seen at Malta. Somewhere a bugle called and a crane swung out to load a barge – all sights, sounds and smells familiar to him. Though a foreign port to them all, it appeared welcoming, a safe haven. He straightened and looked out, the wind cooling his face, the sun warming them all – the horrors of the fog and the *Généreux* fading into a new focussed intent. 'A strange place,' he said. 'But somewhere to begin again.'

'Amen to that, sir,' said Cook.

Rescue

Napoléon Bonaparte, newly invested First Consul, Member of the Institute and former *Général en chef* of the Army of the East, the Army of Paris, and the Army of Italy, was very much the Augustus of his new triumvirate of France – and the recognised *Primus Inter Pares*: very much first among equals. Of the other two consuls, neither was a Mark Antony, and indeed he knew there was no Cleopatra awaiting in Egypt with eager embrace – only Kléber, the Mamluk and a ferocious Ottoman army. Other than this came news of the losses of most of his conquests before Egypt, with reports of the Austrians, Slovaks and Slovenes pushing into Italy, and the Italian city-states throwing off their French shackles. The Helvetian Republic of the Swiss, the Rhine… all had played their best hand in the absence of Caesar. But Caesar had now returned from the Nile, and was ready to march again.

In his fine winter suit of roan corduroy, First Consul Bonaparte strode through to his well-appointed offices, decorated in what the designers had believed was fashionable Egyptian, with black lacquered chairs trimmed with gilt sphinxes and palms, lit by gilded wall sconces of carved Egyptian corn and fine miniature columns – reminding him all too much of where he had just been and what he had left behind.

'To me, it is a simple matter,' he declared in his brittle humour, which few could manage successfully without engaging his white-hot temper, a souvenir, some said, of his tyrannical rule on the Nile. His shoes made no sound across the dove-grey Beauvais carpet, and he slapped down a sheaf of papers onto the large black and gilt *sécretaire* in the centre of the room. He felt the warmth of the fire in the stone hearth with some relief – after over a year in the desert, Paris was a damp, freezing cell, the wind along the Seine cutting through to his bones. 'If the admiral does not abide by my wishes, I will have him *removed.*'

Following behind came Rear-Admiral Perrée and two of his trusted captains. They had all heard these complaints of Admiral Ganteaume before. Perrée was an elegant officer, respected by all and well liked by Bonaparte, who had arranged his promotion personally – Perrée was one of the elite, one of that special band who had shared the hardships of the Egypt and Holy Land campaigns with the general. Whenever he was called in to the Tuileries, Perrée wore the presentation sword granted him by Bonaparte, in recognition of his conduct on the Nile at the Battle of Shubra Khit.

Nevertheless, Perrée gallantly defended Ganteaume's hesitation. 'Consul, it is proving too difficult to put to sea from Toulon now that the British have returned to the Mediterranean, as I know personally all too well…' This was in reference to his own capture by the British, and recent release on parole at the outer roads. 'They have secured Menorca, blockaded Naples and Malta,' he continued. 'They have thirty-one sail to call upon.'

'And Bruix had twenty-five when he came to Toulon,' riposted Bonaparte, 'yet Ganteaume did nothing.' He sat heavily in a bergère chair at the fireside, gazing into the flames in a black mood. He muttered, 'If we'd had that fleet, we would not have lost Aboukir to Nelson.' He hissed with sudden venom, 'What is Ganteaume *about*? Without him I cannot relieve Egypt, or Malta.'

There was a brief silence as Perrée glanced at his captains, who shuffled on the carpet, studying its elaborate design, uncomfortable. They all knew the problems with Ganteaume – everyone did: he was no Brueys or Bruix. He was the 'leftover admiral', with Villeneuve, the rearguard who had crept away from Aboukir once the fighting was done.

The fire crackled. They could hear the muffled voices of officials in the outer offices, heels clicking on the stone floors. Perrée asked quietly, 'Can *Général en chef* Kléber not maintain his command?'

'Of course he can,' snapped Bonaparte. He was convinced of this much, at least. 'He has at least fifteen thousand men. I took nearly all of Syria with fewer. But my soldiers, their families, the *people* demand I send rescue – but the Treasury says *no*.' He shook his head. 'The gold, silver, the plate we sent back home from Malta and Egypt, *gone*. *Ma foi*. It is an *infamy*.'

'And Ganteaume's delay has eaten through his stores and funds…' added Perrée.

'Yes. So I cannot be *seen* to send rescue though I *demand* it.' He stared off into nothing. 'I am damned either way,' he cursed. 'And

Malta is under siege. Most of the mob here do not even know where Malta *is*. But Egypt, yes, they all know Egypt now.' He swooped on a sheet of paper on his desk. 'And this... This from Ganteaume...' He waved it aloft and read from it. 'He is uncertain if the flotilla is to be for Egypt or for Malta, owing to confusion of the order, and could I be so good as to tell him?' He threw it down. 'Idiot! How? How can he be uncertain, *mon dieu*. The order was for Egypt, weeks ago, through the *Ordonnateur de Marine*. The nonsense I endure.'

He got up to pace, hands behind his back, tucked under the warmth of his coat-tails. Perrée watched the decision being wrought before him. He took a step towards the fire, resting a hand on the back of a chair. 'Milord Keith lays siege to General Vaubois, who still holds Valletta. You once said, Consul, Malta must come first,' Perrée reminded him. 'Without it, Egypt cannot be supported.'

Bonaparte stopped and stood still. He stared down, sour, but nodded his head slowly. 'Even Laplace agreed with that. *Ma dame du ciel*...' His mood darkened, his tone bitter. 'So Malta it must be. And Egypt,' he said, 'must wait.'

'The English are stretched thin as well, Consul. And Palermo refuses to supply Malta with grain, so the English must keep contact with their supply ships on the coast. Vaubois is caught, by land and sea. But if he had more men he could conceivably break out.'

Bonaparte nodded. 'Conceivably...' He looked away in disgust at the thought of Ganteaume. '...while the grand admiral dips his big toe in Toulon harbour to see if it's too chilly.'

The captains laughed, and Perrée allowed himself a smile. Bonaparte sighed. '*Alors*, there it is, you all know him. You must see to this. You must.'

Perrée took the compliment graciously, but evaded the question. 'My parole, Consul, prohibits a return to arms yet. And Nelson waits at Sicily.'

Bonaparte stared at Perrée, then shrugged. 'Nelson is done – *ennui, finis*. He is wounded – unfit, they say, resting like an old man in the sun... playing with his pretty mistress.'

They chuckled obligingly, and Bonaparte moved back to the fire, leaning on the mantelshelf and looking into the flickering flames. 'What have they been doing here, Jean-Baptiste, while we have been away...? Thieving from the treasury, losing all we had won. They should be digging latrines in Italy for their crimes.'

The clock on the mantel chimed four. Bonaparte turned about: he had had enough. 'Very well. The *Généreux* shall lead a fleet. You may inform Admiral Ganteaume he will assist you in the assembly of a relief flotilla.' He added with some irony, 'This will not break the terms of your parole with the *anglais*.'

Perrée seemed reluctant but admitted, 'The court martial concerning my exchange recognised my duty to parole, but...' He stood straighter. 'But, my duty to France, and to you, *mon général*, is greater still.' He bowed.

Bonaparte did not shy from such bald declarations of duty, or even affection – and became suspicious if he heard none. He approached him, pleased, a hand to Perrée's arm. 'And we are proud to have it.'

'And Egypt, Consul...?'

Bonaparte kept his voice steady and his gaze perfectly level as he said it, but it was clear there was an unspoken subtext to his orders. 'If Vaubois has a surfeit of troops after his successful breakout from Valletta, then we can consider the needs of Kléber in Egypt. But, above all,' he said specifically, 'no strain is to be put upon Vaubois' stores by extra mouths to feed – and you must judge how best to alleviate that.'

'I am yours to command.'

'If you feel it best.'

There was a brief silence as Bonaparte turned to his desk. They all recognised the curious contradiction, but said nothing. Only Perrée seemed to understand.

'As you say, Consul. And so it will be,' said Perrée. He headed to the door with his officers, but stopped. He turned. 'It is good,' he said, 'to be home, with you at the helm, Consul. If only they could see it, in Egypt. They would have hope.'

Bonaparte pushed his hands behind his back again, his eyes blank. 'Get us to Malta, then we can save them all, *Contre-amiral*.'

'*Mon général*.' Perrée cracked his heels together and the captains bowed in concert, turned, and an official led them out. Bonaparte watched him go and, after a moment, returned to his desk.

As Perrée and his officers passed through the tall double-doors, two men in plain coats and top hats rose from chairs in the corner. No official showed them in, but they entered quietly, the younger at the elder's elbow. They stood silently in the doorway. The more senior of the two cleared his throat.

'Consul.'

Bonaparte did not look up from his work, the pen scratching. 'Controller.'

Controller Vermond was a hard-faced man in his late fifties, in old-fashioned grey wig and a plain high-collared black frock-coat, cravat, waistcoat and breeches, an unremarkable man, a prerequisite for one of the joint chiefs of the *Bureau de renseignements et information*, possibly one of the most powerful men in the Ministry of the Interior. He indicated his junior. 'Citizen Dideron, Consul. Intelligence Directorate, Second Office.'

Bonaparte set down his pen and sat back in his chair, looking up at the pair of them, then waved a hand. 'Close the door.'

Vermond gave Dideron a nod: they could hear Bonaparte's principal secretary conveying Perrée and his officers to the stairs, their steel-tipped boots ringing on the polished stone steps, their voices echoing in the distance beyond the outer office. Dideron closed the doors with a faint click.

'You wanted to see the person responsible for the Levant report, Consul,' said Vermond without preamble. 'Citizen Dideron wrote it.'

Citizen Emmanuel Dideron was roughly Bonaparte's age, had joined Bonaparte's march into Italy nearly four years earlier, serving in the army quartermaster's office, and was clever enough to avoid action. His analysis of intelligence gained from enemy prisoners had proved useful, and he was now a minor functionary in the middle echelons of the counter-espionage service under Vermond. No one had replaced Citizen Derrien, or 'Citizen *Croquemort*' as he had been known – or rather, none had dared. Instead, Vermond had returned briefly from retirement to oversee the restructuring of the Bureau into its two divisions, internal and external, known to all as the *Première* and the *Deuxième*. Dideron was in the new Intelligence Directorate of the *Deuxième Bureau*, producing foreign reports for the Operations Executive. But he was always hoping for more. He bowed with something of the over-eager official, a hint of arrogance and a hint of obsequious servility about him.

'Consul, an honour.'

Bonaparte looked at him, sizing him up, head to one side. 'So… what of the Adriatic fleet?'

Vermond began. 'The Adriatic feint proved useful, Consul,' he said. 'The ploy of a reinforcement flotilla revealed the man Petrides to us, likely an Ottoman or English spy, though I have no wish to bore you with details, but it was he who fed the information to the English blockade fleet under Commodore Sir William Sidney Smith.'

Bonaparte made a hissing intake of breath at the name. 'Mister Smith. Again.' It was Smith who had captured his heavy artillery at Acre before it could be landed – and cost Bonaparte the Holy Land.

Vermond nodded. 'According to dockside reports in Syracuse, the English sailed to intercept the fleet with a single reconnaissance frigate, a Spanish privateer. They found only the *Généreux*, and she was far too strong for them. One ship was lost in the exchange, a Venetian, of little consequence...' He pulled out a pair of spectacles and tugged at a slip of paper from his pocket. 'One of the supposed hulks from Ancona or Brindisi...'

'Renamed the *Hoche*, Controller,' supplied Dideron, his chin down.

Vermond nodded. 'Quite so.'

Bonaparte cut in. 'So? Have you captured this Petrides? Who is he?'

Vermond looked to Dideron and gave him the floor. 'Oh. Yes, Consul,' said Dideron. 'A Greek legal clerk from Athens, in Ottoman Morea, but revealed now to be a member of the English Balkan network.' He added an aside, 'When he tried to make contact with the English blockade at Alexandria, he was captured and handed over to a Citizen Peraud in Egypt. Somehow,' he said, with rhetorical puzzlement, 'Petrides was able to make his escape.'

Bonaparte listened, irritable. 'I did not care for the games of Citizen Derrien, Citizen Analyst, and his reputation far outweighed yours. Do not suppose I shall care for you more so.'

Dideron retreated. 'Of course, Consul. I... I merely wonder how such an agent could escape from... well, from such an experienced officer,' said Dideron, damning Peraud as far as he could. He then took his chance. 'I should like the opportunity to find out myself.'

Bonaparte waved him on. 'Petrides. Be briefer. Is he a threat? Must I change tactics? Must I do anything? Tell me.'

'Yes, I... I traced Petrides from Cyprus to Sicily. We have received...' He glanced at Vermond. 'That is, I received confirmation just this morning that he is expected in Palermo.' He hesitated again, stammering slightly. 'I believe I can combine operations with the relief convoy under Admiral Ganteaume – or Admiral Perrée, such as it may be – and use Petrides to our benefit.'

'How?'

Vermond turned. 'Misdirection, Consul. It is not a bad idea.'

'Misdirection? For the convoy?' asked Bonaparte, intrigued, looking at Dideron. 'Well?'

'Yes, Consul, to confuse the English over its true course and destination, just as you achieved before the invasion of Egypt.' Getting not a jot of response from Bonaparte, Dideron took a step back, flustered, then put his hands squarely behind his back, as he had heard Derrien had been accustomed to do. 'That is, we could convince the English, through Petrides, that the fleet is going to... say, for example, to relieve Egypt, rather than to relieve Malta.'

'They might deploy their heavy blockade ships to the southeast of Malta, to block the path to Alex,' said Vermond. 'This would leave the southwest clear for Perrée to creep in behind the island. Make a clandestine landing on the unprotected coast.'

Bonaparte flicked a perplexed glance at him. 'But Egypt is my intention.' He would change his mind if it suited his purposes, and back again, if need be. 'Do you not understand this?'

'And everyone knows it,' said Vermond. 'Rescuing the brave heroes of Syria and the victors of the Pyramids.' He straightened. 'But so is Malta. It's perfect, Consul. The *anglais* will chase their tails, not knowing which way to go.'

Dideron nodded. 'And a brilliant strategem it is, Consul. Though without Malta, Egypt would surely be difficult to maintain. As I am certain you have already planned.'

Bonaparte considered him, watching his face, his expression, the nervous, faintly effete gestures. 'Indeed.'

'Has Ganteaume mobilised, Consul?' asked Vermond.

'No. The *Commissaire Ordonnateur* and the *Ordonnateur en chef* argue with him over stores – they say they never received orders for Egypt, only Malta.'

Dideron shifted and looked at Vermond, then down, his face glowing hot. Something was clearly amiss, and Vermond had noticed. He snapped at Dideron, 'Your proposal, Citizen?'

Dideron nodded as he swallowed. 'Controller, Consul, I... I have drawn up a list of vessels for Admiral Perrée, and obtained charter of one in particular, for the Petrides operation.' He produced a handkerchief and dabbed nervously at his brow, which was shining with perspiration. His tongue licked at dry, chapped lips. 'One moment...'

He fumbled in his pockets for a folded letter, stepped forward uncertainly to Bonaparte's desk and laid it before him. 'Authorisation to the *Ordonnateur en chef* in Toulon for stores and munitions to be drawn, Consul, and funds for several… deputies, shall we say, as required.'

Bonaparte cast an eye over the sheet, but it was a standard navy order, good enough for the *Ordonnateur*'s office in Toulon. 'Very well,' he said and took up his pen, the scratching of the nib on the page momentarily louder in the room than the spitting of the fire. He handed it back, waved it impatiently. Dideron took it with a bow.

'Thank you, Consul.'

Bonaparte said nothing for a few moments, then looked down at the papers before him. He moved several from left to right, from right to left. 'This should end the Petrides affair.' He still did not look up. 'If it does not, the new minister might see fit to reassign your situation to someone else.' He picked up his pen to renew his work.

Vermond bowed. 'We serve at your pleasure, Consul.'

Dideron could not move, the authorisation letter clattering in his hand as he shook. 'Yes, of course, Consul. I… I seek only to advise, and to assist the Rear-Admiral Perrée in his mission… and bring succour to our troops.'

Vermond threw open the doors. 'Enough, Citizen, the consul is heavily engaged.'

Bonaparte took up his pen, ignoring him. 'I await your inevitable success.'

Dideron bowed, retreating from the desk as if in an *ancien* throne room of old. When at last he was safely beyond the outer office, he weaved on unsteady feet, dizzy, and tried to hurry down the corridor to the light of the grand gallery. He saw Vermond marching onwards. 'Controller, wait… *Je vous en prie…*'

Vermond stopped on the gallery landing, leaning on his tall brass-topped cane, red-faced with anger. The marble floors gleamed all around in the weak afternoon winter sun penetrating from the skylights in the dome far above. Dideron tried to keep himself together, but nearly fell upon the stone balustrade beside his superior, sick to his stomach. '*Mon dieu,*' he gasped.

'*Nom d'un nom!*' snapped Vermond. 'What the *hell* was that about deputies and munitions?'

Dideron could not explain; he gaped at him, his mouth open, his forehead slick with sweat, as if he were mad with fever. He fought for breath. 'I… must get Petrides…'

'*Damn* Petrides,' spat Vermond. 'What has Peraud to do with this? What is going *on*, Citizen?'

Dideron breathed hard, then clenched his eyes shut, a confession about to burst forth. 'The order t-to Ganteaume...' he gasped, his puffy red lips shining and sore. 'I... I do not have our copy.'

'What are you drivelling about?'

With shaking hands, Dideron rifled through the pages in his dossier, searching. 'For the fleet for Egypt – it... It is missing.'

'Missing?' demanded Vermond. 'An encoded order? How?'

'It is why Admiral Ganteaume did not understand...' Dideron looked at him, a snared rabbit. It got worse. 'I changed the destination code. To... To implicate Minister Laplace, as we agreed...' He swallowed and looked at Vermond's thunderous expression. 'I changed it from Egypt to Malta.'

'*You did what?*' Vermond stared at him. 'A coded despatch? How did you...?' He turned away, aghast. '*Putain alors.* You *fool*. There will be an enquiry. It will now look as if the minister himself ordered a fleet to Malta instead of Egypt!'

'Yes, to prove Laplace was against the Consul Bonaparte – that... that the consul wanted to relieve Egypt but had been *prevented*...'

Vermond's face contorted with anger. 'You *utter* idiot. Laplace is out! The new minister will be *Lucien* Bonaparte!' he hissed, dropping the axe upon Dideron's neck. 'You have implicated the *consul's own brother.*'

Dideron was nearly out of breath, a hand on his chest. 'Petrides... took it. He must have—'

Vermond took him by the collar, his twisted mouth at Dideron's ear. 'You will take that damned Corsican rat-scuttle you've found, get down to Palermo, get Petrides, and get this damned order *back*, or see it *destroyed*, do you understand?' He let him go and straightened in revulsion, his grating words the death knell to Dideron's dreams of preferment. 'If you fail, Citizen,' finished Vermond, 'do not bother to return.'

Vermond marched away, the tall cane clicking on the marble floor. Dideron clutched at the stone balustrade. '*Mon dieu... Mon dieu...*' Dideron's assistant, Citizen Boulin, scuttled out from his hiding place in the shadow of a column.

'Citizen...?' asked Boulin in his soft whisper. 'What has happened? What may I do...? Is the rescue fleet ordered?'

Dideron's breath came in panicked gasps; he wanted to get out to the cold streets of Paris, to get out of the palace where he had so fondly dreamt of working one day, as Derrien, Thainville and Robespierre had done. '*Damn the fleet!*'

Not even Vermond understood, but Petrides was nothing – *nothing*: instead, Dideron needed to find that wicked Du Pont-Clair woman and bring her *home*. He knew she had it – *knew* it. Anything to discredit him – *anything*. That she had been captured on active operations in Constantinople by English spies was something Citizen Dideron would never reveal to anyone, let alone the First Consul of France – and certainly not that it was he, Emmanuel Dideron, who had shown her that forged order. Petrides would know where she was. He always did.

It had all been part of the plan – a good plan – to expose Minister Laplace as a traitor to the good heroes of Egypt, and prove that the great Consul Bonaparte had been foiled in his gallant endeavours to relieve them. Oh, how Bonaparte would then reward Dideron with largesse beyond his wildest expectations, overwhelmed with gratitude, for saving his position and raising him aloft once again before the people. But it had all gone terribly wrong.

'*Palermo*,' he whispered to Boulin. 'I can slip down the coast…' It was the only way. He had the authority now. He would go with Perrée … *Yes, then break away, yes, that would work.*

'But… But what of Egypt?' asked Boulin. 'And the rescue…?'

Dideron pushed himself up from the balustrade and straightened his collar. He would leave the Palace of the Tuileries properly, like Vermond – like a true official on state business, a stout man of affairs, upright, and at his own pace. He looked at Boulin, fool that he was, and gave his final word on the matter. 'Damn Egypt.'

–

The captain and officers of the 32-gun Ottoman frigate *Mebda-i Nusret* had been very accommodating, and cleared one of the canvas-walled cabins on the single gundeck for their special prisoner. At first they had grumbled at the unusual inconvenience, but when the genteel lady Celeste Dupuy de Crozes awoke to find herself bound and gagged in an old sack, lying among a heap of fodder ready for the holds, she had shrieked, kicked and raged so savagely the young Turkish officers thought the mad Englishmen had brought a ferocious animal aboard, and backed away immediately.

Soon the frigate set sail, the rattle of cable and line mingling with the shouts and sounds of the deckhands and the cries of seabirds, the rhythmic slap of the waves against the hull lending a strangely reassuring regularity inside the cabin. Still hooded and gagged, Celeste had been bound to a chair; her hands behind her back, she lurched uncertainly, off-balance with the movement of the ship. When an unseen hand plucked the sack from her head, she looked about with blinking, dazzled eyes, but calmed at last with sudden relief from the unknown. The light was streaming in, glinting from the hindquarters of an 18-pound Turkish cannon, its half-open gun-port letting in the fresh breezes of the sea, offering a glimpse of the distant, cloud-strewn horizon. She turned her furious gaze upon her captors. Wayland and Stanford sat opposite, each on a chair, watching her.

'Good morning, madam,' said Stanford.

Her face clouding with outrage and indignation, she struggled against her gag, her teeth biting at it, her protests muffled into the strains of the mute. After a moment she stopped, exhausted, her eyes darting in pain from one to the other, gazing in pitiful confusion at Wayland. When he looked away and gave no response, she sagged, sobbing, her dishevelled hair bobbing before them as she wept. When the tears subsided, she stared down at the floor – almost with resignation, thought Wayland, crushed by his betrayal.

Stanford consulted his notes and cleared his throat. 'You are Madeleine du Pont-Clair, agent of the *Bureau de renseignements et information*.'

She sagged further in the chair, her arms held tight behind her. After a moment she sat up, shaking her head slowly – not that she was answering Stanford, more that she understood now what had happened. She looked to Wayland, and shook her head with incredulity.

'You are, madam?' repeated Stanford. 'Or you are not?'

She looked at him, dark eyes rimmed with fatigue and wet with tears of frustration. It was the hardest look Wayland had ever seen. She shook her head curtly: *No.*

But Stanford continued. 'You befriended Paula Maria Bonaparte on Corsica, and were later found instrumental in seditious meetings in

Spain at El Escorial and Granada, meetings to bring about the Franco-Spanish treaty of 1796 to the benefit of France.'

She stared back at him blankly, unmoving.

Wayland glanced at Stanford. 'I think we can…'

'Yes, sir. Though do be careful,' said Stanford. 'I have heard she bites.'

Wayland considered this, but leaned forward and, as gently as he could, tugged the gag away from her right cheek and over her chin. She closed her eyes and gasped with relief, throwing her head back to take in a deep breath. '*Oh, mon dieu, qu'est-ce qui est…*'

Stanford leafed through his papers absently. '*Si vous préférez, on peut le faire en français, madame.*' *If you prefer, we can do this in French, madam.*

She flicked a glance at Wayland. '*M'sieur le capitaine…? Thomas?*' Her voice almost broke into sobs. 'Could you not have asked me? Was there *anything* I would have denied you?'

Wayland shifted, uncomfortable. After a moment, he asked in a dead tone, 'What can you tell us, Celeste?'

Her head sank and she leaned forward against her bonds, as if to rest, staring at the planks of the gundeck. They sat in silence, the three of them. Then she spoke.

'I need to understand your position, *messieurs*,' she said, not without some authority. 'Your rank.'

Wayland sat up. She spoke with such confidence he hardly recognised her. Stanford hesitated, then repeated, 'Spain.'

Her eyes took on a dull look, as if she knew this by rote. 'I am not at liberty to say.'

'You are Madeleine du Pont-Clair?'

She exhaled softly, as if considering her answer. There was a knock at the door. Wayland called to enter, and the plank door opened on its creaking pin hinges. In walked an older, dark-skinned civilian, tufts of white hair at his temples: it was the Greek clerk who had once been tortured by Citizen Peraud, and rescued by Hazzard – it was Petrides.

Celeste looked astonished to see him, then seemed swept with relief. 'Oh, *mon dieu*. Christos. Of course…'

Petrides stood silent, his lips taut, as if stifling anger. 'The Adriatic fleet was a *lie*,' he lashed, his English flawless.

She nodded, her head hanging. 'Captain Day in Turin believed it. I passed it on to you. What was I to do…?' She looked up at him, then said in Greek, '*Nómiza óti ísastan nekrós.*'

186

I thought you were dead.

'*Oxhi*,' he replied with a hard look. *No.* 'You very nearly cost me my *life*, Madeleine.'

'And you have done the same to me, Christos!'

'Never. *Never*,' he insisted.

Wayland looked back at Celeste. 'I take it this is the lady?'

Petrides nodded and pointed to her left side. 'There is a scar on the left forearm.'

Despite her confidence, she tried to hide her left arm further, even though it was bound behind her, all the while looking at Petrides.

'Celeste,' said Wayland, 'shall we look for the scar? Or should I simply say Madeleine...?'

Petrides glanced at Wayland. 'It was I who gave her the scar, in Spain. She is not Celeste Dupuy de Crozes. Nor Madeleine du Pont-Clair. Her information sent me rushing to the British blockade off Alexandria, where I was captured. Peraud nearly had me beaten to death.' He closed the door angrily and perched on a crate beside Stanford.

'Spain,' repeated Stanford.

Celeste looked to Petrides again. 'Have you told them?'

'No.' He stared at her. 'Because I doubt you myself.'

Her voice became flat, emotionless, the words quick, fluent. 'Very well.' She seemed to come to some sort of decision. She looked at Stanford. 'You are the official? The *secrétaire*?'

Stanford said nothing, but waited.

With some exasperation, she clarified her question carefully, her thick accent lilting and hypnotic. 'Have you the power of an officer parliamentary or do you hold a commission of the Home Office in London?'

Stanford flicked a look to Wayland and he nodded. 'Yes, we do, madam.'

'Then I say to you – *French Committee, Minister Grommier*,' she said with emphasis, watching their reaction.

Stanford cleared his throat and shifted in his seat. The French Committee was strict hush in the Home Office, known only to select senior officials and the Prime Minister. It was run by the Alien Office, and consisted of exiled émigré French government ministers and officials, whose true identities were a closely guarded secret. She could not possibly have known Minister Grommier was one of the

Committee – yet he was. 'I cannot comment upon any such thing, madam.'

The room was quiet but for the creak of the planks and the sounds on deck; a voice called from the foremast tops and a call answered. Seabirds squawked on the wing, pacing the frigate, some lost in the splash of the waves.

She sat back in her chair. 'I am Madeleine de Saëns-Ivry,' she said. 'Niece of Minister Grommier, and agent of William Wickham's Occitan Group. Since we have come this far, take me to El-'Arish. I have a final proof that will make General Kléber sign the peace.'

–

From Katia in the Sinai, the only road had become a scrub track through dark, twisting rocky passes, littered with discarded French equipment: tin plates, canteens, broken bottles, torn canvas tents, shattered posts and poles, shreds of fabric snagged on gnarled desert tree limbs, blowing in the ceaseless wind. They found an upturned pedestal dining table in a ditch, scrubbed raw with dust and sand, a relic from a hopeful officer on his march to glory in the Holy Land the previous year.

Colonel De Bretagne had been right: the roads to the ports had been clogged with French troops and checkpoints, either on the retreat from the Sinai border or moving south to Cairo – they had to move across country, as Masoud had foreseen. Delphine had begun to doubt they would escape, fearing what they were running towards. Their silent Tarabin escort rode stolidly fifty yards out front, his carbine cocked and ready, hungry to meet any French en route.

Half a mile on, they entered blowing clouds of smoke drifting on the wind, the road almost obscured. As they drew nearer they found the remains of a dead horse, startled vultures screeching and flapping their wings, lumbering reluctantly aloft from its whitening bones. Nearby was a broken gun-carriage on its side, one wheel smashed, the other missing, the rest a splintered mass of planks and spars pointing into the sky, the gun itself long gone. The Tarabin stopped, the smoke enclosing him.

Delphine pulled her *shemagh* closer round her face. Masoud slowed his mount beside her, their horses wary. '*Has he seen something?*' she called to him, her voice muffled by the fabric and the whistle of the wind.

Masoud's horse tossed its head, the ears swinging round, pricked. '*Let's follow.*'

They trotted on into the smoke, heads down, coughing, the wind now their best hope as it buffeted them, clearing the air. Off to their left they saw the Tarabin's horse, tied to a shattered tree, but he was gone.

Masoud put a hand out to Delphine's reins, to ensure they were not separated, and walked on, the horses picking their way carefully through the stone and scrub. Masoud pointed. The Bedouin was lying flat behind a line of boulders. After a moment he turned and waved them to join him. They dismounted.

Delphine shuffled forward on her front and lay beside them. A pile of debris burned and smouldered some fifty yards upwind, the track snaking through the humped hills. Beyond the smouldering bonfire up ahead, the area was littered with dead French soldiers, some stripped of belongings, some partially ravaged by animals, but they saw no vultures. The Tarabin tensed and pointed.

On the far side of the bonfire were half a dozen French troops in a variety of uniforms, sorting through valuables. They sat about, drinking, laughing, sharing a flask, assessing the booty they had gathered. One pointed at a corpse, made a ribald joke, and one laughed, smacking at him, knocking him off the wooden chest where he sat; more laughter.

The scene was disturbed by one of them calling out: one of the dead had begun to crawl away, clad in only a torn shirt and breeches, boots gone. With an agonising slowness, he tried to pull himself through the scrub and thorn. Three of them got up from their places, one eating something, spitting stones or pips onto the ground, and walked over to the man, laughing down at him. One nudged him with his boot, miming disgust and darting away, the others roaring with still more laughter, until two of them brought their muskets down upon him again and again, cursing and swearing, beating at his skull until he stopped moving. Delphine closed her eyes, the crack of bone audible even to them. '*Mon dieu...*'

From behind them came the oiled clicks of a firelock ratchet. The Tarabin jerked round to see the shadow of a man standing above them, Charleville musket pointing down. '*Ehi, qui vive là, hein?*' *Who goes there.*

The Tarabin was fast, but not fast enough, his sword flying upwards at the man's groin and connecting, but not before the musket blasted.

The ball smashed into the Tarabin's shoulder and he cried out, but thrust with his short *yataghan*, the blade burying itself into the man's genitals. The Frenchman screamed, collapsing.

Masoud rolled away, dragging Delphine with him, his hands scrabbling for the pistol at his belt as he heard the shouts from the men at the burning camp. '*They are deserters, Delphine, we must run,*' he hissed at her as they clawed their way to their feet. The Tarabin pushed himself up and tore the empty musket from the Frenchman's hands, smashing it repeatedly into his face as he wailed, the unshaven chin disappearing in a burst of blood. '*Allez,*' said the Bedouin. *Go.*

Masoud rushed Delphine to her horse and pushed her up into the saddle, the Tarabin close behind, Masoud helping him, the choking smoke now obscuring them, hiding them from the camp, the cries drawing nearer. A moment later there came a distant shot, echoing flat and loud in the rocky valley – then another and another, four in quick succession, a fifth, a strangled cry, and a sixth. Beyond came the sound of a man gagging, retching – followed by silence.

The Tarabin froze, holding his rein fast, a hand out to them to wait. '*Tschut, tschut…*'

Masoud climbed into his saddle, the pistol slick in his sweating grip. They watched the drifting clouds of smoke.

The hulking silhouette of a man appeared slowly, the long shape of a musket held at the port, a thin matchstick by comparison, a vast robe over his enormous shoulders flapping in the wind. Another came into view, smaller, striding over the rocks towards them, and another, and behind that, horses and riders.

'*As-salamu aleikum,*' called the smaller shape as he drew closer. The smoke cleared momentarily, revealing *Sergent-chef-major* Achille Caron.

Behind him came Pigalle, St Michel, Rossy and Antonnais, and several mounted Tarabin women sharpshooters armed with Turkish miquelet rifle-muskets. A rider moved through them, the horse stepping up carefully onto the rock-strewn track, its hooves thudding softly. The rider removed the dusty *shemagh* from her nose and mouth. '*Ahalan wa sahalan,*' she said to the wounded Tarabin escort. *Welcome.*

The Bedouin bowed his head. '*As-salamu aleikum ya Sheikh.*'

The rider gave the reply, her voice kind. '*Wa aleikum as-salam…*' She looked at Masoud and Delphine. 'I am Shajar al-Durr. You are safe,' she said in French, and looked to Caron. 'One of your newly found army, *m'sieur le sergent?*'

Caron approached Delphine on her horse, and bowed. '*Madame le Chirurgien*. I am *Sergent-chef* Achille Caron, *major* of the 75th Invincibles, a soldier of General Kléber.'

Delphine felt Masoud react beside her. 'Kléber?'

Caron nodded. '*Oui, madame.* I believe we are all here,' he said, 'for the same purpose. As would the *anglais*.'

A hand to her mouth with relief, Delphine almost burst into tears. 'H-he mentioned you... often, with pride and fondness.'

Caron extended his hand to Masoud, who shook it. 'The *anglais*, he is everywhere, *n'est-ce pas*? At Sais with the *diable*, at Embabeh and Aboukir, at Jaffa and Acre.' He glanced over his shoulder. 'And we know him, eh, *M'sieur* le Pig?'

With a deep frown, Pigalle nodded slowly, a mountain moving before them. 'We stood with him at Acre.'

In the midst of her tears, Delphine almost laughed with relief. 'And, he says, he stood with *you*...'

Pigalle sighed at Rossy and shook his great head sadly. 'We are the heroes, after all.'

'*Putain, Chef,*' complained Rossy, 'you promised that would never happen. It is too, too dangerous to be the hero.'

'And I know of you, Masoud *al-Hakim*,' said Shajar. 'The Tarabin speak your name with honour.'

'Tree of Mother of Pearl,' he said, bowing his head. 'We need your help.' He glanced at Delphine. 'Egypt could suffer worse than we imagine. A civil war among the French. We must get word to Hazar Pasha.'

Delphine felt desperate. 'We are trying to reach Captain Smith or...' She hesitated. 'William – that is, Major d'Azzard,' she said with effort, something telling her Shajar al-Durr had more than passing knowledge of him. 'A great man is to be assassinated.'

Immediately suspecting the Bureau, and the ghost of Citizen Derrien, Caron asked, 'Is it my general? Is Peraud behind this?'

'I... We do not know,' replied Masoud. 'But the threat is to the Sultan *al-Kebir*. How could it be Bonaparte?'

Shajar walked her horse closer and stopped beside Delphine, the horses flicking their ears and tossing their heads. 'Are you the Frenchwoman from Jaffa? And Acre?'

Caron squinted up at her. 'This is Chief Assistant of Surgery Delphine Lascelles, my sheikh. She is known as the Angel of Ramla.

She was with the *anglais* at Jaffa and Acre, *madame*, as were you. He saved her life,' he said, squeezing Delphine's hand, 'for succour, for support. 'And she his. As did you save us all, Sheikh.'

Shajar looked her over, assessing her. The two women exchanged some brief unspoken expression of their thoughts and feelings for Hazzard. 'Then come,' said Shajar kindly. 'We ride for Yussuf Pasha and El-'Arish. I know of one there who can intervene.'

'Will you take us?' asked Delphine.

Shajar bowed her head. '*Mais bien sûr*,' she replied. *Of course*. 'To ride with angels must be a blessing.'

Intikam

To a chorus of shrieking seabirds in the nearby port, Lieutenant Pierre Bouchard of the Engineers put a fully extended scope to his good left eye, and looked out from the high battlements of the fort, gazing across the clouded khaki of the winter desert. After his time amid the sea breezes of Rosetta, and then at the lofty interiors of the Institute in Cairo, the fortress of El-'Arish had been first a baking clay oven and now a frigid cold store. The temperature had already dropped from a mild midday to the promise of a cold night – but anything below 30 Réaumur was too cold for him now. Worse, the place felt haunted, the pall of massacre hanging over the town – a massacre wrought by his countrymen nearly a year earlier, the first slaughter on the road to the Holy Land. But now he had other concerns. He stared through the scope.

'*Mon dieu...*'

The horizon darkened before him, but not with raincloud. He traversed the eyeglass slowly from north to south, left to right, seeing the cloudy humps of distant mountains, the rocky outcrops of foothills, and watched an endless line of movement, drawing closer. Among the rising dust, approaching with the inexorability of the tide, were men – thousands upon thousands of men: men with muskets, men with pikes, halberds and spears, banners, flags, horses, carts, the distant earth churned by gun-carriage wheels, all floating in a deepening haze as they came ever closer. Their number was countless. The Turks were upon them: the army of Yussuf Pasha had come.

'Major...!' he called down from the battlements. 'Major Cazals to post!'

No answer came and he turned, stepping back carefully to the edge of the battlement walkway with its sheer drop, and looked down into the inner bailey courtyard below. It was not a proper castle, with outer bailey or a raised *donjon* keep on a mound, but it had once been enough for the local bey to command the region, supporting hundreds of troops – certainly more hundreds than they had at the moment.

Some of this limited number lay sprawled below, swaddled in blankets, one of them sending back up to him a heckling catcall: '*Ah oui, M'sieur Ballon! Can you not fly up and see him!*' Others laughed along, enjoying the joke; upon his arrival at the brigade from the Institute, they had ribbed him constantly about his association with Conté and the School of Aerostatics: 'Mister Balloon' had been his name ever since. That he had flown in the air had brought a mixture of disbelief, awe and envy. Bouchard felt the loss of Conté, who had returned to France with Bonaparte and the other senior *savants* – his scarred right eye was a constant reminder of their fellowship, from a laboratory explosion the pair of them had survived.

'*The major,*' continued the heckler, '*he cleans his soiled breeches, alors!*' Bouchard listened to their childish laughter – some were already drunk – and felt the first twinges of fear. Mutiny was ever a danger in a revolutionary army: having thrown off their leaders once, little prevented them from doing it again. He bellowed back down. '*Soldier! Fetch me the major at once, or we shall watch you piss yourself on the damned péloton once again!*'

Howls of laughter met this, and someone threw an old sock at the moustachioed drunk. The threat of the platoon punishment drill was enough and, bottle in hand, the heckler rose clumsily from his makeshift bed of grain sacks in the shade complaining all the while: '*Putain alors.*'

Eventually, the grumbling middle-aged Major Cazals mounted the worn steps to the battlements, angry, muttering, pulling at his tunic as if he had just got dressed. 'If the *chef-major* will not allocate stores per *company* then what am I to *do*—'

Bouchard cut him short and handed him the telescope. 'They come, Major.'

Cazals took the scope, glancing at Bouchard's hardened face, the scars around his damaged eye. Bouchard was now something of a veteran – a hero, even – slightly older than the average lieutenant and perhaps more confident as a result, but also educated beyond his superiors, beloved of the *savants* and known to Bonaparte himself: the man who had discovered the great stone in Rosetta – a man to beware, or keep down. Bouchard knew Cazals had seen action, but suspected he might be more at home issuing stores at a depot. His unshaven jowls and lined eyes told of a tired man, yet he had a stubborn, mulish nature. Cazals looked out and Bouchard gauged his reaction.

'*Mon dieu...*' With trembling hands the major focussed the scope, then gripped the leather-sheathed tube more firmly. 'All units have evacuated,' he mumbled as if thinking aloud, 'pulled back into Katia, heading for the Delta.' He lowered the eyeglass and looked out. 'We are alone...'

'We have the signed agreement, Major,' Bouchard reminded him, 'of the *Général en chef* Kléber. They were to stay at Gaza. But they have come. Perhaps they have terms.'

The thunder grew more audible, as if the desert around them announced the coming of the host. The soldiers along the wall behind Bouchard stopped talking, and moved to the battlements, muskets ready.

Bouchard watched Cazals carefully. 'The one pasha has written to the other, Major. And Kléber has an accord.' He looked out into the cold wind and shrugged into his collar of his cloak. 'Since the general did not waste us at Acre, he will not forget us here.'

Cazals snapped a look back at him. 'Bonaparte could have been victorious at Acre if we had been braver. If we had tried *harder*.'

Bouchard felt his gorge rise with disgust. 'By murdering still more? I think not, Major.' But Cazals returned his gaze to the host of Babel come to Abraham's Sinai, as Bouchard continued. 'We are the last on the frontier.' He pointed out at the Turks. 'We cannot hold against *that*. No one can.'

It was the wrong thing to say. Cazals stiffened, and stared out at the sand, the scrub, the stunted, desiccated trees. 'We must. We *shall*.'

Bouchard was baffled by his mix of fear and defiance. 'That is madness. As a delaying tactic, it will fail and count for nothing. This horde will swarm around us as if we never existed. The men are in no condition to meet them in the field—'

'Make them so,' ordered Cazals.

'How? With more liquor than they have looted already? We are at the point of mutiny, *ma foi*.'

Bouchard turned to go. As he did so, Cazals called after him, 'You will salute, *Ingénieur deuxième*.'

The title 'Engineer Second Class' was their equivalent for 'lieutenant', its peculiar class distinction rising even to the ranks of generals;

as far as Cazals was concerned, it certainly applied to favoured *savant* academics.

'I did not approve of your transfer, Bouchard. You should have stayed with the luminaries of the Institute, with the ladies in Cairo. And left this to true fighting men.'

Bouchard swung round, his hand snapping to the dusty black leather brim of his shako, his eyes cast in shadow. 'By your command, *Ingénieur principal*,' he said, 'I request your order to discuss terms for armistice under the terms laid down by *Général en chef* Kléber.'

Cazals scoffed. 'You? As emissary? An officer *parlementaire*?'

'Yes. If we do nothing we may have a mutiny, as at Damietta.'

Cazals stared back hard. 'And if you fail? The *général en chef* is no longer here to save you,' he mocked, then looked away. 'Nor is *M'sieur* Conté…'

Bouchard did not reply, but carried on to the steps down to the courtyard below, in his mind tying a tether to Cazals to see how high he might float, given his copious supply of hot air. As he descended from the exposure of the battlements, he called out, 'Douai! *Chef!*'

Sergent-chef Douai appeared, a short, thickset soldier in a time-worn dusty blue uniform open at the collar. He had a lean, mirthless expression, forged by years of campaign – and understood the situation very well. Bouchard strode past him into the enclosed warmth of the quad, the yellowed clay walls rising around them. 'Latest roll?'

Douai fell in beside him. 'We are missing five more,' he said. 'That gives us two hundred and forty-six. Now we are truly doomed.'

'Hm. Stores?' Deserters often looted the stores before going.

'Only the liquor,' said Douai. 'They found the key. *Sous-lieutenant* Casson took it back.'

'Then they're dead already,' said Bouchard. It was common enough for drunken men to run, but they often ran into the desert, to become a dry husk in the sand. 'We need all the grape or buck we can find. Where is Casson or the QM?' They rounded a corner, the dissipating warmth hanging in airless pockets, hitting them as they passed, Bouchard's eye everywhere, assessing.

'Hiding, I presume, Lieutenant. With the shits.' He sighed. 'The quartermaster, I think, took the last horse.'

The courtyard rose to the battlements via several sets of stone steps, but was otherwise open to the sky. They had done what they could, but there was still a terrible sense of exposure. Men had put ladders up to the walls for quick access to the octagonal ring of battlements running round the rising central structure, a thick-walled two-storey tower they had stabilised and extended, to give storerooms, corners, and walls for cover should the fort be overrun.

But the men were in no fit state for anything. Some were lying drunk, claiming heatstroke, sunstroke or *cafard*… anything; others looked on, fearful. Bouchard assessed the scene with some resignation. These were no Spartans, he thought. Cazals would not have his last stand at Thermopylae.

At last he asked a question which had not seemed important until now. 'None of these participated at Jaffa?'

Douai knew he meant the mass executions of the Turks. 'No. Those have all gone, run back to Katia, so they claim,' replied the sergeant. 'It seems no one knows who did anything. I have my suspicions about Martel.' Martel had been the drunken heckler.

They reached a thick wooden door, supported by ornate Ottoman ironwork. Douai opened it with his key, pushing it inwards as its creaking medieval hinges squealed in protest. Bouchard looked in. The dry, stagnant air was heavy with dust, resin and gunpowder. Lit at the rear by a lightwell from the battlements above, he could see the powder-kegs stacked high on the left with crates of pre-packed gun cartridges. Rounds for the 9- and 12-pounder field-guns stood in pyramids, but promised little help. They had some thirty guns, that was all. He did a quick count, totting it up in a small notebook, knowing none of it would be enough. '*Merde alors*,' said Bouchard, scribbling with the stub of his pencil, then slapping the notebook shut. Bouchard marched out and Douai closed the door behind them with a squeal of iron. They stood still, Bouchard staring, thinking, his chest pounding.

Douai watched him. 'They say they have a hundred thousand men out there, *mon lieutenant*.'

Bouchard nodded. 'Sixty, eighty…' He glanced round. The men were watching them. 'More than us.'

Douai's expression gave nothing away. 'That could call for some clever marksmanship.'

They heard shouts, arguments rising, and the smash of a bottle in a distant chamber of the fort. '*Bon dieu*… It begins.'

Bouchard gazed at the red earth beneath his dusty boots. He unbuttoned his water bottle and took a swig. He offered it to the sergeant. 'Any marines with us, from the port?'

Daoui took the bottle, had a small gulp, then shook his head. 'Twenty at most.'

Bouchard nodded. He had studied almost every aspect of chemical engineering, from the testing laboratory to slinging men into the sky. But none of it could help now. 'Do we have any naphtha? Any—' He stopped himself. No, they had no naphtha, no Archimedes, no special weapon to be dropped from on high.

'The men do not trust Major Cazals,' said Douai. 'But they are proud of you...' He looked down. 'For finding the valuable stone, for being at the Institute... with the *général en chef*.'

Bouchard said under his breath, 'Cazals is right... even he cannot help us.' He stepped out and looked round – the faces that looked back were haggard, bleary-eyed, and many were bitter, resentful. They were the ones left behind. '*Chef*,' he said to Douai in a businesslike tone, 'mattresses to the battlements, palisades to the quad. Call them to arms, and muster for *appel*.'

Douai hesitated. The men moved like spectres, watching them, then looking to one another, uncertain. '*Aux armes*,' he called. '*Appel!*'

None moved. Martel appeared from the shadows of the tower, a murmuring group behind him – possibly thirty men in tatters of uniform. He wandered drunkenly into the central court towards them both, bottle in hand. 'Ha... *M-m'sieur Ballon*...' He bowed theatrically, to a murmur of amusement from behind.

'Martel...' said Douai with a note of warning.

The soldier looked at him, paused, put the bottle to his lips and drank, then spat it at him. Douai tried again.

'*Martel!*'

Martel laughed, doubling himself over, wheezing, pointing at the pair. Then abruptly straightened. '*Non. Non, M'sieur Ballon, non*. It is enough, *hein*? *Ça suffit*. We will fight *no more*. Not for this... this *Cazals*, or this *Bonaparte* who abandons us.'

There were shouts from behind him: men who shared this view. Bouchard looked up to the battlements. Some looked down; some were still at their posts, looking out, watching the Turks. One called down in an unhappy voice, '*Two hundred yards*.'

Bouchard put a hand up to his mouth to call out to them and stepped out. 'Listen to me, all of you! *Écoutez!* The *général en chef* has promised us we are going home – but we must sign with *them* out there! We go out for the parley, then we sign! And—'

But Martel interrupted. 'Ah, the *M'sieur* Pierre de Rosette himself, eh? The *grand monsieur* and his great tablet of engravings…' He laughed, belching. 'You should have stayed in Cairo, *M'sieur Ballon*, with the *savants* and your stones.' He looked round, raising his arms to embolden them. 'Eh, eh, citizen soldiers? *Vive la Révolution! Vive la République!*'

With cheers, the men behind Martel started throwing looted bottles of brandy to anyone without. Others piled into the mob, laughing, pushing and shoving to get one. Douai felt sickened. '*Putain – it is too late…*' One man stabbed at a small brandy keg with a knife, gouging a splintered crack, and held it up to rising cheers, letting the long caramel arc splash onto his upturned face and into his gaping mouth as they laughed.

Cazals appeared on the battlements above, his voice shaking with indignation. 'You drunken dogs! You rabble! You will stand or be *shot! Aux armes! Aux armes!*'

Jerking round in surprise, Martel put a hand to a pistol at his belt, but Douai was faster and dropped him with a shot from the hip. Martel crumpled forward, scarcely noticed. But it was all too late. Bouchard was right: it had begun.

–

A cry went up from the Ottoman forward guard as a cloud of dust rose from the direction of the fort's slab walls, a muddied brown in the grey afternoon. Silhouetted against the cloud, a small troop of horse approached.

Exposed on an elevated mound of scrub, an old man in fur-lined robes stood watching them, his long grey beard blowing in the cold wind. Kerim Bey, personal harbinger of the Grand Vizier, narrowed his eyes as he stared into the western glare. Unsettled by the approach of the horsemen, he gripped the ornamental haft of a tall Ottoman halberd, ready to step forward in defence of his pasha.

Directly behind him waited an escort bodyguard of twenty men in two ranks, porting arms, standing stock-still in long red coats, white belts and long-tailed fez. They were the elite New Order Army, the *Nizam-i Djedid*. Behind them, in a protective ring, were a dozen Turkish officers, Albanian Janissaries and cavalrymen in fez, white turbans and helms, not unlike the Mamluk of Murad Bey. In their midst, resplendent on a tall Turkoman horse, swathed in vast fur-lined robes and a tall parti-coloured turban of red and white sat Kör Yussuf Ziyaüddin Pasha, Grand Vizier to the Sultan.

Yussuf Pasha was a heavy-looking man, Caucasian in features, his pale Georgian eyes narrowed as if against the perpetual wind of the steppe, giving him a vague semblance of the Mongol. Mounted either side and behind him were other amirs – among them Nassif Pasha, his younger brother, his chin down, staring at the distant fort, waiting for the order to pounce. To his right was the erstwhile *Sheikh al-Balad*, exiled co-ruler of Egypt and arch-enemy of Murad Bey: the deadly Ibrahim Bey.

No longer the predatory statesman of the Cairo *diwan*, much as Murad had laughed, Ibrahim was the overfed 'caliph of nowhere' with thick grey moustaches and beard, the aged cobra in exile – yet by no means less dangerous.

Yuzbashi Captain Shafik Reiz of the *Nizami* shifted in his saddle, his horse twitching its ears and tossing its head, irritated by the dust. He looked beyond Kerim Bey at the approaching horsemen. One gloved hand gripped the hilt of the ornate *kilij* sword hung from his broad white leather belt, the other brushing down his flowing black moustaches. He looked along the line: the army vanguard stretched in a crescent to either side of them, waiting in their thousands, several hundred yards from the meagre desert fort, but already engulfing the town and port, both taken without a shot fired. All could feel their urge to charge.

Kerim Bey raised his halberd. 'They come!' he called, so that all might hear, then added quietly to Reiz, 'You could shoot them now, young pup, and take the castle.'

Reiz glanced at his companion, likewise mounted on a horse just behind: John Douglas, Major of Marines from HMS *Tigre*, in full Marine scarlet and black cocked hat, worn at a rakish angle, as Hazzard did, fore and aft to shade the eyes, his skin long browned in sharp contrast to his fair hair. Douglas had served with Hazzard, Smith and Reiz in the bloody defence of Acre over six months before, and been praised by the sultan, proud of his British allies. Douglas led a small unit of British liaison officers within the Pasha's army, a miniature embassy, to advise and confer with the Grand Vizier – and doubtless to ensure Admiralty interests were kept paramount. But Douglas was not the typical Englishman, Reiz knew well, and was comparable to

Hazzard, his dearest friend. So well accepted was Douglas that he was now known as the *Pasha'nin Ingilizi* – 'the Pasha's Englishman'. Douglas raised a laconic eyebrow in tacit comment of Kerim Bey, and Reiz stifled a small smile.

At the head of a troop of three dragoons, Bouchard and *Chef* Douai slowed to a trot, the white flag snapping above in the wind. The trot became a walk, and eventually they stopped some yards from Kerim Bey.

Bouchard surveyed the line awaiting them and bowed his head to the figure he took to be Yussuf Pasha. Reiz moved forward to meet them, but the harbinger raised a hand to the Frenchmen, brandishing his halberd. 'Hold!' he cried. 'Those who would approach the pasha shall wait to be summoned!'

Reiz and Douglas walked their mounts forward. Reiz took the lead, and spoke in French. '*M'sieur le lieutenant Bouchard?*'

Bouchard switched his gaze from Kerim to Reiz. '*Oui. C'est moi. Et Sergent-chef Douai. Ingéniuers.*' He paused. '*M'sieur le capitaine Reiz…?*'

Reiz bowed his head sharply in the affirmative. '*Evet.*' Yes.

Bouchard raised his hand to the brim of his dusty shako in salute. Reiz came to attention in the saddle and returned it. Behind Douglas, the *Mulazim* Lieutenant snapped an order and Reiz's men racked themselves back to attention, the dust bursting at their feet. The horses of the mounted officers behind spluttered, their hooves thudding as they stamped in the dirt, the Arnaut Albanians watching Bouchard with undisguised hatred. Of the four thousand massacred prisoners shot, bayoneted, trampled or drowned in the surf at Jaffa, most had been Albanian.

Bouchard saluted Douglas. 'Major? Or, forgive me, is it Colonel?' he asked hopefully, in French.

Douglas touched the brim of his hat, cautious yet genial, and replied likewise in French. 'Major John Douglas, His Majesty's Marine Forces.' Douglas recognised Bouchard for the educated officer he was, no death-or-glory brute soldier at all. 'Be warned,' he continued, with a glance over one shoulder, and for Bouchard's ears only, added in Latin, '*Omnes meminisse caedem.*' *Everyone remembers the massacre.*

Bouchard inclined his head. '*Gratias tibi ago.*' *Thank you.* He glanced at Douai and switched back to French. 'We can fly no flag for our country here today, Major. Only in hope, for doomed men.'

Douglas nodded soberly. 'Well said, sir.'

Douglas and Reiz turned their mounts, and approached the cadre of mounted Turkish officers behind, the harbinger peering at Bouchard's scarred eye. Yussuf, Nassif and Ibrahim drew forward, the dappled grey Turkoman of Yussuf Pasha towering above them all at seventeen hands. He looked down curiously.

'You are… blind?' asked Yussuf in French. *Êtes-vous aveugle?*

Bouchard bowed. 'Only in the one eye, Your Excellence.'

It was then that Bouchard noticed Yussuf's own bad eye, stricken out by some terrible accident.

'*Kör* means "the blind",' whispered Reiz to Bouchard in explanation. 'But beware, for he is not completely so.'

Yussuf peered at him, tilting his head as if examining him. 'Was it a wound…?'

Bouchard hesitated, Ibrahim Bey watching in mute private amusement. 'Answer him, *Français*,' he mocked in French.

Douglas refused to let Ibrahim take control. 'Yussuf Ziya Pasha,' began Douglas, 'this man comes to surrender the fortress and town of El-'Arish into our hands.'

Ibrahim smiled coldly, and spoke to Douglas. 'To us, England. Not to *you*. We shall suffer no Frenchman to live.' Reiz flicked a glance at Bouchard.

Yussuf ignored them. 'How came you by this?' he asked Bouchard, preoccupied by his eye injury. Though he had French, he spoke in Turkish for his officers. Reiz translated each exchange.

'An accident, Excellence, of science.'

'Science?' Yussuf nodded, impressed.

'Chemistry, Excellence. In the laboratory.'

Yussuf was pleased. 'I am often in the laboratory for chemistry. With copper. We have copper mines…' He looked about, the amirs nodding, then became wistful. 'The elements obey the laws of God, do they not?'

'Yes, Excellence,' agreed Bouchard. 'If only men could do likewise.'

As Reiz translated, there came a hush, and Yussuf seemed to appreciate his views. 'If only they did.'

'Do you command the castle?' Ibrahim asked Bouchard sharply.

'I come from my *commandant*, Excellence, with orders to fulfil the terms agreed with our *Général en chef* Kléber.'

Ibrahim looked back to Douglas, as if Douglas and all he represented were somehow responsible for all their ills. He waved a bored hand and said dismissively in Turkish, 'Pah. All of them should die and Cairo shall be ours.'

There came the sound of a distant shot. Someone in the line shouted, and they all looked – it had been the report of a musket. Then another. Someone had opened fire – whether the Ottomans, or the mutineers upon one another, none could say. The line flexed, a great serpent, impatient, bulging and shifting as men started forward then pulled back, their shouts of rage growing louder by the moment.

Douglas cursed, then spoke quickly to Bouchard in French before Ibrahim could interfere. 'I have had sight of letters from your General in Chief Kléber to the Grand Vizier. Do you give your parole to His Majesty King George?'

Bouchard hesitated. 'I do not understand…'

His glance darting from Douglas to Yussuf and the officers, Bouchard accepted Douglas's offer. 'We do gladly, Major Douglas, and wish to discuss terms for surrender.'

Ibrahim realised what Douglas was doing. '*Duggala Pasha…* You *dare* to interfere…!'

But Douglas ignored Ibrahim and carried on. 'Then I accept your parole, and vouchsafe you and your escort the protection of His Majesty the King.' He turned his mount to face Yussuf. 'Great Pasha, His Majesty hereby accepts the parole of these men and their terms for surrender. They are now under my protection, by law, and await yours.'

'Discipline at the fort… it is breaking down,' said Bouchard. 'I fear for Major Cazals, the commanding officer. And that he may do something foolish.'

Douglas turned to Reiz. 'Can we control our vanguard?'

There was another shot and the Ottoman line parted once again, loose groups of men rushing forward, hesitating, stopping, others filing in behind them. Reiz's features remained smooth and inexpressive, but all could sense the army's impatience and desire to attack. 'I can take this platoon to the fore, Major, but if they break—'

Douai pointed. '*Look—*'

In a series of unceremonious jerks, the French tricolour was tugged down from the flagstaff of the fortress keep. There was a deep-throated roar from the Turkish front lines, fists and swords thrust into the air in victory – and the dam burst. A cataract of men poured down the slope towards the fort, a torrent washing over the desert scrub, their enraged calls reverberating across the camp and distant hills – '*Intikam, intikam!*' – the sound of a roaring waterfall. *Revenge, revenge.* Douglas shouted to Reiz and his *Mulazim* Lieutenant, '*Quickly! Tell your men to mount!*'

'*Evet, Binbashi!*' *Yes, Major.* Reiz called to the *Nizami* behind as Douglas hauled on the rein, calling back to Yussuf and Ibrahim Bey, 'We had terms, Your Excellency! They were to surrender.'

Startled by the sudden chaotic charge of his army, Yussuf shouted, 'It is not I who breach the peace, *Duggala Pasha*—!'

'England has taken terms for parley, and if not so honoured, sir, then the Porte shall suffer the consequences—' Douglas hauled his horse round. 'Bouchard, stay close by me! *Dépêchons-nous!* Hurry! Reiz, *Nizami*, to me! *Chabuk!*'

Reiz raised a hand to his *Mulazim*. '*Nizam-i Djedid! Ileri!*' *Forward.*

'We shall honour the terms, England!' cried Yussuf Pasha, turning in his saddle to give his orders. 'All ranks to rejoin formation! All ranks!' The amirs and their entourage began to shout '*Chabuk! Chabuk!*' – *quickly* – and the mounted officers spurred their horses.

Douglas and Reiz galloped down the slope, the remainder of the *Nizami* and others running behind, the sea of men spreading round the fortress walls, encircling it, the clamour inside reaching their ears, panicked shots fired. Douglas rode hard, but nearly brought himself up sharp, unable to believe his eyes – the French were flinging ropes over the walls from the interior, to help the Turks inside.

'Good God...'

One after the other, lines dropped from the unmanned battlements. The Ottoman troops raced towards them, Albanians at the fore. Within minutes, streams of men were scaling the walls, others clambering over interlocked shoulders to find a foothold and reach the top.

Douglas rode just behind Reiz and Bouchard, his words carried on the wind. '*Hurry! Bouchard, with me!*' Soon they reached the rearmost of the Ottoman troops, men jumping aside at the sight of the horses charging through them, some falling beneath the hooves, Douglas calling in Turkish, '*Hold your fire! All ranks to hold fire! Yeter! Yeter!*' *Enough.*

The heavy fortress doors began to creak on their antique hinges under the weight of heaving men – then someone inside opened them. The doors burst inward, Turkish infantry rushing in on a tidal wave as the Albanians swarmed up the ropes and over the battlements. Within moments, the carnage began.

Not fifteen minutes later, Reiz was carried into the fort by the flow of men, his lieutenant behind, their pistols in the air. '*Hayir, hayir! Durun!*' *No, stop!* The Turkish cavalry officers charged into the rear ranks, shouting down at the troops, beating at them with their crops as they passed. '*Enough! Back to your place! Get in line!*'

Bouchard called out, '*We must find Major Cazals—*'

Douglas beat at hands reaching for him, the troops in a frenzy. '*Get back to the officers in the rear, Bouchard! Get out of here!*'

Bouchard and Douai turned their mounts, riding back to the rear as Douglas tried to battle on after Reiz, his shouts becoming desperate. '*Yerine dön! Geç sırana, geç sırana*' – *Back in line, back to your place* – he cried, the French running in all directions, throwing down their arms – *Non, non, je vous en prie* – chased from corner to corner, bayoneted or speared where they stood, a sword flashing, a head rolling. Reiz fired a shot. '*Durun! Dur! Duracaksın!*' *Halt! You will halt!*

The *Nizami* flowed round him into the melee, elbowing their way through the morass of soldiers to protect Reiz, to bring order as only they could, their scarlet coats enough to make them falter – and the power of the raging river ebbed, the sudden storm abating.

Douglas rode in to join Reiz – *Out of the damned way!* – the furious Turkish officers shouting down to sergeants to take names and mete out punishments. Bodies were strewn everywhere, severed heads kicked in the dust, bloody men standing over them – and emerging warily from the shadows came gaunt French soldiers, their hands up, flinching at every shout, eyes darting, faces white.

As the Turkish officers regained control, troops were formed into guards, and the prisoners marched out. The French survivors formed a forlorn column, watching the Turks with their pikes and bayonets. Reiz cast a glance at a Turkish soldier jubilant at their victory. He muttered to Douglas, 'We have overcome them. But this is no glory.'

Douglas looked at the human ruin all around. 'No, sir, it is not.'

The massacre had spent its force. But Jaffa had been only partly avenged.

–

The Ottoman camp was fully established that evening, and the call of the *muezzin* in the minarets of El-'Arish drifted over the vast new city of tents, palisades and cooking fires which lay stretched out across the town's eastern borderlands into the Sinai. The *Nizam-i Djedid* guarded the one hundred remaining French prisoners – one hundred and fifty had been killed outright in the storming of the fort. Douglas's call to the pasha had been heard, but all too late for the French garrison. Few mourned. Bouchard and Douai had been arrested and sent to Damascus, to save them from the same fate, cleverly putting them under the protective law of the sultan. Douglas was satisfied by this outcome, at least.

As the sun set over distant Egypt, Reiz walked the battlements of the fortress, enjoying the rare high vantage point, aware he was missing evening prayers, the *adhan* call wafting around him. But his work seemed endless: fresh ammunition to the fortress powder lockers; new batteries of field-guns on the approaches to the fort; the threat of Kléber ever present, should he change his mind and strike back.

As he looked towards the last glow of the sun, something caught his eye. A distant cloud to the southwest: horsemen. He stooped to a wooden footlocker by the crenellated walls and pulled out a French eyeglass. Sure enough, in a halo of dazzling sunlight he saw a troop of Bedouin horse flickering in the eyepiece – the southwest, he knew, was the land of the Tarabin. He tried to focus on the leader, and recognised her at once. He heard a footfall behind, and Douglas joined him.

'Doing the rounds?' he asked in passable Turkish, a Persian cheroot between his lips, wreaths of fragrant smoke dissipating on the breeze.

'Look,' said Reiz, and handed him the glass. 'It is the Mamluk leader from Acre. It is Shajar al-Durr.'

Douglas looked, the constant approach and foreshortening rendering them into a blur. 'Dratted thing. Who is that behind her…?'

Reiz took back the scope and looked again. They had drawn closer, larger in the vision field. 'It is the doctor, the Frenchwoman, from Hazar Pasha…' He paused for a moment, realising. 'We must stop them. They must not reach the camp – if Shajar al-Durr sees Ibrahim Bey, there will be trouble.'

'Trouble? In which regard?'

Reiz remained as inscrutable as ever. 'She will kill him. Or withdraw Tarabin support from the pasha and harass the army from here to the Nile.' He was certain. 'She blames him for the loss of Cairo. The Tarabin would kill the bodyguard and endanger Yussuf Pasha as well – and she is too valuable to Sir Siddani.'

Douglas did not argue. Smith venerated all local tribes, especially those who served with Hazzard. Such a confrontation could tear the army to shreds as each sheikh made his own alliances, or it could frighten the huge levy of conscripts into sudden flight back to their farms and towns.

Within five minutes they had mounted and were riding out to intercept them, the southwesterly wind in their faces, the glow of sunset fading into the gloom of twilight. The scrub was half-visible, with unseen pits and hillocks, the horses working hard. The Bedouin had seen them, doubtless even when they had emerged from the fort. Now the Tarabin spread out behind Shajar, their number impossible to gauge with certainty, but Reiz thought thirty at most – enough to cause a grave incident, and certainly enough to overcome two lone officers.

Reiz and Douglas slowed. They pulled up behind a low rise of olive rock and sand, a wild thornbush bouncing in the wind. The camp of Yussuf was far behind them, perhaps a mile. The approaching riders slowed, their leader holding up a hand, and Reiz returned the gesture.

'*Acca*,' came the call from the Bedouins.

'*Acca*,' replied Reiz with a brief smile – yes, Acre, the last place they had met. 'Reiz *Yuzbashi, Nizam-i Djedid. Doogalas Pasha ingilizi.*'

The horses approached, dust clouding round their hooves, the Tarabin fighters with hardened faces as dark as the desert, swathed in dusty dark blue and white robes, Zeinab and her women sharpshooters distinguishable only by their long miquelet firelocks slung below their saddles. Masoud and Delphine appeared, and behind them the three Frenchmen Reiz now recognised.

They regarded one another for some moments. Reiz broke the silence.

'*Sergent-chef*,' he said. '*On se revoit.*' We meet again.

Caron raised his hand in salute. '*Capitaine le brave.*' He nodded at Douglas. '*Major l'anglais.*'

'*Chef* Caron,' said Douglas. 'Good to see you well.'

There was a moment's pause as the parties sized each other up, erstwhile enemies now allies – yet still to be held at arm's length.

Delphine approached with Shajar, the Arabian horses hardly puffing, their breath steaming in the growing cold of the evening. 'Captain Reiz,' she said, overjoyed at the reunion. '*Oh, mon dieu, quelle fortune…*'

Reiz smiled and bowed his head. '*Madame.*'

'Major Douglas,' continued Delphine in French, 'we met with Captain Sir Sidney the night of the raid.'

He bowed his head. 'I could never forget your beauty, madam. I am only sorry you have been yet again put in harm's way.'

'Major Douglas, Captain Reiz,' said Shajar with a curt nod. 'So. Yussuf Pasha has arrived.'

There was a brief silence as Reiz looked away with a small smile, acknowledging that, once again, nothing escaped the notice of Shajar al-Durr.

'He has, *madame*,' replied Douglas in French.

Shajar bowed her head once again. 'And when is the peace to be signed?'

Douglas glanced at Reiz, who nearly laughed. *Is there anything she does not know?* 'We are uncertain, *madame* Sheikh, but Sir Sidney is due to bring the French commissioners to meet Yussuf Pasha here, at El-'Arish, very soon.'

Masoud trotted forward. 'Will General Kléber be attending?' He saw Caron glance at Rossy, neither understanding the English, and Masoud repeated in French, '*Vient-il, le général en chef?*'

Douglas knew he would not. 'He has sent his commissioners in his stead – General Desaix and Citizen Poussielgue.'

'You must tell them… You *must.*' Delphine delved into her satchel for the slip of stiff paper they had taken from the little girl at Faiza's brothel in Cairo. She held it out. 'We must get this to Sir Sidney, and to William – I mean, Major Hazzard.' In French she still said *Major d'Azzard.*

Seeing the symbols, Reiz took the slip. 'It is an old style…' he said with awe. 'Antique.' He looked at them all. 'It is a death warrant. And, usually, a promissory note for payment…' He looked at Douglas. '…for old Nizari *hashashin*… what you call *assassin*, an Ismaili sect, or outlaws perhaps, I could not say. But they were banished long ago…'

'Who is it for?' asked Douglas, taking it and examining it. 'Can you tell?'

'If I have understood it correctly, it says not merely a *Sultan al-Kebir*, a Great Sultan,' said Reiz curiously, questioning his own translation, 'but, it says, a *Sultan of Fire…*?'

'I have not heard this expression,' said Shajar.

'No, Sheikh,' agreed Reiz. 'It is from old Persia, I believe – in Farsi, closer to *shah*. I saw something like this during my training, at the *Bab-i-Ali*. It was from Isfahan or Aleppo.'

'But no name?' asked Douglas.

'None,' confirmed Reiz, turning it over. 'It is quite obscure, as if only to impress.'

'We can warn Sir Sidney, certainly,' said Douglas, 'but Hazzard is on operations at sea.'

'But can we learn who is in danger, for certain?' asked Delphine.

'No, *madame*,' said Reiz. 'But there will be those who do not wish for a peace accord. In the wrong hands this order could stop it.' A seabird cried from the port far behind, and it seemed significant to him. He turned to Douglas. 'Major, will London still use the Third Series cipher?'

'Yes, it's old but still used.'

'Then, God willing, we may have a chance,' he said, looking back at the harbour. 'I think I have a way.'

–

That night, Janissary guards stood to arms at the port of El-'Arish, as the captain's gig of HMS *Tigre* rowed into the torchlit harbour. Oars rising and dipping rhythmically, the long cutter passed the swaying lanterns of various trading polaccas and tartanes at the quayside, their lights casting pools of yellow flame on the black water. A group of dignitaries waited at the dock as the crew shipped oars, the boat gliding safely to the jetty. A line was tossed and secured to a mooring-post by a leather-faced Egyptian docker, and the boat slowed gradually on the swell, coming to a gentle stop.

After a moment, Marine Sergeant Dockery clambered out, followed by eight marines, blancoed white belts glowing, musket brightwork gleaming. '*Hup two three, be sharp about it an' look t'yer fronts.*' They formed up and banged to attention as out stepped Sir William Sidney Smith, resplendent in orders, bluejacket and white breeches, complete with pistol and Genoese sword – followed by Citizen Poussielgue and General Desaix. Desaix joined them on the quayside and stood quiet, hands behind his back, Poussielgue very circumspect, bowing to the Ottomans and holding himself low, as he would do at the Sublime Porte itself.

Smith swept off his cocked hat and bowed to the group, acknowledging Yussuf and Nassif Pasha – and Ibrahim Bey. 'Gentlemen,' he said, letting the interpreter translate into Turkish, 'I understand there was some disturbance at the fort. But it does my heart glad to see the sultan's forces are willing to concede a victory, with the grace such power can bestow.' His face wrinkled into a sympathetic smile. With it came a word of warning. 'And that General Kléber will not consider this an obstacle to our endeavours. As neither shall I.'

Yussuf Pasha listened to his interpreter and nodded: Kléber would not exploit the massacre of the French at the fort as an excuse for further hostilities. After Jaffa, Kléber was very much aware that France had lost any claim to the moral high ground, and Smith and Desaix knew it.

Yussuf Pasha exchanged glances with the others. 'You bring the power of your good King Gyorgy, Sir Siddani.' The Russian form was common among the Caucasians of the Empire, and Smith smiled. 'We are glad you are come.'

'Only some are glad—' murmured Ibrahim Bey.

'And some have the courage to be wise,' corrected Nassif, indicating Yussuf. 'And are blessed by God.'

'We shall see where God stands,' warned Ibrahim.

Smith bowed without demur. '*Teshekur ederim, pasha guchlu.*' *Thank you, mighty pasha.* A leather-bound document wallet clutched under his arm, he looked about cheerfully at the ranks of Ottoman guards, the Janissaries and *Nizami*, their torches aloft, lighting the way. 'Now then,' he said brightly, 'where shall we begin? A brandy, I trust?'

Palazzina

De la Vega, Hazzard and Cook were rowed ashore in a gig flying the royal escutcheon of Naples and the Two Sicilies, and were met at the quayside by a lieutenant of the Neapolitan Royal Guard, in plumed bonnet and grey coat, gold epaulettes, brocaded hanger and Savoyard sword. Behind him in perfect file waited an escort of twenty guardsmen, gleaming firelocks at the shoulder. The lieutenant saluted with a crack of his heels.

'*Señor el capitán Don Cesár. Teniente Martino de la Guárdia Reál. Un gran honor,*' he said in immaculate Castilian Spanish, then turned to Hazzard. '*Signor Hasarde, il sergente Cook,*' he continued in Italian. He bowed sharply, his voice taking on a note of awe, bestowing that medieval honour found only in Italy. '*Commendatore.*'

Hazzard and De la Vega bowed in return. '*Teniente.*'

Cook cast a glance over the guards – their polish, their fine Italian muskets, their bright bayonets. They likewise looked him up and down as if they had never seen such a creature, even in Marine scarlet, one of them whispering, *Inglese?* then switching their gaze quickly to their front.

'Very shiny an' all,' muttered Cook.

The three, however, were dressed for the occasion, De la Vega in a fine black-embroidered charcoal grey coat, Cordoba boots and Toledo rapier, Hazzard and Cook each sporting one of De la Vega's tall collars, complete with white cravats. They had slung grey Spanish boat-cloaks over their Bombay scarlet; Cook's jewelled *khanjar* was just visible, jammed in the front of his dark Bedouin *shemagh* sash, the white scabbard of Hazzard's scimitar similarly bright in the evening light. They followed the lieutenant to a carriage waiting at the end of the quay, the guard detachment marching behind.

Once Hazzard had established that Nelson was not aboard his former flagship HMS *Foudroyant*, as would have been the custom, he discovered that Nelson had transferred his flag instead to a small transport moored in the marina far to the south of the inner roads, nowhere near the main harbour at all. The lieutenant confirmed this. 'Palermo has many palaces,' he said with a strange note of irony, 'but never enough for guests, like his lordship, the *ammiraglio* Nelson, the Duke.'

'Duke?' asked Cook.

'*Sì, signore.* He was made the Duke of Bronte by our king. But…' He hesitated, as if aware it were an awkward topic. 'He stays in Bagheria,' he said, which he pronounced *Baaria*, 'at the villa of *lo grande signore, Ambasadore* Sir William.' He looked away. 'And *la signora*… the Lady Hamilton.' He seemed unwilling to discuss it further.

Cook had grave misgivings. 'Shouldn't be so hard findin' yer own flamin' admiral,' he muttered.

'No, it damned well shouldn't…' agreed Hazzard under his breath, thinking of the words of Lord Keith.

They had heard some harbour gossip from the desperate bumboats that had come out to sell food and wine – they had little to offer, coming more in hope of stores. The city of Naples, they had said, was a dark place, still filled with anger, the hatred for the *Francese* yet also now fear of the king. Palermo, by comparison, simmered on some similar brink. Cook had not liked it one bit, but Underhill had shaken his head: *Clucky little hens, eh, lads? Just clucky little 'ens.* Even though bound for shore leave, the marines had seemed tense – Hazzard had bowed to their ability to sense danger, and he could feel it too. 'Sooner we're safe out to sea, the better,' warned Cook. Although he wanted to get to the bottom of it, part of Hazzard agreed.

Their arrival had been trumpeted about the town. By the time the *Volpone* anchored in the roads with the British warships, Hazzard had received a message. It was not from Nelson, but Lady Hamilton. It was an invitation to a reception at the palace. Hazzard had to remind himself that the King of Naples was also King of Sicily, with palaces galore. With her engraved card came a note in a long, sloping hand:

> Dearest William,
>   The conquering heroes come! (Though you would never have me put it so, I know you that well.) Best warlike costume for you and Don Cesár this evening, (it shall be a small affair, worry not, only old acquaintances).

You are quite the catch and I am fearsome jealous of notable ladies about the court waiting to swoon at your feet.

Emma

Her hand, the light-hearted tone, the scent of the paper, all roused sudden memories of his last letter from Sarah: ostensibly from Naples, it had brought him to the doorstep of Lady Emma – it had at once lifted his spirits, yet dropped them so sadly. This did the same. Meeting Emma Hamilton at the Palazzo Sessa in Naples had been intertwined with his search for Sarah, a bloody street fight with Derrien, which in turn had led to De la Vega nearly losing an arm – and the creation of Hazzard's bond with Lady Hamilton. He wondered if it could survive this strange, dark kingdom. But he was disappointed: Hazzard had hoped to find Nelson at some official harbourside rooms or offices – not a palace reception.

They clopped through the streets behind four large bays in royal livery, Martino next to De la Vega opposite Hazzard and Cook, Hazzard feeling very conspicuous, hating it as much as his sergeant. The big man shifted on the cramped banquette next to him, the chassis springs yielding and creaking with his every movement. 'Ruddy mousetrap,' he muttered, his bowed head thumping the pale silk-lined ceiling with every bump in the road, 'built for a tiny piskie.'

The darkening baroque buildings of Palermo reminded Hazzard of what he had seen in Naples on that first tumultuous visit eighteen months earlier. But this was different. Something had happened here. He caught glimpses of disused gibbets in distant squares down alleyways, beggars clustering beneath them, drawing warmth from smoking braziers. Buildings lay abandoned, derelict, their inhabitants crowding their steps or porticos, huddling together, an occasional bare candle in a broken window above. A revolution had come and gone, and this was the aftermath. Nothing much looked better or improved.

Hazzard half-listened to the Neapolitan Lt Martino on the seat opposite, the Italian crisp, educated, though peppered here and there with the musical sounds of the south. He had a plain way of speaking – steady, trustworthy. He was speaking of Nelson and the Hamiltons.

'No, *signore*, they were first at the Villa Bastioni, but this was too cold for *lo grande signore* Hamilton, of advancing years. They moved to the Villa Palagonia. They lost everything with the uprising in Napoli, so he says… like so many.' He glanced out of the window at the passing scenes of genuine deprivation. 'Palermo has suffered, *signore*. The thirst for vengeance after the revolution…' He hesitated. 'Hundreds executed… the guilty, the innocent.' Martino looked down – with shame or sadness, thought Hazzard.

The horses wheeled them round a corner into a narrow street. 'The empty houses,' Martino said, indicating several in fine rusticated stone, 'were taken, their owners accused, imprisoned, goods and titles confiscated, sold for coin by the *pezzomercanti*.' His voice took on a note of disgust. He looked at them frankly. 'The court does this, *signore*. Not the king. The courtiers will know why.'

The native *Palermitani* watched them guardedly as they trotted past; one raised a hand, as if to wave, but another spat. There were resentful looks – looks of the impoverished, of the helpless, in their tattered sacking and cast-off clothes. The lieutenant watched, his voice apologetic. 'Tonight we go to *La Favorita*, the royal hunting ground, by the *Palazzina Cinese*.'

Hazzard murmured to Cook, 'The Chinese Palace.'

Cook watched Martino. The young man stared out, his voice trailing away. 'Such places once spoke of our greatness… but now, what do they say of us? Our greed…' Then, abruptly, he looked back at them, awkward once again, but sensing kindred spirits. '*Mi dispiaci, signore*, forgive me. The soldier, he is never the same when he comes home, is he, *signore*?'

'No, lad,' said Cook kindly.

'He cannot be,' agreed Hazzard.

De la Vega tried to cheer him. 'But tonight, you join us, *sí*? For the good food, the wine? *Un pu da vino, sí?*'

'Perhaps, yes,' Martino said, distracted.

Through the window as they passed, they saw a squad of armed militia confront a man and woman warming themselves by a fire on the pavement. Abruptly they jerked the woman away and seized the man, two of the militiamen striking him with their pikes, her screams ignored by her fellow citizens, who ran from the fireside. They began to kick him in earnest, showering him with blows.

Cook swore. '*Jaysus shite an' all…*'

Martino banged on the ceiling of the carriage. '*Giorgio! Súbito! Súbito!*' Quickly.

The carriage came to a sudden halt and Martino threw open the door and jumped down, pistol in hand. Two guardsmen who had been riding the footboard behind the carriage crashed to the road and ran after the men – '*Halto, halto, Guardia Reale!*' – their iron-shod shoes loud in the cobbled street, brandishing their heavy-bore muskets.

Cook, Hazzard and De la Vega piled out of the carriage in support, but Martino needed none, marching over to the militiamen, shouting, '*Officiere della Guardia Reale, maleditto stronso di merda!*' *Officer of the Royal Guard, you bloody bastards.*

One had the temerity to shout back, at which Martino extended his pistol-arm and barked a command: '*Prete moschette!*' *Make ready!* The two Guards troopers brought their muskets to the aim and cocked the locks. The militiman's comrades rushed forward, hands out. '*No no no, signore teniente, per favore!*' *No, no, please, lieutenant.*

'*Madre, amigo…*' murmured De la Vega to Hazzard. 'Not the good place.'

'*Little shite-bastards…*' muttered Cook. 'Bad as the damn yeomanry back 'ome.'

The militiamen dropped their pikes and ran headlong down an adjoining alleyway, the guards chasing after them. The woman returned, falling to her knees beside the man – *Carlo, Carlo* – cradling his bloodied head. Hazzard and the lieutenant knelt to examine him – it was a broad gash to the brow. 'It's bloody,' said Hazzard, 'but probably superficial.'

'*Sí, amigo,*' agreed De la Vega. He asked the lieutenant in Italian, '*C'e un dottore qui vicino?*' *Is there a doctor around here?*

'Yes, my own…' Martino spoke to the woman in rapid Sicilian, pointing up the road, then back at the carriage, presumably offering to take them to the doctor, but Hazzard could not follow his speech. The woman saw the royal escutcheon and the lieutenant's uniform and shrank back, frightened, her hollow eyes sunken in dark circles, her cheekbones sharp with hunger.

'She will not come in the carriage,' said Martino, digging in his pocket. 'But this will help…' He handed her a clutch of gold *piastres* and counted them out, speaking to her, trying to reassure her as he put the coins into her hand. '*Per il dottore mio, Fra' Angelico, sì?*' *For my doctor, Brother Angelico.*

She nodded, still wary but incredulous at the money in her hand, then wrapped her arms round the man protectively. He blinked awake, his breathing laboured, but he thanked the lieutenant. '*Grazie, signore, Dio vi benedica…*' *God bless you.*

Hazzard waited at the carriage for Martino. 'Well done, Lieutenant. You know these people.'

Martino paused in the doorway. 'The militia… they gamble, owe money, so they extort, they go too far. They get money from city councillors for every so-called traitor they uncover…' He clambered in, sitting with a heavy sigh. 'But only traitors with property. It is an *infamia*. All is *infamia*.'

Hazzard watched him.

De la Vega got in after them. 'No one man can save them all, *Teniente*.'

'No, *signore*… so I have discovered. And no king has tried.' He knocked on the ceiling. '*Giorgio – vai avanti.*' The carriage set off again.

Cook caught Hazzard's eye. Hazzard looked back out at the streets, lost in darkening thoughts to match the settling evening gloom. He recalled a similar snatch of political philosophy lashed into him with a whip by Citizen Derrien: *The time of kings is at an end, Mr Hazzard.*

Looking around, Hazzard was inclined to agree with him. He watched the people passing by, the suffering made more real by the unknown faces in the dark, the firelight flickering. *Where is Nelson in all this*, he wondered, *and what have we all blundered into.*

They passed through a torchlit stone gateway, rolling parklands either side of the road, the bare distant trees dark against the sky, the mountain a black backdrop to the lights twinkling ahead at the Palazzina. For a 'little palace' it certainly seemed big enough, and was favoured over the much grander medieval Palazzo dei Normanni in the centre of the town. They rode in silence, Lt Martino looking out, keeping his seditious thoughts to himself now they were within the precincts of the royal court.

A pillared portico entrance awaited, Romanesque arches over the stone mullioned windows above, a mix of Sicilian Baroque and Norman style. Scaffolding had sprung up around the building, for evident maintenance. They swung into a curved drive behind several other carriages depositing their elegant charges and moving off, music already spilling out into the hunting-park all about them.

A periwigged footman in livery stepped forward and opened their door, and the lieutenant climbed out, his two guardsmen forming up behind him. '*Prego, signori*,' said Martino, 'if you will follow me.'

De la Vega looked about with a frown. 'Something is not completely good here, *amigo*,' he told Hazzard quietly. 'My little hairs, they tell me so.'

Hazzard said nothing, in tacit agreement. Cook loomed behind them. 'Stick close,' said Hazzard.

'*I'll ruddy say like…*' whispered the big man. He was not nervous, but Hazzard could tell he trusted nothing before him.

The foyer opened before them, dulled stone flashing yellow and orange in the torchlight, tall double-doors, liveried guards standing to attention, tall halberds in hand. Beyond was a black-painted room with an ornate ceiling, dressed with painted vine-entwined pilasters, arabesques and acanthus, bright roses rambling up the walls in vivid pinks and blues. Two fires roared in elaborate marble fireplaces at either end of the ballroom, each large enough to swallow the servants feeding them with logs. A Chinese-styled chandelier hung over it all and, beneath, a long dining table surrounded by nearly fifty merry chattering guests. This was Emma Hamilton's small affair.

'*Christ preserve us*,' murmured Cook.

'I agree, *Sargento*…' whispered De la Vega. 'But, when in Rome…'

Lieutenant Martino stepped aside, bowing to Hazzard and whispering, '*Forgive me, signori. It was not of my intention.*'

Hazzard watched him go, now worried. Their cloaks were taken, and heads turned as they entered the room. The crowd began to applaud. De la Vega and Hazzard exchanged glances, Cook looking to see who might be standing behind them, then realising. '*God save Bristol…*'

Among the cheers, a small orchestra struck up somewhere with stirring Spanish music, as if a *torero* had entered a bullring, ending incongruously with strains of 'Rule Britannia'. There were cries of *Bravo! Bravo, bravissimo*, one figure making her way through the crowd along the length of the heavily laden feasting table, smiling, nodding, giving her hand to be kissed, laughing at various ladies as she passed. It was Lady Hamilton – but not the Emma Hamilton Hazzard remembered.

Her hair had been darkened into a mass of Italianate curls, studded with a jewelled tiara, combs and plumes; about her neck hung a host of diamonds and sapphires on shining white gold, her dark dress of flowing and rustling silk glinting with silver thread. At first he thought it was the queen – until she called to him, as much for the attention of the spectators as for his, the hall become a stage, and she the leading lady. '*William! Oh, William!*'

She reached for him, arms outstretched theatrically. The ladies of the court cooed at the display of affection and the men laughed, clapping all the more. '*Brava, brava!*' She embraced him, kissing him on both cheeks. He could feel her heat on his skin, so unexpected after so long a time, his heart lurching as it had done in those last moments in Naples so long before. She whispered in a rush, her breath hot against his ear, sending a *frisson* of nerves down his spine, '*They know you were both at the Nile and saved Nelson, but I tried to keep you free from it all...*'

Hazzard did not understand. 'Free from what...?'

Among the applause and cries of adulation, Prime Minister Sir John Acton appeared from behind her, perhaps less portly than when first they had met, the deprivations of exile and revolution marked in the lines of his face. Pale and balding further, tufts of hair whiter than before, he presented himself well, if a little bowed, in white cravat, collar and waistcoat, his bright blue admiral's sash, his plain topcoat sporting a single large order on the breast. His white gloved hand out, he waited, his frowning gaze perhaps admitting his culpability in their frictive history. 'Major Hazzard, I believe it is now – no longer Lieutenant. I bid you welcome.'

Hazzard shook the hand. 'Sir John. Things have moved on since last we met at Syracuse.' He paused for a moment. 'Or at Naples.'

'They certainly have,' asserted Emma.

Acton met his eye, perhaps still ready to challenge him, but the intent fading. 'And you have covered yourself in secret glory. I believe we have you to thank for Nelson.' He stood closer, half-pulling Hazzard, who still clasped his hand. 'I know you helped evacuate Jaffa, Major, took Bonaparte's artillery from under his nose, and that you had him within pistol-shot, twice. Not many could have done more in the circumstances.'

Emma looked at him, her expression glowing as she clung to his arm. Hazzard did not agree. 'Perhaps they could have fired,' he muttered.

Emma seemed hurt. 'Oh, William...'

'Never,' declared Acton. 'And none would dare say so within my hearing.' He turned and indicated a closed-faced colleague behind him, in dark curled wig and brocaded woollen topcoat.

'This is Count Thurn, or rather the *Graf* Thurn of Austria, a Count of Naples,' said Acton. 'It was he who sat in judgement upon certain of the Republican ringleaders.'

Thurn bowed his head to Hazzard. '*Signore*. Sir John tells me much of your achievements against the French. As does Herr Hammer. You should be recognised for your feats.'

'My only feat is still to be alive,' said Hazzard bluntly. 'And I have these men here to thank for that. *Capitán* Don Cesár Domingo de la Vega, and Sergeant-Major Cook, the Marines.'

Thurn bowed again to them, a grim smile of satisfaction when Hazzard gave no further reply. '*Die echte Sprache der Helden*,' he said. '*Kurz und punktlich*.' *The true speech of heroes. Short and to the point.* 'Rest assured we are not unaware of your service to this kingdom, *Herr Major*, and to the Austrian Empire, even from afar.' He bowed his head to Lady Hamilton, then to Hazzard. '*Madonna. Maggiore, con distinti saluti*.' *My lady. Major, with great respect.*

De la Vega looked about at the tumult – sundry nobles clapping him on the shoulder, offering their hands to be shaken, kissing him on both cheeks – until there came a loud, slow knocking on the stone floor. Sir John stiffened, looking to the far end of the hall, and the voice of an equerry called them to order. '*Ascoltate e avvicihatevi! Silenzio – per il re!*' *Harken and draw near! Silence – for the king!*

All fell silent, the formerly boisterous courtiers now bending double and retreating as a cluster of figures entered from the tall doors at the far end of the hall.

'*Santa Maria…*' whispered De la Vega to Hazzard and Cook. '*Inclín-ante, amigo.*'

'What?'

'*Bow.*'

Hazzard looked down the room and saw why. He and Cook stood to attention, and bowed their heads.

King Ferdinand IV and Queen Maria Carolina of the Kingdom of Naples and the Two Sicilies had arrived. The ageing king seemed less certain than his wife, his pale, almost translucent, skin washed still more sickly by the candlelight and his round white wig – but he perked up when he saw the three newcomers. Acton stood back, his hand out as if he had delivered them personally. Ferdinand raised his arms and called out in his old native Spanish, 'There he is! For the honour of our Spanish blood…!'

De la Vega looked to Hazzard, baffled, but the equerry was already calling his name once again, declaiming his various achievements. '...*for service to His Catholic Majesty of Spain, and thus to His Majesty Ferdinand IV, King of Naples and the Two Sicilies...*'

The assembly roared with applause for the second time, parting and forming a narrow gauntlet leading to the king and queen. De la Vega was still beside Hazzard. '*Amigo*... you should be with me, *por favor*—'

'Never.'

Emma tugged at Hazzard's hand and hissed, '*Tell him to go.*'

'...*for pursuit of the French fleet, from Naples to Malta, unto the shores of Egypt, for the safety of the great Admiral Lord Nelson, Duke of Bronte, at the Nile...*'

Hazzard looked at him and said in Spanish, 'For tilting at windmills. And fighting the winds,' he said. 'Go.'

De la Vega looked at him, and then to Cook, who gave him a nod of the head, rumbling quietly, '*Jaysus shite an' all, Cap'n.*'

'*Sí, amigos.*' De la Vega straightened, put one hand to his Toledo rapier, stepped forward and bowed once again, then walked through the applause of the barons, counts and dukes of the court, the equerry continuing the citation in his staccato Italian. '...*for actions in the Holy land defending our Blessed Virgin Mother of God, scourge of the French, shield of the Faithful, hero of Acca and the Nile...*'

De la Vega reached the royal couple as a footman appeared from one side, bearing a dark velvet cushion. Ferdinand turned and smiled down at it, opening his mouth with delight as if it were a magnificent surprise even to him. He picked up the red silk ribbon edged with white, suspending a medallion – a white enamelled cross on a red foliate escutcheon, sparkling with gems – displaying it first to the crowd at the left, and then to the right, for all to see as the equerry declared, '...*admit you to the Crusader Order of Sicily, in honour of our royal cousin His Catholic Majesty in our beloved homeland...*'

De la Vega met the eye of the queen and she smiled at him, her powdered skin emphasising rouged cheeks, her fine silver wig emphasising her erect posture, her ears hung with diamonds, matching the elaborate necklace nestling in the glowing cleavage of her bosom. He bowed his head to her, and then to the king.

With a childlike joy, Ferdinand looped the ribbon over De la Vega's head, settling it on his collar, then grasped his hands, mouthing a thank you in Spanish – *Muchisimas gracias* – then clapped his hands, the equerry concluding, '…and hereby count thee friend, and honour thee forevermore in the Kingdom of Naples and the Two Sicilies, *Comandante* Don Cesár Domingo de la Vega.'

Hazzard felt Emma's excitement, her hand squeezing his, the heat of her bare arm burning into him, her finger tracing small circles against his thigh as they watched De la Vega return, retreating several steps from the king, then bowing low, one hand sweeping out in the manner of the Spanish court in El Escorial. – '*Su Majestad.*' *Your Majesty* – then turning on his heel, the crowd applauding once again – *Bravo, bravissimo!* – and closing behind him in his wake.

By the time De la Vega returned, hands taking his, various ladies pressing themselves to his attentions, the gathering once again fell suddenly silent and bent itself double as the royal couple made their exit. After a moment's stillness, the courtiers stood, their voices rising like a tide as they burst forward into a free-for-all for the feast, reaching for their seats.

Hazzard and De la Vega looked on as steaming dishes were brought in by a train of servants. The group fell upon the meal at once, the wine pouring into Venetian crystal, their glasses quickly emptied and refilled. The small orchestra which had played during De la Vega's investiture now provided frothy string *concerti* and jaunty popular Neapolitan tunes, not dissimilar to those they might have heard aboard ship, led by Kite and a fiddle.

By the time Lady Hamilton had led them to their carved chairs padded with shot silk, the raucous assembly had laid into the first courses set before them: two sucking pigs, one at either end of the table, a carver complete with a *maestro de cucina* hat laughing uproariously with the countesses as he wielded his knives; pheasants and poussins; a whole roasted lamb, a leg waved in the air by the *Marchese di Gallo* as he gorged himself like a figure in a satirical cartoon, a bib tied about his bulging neck by a laughing courtesan, another dabbing at his mouth. The wine poured from jug to carafe to glass after glass, the clink of crystal in toasts and salutes to one another – '*Salute, il bravo mio!*' – mingling with the delighted shrieks of the women and the guffaws of their menfolk or escorts.

Cook sat rigid on the other side of Lady Hamilton, as did Hazzard and De la Vega. They watched the Bacchanale before them, the preceding events of the evening playing in their minds, each wondering how many mouths such a feast would feed in the streets of

Palermo. De la Vega took up his glass and held it to Hazzard, leaning round Emma to Cook. 'To *mis hermanos del mar*.' He bowed his head to Emma. 'My brothers of the sea. All that is important to me.'

Whatever the circumstances, Hazzard realised De la Vega had not been officially honoured or recognised in any way – other than by his acceptance by Sidney Smuth, Nelson, and the captains. In many ways, there could be few higher compliments from the reticent English. But to this outsider, who had set himself at naught to serve his friends, there should have been more. Cook raised his glass and held it out, and Hazzard brought his up to meet them both. 'Cesár. *Volpone*. And all.'

'Aye.'

'*Salud*.'

They drank. As they set the glasses down, they were refilled by unseen servants from the darkness behind.

'I hope you are not cross,' said Emma. 'I could not stop them when news of your arrival came. It is important he reminds them all of Naples' connection to Spain.'

De la Vega sampled a rich Sicilian Nero d'Avola red and closed his eyes, savouring it. 'I thank you, *señora*... Yes, they are all cousins, beneath the wigs, are they not?' He admired the colour of the wine. 'It gives them less excuse for the wars that make our miseries.'

'I feel awfully privileged,' she said, 'sitting between two such heroes.' She smiled, a lilting hint of her native Lancashire creeping into her accent, looking at Cook to her right. The two scarlet coats spoke of a silent power in a room of luxurious silks and winter wool. But the heroes did not play along, and seemed somehow saddened by it all.

Hazzard glanced at her. 'This is not how I imagined we should meet.'

'Yes,' she said. 'Thought you would hate it.' She looked at him with concern. 'It is not that the king doesn't know of you. He does, truly, but—'

'I didn't mean that, ma'am, really.'

'Oh, you're not calling me *that* again, are you?'

He allowed a smile. They had had this conversation in Naples. 'My lady, then.' He looked round. 'Now courtier to the queen, it seems...'

'Yes, I help Her Majesty, with the little Crown Prince, with the dailies, with decisions, advice...'

She gazed at him and he could not take his eyes from her. At last he understood why Nelson was so smitten. 'Nelson is not on the *Foudroyant*,' he said. 'We need to find him.'

'Oh,' she said, looking down, disappointed by talk of the naval world. 'He's with us. At the Villa Palagonia.'

Hazzard took it in. The gossip seemed accurate. 'With you and... Sir William...?'

She took a nervous sip of her wine and flashed a smile. 'Yes, just so.'

Hazzard caught a glance from Cook. The sergeant then looked away, helping himself to a platter without enthusiasm.

'What happened,' asked Hazzard, 'in Naples?'

Emma looked momentarily confused, surprised. 'There was a *revolution*, William, only months after the Nile – but Lord Nelson saved us all, bringing us here. Did you not hear?'

Hazzard watched her, but that was all she intended to say. 'But after that? We heard of mass executions, mock trials, riot, Count Thurn...'

Again she looked uncertain of what he was asking. 'Oh! That Caracciolo business *again*.' She rolled her eyes. 'The great Prince Admiral Caracciolo, in the end he sided with the rebels, was captured, and... and the count had *no choice*. The rebels were all hanged. Or beheaded.' She drank from her glass again, looking away, almost petulant. 'No more than they deserved.'

'Than they *deserved*?' Hazzard looked at her. 'Madam, people are starving. Not fifty yards from this table.'

Cook stopped eating, fork paused to his mouth.

She put down her glass firmly. 'They were *Jacobins*, William, *traitors*, out to kill the king. And so I told the queen, and my husband agreed. The same mob that... well, that took Paris... and we lost so *much* in Naples – *everything*. Our houses were *ruined*... Sir William's collections... Why, Lord Nelson grew quite purple with hatred for them as we watched the prisoners being brought out—'

'*Bravo Nelsone!*' said a voice nearby: a thick-necked noble in a curled wig, cravat straining at his capacious throat as he raised his glass, slopping wine onto the table. He spoke in English, pinching his fingers together for emphasis. 'They were the *murderer*, the *filth*, the *escrementi* of the world...! *Bravo Nelsone!*'

There were more cheers from further down the table; the woman beside him laughed gaily and clinked her glass with his.

223

Hazzard looked on in confusion. 'Purple with hatred...?' This was not the cool-headed Nelson he had known – nor was it Emma Hamilton, for that matter. 'What happened? What did he do?' he asked, unable to grasp how she had changed.

'The rebels was *executati!*' laughed a rough voice in broken Italian from across the table. Nearby, a man grasped his own throat as if in a noose, stuck his tongue out and rolled his eyes, and people laughed. '*Sì, sì!* Like this! Haaa!'

Hazzard looked over the multitude of dishes, past a swan centrepiece and gleaming candelabra to see a heavyset Turkish senior officer in padded maroon coat, slit like a Renaissance Venetian doublet, gold glinting at the seams and white undercoat likewise fringed with gold; he was dark and moustachioed, with a fine beard, his heavy-lidded eyes staring from beneath a dark brocaded damask turban. He muttered to a younger, paler man beside him, a court interpreter, who added, 'My general says, my sword is dulled with the blood of French prisoners.'

'Ha!' exclaimed the Turk, interrupting. 'What you know of *that*, eh, *Ingalese*?'

Revolted, De la Vega muttered under his breath, '*Hijo de puta...*' *Son of a whore.*

There were thrilled gasps from the audience as the man leaned back, drew a gold-mounted *kilij* sword and held it up for all to see. De la Vega glanced at Hazzard – they could see the dark, dried crust on the angled blade. There was applause from the guests.

Lady Hamilton blushed scarlet, looking at Hazzard, covering her face, mortified, but tried to save the moment. 'This is General Kaya. He visits us from fighting beside our Russian allies...'

'Didn't know we 'ad any,' mumbled Cook with a frown.

'*Eh, Ingalese!*' The general laughed again. 'What you t'ink?'

The other diners watched Hazzard and the conversation faded for a moment as they waited. Hazzard spoke, in Turkish. '*Chok cesur olmalisin, Ferik.*'

You must be very brave, General.

The guests stilled, the general's hand poised over the rump of roasted lamb. The interpreter blanched paler still. 'Y-you speak the Turkish?'

Hazzard watched the general steadily. '*Biraz.*'

A little.

General Kaya crashed the butt of the sword onto the table and the cutlery jumped; the diners sat frozen, waiting, Acton, some seats further along, stiff as a board.

'Oh, do show me, General, please,' cried Lady Hamilton, leaning across to take it. The general handed over the *kilij* and she marvelled at it, holding it over the table, her bust straining at the fabric for the general's pleasure, as she tried to smile at the ladies and they laughed suggestively with her. Hazzard looked on, the bent Thracian-style blade so much uglier in her hand.

'Do you see?' she said to the onlookers, indicating the blood. 'It is here! Truly it *is!*'

De la Vega set down his glass and whispered, '*I like this not, amigo...*'

Hazzard pushed his chair back, threw down his napkin in disgust and stood, De la Vega and Cook following suit. 'If you will pardon us, ma'am. We feel quite ill.'

Emma lowered the sword and straightened, whispering, '*William, please...*'

Another diner took the weapon to examine and pass along, but the general banged his hand on the table and barked a question at Hazzard. The interpreter quavered. 'The general asks... wh-who *are* you...?'

Hazzard looked at them, their sweating faces shining with the grease of roast meat, lips stained with wine and *jus*, their white bibs spotted with food, the half-eaten dishes before them discarded, the same feast to be repeated again and again, night after night.

He replied in Arabic and Turkish: ''*Ana Hazar Pasha, al-Aafrit al ahmer... Kirmizi sheytanim...*' *I am Hazzard, the Red Devil*. He tugged at the scimitar at his hip, unclipping it from its hanger. '*Malta, Shubra Khit, Imbaba, Qahira, Abu'qir, Yafa, Haifa, Acca.*' Freeing the sword and scabbard, he banged it on the table, knocking over several wineglasses in the process. '*Hadha sayf sadiqi, Ali Qarim Sheikh al-Misr.*'

And this is the sword of my friend, Sheikh Ali Qarim of Egypt.

The noblemen and women moved not an inch, looking on, some whispering behind their hands, others murmuring in the background. Acton made to rise, dabbing at his mouth. 'Major Hazzard is not aware, General, of the political upheaval that has been...'

But the general sat back, nodding, satisfied, and replied in English. 'So. You are he. I hear this name. That he with this name speaks in the presence of Djezzar Pasha, and is friend to Murad Bey and Egypt.'

Hazzard felt his face burn. 'I am.'

Putting a hand on Hazzard's shoulder, De la Vega whispered close, '*Do not duel, amigo. It will give only brief pleasure, at great cost.*'

The general snapped his fingers, and a young Turkish servant came forward and bent his ear to the general. He spoke a few words but none could hear, the servant hurrying off. Hazzard looked at Acton and at Emma, and cooled abruptly. 'No,' he agreed with De la Vega. 'No damned duel...'

He snatched up the scimitar, pushing away Emma's hand, but she grasped his again, desperate. 'Tomorrow morning, the Villa Palagonia. *Please*, William... for Nelson, if not for me.'

But he threw off her grasp once more, shoving his chair out of the way. 'Jory.'

'Too feckin' right, sir.'

The three marched to the doors, Cook throwing them open, nearly knocking down two royal halberdiers waiting outside. General Kaya watched him go with a slow nod of recognition, murmuring to himself, '*Chok cesur, inghilizi...*'

Very brave, Englishman.

Trap

Having enjoyed the delights of several waterfront brothels, the marines of 9 Company broke up and investigated the ancient town; chief among their interests after women were drink and hot food. Privates Kite and Warnock found themselves in an old quayside tavern, settled into ornate saloon benches by a tall, narrow stone window looking onto the dark, torchlit waters of the bay beyond. Knife and fork in hand, Kite looked down at a wooden platter.

'Knocky,' he said gravely, chewing in some form of ecstasy, 'I have formed a tender affection for the pie before me.'

His mouth equally full, Warnock pulled at the crust of his own. 'As have I, Mickey, as have I.'

'And I vow never to leave this place.'

'Amen to that, brother.' They clanked tankards of the local ale and drank, the aromatic scents of onion, garlic and olives, anchovies, capers and sultanas rising to their nostrils. Kite closed his eyes to savour them all and put an *arancino* into his mouth, the meat sauce bursting. 'Oh Gawd love us, mate, these little fat rice balls… I could die 'appy right now.'

An old watermen's place, it was noisy and busy, even for a damp winter's evening. A fire crackled on a rough stone hearth, diners and drinkers crowding into nooks formed by wooden posts and low Roman arches of brick and stone; oil-lamps threw their warm yellow light across sweating brows and the bare shoulders of the serving-women. There were shrieks of laughter or shouts of indignation, the girls whacking the occasional miscreant with large wooden spoons, the stout *mamma* bringing in endless trays of steaming portions from the iron ovens in the rear. The customers were mostly foreigners, some in uniform, some not, the tavern geared to service the ships in the harbour.

Familiar figures emerged from the crowd before the landlord's bar and joined them at the table – Underhill, Pettifer, Hesse and Tariq sat down beside them, each armed with a tankard or glass jar of beer, dragging stools and chairs to the booth. They wore a mix of uniform and sailors' coats, jerkins and caps; only Underhill wore his scarlet and stripes, and he passed unnoticed. 'Now then, lads,' said Underhill. 'Mindin' yer Ps and Qs?'

'Yes, mum,' replied Kite, waving a hand to one of the young women and giving his most winning Irish Cockney smile. 'Watch this – she likes me. *Hoi, darlin'!*'

The woman wore a dark cotton blouse ruched at the elbow, a pearl stud in one ear, a broad black leather belt as a bustier, a small kitchen knife in a sheath at one side, her hair spilling over one shoulder in a cascade of dark curls. '*Che voi, mi amore?*' *What do you want, my love?*

Kite was ready. '*Altro arancheenee*-ohs and *calzonee*-ohs for me *amichee*-ohs, awright? Ta, me duchess.'

She put a hand to Kite's face. '*Per bello mio sì*,' – *for my handsome* – then she departed, shouting Kite's order.

'I ain't lost me touch eh, lads?' he asked.

'You should be in the diplomatic, me boy,' said Underhill, and leaned forward onto the black-stained table. 'Now then, I done a deal, see, for some old rum I had brought onto the Don's good ship – shame to lose it but it weren't much cop, as drink goes. I was swappin' it out for some explosive necessaries and some good Jerez brandywine.' He looked at them in turn. 'In the course of so doin', I spotted me some queer fish come into port – Sardinian polaccas, Genoese and such.' He lowered his voice. 'One of 'em claiming Cagliari to the harbourmaster, but actually a Corsican from Calvi – I heard 'em speakin' their argot, one of 'em cursin' in French.'

Warnock looked up. 'You mean we got Frogs?'

'Near as monkeys, Private. I'm thinkin' of the *Gendarme Extraordinaire* again. Got a funny feelin' in me bones we ain't alone.' He took a sip of his beer. 'Seen the major yet?'

'Not yet Sarge,' said Warnock, possibly concerned, but shook it off. 'He'll be all right, won't he? I pity the Frog what meets 'im in a dark street.'

'I'd rather stick with 'im, Mr Knock-Knock. They *knows* him somehows, as I coulda *swore* I 'eard his name spoke, and I don't like it one bit. Drink up. We got us a patrol to do.' He looked at Tariq, smiling strangely with his beer. 'You drinkin that, Ricky?'

The Bedouin gave him a look, and with slow deliberation, drained it dry. He banged it down. 'Yais, mate.'

Underhill grinned. 'He's learnin'.'

Kite took a last bite as they rose and reached for his coat. 'Hoi – wot about me pies?'

–

'Far enough,' barked Hazzard, banging on the ceiling, and the horses clopped to a stop opposite the torchlit arches of the great medieval cathedral. It bloomed orange in the flickering firelight, bright against the black sky. The devout and the hopeless were filing in for late Mass, two curates and a priest in birettas and stoles greeting all at the great doors.

The three dismounted from the carriage they had commandeered at the rear of the Chinese Palace, driven by a nervous stablehand: Hazzard was determined to get as far from the palace as quickly as possible. The great bell tower of the cathedral tolled above them, a line of torch-lamps flickering over the three-storey scaffolding of endless reconstruction.

Diners and theatre-goers hurried past, occasional carriages clattering down the streets, clusters of the homeless huddling round burning braziers in the arched entrances of darkened mews-lanes, noises from hostelries several streets further down by the waterfront carried on the sharp wind. The lights of the fleet-boats criss-crossing the bay winked on the waves, revealing the towering ships of the line – black and stark in the distance, they were anchored beyond the dwindling stone balustrades on the Arenella road, their own tuneless bells clanging a different watch. The wind off the bay rushed up the broad lamplit streets, cold by any standard, especially to the three of them in their cloaks – but given his mood, Hazzard hardly noticed.

Bloody fool, he told himself, furious that he had let himself imagine a nonsensical fantasy of Emma Hamilton in the fragrant rose gardens of Sicily or Naples, the scent of her heat still glowing in his mind, her hand on his shirt-front. *Promise me you will live and try to be happy.*

'Damn her,' he swore under his breath, striding down the pavement ahead of the other two. '*Damn* her. What was that disgusting display in there? That bloodstained *kilij*, for God's sake…'

'Not the Lady Ham I recall, sir…' said Cook.

229

De la Vega was more thoughtful. 'Acton, their Englishman Prime Minister, and *el Conde* Thurn from Austria, all of them there… with the Turkish general,' he wondered aloud, one hand to the order round his neck, bouncing against his coat as they walked, 'and this, all, *todos in Español*. Was it all for the *diplomacia*? To join with *España*? To please *los Ottomanes*, for the grand alliance?'

Hazzard begrudgingly allowed it. 'Possibly. Possibly they have to please everyone. Sicily is vulnerable. But what in *hell* is *she* to do with it? Ambassador, counsellor? I damn well think not.'

De la Vega made a gesture and said quietly, 'Perhaps just… ehh… vulnerable, as you say, *hermano*.'

Hazzard marched onwards, angrier than ever, his heels catching on the slick, uneven cobblestones. He ignored the sounds of the taverns, the sounds of music, song and laughter. Horses' hooves echoed ahead as he drummed at himself over and over, wanting only to get to his billet and end the wretched day. Perhaps, yes, he would damned well go to the Villa Palagonia and see Nelson – not her, but *Nelson* – and if she were there, all fine and well, but otherwise…

'Sir,' said Cook. 'Company.'

Hazzard turned, alert.

'We are being followed, *amigo*,' confirmed De la Vega, glancing behind.

Up ahead, Hazzard noticed two men on the opposite pavement, about thirty yards further on, meeting a militiaman with a tall pike. The men carried on, heads down, but looked back at Hazzard repeatedly, doubtless noting the scarlet under the cloaks. 'And those ahead?'

'Ahead and behind…' said De la Vega under his breath.

Hazzard put his left hand on the scabbard of the scimitar. He was just in the mood. They approached the corner. 'Ready. On me.'

He turned the corner into a narrow road, tall terraced houses either side, most shuttered, some with broken windows, more homeless families in the street, the nearby taverns louder, drunks propped against walls, laughing. To the right he saw a darkened archway leading to a mews, possibly of the block they had just walked. They hurried, their boots padding quickly on the earth, and ducked into the shadows, watching the quiet road from the arch.

Aided by a stout girl in voluminous skirts dragging in the dirt, a tottering pair of men staggered past, one laughing, the other cursing, half propping each other up, the girl on the far side with a bottle in her hand suddenly laughing and coughing. Hazzard sank into the shadows and watched, right hand on the grip of the scimitar.

De la Vega murmured, 'I see why I do not go on the evenings out with you, *amigo…*'

'Better'n Cairo,' said Cook.

'Evenings out?' asked De la Vega. 'You say this?'

'Sh.' Several minutes passed in silence. They waited. Then Hazzard heard running feet. '*There*—' he hissed to the others. They listened.

Hazzard heard whispering voices, urgent, accusatory. De la Vega had sunk deeper into the mews' shadows and all but vanished, but he heard the ratchet of his pistol lock. Hazzard saw Cook on the other side of the passage only by the reflective glow of his brass buttons in the shadow of his cloak; his sword-bayonet was out, concealed behind his forearm, ready. A shape appeared at the arch, peering in furtively.

The figure turned and called to someone behind, and another man joined him, looking back, looking up the side-street – they hurried into the archway, then advanced cautiously, conversing in whispers. Among the dark bulk of long coats, Hazzard could see on one the outline of a turban, and baggy *shalvar* trousers – they were Turks. The general had taken offence after all, and sent retribution. But something was wrong: they too were hiding.

The Turks stopped. One of them whispered tentatively, '*Binbashi…?*'

De la Vega stepped out into the pale moonglow, the Toledo blade suddenly bright. '*Señores.*'

Cook grabbed the man closest as Hazzard seized the leader by the neck, hauling him off his feet and dragging him back to the shadows of the wall, the edge of the scimitar to his throat.

'*Binbashi…!*' hissed the leader, his hands out. '*Hayir, hayir, dost, dost, dost!*' *No, no, friend.*

Hazzard paused. The Turk knew his rank of 'major' – *binbashi*. Hazzard had not said this to the general, though it was possible he might have picked it up elsewhere. He could smell the man's food, the oils in his hair, but above all the sea, the salt embedded in the wool of his coat. *A sailor, from the general's ship?* Hazzard whispered in Turkish, '*Sen kimsin? Kim!*' *Who are you? Who?*

The Turk put up his hands, waving them out to show they were empty. '*Hazar Pasha…?*'

De la Vega advanced, but Cook's man thrust his empty hands out, and gabbled, '*Reiz Yuzbashi…! Reiz!*'

Cook relaxed his grip. 'Reiz? *Captain* Reiz?'

'*Evet evet evet!*' whispered the Turk. *Yes yes yes.*

They could have heard 'Hazar Pasha' from the general at the feast – but no one had spoken of Reiz. Hazzard released the man.

Diffuse light from the empty mews yard behind casting deep shadow on his bearded features, the Turk peered at Hazzard. '*Binbashi…? Hazarbash'…?*'

Hazzard nodded. '*Evet.*'

The Turk tapped his chest. 'Rafik *Chavush.*' *Sergeant Rafik.* He reached into his inside pocket and handed over a folded note. 'Reiz *Yuzbashi.* El-'Arish.' He pointed at his companion. 'Hassan.' Hassan bowed, and Rafik clasped his hands in prayer, much as a Hindu in greeting. 'Kaya *Ferik. Friend…?*'

General Kaya, it seemed, was no enemy. Hazzard nodded. 'Friend. *Dost.*'

Hazzard then remembered the Ottoman ship in port. They were couriers. They must have followed them to and from the palace, waiting to get them alone, whereupon their pursuers had picked up their trail. He sheathed the scimitar and took the note. '*Choq teshekur, Rafik Chavush.*' *Thank you.*

Hazzard opened the page and held it to the eerie half-light around De la Vega. It consisted of eight lines of numerals in groups of three – a typical Admiralty code. Hazzard cursed; Reiz had clearly taken no chances.

Rafik pointed back to the streets, and put a finger to his lips. They too were hiding from someone – then Hazzard remembered the other men he had seen in the street, with the militiaman. He could hear running feet echoing in the road.

Cook moved to the archway and took a quick look. '*Jaysus shite…*' He looked over his shoulder. 'A dozen, I reckon, comin' this way. A few o'them militia, and a bunch o'wharf-rats, most like.'

Rafik snapped a word at Hassan and moved to the entrance. De la Vega said to Hazzard, '*Amigo*, a dozen. And we are but three. We must *snic* and *snac*, make for *Volpone* at the port.'

Rafik looked round at Hazzard, shaking his head, and proffered a long straight-backed *pishkabz* dagger. '*Binbashi.*' Hassan nodded and lifted his cloak to show a similar weapon.

Hazzard put the message away and joined Cook at the archway. '*Fransaya?*' he asked Rafik.

'*Evet. Denizciler, casuslar.*' *Yes, sailors, spies.*

Hazzard understood the '*denize*', but not the latter. He thought of the ambush in Naples all over again: the swagger of the swordsmen, his first clash with Derrien, and his lunge missing, only scarring him. The bullet in De la Vega's arm.

Not again, never.

He felt his body tense with the familiar indignant rage, and drew the scimitar. *A dozen will do.* Its curved blade glowed dully. 'I want them in the open...' He shrugged off his boat-cloak, immune to the winter night, Cook watching him. 'India Rules, Jory...'

'The last shall be the first – aye,' murmured Cook.

The dark silhouette of the archway became a great frame, figures flitting across it as if in a magic lantern show: four men, torches in hand, running past, the scene flaring with light as they went, windows of buildings opposite appearing then darkening once again. They were dressed as sailors or dockers, thought Hazzard, as Cook had said, but he remembered Derrien's men in Naples – professionals.

Then another few went by – crooked militiamen perhaps, including the one he had seen earlier – jogging past with torches and long pikes, the light flashing and dying away, a face turning towards them, then ignoring the arch. Another went by, better dressed in a dark coat and top hat, in charge. '*Regardez bien alors,*' he called in French – *look carefully* – holding up a shutter lamp, its beam swinging across the street. Hazzard had no doubts: it was another Derrien, from the *Bureau d'information*.

Bringing up the rear came the last two, older, heavier, more experienced, both in long-tailed sailors' caps and tattered dockers' coats, ankle boots and short *culotte* trousers, calling to the Bureau man with mockery in their own language, then in French '*Ehi! Induve sò andati, eh?*' *Where they go, eh?*

Hazzard watched them through the arch. The men continued past, muttering to each other, a battered leather sheath noticeable on a sagging belt: these were not professionals. He heard Rafik breathing next to him, slow and steady. A moment later the pair of men reappeared, and stopped. They looked at the arch curiously. The heavier of the two moved closer, shielding his eyes from the torch overhead as if from the sun, his face cast in flickering orange light as he frowned. ·

In the shadows, Cook shifted his weight, wanting to get at them. '*C'mon, ye shites…*'

The pair then turned, hearing a noise from a cluster of frightened onlookers in the shadows opposite: gaunt, starving, rags for clothes, their belongings in a heap, several tried to run. One of the dockers snatched at them, catching an elderly woman, snagging her bedraggled hair in his fist, pulling her down, shouting at her. '*Dove? Dove sono andate? Induve sò andati?*' *Where? Where did they go!* Two of the men turned back to help, calling out, one hobbling on a crutch for a withered leg, the other elderly. The heavier man gave them a lazy swipe with a club studded with short nails, the old man going down, striking his head against the kerbstones, the woman crying out as they kicked at the crippled man with the crutch. '*Cazzo di stronzi! Bastardi!*'

It was not a dialect Hazzard recognised – *Genoese? Corsican?* – but he knew what it meant. '*Going right!*' he called, and charged out of the archway into the road straight at them.

'*Going left, aye!*' replied Cook just behind, and they parted left and right, the two men now staggering back in alarm, holding their torches aloft, trying to find their footing. '*Sò qui! Sò qui! Inglesi! Aiutu, aiutu!*' *They're here, English! Help, help.*

Discarding their torches, the heavier man to the left tugged at his broad-bladed knife in the sheath, but not fast enough. Hazzard dropped below a wild swing of the man's club and skidded low in the dirt past him, the scimitar blade slicing as he lashed it round at full strength, the man's near leg shearing open at the knee, the bright white of bone gleaming as he screamed and the limb dropped to the ground. *One.* The other lunged at Cook with a smallsword, but Cook scooped it aside with his heavy sword-bayonet – '*Ye shite-bastard!*' – and took the sword-arm under his, lifting him up and twisting with a sudden jerk. The man's shoulder socket splintered, and he screeched, spinning about, Cook dropping him like a felled ox. '*Let's have 'em all!*'

There were cries from the makeshift shelters on the far side of the road, and the terrified bystanders ran, the old woman trying to drag her prostrate husband from the scene. The other assailants came at the run, weapons drawn, a pike running at Hazzard, too low, scraping the ground as Hazzard rolled away, blood hot on his hands. He swept the pike upwards, exposing the man's midriff, the scimitar flying across the ribs, and the pikeman clutched at himself and crumpled forward. *Two*.

Dropping their torches as they ran, the road was alight with pools of flame. One of the running militiamen swung his polearm at De la Vega as if to trip him up, but De la Vega shot him dead with a 40-bore pistol. He drew his Toledo rapier and pinned the pike of another and stamped down with his boot, shattering it, and thrust the rapier straight into the man's eye. Another tripped over the broken pike as he backed away, only to be caught by Sergeant Rafik who held him from behind as Hassan leapt on him, driving his *pishkabz* through his chest and out again. '*Tamam!*'

Hazzard charged two more; they were backing away, stumbling, running, swinging short curved swords in panic. Hazzard parried one to the left, his blood rising. '*Appel! Allez vite hein!*' *Come on!* He flicked the scimitar over the blade and took the man's throat and jaw, the blood spraying, and cut down on the right, across the second man's face and swordarm, charging between the pair, swiping backwards in an arc to cut at his hamstrings. The man arched his back in pain and fell to his knees and Hazzard seized him by the hair, shouting at him in French and Italian, '*Qui êtes-vous! Chi sete! Chi?*' *Who are you? Who?*

From several streets away they could hear whistles blowing and the sounds of running boots, calls in English, in Italian, drawing closer.

Blood bubbling at the corner of his lips, his head back, mouth wide, his face white. '*Semu… de l'Acellu d-diu Norte…*' *We are from the Bird of the North*, the man gasped, '*De Calvi…*'

There was an echoing bang, and the Corsican was thrown to one side, a bullet missing Hazzard and smacking into the man's chest just below his throat. Hazzard turned to see Dideron, the Bureau man in coat and hat, pistol in hand, already running to make his escape. He then heard Underhill's voice – '*Nine Comp'nay! Let's be 'avin' ye,*' and Pettifer ran past him. '*We got 'em, sir,*' followed by Warnock, Kite, Tariq and Hesse, chasing the remainder up the road, among it all the clatter of horses' hooves. Half a dozen mounted *Guardia* came charging up the side-street, at the forefront Lt Martino, sword out, blade held low. '*Guardia Reale! Fermati! Ti fermarai!*' *Royal Guard! Halt! You will halt!*

Dideron ran for his life, the shutter lamp flashing in one hand, shadows leaping along the darkened buildings either side of him, his companions just behind. One of the horsemen fired a long shot and

Dideron threw his arms out with a cry and spun, falling, his lantern smashing to the road. Its oil spilled and flared into flame, his sleeve catching, his collar, his hair. Screaming, he staggered to his feet and stumbled onwards, Martino and his men giving chase, the surviving Corsicans scattering in different directions.

Hazzard stormed up the road after the marines, his chest heaving, his left arm bruised, the hand heavy, the scimitar slick in his grip. The road was littered with dead men, but he felt no satisfaction, his hands trembling with frustration; he had wanted them all. After the sickening feast, it had come upon him: the anger, the losses aboard *Volpone*, Renaudin, Emma bewitched in this place – this miasm of vile privilege – and the monumental unconcern for the wretched. Hazzard had *wanted* them – wanted these men to *pay*.

Underhill and the others trotted back, puffing. 'Who was that little shite in the coat...?' He glanced at Hazzard. 'Y'awright, sir? Hit?' Hazzard stood staring down the street, forehead streaked with blood.

'Wasn't Derrien,' said Cook. 'Dead and gone. Fed to the birds...' He looked at the dead around them. 'If they ain't coughed him up and spat him out.'

'Too many ghosts,' said Hazzard. He checked them as they came in. 'Where did you all come from?'

'Tavern round portside, sir, down there,' reported Underhill, pointing. 'Had a feelin' in our bones, we did. Heard the ruction and come runnin'.'

Hazzard nodded, his blood cooling. 'Glad you did.'

'Aye sir,' said Underhill, looking at the bodies. 'Ye' scarce needed it, sir.'

Hazzard turned to Cook. 'Why were they after the Turks? It makes no sense just for a message...'

As they gathered, three of the horsemen slowed at the end of the street and came back, trotting, slowing to a walk, the horses' breath steaming in the cold air.

'What were they?' asked Cook. 'Frenchies? Sounded like ruddy Eyeties...'

Hazzard shook his head. 'Corsican. This one...' He waved a hand, looking for him. 'He said they were from Calvi... but the man in the coat was French. Bureau probably... like Derrien.' He met De la Vega's eye.

The Spaniard shook his head. 'Not Derrien this time, *amigo*. No bullet in the arm.'

'No...' It was something, at least, he thought. He looked up as the first horse stopped before him.

'I do apologise, sir,' said the rider, looking down, touching the brim of his top hat, nodding to the marines. 'Gentlemen. I rather think he was looking for us.'

He was English – young, a civilian in a dark coat, gentleman's boots and dark breeches, the glint of a pistol at his waist. Hazzard was immediately on his guard. 'And who are you? Admiralty?'

Another rider joined them, the one who had shot Dideron at forty paces, the hooves of his bay thumping slowly on the road surface – another civilian in a gentleman's coat, a sword at his hip, a Turkish *kilij*. He removed a dark, broad-brimmed felt hat, revealing blond curling hair and a tanned face, bearing a few slight scars more than when he had fought at Karnak with them. 'No sir. Alien Office, actually,' said Acting Captain Wayland. 'Like all of us.'

It took Hazzard a moment, but his frown melted away. 'Mister Wayland...? Good God... but how? You're in—'

'Yes sir.'

The three could all see indeed who it was, De la Vega laughing, patting the horse. '*Caramba, Teniente!* Well met!' He slapped him on the leg. 'You say this, in *inglés*, yes?'

'Yes we do,' said Wayland with glad heart, dismounting. 'Sar'nt-Major Cook. You've grown.' He took his hand, nodding to the others.

Cook chuckled. 'So have you, sir... By all that's holy in Bristol,' said the big man, pleased to see him. 'Lovely timin' an' all, as ever.'

'Sorry not sooner. But you had the chaps with you, I see. The steady red line. Underhill... Pettifer, where's your blunderbuss? Hesse and Tariq, *as-salamu aleikum*. And Kite and Mr Knock-knock himself...' He smiled. 'You two have quite the reputation with the Turks, they tell me.'

'All 'is fault, sir.' Kite grinned. 'But good to see the Professor back again, sir.'

After a moment they stood aside and Hazzard took his hand, noting the glove on the prosthesis on his left once again. 'So very good to see you, Mr Wayland – so very good.'

'And you, sir,' said Wayland. 'Very much.'

Rafik and Hassan appeared and bowed to Wayland, who spoke in rapid Turkish. 'Rafik *Chavush. Mesajımı ilettiniz mi kendisine?*' *Sergeant Rafik, did you give him the message?*

Rafik bowed. '*Evet, Yuzbashi.*' *Yes, Captain.*

Hazzard looked at them. 'How did you find us?'

Wayland continued, 'Syracuse told us you were going to look for Nelson or Keith. I trumped for the former.' He smiled ruefully. 'Took us a lot longer than expected.' He hesitated. 'They said you had engaged the *Généreux* in the *Volpone*. Had some trouble?'

'We did, *Teniente*,' said De la Vega. 'It was the bad night.'

Hazzard indicated the Turks. 'Who are these men, Hassan and Rafik *effendi*?'

Wayland introduced them. 'Sergeants Rafik and Hassan, Ottoman Marines, sir, part of the *Nizam-i Djedid*, the best. They were part of General Kaya's troop on our frigate from Cyprus. Some of their number rowed out to us from El-'Arish with a despatch from our good Captain Reiz, now in the army of Yussuf Pasha.' He sounded proud. 'Apparently he had told them to deliver it to you personally. They insisted. I have no idea of its contents – apparently Major Douglas helped encipher it.'

Hazzard dug out the folded note and Wayland held the page to the firelight from the discarded torches and saw the numeric cipher. Hazzard said, 'I'll need a key. It could be Second or Third Series.'

Wayland's companion reached down from the saddle with a diffident hand. 'Perhaps I might help, sir…?'

Wayland indicated the rider. 'My apologies, sir. This is Mr Stanford, British Embassy, Pera, Constantinople.'

'An honour, sir,' said Stanford. 'I've heard a great deal.' Hazzard handed up the note. 'If I may, sir, to put your mind at rest, *Généreux* put into Toulon for repairs…' he said, making quick strokes of a pencil on the note, '…and we believe she's headed this way soon.' He looked up from the message. 'Most likely Third Series, sir, a vertical code. Arrange the integers vertically by threes, then read the bottom of the first column to the top of the second, bottom of the second to top of the third, and so forth, the middle numbers being blinds, then apply the key. I could decipher it for you if you wish, sir.'

'Thank you,' sighed Hazzard, and looked to Wayland. 'What has the *Généreux* to do with this? Why were these Turkish marines being followed by these Corsicans, and who was the Bureau man?'

'I fear that is our fault, sir,' said Wayland, stooping beside one of the bodies; he rolled it over, noting Dideron's shot, and the deadly sword-cuts that could only have been delivered by William John Hazzard. He straightened up, dusting off his gloves. 'We suspect the Frenchman was a Citizen Dideron of the *Bureau d'information*, straight from Paris. Yesterday night his men tried to get aboard our frigate in the harbour, but failed, and when we heard you were in port and attending the Chinese Palace, Sar'nts Rafik and Hassan set off with your message and joined Kaya, being accommodated in the Palazzo dei Normanni. But they were shadowed by Dideron's mob – hired hands, disposable. Stanford and I tried to draw them off, but lost you just before you arrived at the cathedral.'

'What was this bloody Dideron up to?' Hazzard looked away, seeing the homeless families returning, beginning to congregate, gazing at the torchlit bodies in the street, disturbed, uneasy with the violence lying before them, though inured to so much of their own. Further down the road, Lt Martino and his sergeant came riding back with a platoon of the *Guardia*, Martino issuing orders, a horse and cart plodding behind, gloomy in the flickering torchlight, ready to carry off the dead. Two other horses broke off from his group and approached. One rider was a smallish, older man, tufts of white hair at his temples, yet with a hard, grim expression, and was strangely familiar to Hazzard. It was the Greek spy, Petrides.

'*Kalisperah*, Mr Hazzard,' he said. *Good evening*. He gestured at the dead men. 'They wanted our passenger,' he said, Hazzard noting the perfectly good English, 'very badly.'

'Petrides...?' Hazzard looked at him, at Wayland. 'Which passenger?'

'Here...' Petrides indicated his companion. Though dressed in breeches, boots, coat and small-brimmed top hat, Hazzard now saw it was a woman. It was Madeleine de Saëns-Ivry.

'*M'sieur* d'Azzard.' She bowed her head slowly. '*Une honneur.*'

'Perhaps we can explain all, sir,' suggested Stanford, glancing at Wayland. He then handed down the deciphered note to Hazzard. 'If I am correct, sir,' he said, 'this could be rather serious.'

–

An animal screeching in confusion and pain, Dideron threw himself into the gutter in his frantic efforts to put out the flames, tearing at his coat as hands kept beating at him, trying to control him – '*No, no, signore*' – the very air burning, and he ran and fell and ran again, until he stumbled and tripped on the shingle of the shore, women with blankets beating him down, the smoke choking his lungs – '*Fretta, fretta, brucia, brucia.*' *Hurry, hurry, he burns, he burns* – clawing his way to the foam of the surf. The winter sea rushed over him and he cried out, the stinging seawater searing amid his sobs. '*Forgive me, forgive me...*' wailing in French, uncaring now who knew. '*Mon général... Mon roi...*' *My general, my king.*

Carefully they pulled him from the water; arguments overhead – an old woman, a younger woman, bargemen, boatmen – the footsteps of others approaching, and he cared nothing, *nothing*. It was gone, all of it – his dreams of serving the new king Bonaparte, as once Derrien had done, flew from him, and his tears burned anew. With the sudden stillness, the small gathering backed away, afraid of his fear, afraid of the evil eye that had caused such anguish. Silence fell, the only sound in his ear his breath sawing between his sobs of pain. Someone knelt beside him. He felt a hand on his neck, feeling for a pulse.

'*E vivo,*' said an Italian voice with a sigh, almost regretful at this sad discovery – *He's alive* – not from malice, but from a knowledge of what horrors come with survival.

His burning face caked with the salt mud, one eye gummed closed, Dideron blinked into the blur of bobbing lights on the water, the shape of an older man leaning over him. *Doctor?* he wondered. The lined unknown face looked down upon him, glowing with light from approaching torches, reflected in the wet shingle. Then Dideron remembered: he was from the Corsican polacca – the captain. They had not exchanged two words throughout the voyage.

'Citizen,' he said in French.

Dideron blinked again, his lips moving, but producing no sound other than a low moan.

Hands moved him, rolling him onto his back, and he gasped, eyes wide. The captain shook his head, as if weary of suffering. 'I should put the knife to you, for your own sake. But I must not. You may curse me later for my orders to keep you alive.' He looked at the men around and nodded. '*Prendilo,*' he said. *Take him.*

Rough hands grasped Dideron by the ankles, under the knees, under the arms and waist, firmly, yet with some concern, the smouldering of the woollen coat sharp in his burning nostrils. '*Tell the old* one,' the captain continued in Corsican to the crew. '*Find me fish skins, heads, any remains, presto, sùbito, sùbito.*'

Dideron felt the world slide from under him as he rose, weightless. '*Wh-who…?*'

But there came no answer other than this sense of mercy. He felt the air on his blistered skin, burning his molten cheek and brow, the harbour lights hypnotic as he was laid in a horseless barrow waiting on the dock road. The torches left Dideron staring upwards into darkness, the stars slowly reappearing as he bumped his way along the uneven ruts of countless cartwheels, a blessed numbness passing over him, and he thought there was only one way, just the once chance, to serve Bonaparte:

'*P-Perrée…*' he slurred, his breath in tight gasps. '*Portami dall'ammiraglio… Portami alla flotta.*'

Take me to the admiral. Take me to the fleet.

Captain

Some weeks earlier, a longboat had slipped silently across the black waters some twenty miles offshore from El-'Arish. Oars dipping rhythmically, the boat rose and fell on the light swell, the lights of coastal Palestine closer than those of Sinai. Their destination loomed large above them: a dark castle of wood and iron, the portside quarter of Sir Sidney Smith's HMS *Tigre*.

The cox'n of the boat opened the shutter of its swaying lantern, suddenly illuminating the oarsmen and passengers, and the *Tigre* responded, a figure at the portside rail opening a lamp. Other lights flared into life, the quarterdeck and midships leaping into view; lamps were lit in her open gun-ports, showing her teeth. Guidelines were dropped down the boarding steps and the boat's gunwale knocked hollow against the painted broadside.

On the quarterdeck waited Marine Sergeant Dockery and Marine Lieutenant Yolland, a brace of marines behind, porting arms. Out from behind the glow of the binnacle stepped Smith. He stood in his evening mess dress of bluejacket, tall collar and white cravat, and led the way for Citizen Poussielgue and General Desaix. They watched the guidelines twitch as the first boarders made the climb.

'Ah, Mr Wayland...' declared Sir Sidney, stepping forward with Yolland to help him aboard. 'And Mr Stanford, I presume? Good of you to pop by.'

Puffing slightly, Wayland made the rail, his stiff leg playing up, but he ignored it and climbed stiffly onto the deck. 'Sir Sidney.' Stanford struggled up the last step, helped by Smith and the young Marine lieutenant. Stanford doffed his hat as Smith shook his hand. 'A pleasure, sir... Life on the ocean wave, and so forth.'

'Ah, a born sailor at last,' said Smith and smiled broadly. 'My dear fellow,' he said to Wayland, 'you've missed the fatted calf, but we may rustle you up a rather good port.'

'Perhaps a cognac might be more appropriate, sir.' Wayland turned and helped the third and final passenger. Her top hat with bouncing plume appearing first, Wayland helped the lady aboard. 'May I present *Mademoiselle* Celeste Dupuy de Crozes. Agent of the *Bureau de renseignements et information*, and our prisoner.'

Wayland knew the deception with Madeleine's name was crucial for what was to come – the intelligence services, both French and British, knew her as Celeste. And Wayland had no wish to force Smith into a lie if tested. Smith examined her swiftly from head to toe, in her Turkish silks and fur-trimmed cloak. 'From the dread Bureau?' He cocked an eyebrow. 'My, my. I believe I know that name.' His eyes twinkled as he looked from her to Wayland. 'Do I?'

'Yes sir.'

'As you say, my dear fellow,' he grinned. It suggested to Wayland that Smith knew 'Celeste' was a very special French agent indeed.

She gave a brief curtsey. 'Sir Sidney,' but her eye caught the figure of Desaix behind, his eyes fixing on her, puzzled. She reached into the silk clasp-purse on her belt and withdrew a folded piece of paper. She moved past Smith and handed it to Desaix. '*Mon Général*,' she began, speaking in French. 'For General Kléber, and the commissioners.'

Desaix took the paper. 'What is this…? What goes on here, may I ask?'

The lamplight played on her dark hair, her pale skin in part shadow from the hat brim; though she seemed fresh and invigorated, even after ten days at sea, she bore the same lines of her trade that were visible in Wayland. 'It is from the Minister of the Interior, Minister Laplace, through the *Deuxième Bureau* and *Gendarme Extraordinare*.'

Wayland explained, in French, 'We supply this to you, General, in the interests of a peace accord. Just like Citizen de Crozes, we are unaware of its precise contents, but understand it to be of mutual importance.'

Desaix considered his words, weighing the paper in his hands. 'When do the British Admiralty trust the word of an agent of the *Bureau d'information*?'

Wayland had been ready for this. 'When the agent provides a third-party message they cannot read.'

'You take a risk, Mr Wayland,' said Smith with a note of warning. 'I have not read this.'

'Nor could you, sir. As you shall see.'

Desaix unfolded the note and cast his eye over it. '*Bon dieu*... It is in cipher.'

Poussielgue grew wary. 'Can you read it, General?'

'It is the senior command code used by the Ministries...' Mumbling to himself, Desaix decoded the page at sight. He gave no visible reaction – but as he read, he swallowed, as if his mouth were suddenly dry. '*Sacre*...' His eyes flicked up at Madeleine and fixed on her. She raised her chin, in defiance, playing her role as Celeste Dupuy, agent of the *Bureau de renseigenements et information* as well as she ever had.

Desaix held out the letter for Poussielgue. 'I cannot believe it...' said Desaix, looking away.

Poussielgue took it and read. 'What does it say?'

Desaix looked out sightlessly at the shrouds, at the sea. 'I can read *Ganteaume*, I see *Toulon*, and I see *fleet*. I also see *Valletta*.' He said it almost as a curse. 'I see *Malta*.'

Smith held out a hand to Poussielgue. 'May I, *m'sieur*...?' As he glanced over the lines of numerals, he shook his head ruefully. 'Is this *le Grand Chiffre*?'

'And then some, Sir Sidney,' said Wayland. 'The Great Cipher had six hundred numerical associations in its key. This government code has twelve hundred.'

Smith seemed lost in admiration. 'Can none of our fellows crack it?'

Stanford confirmed, 'Not Admiralty, sir, and not Abchurch Lane.'

Smith understood: the chief codebreakers of William Wickham and the Alien Office inhabited small premises on Abchurch Lane in the City of London.

Desaix looked to Madeleine. 'Do you know its contents? I can decode it myself, but it will take me some while.'

Madeleine was prepared for this as well. 'I have this from Citizen Dideron, director of Toulon-Venice, *Deuxième Bureau*. It is from the Minister of the Interior...' It was the missing naval order of Citizen Dideron – which he had so eagerly amended.

Desaix wandered to the midships rail and looked out into the night, his head lowered, nodding, as if expecting the worst. 'And what further...?'

Madeleine took a moment and glanced at Wayland, then delivered the bad tidings. 'It is confirmation, General, of a relief convoy under

Admiral Ganteaume,' she said with regret, 'but bound for Malta. Not for Egypt.'

There was silence. It was the death knell for Kléber, Desaix and the army. Poussielgue looked crushed.

'*Mon dieu*... We are lost.'

'*Vaubois*,' hissed Desaix in a faraway voice. He almost laughed in disbelief. 'Of course. It goes to the great General Vaubois...'

Madeleine glanced at Wayland. 'It was to be used by Minister Laplace against General Bonaparte,' she said, 'as proof that he never intended to reinforce the colony, but only to relieve Valletta, on Malta.'

Wayland caught Smith's inscrutable eye. He seemed somehow to have guessed. The missing order had at last served Dideron's purpose – but in the worst possible way, thanks to Petrides and Madeleine.

'And now you play into the hands of the *anglais*?' snapped Desaix, uncharacteristically bitter. 'Like *this*?'

'No, General, I present it to you here,' she said with honest anger, 'because I could not bear to leave my countrymen in such a position... to suffer in vain hope of aid that would not come.'

She paused, the fragile veneers of half-truths cracking and splintering as she tried to sort them in her mind – but Wayland had been clear:

Desaix must be convinced.

She delivered the *coûp de grace*.

'*Général en chef* Kléber was right, *mon général*,' she concluded, voicing the single truth Desaix had not ever wanted to acknowledge. 'The *Armée d'Orient* has been abandoned. Not merely by neglect, but by design.'

–

Hazzard rode the foothills of Monte Pellegrino, looking down abstractly upon Palermo, strung out along the river to the mouth of the broad bay, his mind scattered by Wayland's sudden appearance, by the scenes at dinner the previous night, the blood in the streets – and by the tale of Madeleine de Saëns-Ivry.

Though the sun shone through the winter's morning haze, he was cold, the bay's breath blowing in steaming clouds like his own, and he nestled into the tall woollen collar of his dark boat-cloak. He settled the crushed black fore-and-aft cap on his head, putting himself in deep shadow. '*Come on now, boy…*' He touched his heels to the belly of the bay and urged him onwards, nimble hooves finding the path among the rocks, the tall grasses waving in the cool northerly breeze.

A royalist French spy, worked by Wickham – and by Sidney Smith, no doubt – to bring down the Revolutionary government. How ironic, he thought, since Bonaparte had now seized power; he could hear him, loud as life: *the Revolution is over.*

D'Ivry's tale explained Petrides' information of the flotilla, and the appearance of the *Généreux* and the Venetian – and with that thought he found himself once more clinging to the heaving broadside of *Généreux* as the guns battered at his senses, the spray blasting his eyes as the bomb *wouldn't fit wouldn't fit damn them damn them*—

He was almost at a gallop before he realised it, the hooves thudding at the hard ground, faster and faster downhill, the bay's ears back, the light flashing overhead through the tall pines, his breath sawing through clenched teeth. He slowed to a stop and fought it off, slowing, breathing. *A nervous attack, sir*, Porter had said, *recurring memories the soul never forgets.* His shaking hands clutched the cold reins, the tang of the leather sharp in his nostrils, and it seemed to bring him back. He leaned forward over the horse's neck, catching his breath, and just wanted to lie there. '*Sorry, boy… sorry.*'

What hope was there for any of us, he asked Porter in his mind, *if our souls can never forget.*

The light played across the waves in the bay below, and Palermo looked a golden city, but its scathed beauty brought no pleasure to his torrent of thought: thoughts of Emma, or Sarah, and a betrayal – but by whom? *By whom?* It hung there, before him, a foreboding Ides of March, but he could not fully grasp it.

And now peace could fall upon Egypt; but he had heard that all before, from Mughals and Marathas, generals and princes, in Kalikut, Mahe, Karnataka – a hope for all in India that a divine blanket of mercy would descend upon them and smother the violence and discontent of years. Yet nothing would follow, he suspected, but recrimination, bitterness and the vicious injustices of some new tyranny. Now they talked peace, yet hated those who would deliver it. That was the betrayal to come. How had Lewis put it once to him? '*Treatified, speechified, making excuses for kings and cowards.*'

Betrayal by everybody. Bonaparte, Nelson, Emma, Sarah, Blake. Everybody.

Down in the bay he could see the ships of the line – HMS *Foudroyant* in particular, Nelson's flagship, abandoned in favour of the undignified scow in the lower harbour. It now served as 'the Admiral', a floating post-office for the despatches of outrage from Keith and the Admiralty – despatches Nelson chose in his mad fever to ignore, while he warmed his chilblains in the soft bosom of Lady Hamilton, self-styled adviser to a cruel throne.

Damn them all.

The horse took a cautious jump over a tussock of grass, a leafless birch shivering as he passed, its dew and night rain spattering his shoulders, and soon he reached the beaten track leading down the hills to the southern stretches of the city.

Of it all, Reiz's encrypted message had thrown him the most. Douglas had signed it with Reiz, so that Smith would know it was genuine: a death warrant, a promise to be fulfilled. Djezzar Pasha of Acre was certainly mad enough, and paranoid enough: he had watched Bonaparte's forces march off in disarray, the cratered landscape littered with dead and dying, the wounded and plague-ridden. What must the old man have sworn to himself in the dead of night? *To throw him into the fire*, he had once vowed, yet Bonaparte had escaped.

And Al-Djezzar had pricked the name of only one, called him *al-Kebir* but named him a Sultan of *Fire*.

If Bonaparte had been the Great Sultan, there could be only one 'Sultan of Fire' in the French Command, a target worthy of a warrant as described by Reiz: the man who wanted peace, and to get his men home. Jean-Baptiste Kléber.

Al-Djezzar, you fool, you mad old fool.

And the key, he realised was not Al-Djezzar, or Kléber, but *Généreux*, and a reinforcement fleet. Kléber was holding out for that. That it was headed for Malta, Hazzard had no doubt; it made sense. Just as with his invasion, Bonaparte had secured Malta as a supply chain first; ergo, he would do the same again.

But what if the fleet did not stop there?

If the French continued onwards from Malta, there could be only one destination. This could be the last convoy to Egypt. If Perrée were in command, and not Ganteaume or Villeneuve, then Hazzard was *certain* the intention was to head for the Nile, where Perrée had bled for Bonaparte, where Perrée knew the waters.

Généreux.

And there was only one man in the Royal Navy who should sail out to challenge her.

Hazzard descended the hill towards the edge of the great hunting park, *La Favorita*, and continued south to his destination: the Villa Palagonia, and Admiral Horatio Nelson. He was to meet Cook and a despatch rider – a boat had come in with orders after the Mid Watch. What orders they would be, he did not wonder.

Soon he was cantering along a beaten road lined with Mediterranean pines, their thick woollen evergreen canopy soaring far above. He passed stone dwellings, then walls, swathes of parkland and sudden streets of cheap, tottering baroque tenements; then carriageways, a tavern, marketplaces, and was soon among tradesmen's carts, and customers going to market, looking up at him, the flash of his scarlet enough to rouse curiosity – *Commendatore, commendatore* – the white Egyptian scimitar bright against his hip as he trotted through them, doffing his hat, '*Giorno, giorno, scusi, grazie.*'

Eventually he came to a set of tall gates on a curving road, a Romanesque pantiled roof high above matching the curve, a gate affording a glimpse of order and geometry, cypresses, gardens and a mews before a tall, compact palace of neoclassical stone. Waiting on a black mount was Cook, shrugging into a boat-cloak, a hard-bitten Royal Navy despatch rider beside him in full bluejacket and cocked hat.

'Mornin', sir,' said Cook, then gave a nod at the house and gates. 'Welcome to God knows-bloody-what.'

Hazzard slowed to a halt and looked up at the villa. Lt Martino had called it the *Villa dei Mostri*: the Villa of Monsters. Hazzard then saw why.

The Villa Palagonia summed up all that Hazzard felt of his experiences so far in royal Palermo – this once grand seat of Norman princes and crusader knights, now twisted by kings and knaves. The villa peered back at the world from behind high walls topped with freakish grotesqueries, figures with gaping mouths and bulging eyes, their elongated limbs and contorted features the stuff of an opiate-fuelled nightmare. Gargoyles in human form, to Hazzard they became demonic souls frozen in mid-howl, their personal hell fixed for eternity in stone. This, surely, was the new home of Nelson and the Hamiltons. *What have they become*, he wondered, gazing at the horrors before him. 'Good Christ, Jory…'

Cook shook his head as he looked up at it. '*By all that's ruddy holy in Bristol…*' he muttered. 'Felt more at home with the Bedoos in the damn' desert, I did.'

The despatch rider touched the brim of his cocked hat in salute. 'Major Hazzard, good morning. Lieutenant Hardridge,' he said, with a strong Northumbrian accent. 'An honour, sir.' He glanced up at the villa. 'Looks worse than it is, this.' He manoeuvred his large roan horse sideways on to the gate and shoved the iron rails with a boot. The unlocked gate swung inward with a rusty moan, and he led the way in, hooves clopping loud on the stone-flagged walkway. Hazzard and Cook followed, the three of them entering warily, visitors to an alien world.

A dishevelled groom in battered leather jerkin and shirtsleeves ran out to greet them, fussing and rabbiting in *Palermitano* Sicilian, that they should have 'gone round behind', but Hardridge ignored him, dismounting. 'He all'ays says that, and all, sir.'

'How many times have you been here?' asked Hazzard, climbing down and handing the bridle to the groom.

'Four times, sir. Turned away each time, with a flea in me ear.' His Durham twang bore a note of condemnation. 'But this time it's different, sir, if he'd but read it. I'd gladly show ye', sir, as yer'll more likely take action as not.' He reached into his shoulder-bag and handed the open pages to Hazzard. They stopped on the path, the tall cypresses either side, casting slanting shadows as the morning sun warmed the stone of the villa before them.

Hazzard handed one page to Cook and asked Hardridge, 'How old is this?'

'One day, sir. Received ten hours ago off Capo Gallo from HMS *Success* herself.'

Cook looked over his shoulder and sighed, '*Jaysus shite*… It could be her, sir.'

'It just says he's sighted a 74 in escort.'

'Aye, sir, but we all know who she is,' said Hartridge. 'His report to his lordship was much clearer.'

'And he's sure? The captain of *Success*?'

Hardridge gave him a look and a wintry smile. 'D'you know Cap'n Peard at all, sir? He doesn't muck about. We all know it's the *Généreux*. And he'll have her if Nelson won't stir himself.' He nodded at the house. 'But will he listen to me? Ah doubt that, sir.'

Généreux. Captain Peard of HMS *Success* had found her.

On the side elevation of the villa, a footman emerged from a door at the top of a flight of stone steps glowing in the sunshine. He bowed as they approached and indicated the way. '*Commendatore Hassarde, signori, in giardino, il duce e la mía donna della casa.*'

They were in the garden, the lady of the house and 'the duke'.

Hardridge marched round the side of the building and Hazzard and Cook followed. Ornamental beds, herb knot gardens contained behind box-trimmed rosemary and lavender, and red-leafed maples painted a palette of winter colour, the occasional shocked and salaciously grinning statuary revealed among alder and thorn. Hardridge led them to a high wall of deep green hedge surrounding a small lawn, accessed through an arched arbour of fading winter roses.

'Lieutenant,' said Hazzard, and Hardridge turned. 'Would you allow me to present the despatch concerning the 74?'

'Sir.' He dug out the page again and handed it to him. 'You are welcome to it, sir, for it'll do me little good – as yer'll see.'

Hartridge marched in and left them, an unpleasant routine task to fulfil. Hazzard folded the page and tucked it into a pocket. They waited at the entrance. They watched three figures in a sunlit corner on the far side of the lawn: at an ornate cast-iron garden table, a blanket across his knees, sat what appeared to be an elderly invalid. With a start, Hazzard realised who it was: Nelson, being tended by a manservant in plain black coat and breeches, white cravat and collar. The man bent low to listen, perhaps to a request, as they spotted Hardridge. In the chair opposite, in morning frock, bonnet and fur-trimmed cloak, was Emma Hamilton, her devoted footman approaching already with a tray of coffee and cups. The manservant took the tray and set it out before the admiral.

Cook stared at the scene. 'By Christ a'mighty... he looks an old man, an' he's only got five or six year on me.'

Hazzard looked and agreed. 'You're a model of rude health, Jory...'

Nelson had become shrunken, hollow, his shoulders rounded forward, his head low, yet bright with Emma's company. Then she turned, saw Hazzard, her chin lifted in hopeful expectation, and she rose from her chair.

Hazzard jerked back. '*Dammit...*' He pulled the crow's beak of his cap further over his eyes, and he and Cook moved back into the main garden.

'Ye can't not see her, sir,' murmured Cook. 'This is all her, they say, all o'this. His man there, Tom, he's givin' her a look, by God.'

Hazzard watched again. Emma passed Hardridge, who stopped and bowed, then carried on to Nelson in his chair. Tom took a pace back and stood behind Nelson, waiting in support. Emma hurried towards them, waving an eager hand at Hazzard, all smiles. Cook cleared his throat. 'I think I saw one of me favourite types o'shrub round the corner, sir...'

Hazzard nodded. 'All right, all right. *Damn.* I did not *want* to see her.'

Cook loomed next to him, looking across at her. 'She helped us once, sir. Maybe again.'

Hazzard watched her approach, his mind in turmoil. Cook made off just as she reached the arbour archway. Hazzard waited.

'William,' she gasped, as if stating a fact, and without hesitation kissed him on the cheek and embraced him, breathless.

Hazzard felt tense, coiled like a steel spring. 'No Sir William today.'

'At the Palazzo dei Normanni,' she replied brightly, one hand to her bonnet as if there were a high wind. 'He's politicking.'

Over her shoulder, Hazzard watched Hardridge deliver the despatches to Nelson. Nelson seemed to slump further, raised a slow hand to take them, then tossed them, unread, onto the table. Hardridge stood stolidly, waiting, delivering further verbal messages, Nelson shifting uncomfortably. Tom poured Nelson some coffee and offered Hardridge a cup, but Hardridge declined.

Lady Hamilton turned to look as well, the curls of her hair brushing Hazzard's cheek. He closed his eyes for a moment, conscious of her scent once again, her warmth, his head swimming. 'He does this every so often Arthur,' she said. 'I mean, Mr Hardridge. Delivers his threats and letters, makes Nelson feel worse, then goes.'

'My lady,' said Hazzard.

'And Tom there...' she said, leaning closer. 'Well, Mr Allen, I call him. Norfolk. Strong as a drayhorse. Always with him. When King Ferdinand met him, he offered the royal hand to be kissed and Tom shook it, saying, "How d'you do, Mr King?" He's...' The words caught in her throat as she searched for things to say. 'He's... awfully *good.* Yes. For... For him... some memory of... of home...'

'Emma,' said Hazzard.

With a jolt, she turned to him, startled, flushed. 'You called me Emma.'

Hazzard looked into her eyes. He could not understand the previous night – the villainy of the palace, her vanity, her harshness: *They were rebels, all they deserved, William.*

'I did.'

She put a hand to his neck, the side of his face, her silk gloves warm against his skin, and he closed his eyes again, his head down, taking a controlled breath, unable to bear her proximity.

'My God, William, what have they done to you…'

Abruptly he broke away from her, hearing with horror the same words in his memory, the *very words* spoken by Sarah when he had arrived home, hacked and battered at the Cape, unable to stand, unable to walk. '*No…*'

'Oh no no, forgive me,' she said in gentle urgency, her arms taking him, holding him. 'God, no, this world of men… You tear each other apart and… and no one questions, thinks of the *cost…*' She put her head against his chest. 'Oh, that you are alive. Just *alive.*'

Her hair crushed against his face, his nose, filling his mouth, and he breathed her in. 'And you… my lady.'

'I know you think it, but I've not changed,' she said, not looking up, her voice thick with some great sadness. 'I've *not*, you see, I am, I'm just…' She looked up at him.

'Alive.'

Her voice a whisper. '*Yes.*'

He looked over at Nelson and Hardridge. 'Do you love him?'

She did not hesitate. He could feel her sobs, her breast against his, the convulsion as she wept. 'Yes…'

'And you love your husband.'

'*Yes,*' she sighed, trying to collect herself. 'He knows. He bought me, William. He *bought* me and my troubles, at *cards*, only to save me from that dreadful house Uppark…' She sniffed, a kerchief in hand. 'They used to *strip me* and make me dance on the table… but William saved me,' her weeping a small cry. 'And they blamed me, they always *blamed me*. And all I do is *love.*'

He looked down at her and, without making the decision, his fingers delved into her hair, to capture her, as they all had done to her, and he was bringing her mouth up to his. '*I don't… I don't care what they think…*'

252

Her silken hands holding him still while she tried to consume him, and he her, his arms tight round her waist, the pair sank into the green leaf of the arbour, her grace lifting from him the burdens crushing him, driving him – and he felt free, weightless, floating in calm waters and no longer struggling in the depths – until he resurfaced, and pulled away slowly. He gazed at her, his voice soft but insistent. 'Stop all this, Emma. Stop it all now. Leave him be, for your sake as well as his,' he said gently. 'You will destroy the world. Only he can save it.'

She shook her head, imploring, wanting to understand, yet refusing. 'Whose world, William? Yours? His? Mine?' She kissed him again. 'My world hangs always in tatters. I am in tatters...'

It was the truest sorrow he had yet heard, and he felt her anguish, but had no balm to offer, no cure. He could hear the harsh footfall of Hardridge across the lawn, his steady march, and they separated, a feeling of something tearing apart between them, ripping away from him, a clotted bandage from a dried and bloody wound. When he looked up, he found Hardridge watching them in the archway of green.

'I have done my all sir,' he said quietly. 'My all.' He removed his hat, his eyes blinking, confused, having visited a benign grandfather slowly slipping away from a loving family, his care bringing him nothing but pain as well. 'Damn this place,' he whispered. He replaced his hat, his gaze swivelling like guns to bear, as if making a decision never to return. 'I can do no more.' He glanced at Lady Hamilton. 'Though others clearly have done too much.'

Hardridge bore off back down the path to the stables, shouting for the groom once more, '*Presto, ye dam' basta'd!*' Hazzard watched him and wanted to call after him, but looked instead to Emma. 'It will end, you know. All of this.'

'I know,' she said, tearful. 'It always does.'

'And I shall end it.'

She shook her head, one gloved hand before her mouth, weeping again, her words pleading. '*Please do not.*'

He spoke his last to her, the pain cloying in his throat. 'I must.'

He pulled further from her, her hand taking his and she cried her small cry again, '*William...*' But Hazzard had gone.

He walked across the lawn, the figure in the corner growing as he drew near. Tom Allen looking up, the table, the chairs, the coffee-pot, the cups, the despatches, Hazzard noting all in some strange disconnected vision – until suddenly he was there, looking down at the admiral.

Nelson looked up.

'Sir,' said Nelson. 'You are come, I see.'

'Sir,' replied Hazzard, with a bow of the head, his face set and grim, the crow's beak of his hat casting him in shadow. He nodded in compliment to the valet. 'Mr Allen, a good morning to you.'

'And you, Mr 'Azzard,' said the servant in the broadest Norfolk. 'Glad you be with us still, after all your travails.'

'And you, with his lordship.'

Allen nodded his sturdy, rock-like head. He looked down at Nelson. 'My lord.'

Nelson nodded. 'Thank you, Tom.'

They waited till Allen had made his way back to the footman at the house, giving them time alone.

'You seem well, my lord.'

Nelson regarded him warily. 'Good heavens. A courtesy and well-wishing. This is not the Mr Hazzard I recall. Where, I wonder, is the fire gone.'

'There seems scant fire here either, sir.'

Nelson's face nearly clouded with anger, but cleared with understanding. 'Ah.' He nodded. 'So. Young Hardridge fails, spent, and you cut in astern with fresh powder, point-blank. A fine tactic.'

Hazzard watched him. He recognised perhaps what others would not: the remnants of some deep wound, both injury and insult. Giving the Levant to Sir Sidney Smith after the resounding victory of the Nile had been bad enough, but being leap-frogged by Keith for the command of the Mediterranean Fleet was clearly a slight too far. Keith was respected but unloved. This man, however, as Hazzard knew very well from that evening on HMS *Vanguard* at Alexandria, was worshipped.

Yet Hazzard suspected that Nelson was not being kept fully informed in his present condition, perhaps for fear of information being leaked to the Neapolitan court through Lady Hamilton. It seemed unlikely that Nelson would have heard of *Volpone*'s attack on *Généreux* out here in isolation – he would have mentioned it to Hazzard, if not from simple curiosity, or perhaps even out of envy.

Nelson sat forward, wincing, touching his head. 'Constant headache,' he gasped. 'Constant.'

Hazzard sat on the chair opposite, the cold of the cast iron creeping slowly through his woollen boat-cloak and breeches. He removed his hat, the sun warming his face. He watched Nelson. 'Your head wound, sir? Is it your vision?'

Nelson nodded, tired. 'One good eye, one bad... Physicians think five bowel movements a day will cure it.'

Hazzard looked across the garden, at the sunshine advancing gently across the lawns, the shadows of the hedge wall around them diminishing by slow degrees. 'If my right arm is exposed to the sun too much...' he murmured, 'I feel the fire from *Orient*.'

Nelson watched him in turn. 'Time is not the greatest healer, it seems.' He dropped his remaining hand from his face. 'Our St Crispin's Day, what?'

'Sir.' Hazzard thought of Wayland – these were the words he had used when last they had parted on the *Tigre*, nearly a year ago. 'I must ask, sir...' He hesitated, as if he had no wish to learn the truth, deep down, if it were bad news – it would be simply too much now. 'Have you heard of Lt Tomlinson since? Had any news of *Valiant*?'

Nelson frowned and sat back with a sigh, trying to recall. 'Since her journey home...? I believe so,' he mumbled. 'I believe so... to Motherbank, to Spithead with despatches, then round to Deptford... Tilbury, I had thought, but...'

Motherbank at the Solent and the Isle of Wight, the sandbar which all captains knew, the anchorage of merchantmen and old hulks and the gateway to Portsmouth, Spithead and Southampton docks; then round Kent to the Thames and upriver to Tilbury, her final disport in Essex – followed by a mournful carriage drive north to Suffolk and Minster House, and a grieving family.

Hazzard felt a lurch of sickness, a recurrence of his worst fears. From Nelson, it was neither a yea nor a nay, and perhaps all he could offer at the moment in his state. The uncertainty was, in a way, a relief for Hazzard, as if there were some safety in ignorance.

After a considerable silence, he asked, 'Do the events of Naples still trouble you, sir?' It was something Hazzard wanted to understand: what had happened to Emma, what had happened to the fleet, the royal court, to all of them – to uncover what had brought them to be overtaken by such bloody vengeance, and for the Navy to have cast out their greatest commander. 'The Admiralty seems reluctant to forgive. Or understand.'

Nelson let out a long, drawn-out sigh, a man in need of confession. 'I *know* Hardy and Troubridge were disappointed at our position... and poor Foote was placed in a terrible spot. But rebels took up arms against our ally, a *king*, whose ports and good graces we *need*.' Angry again, he slapped his thigh. 'We were bound – *bound*, I say – by law, and... and, yes... expediency, I admit.' His eyes closed, and he took a steadying breath. 'I must leave this place, but I... I cannot. I am... tied. Bound as well, by the expediency of others.' He looked at Hazzard, his eyes frank with some realisation. 'Smith wrote to me of you, you know. That you were a good man. A good man.' He considered his own words and looked away, lost in thought. 'I wrote to him that I had known this the day you fell onto my deck from a fisherman's net. And I knew as I saw *Orient* and the French line, that this was your doing. And someone swore they saw scarlet on the French quarterdeck. Swore it, and I knew. I knew. This was your tethered goat... for my tigers.' He had never admitted as such before – not to Hazzard. The memory seemed to bring back his pain. 'I must leave, yes. But not to serve under an... an *old maid* whittering on about command and tactics, yet who has never wielded so much as a skiff in battle.'

Hazzard thought of his own resignation, his disgust with the Admiralty, with Blake, and Sir Rafe Lewis. Of all things, Hazzard understood Nelson's frustrations. 'Lord Keith sir?'

Nelson cursed and snapped, 'How many times must I explain to that dull-witted Scot, that Jack Jervis called the Mediterranean the French Lake for good reason!' His face screwed up in anger. 'When the French treated with Naples to close their doors upon us, we had nowhere to go. Nowhere, sir! And now I am sworn to keep those gates *open*.'

'And there an end to it.'

'Yes by God. I shan't be wheedled at to guard Malta like a... a prize eunuch, to please the dour, *untested* George blasted Elphinstone-cum-Keith.'

This indiscretion alone was unlike Nelson, thought Hazzard. He was angry. Perhaps he was more restrained with naval officers such as Troubridge and others; Hazzard was, he knew, an outsider, not a member of the tight-knit Navy family. Confession to a stranger was infinitely easier.

Nelson drifted off again, looking away, and Hazzard knew it was time to bring him round. 'Do you recall a Captain Peard, sir?'

After a moment, Nelson did. 'Shuldham.' He said, glancing at him. 'Shuldham Peard, yes. Believe I shook his hand.'

'Captain, HMS *Success*, sir.'

'Yes. Thirty-two guns. Swift frigate. Good lines.'

'Yes sir. Have you read his report about Toulon?'

'Report?' Nelson sat more upright in his chair. 'Which report?'

Hazzard was right: Keith had not told him everything, only snapped orders at him. He glanced at the despatches lying on the table, the pages bouncing gently in the slight breeze. Hazzard picked up one of them and read through it: a private letter from Sir Thomas Troubridge, entreating him to return to the fleet. Another was an imperious demand from Lord Keith, summoning 'the Rear Admiral to come to duty' – as if he had previously been shirking. Hazzard read the second page and the Admiralty order: ...*heavy battalion of said 500 Portuguese Marines to be replaced by 1200 Neapolitan Foot vouchsafed by King Ferdinand, to be conveyed to Commander Land Forces Malta, by Vice-Admiral the Lord Keith, Rear-Admiral the Lord Nelson to support in HMS Foudroyant (74), with HMS Northumberland (74), and HMS Audacious (74)...*

This too he put down. He looked at Nelson. The moment was right. 'I see there is something they have not explained, sir. About the Nile.'

'The Nile?' Nelson's interest was immediately piqued, a new energy rousing him to curiosity. 'What news of the Nile?'

Hazzard took out the folded despatch given to him by Hardridge. 'Lord Keith believes this is solely a mission to reinforce our troops on Malta by the King of Naples, nothing more. However...' He opened it for Nelson to take in his left hand. 'Captain Peard has found a 74 in escort with several frigates and troop transports. She's now been sighted off Trapani, heading south.'

'A lone 74?'

Hazzard gave it a moment. 'Peard says it's the *Généreux*, sir. And we can get her.'

Hazzard knew how Nelson would react. After the Battle of the Nile, Hazzard would have reacted in the same way.

Généreux: the one that got away.

Nelson took the letter in his left hand and held it out to read, favouring his good eye. Hazzard watched him. After a few moments the page shook slightly in his grip, and he lowered it. Hazzard's heart sank. Clearly it had been too much – this was now something beyond even Nelson.

But Nelson gazed through the stiff page into the unseen, his mouth tightening. 'Yes... *Yes*, by God...' Hazzard watched with renewed hope as Nelson rose slowly from his chair, reading it again, the blanket slipping from his lap to the grass. 'A 74... in close escort, frigates, three, transports to lee. So. She comes not alone. She brings a *fleet*, sir... a *landing* fleet.' He looked at Hazzard. 'What else do we know?'

'Intelligence reports this flotilla from Toulon will likely be under Rear-Admiral Perrée, sir. Bonaparte's commodore from the Nile.'

Nelson leaned on the edge of the ornate table and Hazzard rose to offer support. Nelson looked round sharply. 'Perrée? He may *not*. His parole to Markham specifically forbade him. Else this is an actionable crime—'

'Precisely, sir. The French believe you unfit, unable to intercept, no longer in command. What else could entice Perrée to break his parole but this rare chance?'

'And Ganteaume sits idle in harbour,' Nelson mused, something within him rekindled. He looked down at the page, his eyes drifting again. '*Généreux*...'

To avenge the Nile. To avenge Captain Thompson of the *Leander*. To avenge Sarah and the *Valiant*... he could not be sure. Hazzard thought of Shepherd on the *Volpone*, and his wretched fate. 'Given the chance, Captain Peard will try to bring her down himself in the *Success*, sir, I know it,' he warned. 'He could sail rings round her, but not without the Devil's own luck, sir.'

Nelson grew angry once again. 'Not while I am here, sir. A *flotilla*. It is only right Perrée be met with an admiral, not a scout captain. And the *Généreux*, sir, is one of mine.'

Hazzard collected his hat, tucked it under his arm. 'Sir, I would like 9 Company and *Volpone* to join *Foudroyant*'s squadron,' he said. 'With Mr Wayland we'll take the Ottoman *Mebda-i Nusret* frigate, meet the *Success*, and flush *Généreux* towards your guns.'

'If she reaches Valletta it could be too late, sir.'

'Perhaps, but she could help break the *Guillaume Tell* out of harbour. The pair could run with the wind to Egypt.'

Nelson's lips compressed and he almost smiled. 'By heaven, that would be a thing, to bring them both to battle at once.' He looked at Hazzard, with a new determination. 'By God, we shall.' Nelson was afire: the game was on.. 'So, Keith will have his way after all. Armed troop transports. Whether for Malta or the Nile, Perrée could tip the balance for Vaubois or for Kléber. He could slip past our blockade and hare all the way to Alex…' He looked at Hazzard. 'And we shall not allow that a second time, shall we, sir?'

'No sir.' Hazzard shot his final bolt. 'But we must send word quickly, sir – lest Lord Keith shift his flag and lead the chase in *Foudroyant* himself.'

Nelson rounded on him. '*Foudroyant* is my flagship, sir. I would have him for that.'

Hazzard had hit the mark.

'Sir.'

Nelson dropped the despatch on the table and clutched for his walking-stick, hooked on the arm of his chair. He stood and slowly straightened, the slightest smile playing at the corners of his mouth, and nodded. 'Point taken, sir. For a shot across the bows, Mr Hazzard,' he said quietly, 'you cut exceeding close.'

'Would you trust Lord Keith not to, sir?'

Nelson considered it. 'No, sir, I would not. Let's be about it.'

Hazzard steadied him on his stick and Nelson turned from the table, his voice low. 'And if *Généreux* turns to meet you? You might buzz round her like hornets, true, but…'

'We pack a nasty sting, sir.'

'Indeed you do.' Nelson's gaze flicked to a movement at the corner of the garden. In the arbour archway in the hedge stood Cook, and Hardridge looking on, amazed; beside them was a tearful Emma Hamilton, her face streaked, kerchief in hand. Hazzard had warned her and he had meant it: he would end it all, and he had.

'Lieutenant Hardridge!' Trying not to lean too heavily on the stick, Nelson began to walk stiffly across the grass towards them, raising his voice. 'You may signal the line. *Foudroyant* to raise my flag, and compliments to Cap'n Berry, she is to prepare to weigh anchor. We are for Malta and the hunt once more.' He glanced at Hazzard. 'Kismet, it seems, and Mr Hazzard, have called the tune once again.'

Hardridge seemed to regain something of the hope he had lost, and strode off with renewed vitality, bellowing through the garden for the carriage, Cook wearing the ghost of a rare grin. As they neared the archway, Nelson cocked an eyebrow at Hazzard by his elbow. 'I hear you near sank her yourself, sir. Seems we both have unfinished business.'

Hazzard nodded. 'Sir.'

Touché. Nelson had known all along.

Nelson walked off. 'But this time we shall damn well have her, sir.'

Chase

The wind blew fresh at their backs as they left the island of Pantelleria behind, and for the first time in a while *Contre-amiral* Jean-Baptiste Perrée felt things might be going their way. He stood at the starboard shrouds on *Généreux*'s quarterdeck, feet astride, riding the ship as she rolled and dipped, an eager steeplechaser on the flat, her fore and mainsail coursers billowing bright above, the morning sun flashing from behind them as the great warship forged ahead. He raised his eyeglass and scanned the horizon. So far, there had been no sign of the English.

'We might yet do it,' he said to himself and the officers nearby. 'We just might...' Then, with a memory of the Nile, he whispered, '*Insha'allah.*'

God willing.

He heard a slow, steady footfall behind as Captain Cyprien Renaudin joined him. Renaudin took a long look at Pantelleria disappearing off the port quarter, certainly knowing how much further they had till Malta – and how many English, Portuguese or Neapolitan ships might lie in their path.

'If we do,' murmured Renaudin, hands behind his back, his glowering eye ever on the horizon, 'it will be in defiance of fate and the gods...'

Perrée glanced at him. Renaudin had been in a foul mood since the launch from Toulon. With typical ill-favour, contrary winds had taken their mizzenmast and snapped their tops on the first day, and they had been forced to turn back for repairs. Since then, it had seemed a cursed enterprise to the old hands below decks. But Perrée refused to see it that way – Renaudin muttering about fate and gods did not help matters. Renaudin was a strong-looking younger man, with hard eyes set deep in a carved oaken face, as if he had seen so much more than most. Of all who had fallen aboard the *Vengeur du Peuple* that day, here was the solitary hero: the man who had stayed, *l'homme d'honneur*. 'You believe in the gods, Captain?'

They had dispensed with 'citizen' in these last months – there was a new force in France, and its name was Bonaparte. The churches had reopened and the people felt free once again – what had been torn down was slowly being rebuilt. There was a strange hope.

Renaudin nodded slowly, a disconsolate Gallic shrug. 'Gods, *oui*,' he admitted, then with sudden memory, 'And demons.'

They had spoken of this over the previous days, over cognac after dinner, into the late watches. Renaudin was a fatalist, as much as any Egyptian Perrée had encountered. 'The English breed a particular type of madness,' said Perrée. 'They have honour, but no soul, no religion or fear of God… and a violence incomprehensible to most.'

Renaudin looked off, unwilling to discuss it. 'We have all seen it.'

Perrée knew the particular demon Renaudin had spoken of – had seen it himself, on his gunboats at Shubra Khit, fighting off the Mamluk *to save the savants*. A madman in red, fighting for his *enemies*. Why? What drove him to fight for no flag? Honour alone? Had his dishonour been once so great that he sought constantly to remedy it?

And he had since learned its name, this English madness, as Sir Sidney Smith had swooped on their heavy artillery at Acre, and Frenchmen had spoken of Arab assassins and Englishmen with scimitars – Englishmen who threw themselves at holy mountains and ships under fire. Its name was Hazzard.

Perrée had seen the repairs to *Généreux*: to the rails, bulwarks and broadsides; the new reinforced softwood gun-port shutters; the renewed planking and fresh paint. The gaping 60-pounder *obusier* carronades had been removed for speed, and her guns had been reordered, 36s below, 24s above, 18s on the upper decks. *Généreux* had been returned to her original state, the fine 74 she had once been before the Battle of the Nile, before Nelson and the unfavourable wind had tarnished her as coward, forcing her to sneak into the night as her sister ships burned, settling in shattered heaps into the shallows of Aboukir Bay.

This convoy would redeem her honour. Malta would redeem everything – and Perrée needed so much more: captured off Jaffa, paroled at Toulon by the English, he too had honour to reclaim. And so far, honour seemed to lie at the Nile, where he had sailed in support of Bonaparte's army in everlasting glory.

Beyond the great 74's taut sheets and braces, three jibs strained above her broad bows, plump with God's good winter winds. Sighting along the 74's starboard rail, Perrée saw their keen escort frigates, the *Badine* and *Fauvette*, both leaning to leeward as the flotilla flew southeast to Malta on their rescue mission. Perrée leaned out past the shrouds to look astern on the flank, to see three transports, the largest the *Ville de Marseille* and, dodging far behind, the lean and swift 16-gun *Sans Pareille*, the rearguard escort. He wished he had more. He wished he had but one third of Ganteaume's idle warships. But Bonaparte had been adamant: *Quickly in, quickly out. I must, yet cannot, reinforce Kléber in Egypt.* 'We must plot a course to get us between the English and the shore,' he said, as if thinking aloud.

'Yes,' said Renaudin warily. 'It is a risk. But if we approach by night—'

'We may not have the time. General Vaubois needs us at once – he can wait no longer. If we make the shore in daylight, so be it.'

'If we do so in daylight,' Renaudin said, shaking his head, 'we cannot do it with safety.'

'The English did at Aboukir.'

'Aboukir was sand shallows,' said Renaudin, looking away again. His petty officers and lieutenants watched him, the sharp tone of his voice not passing unnoticed. His hair flew loose round his face from under the brim of his soft cocked hat, slouched over one eye. The bo'sun called up to trim the lower maintopsail and clear a fouled block rattling on the port side topyard – Renaudin used it as cover. 'Malta is rock, *Amiral*. If the English are at Marsa Sirocco we cannot offload the men. If we lay off at night we may succeed…'

'You continue to press me on this?'

A signal gun banged, snatched by the wind and a reply came from *Sans Pareille*, some of the deckhands cheering at the rail as she sliced past. 'This is your convoy, *mon amiral*, but this is my ship. If we meet the English head-on, we will have to run with the wind and not stop until Egypt. What then? Men lost in the marshes of *le Marse*? Then no breakthrough to Valletta, no *Guillaume Tell*, no Admiral Bedout or Decrès to help us. You want the grand battle with the *Alexander* and *Zealous* and *Audacious*, all those who destroyed our line at Aboukir? They will be there waiting, and we are but one ship.' His words were hard, delivered like the rapping of musket-fire. He turned away, his lip curled with anger, the bo'sun and deckhands looking over at the pair, the display off the port beam no longer sufficient distraction.

Perrée raised his eyeglass once again, gave an order to the Second Lieutenant some way off: '*Sans Pareille* to maintain station off the larboard quarter.' It was a neat deflection, avoiding Renaudin's slight, his insubordination. 'The reason I am not concerned, Captain,' he said quietly, 'is that we shall offload only the stores.'

Renaudin watched him for a few moments, aware all eyes were on them. They had been at sea for over a week and this was the first time Perrée had mentioned this. 'The stores *alone*? What of the men – the three *thousand* men in—'

'Yes.' Perrée slapped the eyeglass shut and faced him. 'The men shall continue onwards.'

'Onwards? To wh—' Renaudin stopped himself and cursed, his hard expression unchanging and said carefully, 'My orders say Malta, *Amiral*.'

Perrée reached into his inside pocket and produced the envelope given to him by the official in Bonaparte's office. He handed it to him.

Renaudin looked at it as if it were a contagion of plague. 'Sealed? *Ma foi…*.' He flapped open the broken wax seal and read the few lines as Perrée explained.

'What value is there in taking food to a starving garrison, and then leaving three thousand extra mouths to feed?'

The sun flashed across Renaudin's face as he read. '"The distribution of forces is at your discretion…"? What is this to mean? Bonaparte's signature here means nothing, *Amiral*. This is contrary to our orders given by *Ordonnateur* De Sucy, signed by Minister Laplace, and is not—' He broke off, a light dawning. 'This is why you plotted our course via Lampedusa – for water, in case we cannot make landfall at Malta… This was the intention all along. *Mon dieu, quels salauds…*.'

Perrée turned away. 'We shall never know. But the First Consul cannot send men to Egypt before Malta.' Perrée looked at him, very direct, his dark curling forelock bouncing in the wind. 'But at sea, authority falls to the senior officers.'

'And if Nelson has left Palermo? What then? He will not stop, they say. Brueys learned this, Decrès learned this, hiding in Valletta in *Guillaume Tell*, and so did Villeneuve and Ganteaume, yet you seem not to care, *Amiral*. Bonaparte has doomed us – doomed us with the burden of decision. *C'est un infamie.*'

'If Nelson comes, we shall face him.'

'De Suffren himself would never have attempted this folly without a second ship of the line.' Renaudin shook his head in wonder. 'You will force us into an impossible position.'

'No, Captain,' said Perrée stiffly. 'We shall perform a miracle – Linosa by nightfall, Lampedusa by midnight, and a clear route to the southwest coast of Malta the next morning.'

With that, Perrée walked back to the binnacle and the men at the wheel; an ensign was taking the noon, aiming the sextant over the portside rail, another assisting, a lieutenant supervising. Renaudin watched Perrée, then stared off at the bright blue sea, shaking his head in dumb wonder. After a moment he barked, '*Lieutenant Rou!*'

Within a few moments the lieutenant appeared at his shoulder: a red-haired Norman a full head taller, known by his nickname 'the Red' throughout his long years with Renaudin. '*Capi.*'

Renaudin seemed to have a sour taste in his mouth. 'Clear for action at change of watch. A drill. I want them confused, afraid. I want them to fear the devil incarnate...' Renaudin looked at the deckhands at their tasks, their uncertainty, their youth. He headed down the quarterdeck steps. 'For he shall be upon us soon enough.'

–

His old-fashioned gold-brocaded Navy coat flapping and swinging as he went, Commander of the Mediterranean Fleet, Vice-Admiral the Lord Keith, strode to the portside rail of his flagship the *Queen Charlotte*, and took a despatch from the Signals officer just climbing in through the open gate. The *Queen Charlotte* was riding a heavy swell patrolling the coast just south of the capital port of Valletta, and far below, the despatch-runner's boat bumped and knocked impatiently against the broadside. The horizon heaving, a young seaman vomited under the starboard shrouds, doubling over, one hand on the rail. Captain Todd paused on his way from the binnacle to join Keith. 'Get him for'ard to the fo'c'sle, Mr Clarence, and clear that away...'

The boy was taken along the gangway by the bo'sun – '*Off wi'ye, laddie, and bend yer ruddy knees*' – and two deckhands appeared with a swabbing bucket. Keith re-read the signal and showed it to Todd. It was from HMS *Success*: *Enemy squadron sighted bearing south-southeast Trapani, Malta relief flotilla, Genereux (74) frigates, transports.*

'They're coming,' said Todd with relief. 'At last.' He glanced off to starboard and the seaward silhouettes of the *Alexander* and *Northumberland*, mainsails furled, topsails shortened to help maintain station with the admiral.

'Aye sir,' replied Keith. 'Men o'war and transports, if Peard is correct, and I don't doubt he is.' Marines and officers stepping aside, Keith leaned over the rail to call down, his Scots booming through the three gundecks. '*Can ye'hail the Lion off Valletta, sir?*'

A young midshipman stood in the pitching boat below, one hand hanging on to a guideline by the boarding steps, one hand on his hat. '*We can, sir!*'

'*Very well then sir!*' Keith patted his coat pockets in frustration, then accepted a pencil from Todd and began to write furiously on the despatch.

'Dixon's dashed quick, my lord,' said Todd, 'but he alone to intercept?'

'The *Lion*'s 64 can roar louder than the *Bellerophon*, so I'm told.' He thrust the note back at his Signals officer, who pushed through the gate hands reaching for the sopping guidelines, and fairly leapt down the steps to hand off the despatch to the young cox'n. Keith bellowed down all the while, '*Compliments to Captain Dixon, HMS Lion to guard the channel 'tween Gozo and St Paul's and to be smart about it!*' The young officer took the note and near fell back into the lurching boat. '*And make yourselves available to Lord Nelson!*'

After a moment's pause, the news was met with some excitement. '*Aye-aye sir!*'

With the glad news of Nelson's return, the boat charged into the growing swell, the oars digging deep as the excited crew pulled hard and fast for the anchored brig rocking fifty yards off the port beam. By the time the boy had scrambled aboard the sloop, all on the *Queen Charlotte*'s quarterdeck could hear the three cheers. Keith knew it was for the promise of action, but chiefly for Nelson, as it always was. Todd watched him with a weather eye, not daring to wonder whether Nelson would appear like a force of nature, a gale from a clear blue sky.

Keith scribbled again for the Signals officer. '*Northumberland* and *Alexander* to guard southeast approaches with *Audacious* and *Foudroyant*,' he continued, 'if she comes.' And, as if he had thereby cast a spell, a call came down from aloft.

'*Deck, lookout! Two sail of the line, three mile a' north o'larboard quarter, coming to intercept!*'

Keith stopped writing and stormed over to the mainmast, shouting upwards, 'Masthead, deck! Identify!'

'*Deck, lookout! No sight, my lord…*' Then his call was nearly drowned by the cheers of the rigging hands. '*Signal, sir! Admiral's signal! Foudroyant and Audacious, sir! It's his lordship! It's Lord Nelson!*'

Keith looked out to port, the specks on the horizon growing bolder. 'Very well…' He harrumphed at Todd. 'Captain Todd, with your leave, make reply and convey station order. Make your helm nor'nor'west for Valletta. We shall sit outside their cave lest the bear venture out.'

'Aye sir.' He looked at the wind. 'Freshening, sir, north by west. We'll beat to wind'ard on the starboard tack, but will keep as close as we dare.'

'Very well, Captain.' Keith stood at the quarterdeck shrouds and watched as *Foudroyant* passed in line with *Audacious*, signal flags rising on the masthead – *Division will form line on the admiral* – the crews waving their hats as if it were regatta day. 'He can beat round the point to wind'ard himself, should the French appear, and follow down the sou'west coast with leeward speed…'

Todd bowed, evidently used to the gruff manner of Uncle George. It was a good plan: guarding Valletta and the trapped French garrison with the 100-gun *Queen Charlotte* to catch the *Guillaume Tell* if she tried to break out – leaving Nelson and his captains on the southwest corner watching Marsa Sirocco. 'Very good, my lord.' He turned to his First Lieutenant at the binnacle. 'Make your helm nor'nor'east a quarter east, Mr Clarence. Prepare to come about.' He paused and warned Keith, 'They cannot land troops or supplies but on the marshes or beaches, sir. He might meet them head-on.'

They both knew 'he' meant Nelson, and Keith glowered out at the two battleships as they set full sail. 'Indeed. And I want us in position to contend hard with the French should they approach from the north. If Peard is right and it is Perrée, I want him captured and arrested for violation of his parole, *instanter*.' Keith marched away down the passage to the Day Room, muttering, 'And if Nelson does not live up to all his blather… I shall send him packing back to his punt in Norfolk…'

That night, the *Volpone* heeled from the strong northwesterly in full sail, braced to port, slicing ever southward across the wind on the black sea. Hazzard looked off into the thick pre-dawn darkness, a glow from the flying bow-wave of the Ottoman *Mebda-i Nusret* off their port beam.

The Ottomans had agreed to hurry onwards to Smith in the *Tigre*, so that Stanford and Petrides could warn him, and the blockade could prepare for the potential threat. The Turkish Captain Farah had been eager for action with the great 'Nelsoon Kapudan': with curling moustaches, wearing a battered Macedonian slouch hat, and festooned with pistols, twin daggers and a short *yataghan* sword, Farah looked ready to board an entire pirate fleet alone. Yet he understood the dangers should the French troop transports reach Alexandria – and had determined to intercept them on his own. A few dim lanterns glowed on the Turk as she heeled off to the southeast along the Sicilian coast, hands waving from the quarterdeck, Wayland and Madeleine watching them go.

Once alone, the crew of the *Volpone* turned to their stock-in-trade: the hunt for prey. The cool winds ignored, all eyes were trained on the dark southerly reaches, peering through night-glasses, looking for the telltale glow of canvas, looking for HMS *Success*. Peard's frigate would likewise be cutting across the wind, holding back, haunting *Généreux*'s trail, constantly shortening sail to maintain distance lest she overtake the slower-moving flotilla and be surrounded by the escort frigates. Of them all, *Success* would be the first ship De la Vega should sight, and she would point the way to *Généreux*.

After that, Hazzard had only the kernel of a plan. As he gripped the stays on the quarterdeck beside Wayland, the wind buffeting them, he knew what he wanted to do – and that neither Cook nor Wayland would permit it. But he had done worse.

'Do you think Nelson will reach Malta in time, sir?' asked Wayland, his eyes narrowed against the wind.

'We've got him out at last,' said Hazzard, 'and he needs as much glory as any captain.' He adjusted the scope, its broad lens heavy. 'This is more than duty for him now.'

Wayland nodded. They all understood the personal war. Wayland took a breath. 'I shall see to the men.'

Hazzard took his eye from the scope. 'It's good to have you back with us.'

Wayland turned, with a rueful smile. 'Wait till I start timing their firing drills.'

'Kite has missed those.'

Volpone had parted from Nelson on *Foudroyant* while rounding the Sicilian headland near Trapani, when they had met the 74-gun *Audacious*, and she fell in behind the flagship. While *Volpone* had headed south to spread the search, the pair of battleships raced down to the southeast to Malta. If *Généreux* ever did reach Valletta, and managed somehow to break the giant *Guillaume Tell* out of the harbour, the full might of Keith's blockade fleet would fall upon them – Perrée would not expect a confrontation with four 74s and a First-Rate 100-gunner. If engaged, his only hope would be to evade, and if all went awry, he would run tail-high for Egypt.

Nelson knew this, but Keith would never guess at it. However, if Perrée bore up, turned *Généreux* to windward to try to claw his way back to Malta, he would lose headway, and Nelson would have him. Hazzard was banking on Renaudin doing just that – not to escape, but to fight. And Hazzard had an idea of how to make him do it.

A cry came down from the foremast. Ezau and Pau sat on the foretopgallant yard, each with one hand on the foremast, calling down in Catalan, '*Allá! Veles tot recte!*' *There – sails dead ahead.*

De la Vega and Cook hurried down the tweendecks and leapt up the fo'c'sle steps to join Hazzard at the forward rail. '*Todo derecho?*' Hazzard called up in Spanish to confirm – *Dead ahead?* – and down came the answer: '*Sí, sí!*'

Wayland emerged from below with Kite, Hesse and Tariq, others emerging from the midships hatch, all eyes searching the dark. Hazzard and De la Vega peered through their night-glasses, the four large jibsails rattling overhead, billowing out to the portside.

'Where?' demanded Hazzard. 'Can't see a damned thing.'

At the starboard corner of the fo'c'sle rail, De la Vega hunched behind the eyepiece, traversing the horizon slowly. 'It takes *la paciencia*, *amigo*... which you do not have in the abundance...' He looked briefly to Wayland. 'Do you say this...?'

Wayland's face creased into a tight grin. 'Yes, we say this.'

After a moment De la Vega stopped, one hand out. 'Ah, *mira mira*... Look...' He straightened, his arm laying the course for Hazzard. 'There, *amigo*. A phantom on the waves...'

Hazzard peered through his scope. A flickering blur in his sights slowly sharpened to a distant pale smudge against the darkness, so faint he was unsure if it were a trick of the light. The image grew, then shrank, as if flashing. 'The ensign is flying astern,' he said. 'She's English.'

Even as he watched, it grew larger in the viewfinder. Low-slung, a frigate, the dark ensign flapping, obscuring the glow of white from her mizzenmainsail, creating the illusion of flashing. It had to be HMS *Success*.

De la Vega frowned. 'The heading... It is... how you say? ...all *wrong, hermano*. She is far off course for Malta.' De la Vega looked up at the dark, starlit skies, thin cloud in a hazy film racing high above. He called to Carlos and snapped a finger. Within a few moments, Alfonso arrived with the chart and spread it out over the curved fairing of the bellhouse, straining to see by the dim glow of a shuttered lamp. 'Why does she go to the south so soon...?'

Elena appeared at the steps, at her side, Madeleine de Saëns-Ivry. They could not have been more different, the dark-eyed Spaniard and the pale-skinned Frenchwoman in her bodice and skirts. '*Permets?*' she called quietly up the steps. Wayland turned, and De la Vega looked up from the chart and nodded, bowing.

'*Señorita,*' he said, inviting her up. It was a peculiar situation to have her aboard – a known French spy, even if a royalist – and though De la Vega was uncertain of her, he went out of his way to make her feel welcome. She moved to Wayland and looked out.

'A ship?' she asked. 'The *Généreux*?'

'Not yet,' said Wayland, noting Hazzard's unmoving back before him as he peered over the rail.

'She's dousing sail...' Hazzard looked up. 'Cesár, the lamp?'

English ensign or not, De la Vega hesitated, smoke curling round his chin. Once they lit the signal lamp they would reveal their position. '*Otros barcos?*' Other ships?

'*Nada, capitán,*' confirmed Carlos, his gloomy eyes hooded in the darkness, the indigo glow from the skies leaving his black hair in a halo of half-light. *None.*

De la Vega nodded. '*Listo los cañones.*' Ready the guns.

Carlos nodded. '*Listos.*' Ready. He whistled up to Handley.

Up above in the mainmast tops, Handley opened a shutter on the masthead lamp, illuminating the blockade signal, a white flag bearing a blue cross. Ezau and Pau then hoisted the red Mediterranean Fleet ensign, and in moments it snapped open over their heads. De la Vega nodded to Carlos.

'*El faro.*'

Hazzard stood aside as Carlos approached the shutters of the bright lantern and opened and closed them several times, the mirrored light momentarily dazzling, the return of darkness blacker than ever.

'*Amigo,*' said De la Vega, 'let us hope we are right, hm?'

Hazzard watched the frigate. He saw a burst of white foam, a heavy splash on the dark surface off the broadside: an anchor. The ship was waiting, sails doused.

Alfonso stabbed a finger at the chart. '*Padre.*' De la Vega bit into his cheroot and looked. There could be no doubt. 'She is for Lampedusa, my friend,' he said to Hazzard, 'or little Linosa. Not Malta.'

'Lampedusa…' Hazzard lowered the eyeglass and handed it to Cook. 'Are we right, Jory?'

The big man put it up to his eye. 'S'as dark as a tin pit… That could be a 24, aye… or a 32, sir,' he confirmed. 'She's squared away. Single gundeck, tight abeam, tight little arse up high, a right fast bugger.'

They had come far beyond Pantelleria now, and the Pelagie Islands – Lampedusa, Lampione and Linosa – lay more or less due south, between Malta and the Tunisian coast, Malta roughly a hundred nautical miles to the east. If the *Success* were following Perrée's convoy close behind, then the French had made a wide diversion, to slide in behind Malta from the western approaches using the full speed of the prevailing winter northwesterly – perhaps to land his troops and stores with agents or sympathisers ashore. This way Perrée would avoid direct confrontation with the Valletta blockade. Unless there were another reason.

'Water,' said Hazzard.

De la Vega and the others looked up, the chart rustling and flapping in the wind. The Spaniard nodded in slow agreement. 'Water… *Sí, posibilamente.*'

Madeleine watched the exchanges, and Wayland watched her in turn. '*De l'eau?*' she asked quietly, and he nodded.

'*Sí, agua,*' Hazzard continued in Spanish for the others. 'Why come so far out unless he means to stop in the main port? He needs water. Why? Why would he need more water?' He looked to Wayland. 'Unless he planned to go further?'

Cook lowered the glass and considered this. He would need water for only one reason. 'By all that's holy in ruddy Bristol,' he rumbled. 'The bloody buggers…'

Within barely fifteen minutes, *Volpone* caught her up, angry signal flags rippling up the Englishman's masthead as he slowed. *Volpone* drew in astern of the *Success* on the port quarter, riding the swell, Handley calling adjustments to Carlos as they crept along her port broadside. A lantern was lit on *Success*'s taffrail and at her prow, illuminating the gusting drizzle, but none on any of the three masts for fear of detection, their skeletal structure discernible only by the gleam of their woodwork in the lamplight and the glow of furled canvas. All eyes surveyed the English frigate's lines, the Spaniards' heads nodding, impressed – the little ship low at the bow, potent, keen to sail. A fine rain began to blow.

'Gun-ports are open, sir,' warned Handley, hunkering into his collar, his wool cap beading with rain. Despite the red ensign, *Volpone* was clearly a Spaniard, and HMS *Success* was taking no chances: Peard would give the order to fire nonetheless if he felt threatened. De la Vega had felt the same, and though *Volpone*'s gun-ports were closed, the guns were loaded and rammed.

The squall continued to blow, but the rain died off, and they gathered behind Hazzard at the starboard fo'c'sle rail between the shining wet carronades, the marines of 9 Company crowding with the Spanish and Catalan deckhands, peering into the dark. 'Steady as she goes, Cesár,' murmured Hazzard.

'Carlos,' whispered De la Vega. '*Tirantes a babor.*'

Carlos snapped his orders, and *Volpone*'s mainyards swung slowly overhead to port, to avoid fouling the Englishman abeam. Though practical, it was also a clever point of diplomacy. *Volpone*'s portside sea anchors splashed over the side, both fore and aft. A vigorous figure in Navy bluejacket and cocked hat appeared at the opposite rail, megaphone in hand.

'*Captain Shuldham Peard! His Majesty's Ship Success! Who in hell are you!*'

The voice was hollow, but the anger was clear for all to hear. De la Vega gave Hazzard the nod, and he raised their own megaphone, an antique brass-mounted contraption. '*Major William John Hazzard, 9 Company the Special Landing Squadron! Captain De la Vega, the Volpone, Levant Squadron, the Mediterranean Fleet!*'

Despite the tension, Warnock nudged Hesse and De Lisle when they heard their title called, Underhill growling, '*Bloody tell 'im, sir...*'

There was a muffled curse from Peard opposite, now looking down, hands on hips, shaking his head. Abruptly, he raised the megaphone. '*So recognised. Compliments for Acre. Ceased pursuit to signal you!*'

Hazzard ignored his resentment. 'Have you the heading of the French flotilla?'

Peard was unshaven, his lamplit face dark with stubble, and they could see his teeth flash with a grim laugh. '*South by east a quarter south! Linosa or Lampedusa!*'

Not Malta. Hazzard glanced at De la Vega. The Spaniard whispered, '*Bravo, amigo. Agua.*' Water.

Hazzard lifted the cone on its engraved handle. '*Nelson's compliments. We are to beat them towards his guns off Malta.*'

There was a pause as Peard conferred with his First Lieutenant, the pair considering these words. '*Nelson's own orders, sir?*'

Hazzard understood his suspicion: the entire fleet knew Nelson had been refusing to leave Palermo. '*In person. He leads the Alexander, Audacious and Northumberland from Foudroyant.*'

Peard shouted something to the crew, and Hazzard thought he heard, '*Nelson has sailed.*' They roared, their fists in the air. Peard shouted back, '*Very good, sir! How shall we proceed?*'

'We shall go to the southwest of Lampedusa and cut round the south coast. You can rush them from the north once you see us driving them from astern.'

'*They'll fly to the east! Very good, sir, we shall beat the bushes!*' The figure lowered the megaphone, listened to his First Lieutenant, nodded, then turned back to the rail, another lamp shutter opening. Hazzard was able to distinguish his brass buttons and epaulettes. '*Sir Thomas sends regards to the pirates! Anything further?*'

The marines laughed and some cheered back, Hazzard thinking of Troubridge, of their tense briefing before they had left the blockade: *Come back, William, pirates and all.* He raised the megaphone. 'Chase her like the Devil, Captain, and we shall bring her about to windward. If Nelson cannot reach her, you shall have her, sir!'

Peard nodded his head and raised an arm. '*Then we shall cook her damned goose sir!*' There was a further cheer from her crew and he signed off, doffing his hat: '*HMS Success, on the wind!*'

With that, Peard marched back to the helm, his officers around him, and the cheering crew leapt to the sheets, deckhands to the anchor rising up the port bow, the braces pulling the yards round to port, the sails dropping and filling.

'Good oke,' said Cook. 'Must be a terror.'

'Aye, Jory boy,' muttered Underhill beside him, his face still dark in the gloom. 'But he wants the kill now, havin' flushed the quarry.' He tapped the side of his nose. 'We'll 'ave to be quick if we want our share. Winky-winky, monkey-monkey.'

HMS *Success* leaned forward, heeling to port as she caught the wind, her jibs filling as the northwesterly propelled her through the grey dark of the choppy sea. Madeleine looked out past Wayland at the disappearing shape of the English frigate, her eye catching Hazzard as he conferred with De la Vega. She put an affectionate hand to Wayland's shoulder. 'He is quite the captain,' she said. '*N'est-ce pas?*'

'Peard is a typical frigate captain.' He looked back at her. He found her still beautiful, despite their peculiar star-crossed path, despite everything that loomed in his mind when he so much as thought of her. 'He is a terrier. He does not let go. Like another I know...' He smiled grimly.

She looked forward again, at Hazzard, moving among the marines. '*M'sieur* d'Azzard.'

'Mm.' Wayland watched the glowing sails and wake of the *Success* as *Volpone* lurched, her sails filling, turning to the south to head into a dark curtain of grey and white, of cloud and distant rain. 'One day he will go too far,' he said.

Madeleine touched the side of his face, his curling hair. '*Tu t'inquiètes.*' *You worry yourself.*

He clutched her hand and kissed her fingers. 'They are your countrymen, Madeleine, and we are sailing to destroy them. How awful it must feel for you... I am sorry.'

'We did not do this,' she said with a sudden frown – not for Wayland or Hazzard, but for the circumstances. 'They did this. Bonaparte did this. Admiral Ganteaume, he did this – his cowardice did this.' Then, with a simmering anger, she added, 'The guillotine – it did this.'

Wayland noticed her eye flicking forward as Hazzard moved down the fo'c'sle steps and approached along the line of guns, the deckhands bracing the yards, Carlos speaking to him, pointing off into the distance.

Wayland said, 'Kléber is desperate. He will break Sir Sidney's peace if he must – then God help them, French and Ottoman. God help us all.' He looked at Madeleine. 'If the convoy heads southeast of Malta, we shall know,' he said. 'And it must not reach Egypt. If they escape Nelson, the major will not stop till he has put them all to the bottom of the sea.'

She watched him thoughtfully. 'You think much of him.'

Wayland glanced at her. 'I have very good reason to.'

The rain began to drift over them again, a fine mist clouding in the lamplight. She raised the hood on her cloak and leaned up towards his cheek. She kissed him, and he looked into her blue eyes – and wondered, not for the first time, when it might all end: when she might at last betray him, or he her, out of duty, out of necessity. He prayed it would not come. He had prayed ever since Palermo, when Stanford had handed him the letter from the consul in Turin, telling him that the Occitan Network had long since collapsed – and that Madeleine de Saëns-Ivry had been feeding Petrides false information for some time.

Madeleine drifted off back to the cabins and disappeared into the lamplight of the interior. Wayland watched her go, wondering what she might attempt at the last moment.

Battle

The island of Lampedusa squatted on the southern horizon. They had passed the isle of Linosa to port, and Lampione lay further west, closer to the Tunisian coast. Lampedusa, by contrast, was unmistakable: long and low, stretching from west to east, black against the dark, swollen cloudbanks of the pre-dawn skies, pinpricks of light on its shores, breakers foaming on its jagged coastline. *Volpone* had outstripped the *Success*, which had gone further out to sea to the east to intercept Perrée and the convoy en route to Malta. Hazzard knew Peard had invested too much in the hunt to stop now, but the rough plan might still work, and *Volpone* would harry the French from astern and drive them to Nelson.

There was no sign of life; nothing but the heave of the dark sea, the waves lit by their phosphorescent whitecaps from the strong north-westerly driving them onwards, the black headland cliffs of the island before them unyielding.

Hazzard felt the cold wind at his neck over his Bombay Scarlet, his shirt damp with the constant strain – but he would not lower the night-glass, resting it on the fo'c'sle rail, one boot on a gun-carriage, haunches on a stool brought to him by Elena. She stood behind him endlessly, murmuring incantations, Iphigeneia hoping to cast spells to Poseidon.

'*Hola…! Veles!*'

Hazzard jerked round, as if woken from a half-sleep. 'Where away? *Dónde?*'

He swung the glass to the port bow and traversed slowly, the bare spritsailyard fouling his view, the spray clouding his vision. He stopped.

There.

Movement.

'*Veles!*' Pau, far above at the mainmast lookout, calling down in excited Catalan. '*Veles tot recte!*' Sails dead ahead.

Hazzard looked to the foremast tops above, and behind him to Cook and Handley. '*Jory! Handley! Identify!*' He stood up abruptly, knocking over the stool, trying to steady the glass at his eye. 'Christ, by God... *where...*' It was still dark, the pinpoints of light growing in number with the parallax of their own headway.

Handley took up the call. '*She's a transport, sir!*'

Then Hazzard saw it: a merchantman, broad in the beam, riding heavy in the swell, nosing out from behind the eastern headland of the island at the left. Hazzard knew what it meant: *Troops.*

But for Malta, or for Kléber in Egypt?

'*Aye sir! A fat bugger listing to larboard!*' confirmed Cook high above, leaning forward, hands on the rail of the foremast tops next to Handley, a field glass to his eye. '*Looks a Leghorner to me!*'

Handley was more specific than Cook's Ligurian suggestion. '*Genoese polacca, most like, sir, making three knots at best, overloaded, two Long Nines to bow and poop and four 18-pounders on her top deck, but no gun-ports, sir!*'

Hazzard tried to see the same detail, but their elevated position in the tops gave them the advantage of twelve miles' line of sight. '*Deck looks crowded... Crew... Could be butts, stores or...*' He considered for a moment, straining through the darkness. '*Or men, sir! Could be Frog troops on deck!*'

'*It's men arright, the buggers!*' shouted Cook. '*Ruddy 'undreds of em!*'

Hazzard looked round over his shoulder at De la Vega on the port-side shrouds of the quarterdeck, also looking out. '*Carlos! Oscurecemos!*' *Darken us.*

Alfonso snapped his fingers and called, '*Linternas!*' *Lanterns.*

One by one, the lights went out, on the quarterdeck, taffrail, masts and midships hatch; the lantern shutters snapped shut, leaving barely a dim glow leaking into the night. The *Volpone* was now running dark, stalking the convoy.

Hazzard looked out forward as the humped black shape of the island began to grow fast, the angle blotting out his view of the Genoese transport. A dull glow from the port on the south coast silhouetted the island against a black sky. The wind freshened, black night bringing that rare cold before day, and Hazzard shrugged into his jacket. Underhill moved somewhere to his right, looking out, one boot on a carronade truck. Hazzard caught his eye.

'Assault kit clear, Sar'nt?'

Underhill replied with a grim laugh, 'Aye sir. Boats, blades an' bombs, for the use of, clear aye.'

The *Volpone* heeled heavily in the strong northwesterly wind, the jibs flaring over her port bow, the island growing steadily as the frigate arced towards it. They wanted to weather the island's southwest promontory as tightly as possible with as much speed as they could; they had no idea what could be waiting, and De la Vega wanted to be ready to engage.

A Ship's Master would demand a calling of knots and a measurement of the wind at intervals, but Handley stood stock-still in the foremast tops, night-glass to his eye, staring at the island and the breakers on the outlying rocks, calling in his new-found Spanish to Ezau or Pau to adjust the topyards or down to Carlos on deck. '*Alivia los tirantes... más más más!*' *Ease your braces, more, more, more.*

Heaving before them, Lampedusa loomed on a collision course as they sped towards it, the rush of the sea roaring back at them, the jibs straining far out over the port bow. '*Handley...!*' called Hazzard in warning. '*Keep her down, man!*'

'*Diez!*' came a call from Alfonso, measuring the knots as the frigate ran with the wind. *Ten.*

Volpone had a deep keel, allowing her to heel over at a sharper angle than most, but Handley did not slacken the speed and Hazzard watched the island race towards them.

'*Doce!*' *Twelve.*

The marines assembled weapons on deck, the deckhands readying the blackened boats on their davits. All could taste the coming action, and knew their tasks – hands flew across chests as they crossed themselves and checked locks, oilcoths and daggers in sheaths.

'*Jory... Mr Wayland...!*' Hazzard stared forward, one hand to the stays. '*Stand by when we pass the headland!*'

Hands behind his back, Wayland stumped along the line of guns and gun-crews and called back, '*Cañones claros! Guns clear aye!*' The marines were now assembled in an assortment of navy blue and black, their Egyptian *shemagh* headdresses wrapped round necks, heads, across chests or round waists: Kite, Warnock, Hesse and Tariq, Pettifer and De Lisle, Cochrane and Napier, streaking pitch in stripes over forehead and cheekbones. Some of the Spaniards crossed themselves again and again. '*Los diablos ingleses.*' *English devils.*

'Wha'ss the plan then, Knocky…?' murmured Kite, riding the sloping deck, checking the lock on his short sawn-off tar-coated Charleville.

Warnock dragged a blackened thumb under his closed eyelid, across his nose and down his chin, and blinked, the white of the eye bright by comparison, his teeth savage and animal as he grinned. '*We gonna kill 'em, Mickey.*'

Napier clapped the priming-pan of his musket shut and nodded his big head firmly. 'Too bloody right, Knock-Knock. For Sheppy.'

'Prayers to be shriven, Art'ur,' said Cochrane quietly to the big boxer in his Derry twang. 'Let us pray…' They obeyed and clasped hands at their fronts, heads down, eyes closed, the ship heaving forward in the hunt. '*O Lord, watch over these Thy children, who strive to serve Thee within Thy mercy…*'

Now the fully fledged surgeon's assistant, Porter was to remain aboard, but moved among them, checking their oilcloth packs, tightening belts, paying attention to Tariq: 'Come now, lad, your sundries'll fall out and then where will you be?' Tariq was puzzled, but refined the points on his moustaches like a Prussian general, like Hesse, who nodded to him firmly.

'*Bereit?*' Ready?

'*Nahm. Rabbena ma'ak.*' Yes. God be with you.

'*Du auch.*' And you.

Pettifer got them roughly in line. 'Sections, look t'yer fronts.' They moved into two files of four and faced forward, legs braced at ease, the ship heeling, Handley calling down, De la Vega answering, the marines letting it happen over their heads. Pettifer nodded to Cook. 'All yours, *m'dame.*'

Cook turned to the foot of the mainmast and hefted up an object: it was a Turkish blunderbuss. 'An' this is yours, milady.'

He tossed it to Pettifer, who gazed at it in wonder: foliate scrolling along its dark mottled barrel, the wooden stock inlaid with striped bands of rosewood and sandalwood, its miquelet lock larger than most and easier to thumb back. 'Blow me down, Cookie, it's a beaut.'

'Y'can thank Mr Wayland – got it from that general in Pall'a'mo.'

Hesse agreed with an appreciative nod. '*Ausgezeichnet.*' Excellent.

'Bless you an' all, and use an 'andkerchief,' said Kite. 'Your berfday, then, Corp?'

Pettifer glowered, shouldering the weapon. 'Well, it is in two month.'

"Appy returns,' chimed Kite. 'I'll pinch ye somefink nice.'

'P'rade stand-to,' rumbled Cook. 'Mind the natives, mind the furniture and wait fer it.'

Handley called down from above, '*Range two thousand yards, closing! Captain! Helm a-starboard and brace a-larboard!*'

De la Vega bit down on his cheroot at the wheel and called, '*Timón a estribor! Tirantes a babor!*'

The deckhands close-hauled the yards to port, the mizzenmainsail gaff coming round like a great tailfin, spinning the ship hard to starboard, the arc tight with the strong wind. The island of Lampedusa seemed to rush towards them, suddenly large, a black mountain, her low jagged cliffs a rising wall, the breakers bursting bright at the bows and port broadside as *Volpone* shrieked past in her heeling turn, cutting south across the wind, Handley shouting down, Hazzard unable to hear as he held on to the rail. '*Jory! Marines to brace!*' Deckhands clasped forearms as the masts tilted, the sails rattling and straining as *Volpone* sliced round the headland, the spray flying in clouds as the wind shuddered along her planks from stem to stern, the island sliding past, impossibly close, impossibly fast.

After the engulfing darkness of the island towering above them, they rounded the point and burst upon a new dawn, easing the helm to midships and round to port at once, the yards swinging about, Carlos whipping them into action. '*Estribor, estribor!*'

Lampedusa now on their portside, they shot round the promontory, the distant dawn a low grey streak to the fore. The small harbour was dotted with torchlight: oared boats coming in, fishermen going out, a low-slung Berber galley taking on provisions. The crew cheered, '*Viva, viva!*' and Handley called down, '*Clear to run with the wind, lads!*'

But of the French there was no sign. The convoy had vanished.

On the quarterdeck, De la Vega clamped a new cheroot between his teeth and shouted, '*Tirantes al médio y todas velas!*' *Brace amidships and full sail*. The gaff swung and *Volpone* straightened as she skidded across the sea, her bowsprit aimed towards the clouded grey of the east and an approaching sunrise.

Handley leaned out from the tops and called up to Ezau, still clinging to the mast on the topyard. '*Ezau! Get us a sight! Todos a buscar! Mira, mira!*' *Everyone search, look, look.*

'*Sí, sí, Handeleh!*'

But of the Genoese freighter there was no sign, visibility in the half-light so poor that not even the glow of sail could be found. Hazzard extended the night-glass again, looking forward into distant clouds of rain, blackness and mist-obscured stars above, a dull white across the horizon before him, and he cursed his blindness, cursed the wind for its strength, and cursed his plan. He looked back and called in Spanish, '*Cesár! Where away? I can see nothing!*'

On the quarterdeck, the Spaniard was locked against the shrouds with his own glass, searching the horizon. '*No se, amigo!*' *I don't know.*

The ship leaned into the swell, her bows devouring the waves before her – to Malta, just as Perrée would have done; there was little choice. De la Vega's shouts to Hazzard were carried on the wind – '*Buscan la blanca! La blanca!*' *Look for the white* – when Hazzard spotted a distant cloud of swirling specks against the dark of the clouds, rising, falling, mere dots, a caravan of travellers in the desert of the sea. Hazzard thought of vultures, wheeling, soaring, betraying the signs of recent life. Then he had it, and cursed himself again for having been too long on land, and not at sea.

'There...'

The birds.

Out to sea.

'*Gulls! Seagulls larboard bow! Range, Handley?*'

Handley sighted his own glass. '*Got 'em, sir! Diving on the white 'orses—*' He cut his commentary short and exclaimed, '*Ho there! Ship of sail, frigate, one! Eight... no, ten... no... sixteen guns!*' He shouted from the tops as the Catalan was rattled down to Carlos and Alfonso on deck. '*Runnin' with the wind, bearin' east by nor'east a-larboard bow, range three miles!*'

Hazzard swung the glass and followed the birds: one of the ships in the convoy must have been casting off scraps from the galley. Then he saw it: a low dark shape, the white dots above, swooping around a block of shadow among the heave of the dark sea, now visible, now hidden, her sails a shifting dull glow. It must have been one of the convoy escorts. '*Got her! No ensign!*'

'*Second sail,*' Handley called down. '*Twenty guns! Off larboard bow of first! And a third... Twelve... correction, twenty-four guns, one 'undred yards starboard abeam the first! Range three miles and an'arf! Loose order, they're all over the ruddy place!*'

281

Carlos joined Cook and Hazzard as they peered into the half-dark of the waves, the skies yielding slowly to a spreading grey dawn on the horizon. 'Is them…? Is… the *Franceses*?' he asked in his broken English.

'*No estamos seguros,*' said Hazzard. *We're not sure.* 'We wait.'

Cook nodded. 'If'n we keep dark and get close enough, we'll know. Then Cap'n Caesar can bring her about and rake the lot o'them.' He looked out again, lifting his eyeglass. '*And where's the buggerin'* Généreux…'

The French lookouts might be focussed more forward than astern, thought Hazzard, for fear of Nelson and the blockade fleet – not thinking of an intruder creeping in behind. Hence his plan with Peard: *Success* would charge in from the north, and none would notice the *Volpone* astern. They sped into the darkness on the hunt, now making at least eight knots. They would soon catch them. Then Handley called from above.

'*Ho there!*' he cried. '*Enemy ship o'sail, 74 guns dead ahead! Enemy ensign flyin' astern!*' He leaned over the edge and hallooed down to them. '*She's our Frenchie all right, sir!*'

'*Confirm the ensign!*' shouted Hazzard, unwilling to believe it simply because they wanted it to be true, but Handley crowned the moment: '*Ho there! Transport, Genoese, enemy sail! Larboard bow of 74, strugglin', four miles off …! Enemy transport second, enemy transport third, biggest farthest off, range five miles! You got 'em, sir! It's the ruddy convoy! You got 'em!*'

Underhill roared out to the marines, 'Frenchies by the dozen, for the use of! Ram yer rocks and lock yer cocks, me beauties! Three cheers for Cap'n Caesar!'

They replied without hesitation, the crew joining in, '*Viva, viva! Viva el capitán!*'

De la Vega gave the word, cupping his hands to his mouth in the strengthening wind. '*Listos para la acción!*' *Clear for action.*

Underhill and Pettifer led the marines on the lines with the deck-hands, the tackles heaving the tar-painted boats into the air, swinging out to the portside rail amidships. Cook led the first section of four, Underhill the second. They stowed their equipment and prepared to board.

Wayland helped the gun-crews as best he could, his stiff leg no help, his prosthetic left hand weighing heavy as he swore while trying to haul the restraints of an 18-pounder, one of the Spaniards taking the line from him. '*Preparanse, amigos!* Our captain can smell the Franceses!'

They laughed as he leaned on the rail, watching the marines as the boats swung down for boarding. He felt a presence nearby, a hand taking his left arm gently, and the soft warmth of her proximity – Madeleine was standing beside him. 'What do they do, Thomas?'

They had come this far, to Christian names, and he felt reassured by her kind beauty, and he touched her small hand. 'The marines,' he said close to her, to be heard over the wind. 'They're going to take the *Généreux*.'

Her eyes widened, and she looked across the decks at the Englishmen in war paint and Arab headdress. 'Take her?'

'Capture her,' he explained in French. 'Come from behind her, and take captain, admiral and all.'

She met his eye and Wayland knew that, somewhere inside, she shivered with horror. He thought of Stanford, and the Occitan Network. He pushed harder.

'Or kill them all.'

As he said it, he knew Hazzard would.

–

'*Enemy sail off the larboard quarter—*' The voice of the mizzen lookout had nearly cracked with fright, and Renaudin turned about, cursing.

'Details! How many, *tu crétin*? *Tabernac maudite!*' he shouted up into the grey darkness, angry, looking up beyond the gaff rig of the tall mainsail, lamps lit at the tops, seeing the boy pointing. An older hand was with him, pipe in mouth, who called down, '*One enemy sail, capitaine! Frigate, anglais, 32 guns, two leagues off to larboard and gaining!*'

'Very well…' Renaudin turned and barked, '*Helm two points to larboard! Clear for action! Beat to quarters!*'

The drums began to rap fore and aft, and Perrée emerged from the quarters behind the binnacle, pulling on a sleeve of his jacket, acknowledging the marines who cracked to attention. 'No breakfast then, Captain. Where away?'

'English frigate approaching from the north-northwest, *mon amiral*, our shadow from Trapani and Mazara.' He looked at him hard. 'She will not give up.'

'Very well,' said Perrée, doing up his buttons. 'Larboard guns to stand by, and the *Fauvette* frigate to intercept.'

Renaudin almost seized him. '*Amiral*, we cannot land the troops. Not even the stores.' He pointed out to the dark sea, the whitecaps whipping and cracking in the wind. 'Where there is one *anglais*, there will be others. *We are discovered.*'

Perrée would not yield. He studied Renaudin's face, the grey dawn behind, washed yellow in the lamplight of the quarterdeck – his harsh expression, his hard eyes – and quietened his own by contrast, speaking softly. 'When you have Mamluk swimmers crawling up the broadsides with knives in their teeth and axes in their hands, *capitaine*, then, and only then, you may consider you are discovered. But never presume you are lost. You, above all, should know better.'

The slight was savage, and cut deep. 'We have three thousand men exposed in slow-moving transports! Let me turn and engage this *anglais* and blow him from the water.'

Perrée remained patient. 'We cannot, lest the transports outstrip us – they would then become vulnerable to the blockade fleet at Malta, should it appear.' Perrée straightened his jacket, the silver thread glinting in the grey dawn. 'I will not abandon them for the sake of a small frigate of no consequence.'

Renaudin stared back. '*Mon dieu*. They were right about you.' He hissed at him, 'These are not Mamluk assassins, but *Englishmen*. They do *not* stop. *Comprenez?*'

'Neither did Bonaparte. And we won. Make your course for the cove headland west of Marsa Sirocco as agreed.'

'Still to put ashore on Malta?'

'Yes, Captain.'

Renaudin watched him, unmoving once again, then shouted, 'Lieutenant Rou! Evasive manoeuvres but maintain course to Ghar il-Munxar!'

The response came at once, the tall Norman coming to attention. '*Oui, mon capitaine!*'

Renaudin moved to Perrée at the quarterdeck rail. 'We are so few, *Amiral.*'

'Enough to do our country loss,' said Perrée. He extended his telescope and glanced at him. 'I believe an *anglais* said that, some time ago.'

Renaudin had the last word. 'I am sure Voltaire had a response, *Amiral.*'

Perrée headed up the steps to the poopdeck, heavy eyeglass in hand as the crews loaded the carronades, gleaming black in the lamps, the skies streaking with grey light.

But Renaudin knew their plethora of guns could not help the transports. The *Ville de Marseille* was crashing through the swell faster than expected, its spread of sail greater than the others. He shouted up to the masthead lookout, '*Range to the Ville de Marseille!*'

'*Two leagues, mon capitaine!*' came the reply from above; then, after a moment, '*Too far.*'

'Reply to our signal to shorten sail and maintain station?'

'*No response, capitaine.*'

They had let her leave the island port first to gain some distance, assuming the northwesterly would fill their sails faster and the bigger *Généreux* would catch up – but they had not, and the wind had freshened, the *Ville* making too much headway. All was contrary to proper convoy procedure, but Perrée had been supremely confident. To clear the decks, the deckhands swung the small boats outboard. The first splashed into the darkness of the waves below, pitching and bucking, each tied in line to run astern.

Renaudin thought of Brueys at the Nile, who had looked at the shoals of Aboukir and felt safe – until he had spotted Nelson. What had Brueys thought, he wondered, at that moment? '*The English come,*' his brother had said on the *Vengeur du Peuple*, also supremely confident. My God, but they did. Renaudin knew them well.

As if to confirm all he had ever suspected of deceitful fate, a call came down from the mainmast lookout. '*Two enemy ship of sail dead ahead! Of 74, English, heading to intercept, range six leagues!*'

Renaudin froze, his hands ice-cold on the quarterdeck rail, his eyes dead, his breath catching.

No.

Nelson.

–

'*Frigate to larboard beam, heading south by east! Runnin' with the wind, intercept course convoy!*' Handley called down. '*It's the Success, sir and she's coming in to attack!*'

Hazzard rushed to the midships portside rail, the marines waiting at the boats as HMS *Success* came streaking in full sail from the north, far off the port bow, flashes popping from the forward battery of her star-board broadside, aglow with the flat glare of the sunrise, waterspouts bursting around the nearest of the French frigates.

'He's heading for the *Généreux*,' said Hazzard.

'Through them frigates?' scoffed Cook. 'Ruddy mad...'

The *Volpone* tore into the waves, plunging into the swell, the grey line of the dawn widening on the horizon with every moment, the gloomy half-light tricking the eye. Dead ahead, the two French frigates running astern of the *Généreux* rose and fell on the waves, their lamps bright, darkening their decks by contrast, barely a hundred yards ahead. *Volpone* had caught them up.

'*Hurry, amigos!*' cried De la Vega. '*We shall be among them!*'

'Jory,' urged Hazzard. 'We've got to get up to *Généreux* and Peard will make her veer off, or blast him with a broadside.' He turned for De la Vega on the quarterdeck. '*Cesár! We've got to give him support! He'll be shot to pieces!*'

Wayland watched, dumbstruck, as the frigate roared into battle, grey geysers erupting around her as the first of the three French escort frigates replied while trying to draw Peard's fire from the *Généreux*. Wayland turned to Madeleine. 'They're brave,' he said, 'doing their best to stop Peard...' But she had gone.

He looked round for her. Instead he found Christina, in her dark Moorish habit, her face pale, disembodied and floating among the black headdress. She was murmuring to herself as she stared forward – Wayland turned to follow her eye. Christina was staring at Madeleine.

In the mayhem of clearing for action and the arrival of the *Success*, Madeleine had ascended the steps to the fo'c'sle deck. Wayland moved forward, a frown gathering as she stopped by the bell and the foremast.

Wayland moved forward along the deck, the cries of gunners and the marines fading from his perception as he went – wondering what she might want with the bell. He began to hurry, stumping along the deck faster.

'Madeleine...'

But she passed the bell and the foremast and moved to the forward rail, her arms hanging almost dead at her side, as if she were sleep-walking. She stopped beside the binnacle – the powerful *faro*.

The crews around her busy with bow-chasers and carronades, none paid her attention.

She studied the light seeping from its closed shutter doors, casting its muted glow, even in the dawn. The decks rising and falling, she put a hand to the shutter doors as if to keep her balance. Wayland's voice cut through to her.

'*Madeleine.*'

She turned. Wayland had stopped halfway up the steps, his pistol out. One of the forward gunners looked at the dark French ships ahead, the sea, and Madeleine, by the *faro*. There seemed little doubt what might happen. He moved towards her, but her left hand pointed a small pistol at him, and he stopped. They all did. He cried out, '*Securdo, securdo! Capitan!*'

By the boats, the marines looked up, Hazzard and Cook unmoving.

The spray burst from the bows, the wind blowing Madeleine's dress in swirls about her legs, her hair pinned in her tight bonnet, its plumage bouncing in the northwesterly as the *Volpone* heaved and heeled. The lightening streak on the distant horizon left her in silhouette, her face in shadow. Her hand had not moved from the *faro*.

Wayland looked at the two French frigates dead ahead – and, just beyond them, the *Généreux*. A burst of gunfire from *Success* was a mere dull rapping in the distance as Peard continued his first run. In the commotion up ahead, the French had not spotted the *Volpone* creeping upon them from astern. Madeleine's hand clutched at the *faro* shutters. There was no question what she intended.

Wayland cocked the pistol and aimed.

'Do not,' he said to her.

Madeleine did not move. But neither did she take her hand from the shutters.

'You would shoot, Thomas?' she asked.

'Do not,' he repeated.

The wind was pushing the *Volpone* at nearly ten knots – within five minutes they would outstrip the French ships ahead and sail between them.

'*Madre de Dios…*' De la Vega watched from the quarterdeck, taking the cheroot from his lips, his long tied hair flying round his shoulders. 'Alfonso…'

Alfonso had the same thought and handed him a Turkish musket. De la Vega cocked it and slowly brought it to the aim. '*Listos, filio mio…*' *Be ready, my son.*

'Why?' Wayland asked her. 'All of this. Not your fault.'

She raised her chin, shaking her head. 'It is. Kléber needs our troops.'

Watching behind Wayland's shoulder, Hazzard slowly drew the Lorenzoni pistol from its sling. Wayland did not notice, his gaze fixed on Madeleine.

'To surrender?'

'To guarantee the peace, Thomas!' she cried. 'To withdraw with honour.'

'*Honour?*' repeated Wayland. 'Putting these good men and women at risk? My friends? That will gain no honour.'

'*Généreux must get through…!*'

Hazzard watched her, his thumb on the lock of the pistol, but he knew it would never be fast enough. One shutter door would be all that was needed. A lookout would turn, the alarm would be raised, and both frigates would adjust their helm and fire their broadsides into *Volpone*'s bows, the perfect rake.

Wayland took a steadying breath, the ship rocked and plunged, the horizon rising and falling, the French ships getting larger. 'And Petrides?'

'One of yours.' With her free hand she wiped away tears, then waved a dismissive hand. 'I had given him false intelligence. For many years…' Her French was almost lost on the wind, her voice choked with misery.

Underhill moved slowly past the mainmast, his hand slipping into his waistband and retrieving a pistol. Hazzard put out a hand to stop him, shaking his head slowly – *Wait*.

'Madeleine,' pleaded Wayland. '*Je t'en prie.*' I beg of you. 'Come down.'

He could not see, but she was weeping again, her head drooping in sadness, in regret, the wind in her face. The sterns of the French frigates grew steadily larger at the bows, a maddened team of lashed horses unconcerned with what lay behind. Suddenly she pulled herself straight and said, '*Pour l'honneur*,' and dropped her hand, throwing open a single *faro* shutter just as Wayland fired.

The crack of the report snatched by the wind, she pitched backwards in a sudden mime show, arms flung forward as if trying to reach for him – to catch something to stop her fall – but she struck the deck, a broken doll. The French ships leapt into sharp focus, blasted with bright light, their decks and rails and arched taffrails floating spectrally against the dark sea, their names *Sans Pareille* and *Badine* bold in large Romanesque gilt characters across their curved haunches, the dawn lost and insignificant in the *faro*'s glare.

Admiral

Bells clanged in alarm as the French lookouts cried, '*Anglais, anglais, ennemi s'approche,*' as *Volpone* reared on a cresting wave and plunged half a length closer, her bows passing their exposed flanks. The French crews raced to man the guns amid calls of '*Arrêtez, arrêtez,*' to stop, to hold fire – '*Tirez pas*' – for fear of hitting their sister ship opposite. They had been caught in a death-trap.

De la Vega tossed Alfonso his musket and bit on the cheroot. '*Cañones a babor y estribor! Fuego!*' Guns to port and starboard, fire.

As she overtook the stern quarters of the two frigates, *Volpone* opened up with her forward guns from both batteries, carronades, 18-pounders and 24s, as the two frigates drew past, the *Volpone* a mass of muzzle-blasts between them. The sea erupted around the two smaller ships as they hauled away to the north and south to escape, the decks of *Sans Pareille* bursting with clouds of shot and wood, men flying from the exploding rails. Several gunnery crews tried to reply, firing low with 9- and 12-pounders, the rounds thrashing the water or bouncing off *Volpone*'s hull. The *Badine* gave a withering fire from her stern chasers, and Hazzard shouted, '*Down!*' the marines throwing themselves to the decks as the splinters flew, the small rounds whistling through the rigging and rails.

Volpone slewed to port to make for the *Généreux* just ahead, and the gunners let go with both port and starboard broadsides, the regularly pounding blasts driving the wind from Hazzard's chest as he gasped, '*Marines! To the boats!*' The air thudded and boomed in a raging storm of sound.

Far off the port bow and lying abeam of the *Généreux*, the *Fauvette* had tried to turn to windward to meet HMS *Success*, but could rally only a desultory salvo as Peard streaked past, heading straight for *Généreux*. In her haste to evade the *Volpone* astern, the *Sans Pareille* bore up and nearly fell off the wind as Peard charged the gap between her prow and the stern of the *Généreux*.

Close-hauled to port, Peard sliced across the wind, heeling sharply, firing at *Sans Pareille* from her starboard guns, while passing the *Généreux* barely twenty yards off her high stern galleries and firing a sixteen-gun broadside, raking her with double-shotted 18-pound rounds.

The gallery windows burst into clouds of silvering crystal, splinters, and charred iron, men crying out on the taffrail as *Success* ploughed straight past with impunity, passing the bows of *Badine* to starboard and firing a rake from the bows. Within minutes she was coming about, ready to make a second dash. Rocking from the impacts, smoke drifting from her scarred rump, *Généreux* rose before Hazzard's eyes, her towering masts and spread of sail dwarfing her escort frigates, huge before them: *Volpone* had caught her up.

'Sail ahead!' Handley called down. '*Seventy-four! Beating to wind'ard… and a second…! Third beyond, and a fourth! Four sail of the line!*' He was almost clambering out of the tops in his excitement. '*They're ours, sir! It's the Alex,*' he whooped, '*…and Foudroyant! It's Nelson! It's only Lord bloody Nelson, sir!*'

With the marines, the Spaniards and Catalans gave a cheer – *Nelsone, Nelsone!* Hazzard scrambled to his feet, fearing the distraction aboard the *Généreux* would not last long enough. '*Nine Company in the boats! We have one chance!*' He called to the quarterdeck as he ran, '*Cesár! Más cerca!*' Closer!

Dela Vega waved an arm. '*Sí, sí, amigo! Carlos, timón a estribor!*' Helm to starboard.

Four small attack boats freshly tarred and blackened at Palermo were slung two a-side of the quarterdeck, large enough to seat eight; but both of the starboard boats had been shattered by small-bore shot. The remaining two still hung suspended from the portside quarterdeck booms, the marines guiding them to the rail. Hazzard threw himself into the first portside boat. '*Jory! Move!*'

Cook roared out, '*One Section to forward boat! Two Section to aft boat! Move yer arses!*' He, De Lisle, Kite, Warnock and Hesse followed Hazzard, falling in as Carlos and his deckhands jumped to the lines – '*Suelta el bote.*' *Drop the boat* – and dropped them below the rail and the muzzle of the quarterdeck guns. A salvo from *Sans Pareille* rapped out across the water, the flashes suddenly bright in the early morning gloom, the rounds howling through the air, banging into the *Volpone's* hull plate not ten yards away from Hazzard in the prow of the lead boat. He flung himself down and ducked as a gun–port door splintered, cracking and sagging as the boat smacked into the waves. Paddles in hand, Cook shouted, '*Dig for Davy, lads! Dig for the Jenny Rooks!*'

His cheeks daubed with two white and red stripes, Warnock raged at the ships, '*For Sheppy and Leander!*' The others took up the call: *For Sheppy, for Sheppy!*

Underhill, Pettifer, Tariq, Napier and Cochrane dropped from the davits in the second black boat, Pettifer calling, '*Right be'ind yer, Cookie!*' but Cook bellowed back over his shoulder, '*Move yerself, Pet, and make for that fat arse!*'

'*Whose? Hers or yours?*'

Underhill cackling far behind, Hazzard paddled hard for the *Généreux*, hearing them call the time behind him – *One two, one two, one two, dig!* The grapple was sharp and clumsy in his lap, the rope coiled at his feet, his one hope that they could make the ship before they took fire – or before Renaudin accelerated away. They paddled up the crests and harder down into the troughs, *Volpone* bearing off to port behind them, holding fire, the boats caught between her starboard broadside and *Généreux*'s stern and a perfect raking shot.

'*Twenty-five yards!*' called Cook. '*Faster, ye buggers! Put some juldee in it!*'

Hazzard dug with his paddle, the shattered galleries of the 74 rising and falling before him, limned by the brightening horizon glowing behind – *Faster, faster* – the grey swell launching them forwards, the boiling wake of the great ship pitching them up and rocking them abeam. '*Dig! Dig, dammit!*'

Hazzard focussed on the target: the stern gig he had seen suspended from her poopdeck taffrail had gone, blown to smithereens by the *Success* in the same passing broadside rake that had blasted the gallery windows, the broad gilt name across her stern – *Généreux* – scarred by impacts and flaming powder.

The feeling of exposure was terrible, the bark of the guns and churning roar of the wake deafening as the waves clashed and chopped, rising and falling, the nausea filling his gorge. He felt a shudder in the air overhead and heard Cook – *Down!* – as a 9-pound round screamed past and smacked into the water ten yards off. *Sans Pareille* and *Badine* had swung their prows back towards them, a lookout standing on the rail of *Badine*, pointing. '*Fantassins! Marsouins!*' Soldiers, marines.

Hazzard realised it was his Bombay scarlet: *Good*, he thought, *now they know what to expect* – and the lookout gave the dread alarm: '*Anglais!*'

The water hissed, another blast from a 9-pounder shivering the air overhead, waterspouts pluming, the spray soaking, Hazzard's vision blurred, water sheeting off his face, the salt stinging the eyes. '*Stay with me! Keep going!*' The *Badine* plunged against a bright sky to the right as if racing him, the *Généreux* looming, Cook's voice muffled in Hazzard's ear: '*Fifteen yards, stand by!*'

A figure appeared at a smashed gallery window above, then vanished as the air shrieked with rounds, chopping the water, someone crying out, *Hesse, he's hit,* musketry thwacking into the gunwale of the dark boat—

Ten yards.

De Lisle hauled on the tiller and kept her lined up with the stern. '*Climbing party ready! Mickey, Knock-Knock, on yer toes!*'

His right arm dark with blood, Hesse called out, '*Alle einsteigen!*' – *All aboard* – his anger cutting through clenched teeth and he cursed. '*Verdammt noch'mal, monsieur, you will pay for this! Gott save der verdammte king!*'

They leaned into their paddles. '*God save the King, God save the King!*'

'*Never give up the boat!*'

'*Clear aye!*'

'*Sir!*' Warnock reached forward to Hazzard at the prow, handing him his tomahawk. '*For the climb!*'

Hazzard glanced at it – the sharpened head, the deadly hook behind. He took it, stuffing the beaded and bedraggled feathered haft into his belt. '*You'll get it back!*'

Hazzard threw his paddle into the scuppers with a clatter and gathered up the grapple. '*Steady as she goes, Lil!*' The prow of the boat was rising and falling with such regularity he would use it for timing, trying to calculate the periodicity, angle, the soaking coil of line in his left hand, the hook swinging from his right, the towering block of the *Généreux* rising before him, shouts aboard: *Anglais, anglais!*

Because she was a *Téméraire*-class – and not an *Arrogant* like HMS *Bellerophon*, or even *Ardent*-class like HMS *Agamemnon* – she had no curving balcony to the stern to hook onto, only the flat-faced window galleries. He would have to get the grapple into a broken window or the smashed taffrail above.

HMS *Success* came to the rescue, firing once again from far off, partly obscured by the *Badine*, and *Généreux* replied, her 24-pounders booming, the sky thumping to the blasts. Hazzard slung the grapple just as the 74 heeled to starboard, the hooks snatching at the broken glazing bars of the shattered windows to the port quarter, where the captain's Great Cabin should be.

Pettifer called from the second boat some ten yards behind, '*Whale ho! We got 'er!*'

The rope was yanked from Hazzard's hand as the coil unravelled like a whip. Secured to the boat's painter ring, the line tautened and the boat jerked forward, Hazzard nearly flying off his feet into Cook and Warnock behind, the musket-fire now fizzing and snapping off the waves around them from the *Badine* and *Sans Pareille*.

'*Line!*' cried Hazzard. The boat bucked and skidded across the water, slamming against the waves, pulled now at seven knots by their prey running with the wind. Kite passed the other grappling line forward and Hazzard swung it, and launched.

The hook travelled upwards, the knotted line looping out behind in crooked waves. The grapple bounced from the taffrail, but snagged the frame of the topmost windows to the port quarter.

Volpone opened up again on the *Badine*, and the small frigate heeled away to starboard to engage *Success*, the morning now bright on her sails as she bore off – but *Sans Pareille* maintained fire, the water around them shattering into leaping spouts, De Lisle calling out, hit, Hesse shouting to Kite, '*Take his arm, hold his arm!*'

The boat flying in the wake of the battleship, Hazzard looped the line round his waist and Cook called out, but Hazzard only shouted back, '*Get them under her tail, Jory, or get out!*' – and jumped.

He heard Cook shout, '*Covering fire! Unwrap yer locks...*' but no more. He knew the line was effectively the hypotenuse of a right-angled triangle, and when he jumped, this would collapse and he would be dragged through the water – but he had no idea how bad it would be. He hit the cold surface and gasped, the constant pummelling of spray choking, his head going under, his lungs bursting for air as he tried to pull himself along the knotted line – *Up, up* – panic setting in as he fought for breath, taking great gulps when he could, the salt burning his throat as he coughed it up and hacked. *Drowning, Christ God, drowning.*

Jettied over the water, the stern was so very close above – *Three men, that's all, height of three men.* The blasted gallery windows hung like a great mountain bluff over his head, just out of reach, the massive yard-thick rudder swinging close as he skidded through the wake – *Watch it, watch it* – its scored gauge marks bright, the grey foaming water sheeting off the Roman numerals as the ship rose and fell before him, a dangling fish on a line, exhausted. *God, God, God.*

Fighting to breathe, Hazzard turned onto his front, shouting as he pulled with his arms and struggled to stand on the rope in the flying stream, his boots heavy with seawater. Cook's voice called loud nearby, their towline taut and snapping somewhere to his right, his arms burning with the strain of the relentless drag and he wanted to call for him: *Jory.*

The rudder swung with a creaking groan beside him and he was pulled into the turn, *Généreux* dipping and heeling as she turned to starboard to face the *Success*. This gave him sudden relief, the drag decreasing, and he sank like a stone. But the swelling waves raised him up, and the hind of the great ship seemed to sink towards him. He lunged upwards. *Now.*

Standing on the knots of the sodden line, he rose from the sucking clutches of the water, his shoulders roaring, and swung free. He climbed, rising one full length at a time, feeling his weight, boots full, his Bombay jacket heavy, and the *Généreux* unwittingly reeled him in. He craned his neck to look up, the rim of the lowest gallery just two yards above, his boots kicking out in panic, trying to find the wooden hull, the rudder chains and a torn remnant of the stern rope-ladder smacking at him, his body swinging, his hands wanting to open and let go. *Come on, come on.*

The ship lurched back to port and flung him outwards, away from the gallery windowsill, then swung him back. *Christ above.* Someone was calling from behind or in his mind, urging him on – *Renaudin, I'm coming* – the pumps disgorging tons of water into the sea far below as he dangled and swung like a spider. *Frame, take the frame.* He reached up, his fingers feeling the edge of the splintered wood. It was enough, a gift of hope, and he seized upon it, launching himself further – *Now your hand* – when a grizzled face in a woollen cap stuck out of the broken window and looked down at him. He looked at the shaking rope hanging from the hook above him and cried out, '*Anglais! Anglais! Ici, ici!*' Here, here.

He ducked back inside and Hazzard struggled upwards, but the sailor reappeared within moments, the long barrel of a Charleville musket emerging, the stock catching the broken frame awkwardly, the crewman trying to lean out and angle the muzzle downwards, voices from inside calling, '*Tiens alors, tirez, tirez!*' *Come on, shoot, shoot!*

The timbers around the seaman leapt with shot and splinters, and Hazzard shielded his eyes. The man cried out, the musket plunging past him to splash into the water below, the Frenchman sagging in the window, one arm hanging, a belated offer of help to Hazzard.

He heard the marines in the boat below – '*Go on, sir, go on!*' He hauled himself up the line, slipping on the knots, until his hand felt Warnock's tomahawk at his belt. He swung it up, smashed the sharp hook into the woodwork and felt the firm grip. He pulled himself up, hearing himself shouting with the pain as he found it, a firm edge – *windowsill* – and he heaved himself up, catching a glimpse of Cook and the others below, Kite and Warnock reloading.

Officers' gunroom.

Half a dozen men of the lower-deck gun-crews struggled with their dead crewmate, smoke drifting in the cabin, the 24-pounders being swabbed for reload. They stared at Hazzard, a frozen tableau. Then one shouted, '*L'anglais, l'anglais!*' They dropped the feet of their crewmate and one lunged with a knife, but Hazzard swung the axe upwards and sprang for the next level, his legs frantic as they called after him, '*Vite, vite.*' *Quickly.* Finding a purchase on the blistered gilt arm of a carven Neptune, he clambered up to the shattered remains of the Great Cabin above.

The place was dark, furniture upended, a table with a broken leg, chairs thrown back against folding bulwarks shattered by the blasts. The senior officers were on deck engaging the *Success*, but the alarm had been called – an *anglais* had climbed aboard – and in his mind he could already hear running footsteps on the stairs, and he imagined French marines leading the baying pack.

He heaved himself up – *Get in, get in* – hanging momentarily half in and half out of the broken casement window, its hinges laid bare, his hands already bloodied by splinters, glass and twisted metal. He fell inside, collapsing to the plank floor – *Too dark, can't bloody see* – to the cries of '*Arrêtez! Aux armes!*'

A door burst in from round a collapsed bulwark, and he heard the sound of pistols being cocked. '*Le voilà!*' *There he is.* But Hazzard could do nothing, and lay face down, gasping for breath, arms afire, as a rough hand took him by the collar and he thought, *What a damn fool thing to do.*

Drums rapped as the crew of the flagship HMS *Foudroyant* cleared for action, the call coming down from the lookout above, '*Deck there! Unidentified ship of sail! Range three miles, closing!*'

Pacing the quarterdeck from binnacle to the portside shrouds, watched in awe by his junior officers and crew, Rear-Admiral Horatio Nelson strode angrily to the mainmast and called up, the bo'sun and a brace of scarlet marines stepping aside. 'Lookout, deck! Identify ensign! At once, sir!'

When the reply came down in the negative, he strained to glimpse the warship in the distance. Seething, he turned to Captain Sir Edward Berry peering through an eyeglass at the portside shrouds, his First and Second Lieutenants close at hand, 'What *is* she, Sir Edd'ard? Is it *her*?'

A young and trembling midshipman stood beside Nelson on the crowded quarterdeck, holding a cumbersome eyeglass, waiting. He offered it, ready. 'S–sir? I mean, my lord?'

They could hear the flat reports of gunfire carried on the wind. Barely able to contain his agitation, Nelson marched to the shrouds to join Berry, Parsons hurrying behind; he raised the glass for him and Nelson steadied it with his remaining hand. Sure enough, reflecting the dead white of the grey morning came the bright sails of a ship far off the port bow.

'Unknown as yet, my lord,' said Berry, trying to refocus his eyeglass as he peered beyond the port bow. Braced to starboard as they tacked in the brisk wind, they had a clear view out to sea, the bright sails of an approaching ship mere specks of white in the distance to the naked eye. 'What do you make of her, sirs?' demanded Berry.

The First Lieutenant focussed his own glass and reported, 'Mains'ls shortened, sir,' he said, 'tops set, trying to keep her speed down…'

Nelson looked up from his eyepiece, squinting into the lightening western skies, 'It *must* be her… it *must* be *Le Généreux*…' he said, 'Mr Hazzard…'

Still watching through the glass, Berry grumbled, 'Let us pray he was right, my lord.' He looked back at Nelson over his shoulder. 'I took against him when he dropped to my deck amid all those damn fish—'

The Second Lieutenant pointed. 'Sir, *look*—'

Berry turned back to his eyeglass, and reacted suddenly to what he saw. 'Change of course, my lord, I believe she is bearing up, heading away—'

A second call came down. '*Deck there! The stranger… is a line-of-battle ship, going large on the starboard tack!*'

'Very well Sir Edd'ard,' said Nelson, concealing his relief, putting his left hand behind his back. 'Squadron signal,' he called, turning about so all could see him. '*Enemy in sight.*'

The lieutenants bent to their tasks as the call went up, *Enemy in sight, stand by your guns, upper and middle gundecks ready to run out* – and the ship thrummed with activity, gun-crews loading the quarterdeck 18-pounders beside them, *Step to it, sharply, move yerselves* – Nelson looking off to port, the distant ship drawing ever nearer, as he murmured, '*Mr Hazzard… have you done it again…?*'

His musings were confirmed by the call from above. '*Deck, lookout! Convoy dead ahead! Enemy line-of-battle ship, three enemy corvette frigates, and three enemy transports in sight! HMS Success engaging!*'

Nelson bent to the eyepiece of Midshipman Parsons' eyeglass once more. In the distance was the fast-moving frigate of Captain Shuldham Peard, puffing white clouds of gunsmoke, tattoos of percussive thuds reaching their ears moments later. Nelson stepped away from the glass. 'Signal for general chase, Sir Edd'ard – we *must* catch her.'

HMS *Alexander* surged ahead off the port beam, going in for the attack, *Audacious* and *Northumberland* coming hard astern. The first heavily laden transport ship tried to turn away to the north, but she was poorly positioned. HMS *Alexander* had caught her in her tack, her warning shots booming in their ears. Berry leaned forward, excited. 'Could be the *Ville de Marseille*, as we heard tell, my lord,' said Berry, cries of jubilation coming down from above, 'Young Harrington's got her, my lord – the *Alex* has got her, and she's striking! Well done, not a shot in anger.'

Nelson gripped the rail before him tightly. 'Let him have his prize, Sir Edd'ard, we want *Le Généreux*—'

Berry remained circumspect. 'We are not wholly certain she is the *Généreux*, my lord—'

Nelson looked to the flank, *Northumberland* gaining astern. 'It is most assuredly *Le Généreux*, Sir Edd'ard, as we know *Le Guillaume Tell* lies in port, and to me alone on the flagship can she surrender! We must – and shall – *beat* the *Northumberland!* Make *Foudroyant* fly!'

The bo'sun bellowed from the mainmast, *Come on, lads, make 'er fly for his lordship! Let's beat the Thumberland!* The rigging hands cheered and Berry replied to Nelson, 'We shall, my lord! Signal *Northumberland* to maintain station! We shall cross her path!'

The helmsmen answered grimly, '*Aye, sir,*' but knew they could do little more than they were, but Nelson turned, catching the tone. 'And you, sir – I shall knock you off your perch if you are so inattentive! Sir Edd'ard, your best quartermaster to the weather-wheel at once. We shall catch her, by God!'

Berry raised topgallants and staysails, and even considered the blinds on the spritsailyard, as *Foudroyant* rocked and fought her way through the waves. Nelson stormed to the rail, his severed arm twitching at the elbow, a sign of his greatest agitation. Berry glanced at the First Lieutenant at his side, and added quietly, 'Careful now, the admiral is working his fin.' The lieutenant doffed his hat – '*Aye, sir*' – and jumped to it. '*Prepare to come about, ease your braces!*' Nelson watched in frustration as they tried to claw their way upwind to the battle being enacted before them – their only consolation, that their prey was being drawn inexorably into their opening jaws.

–

Hazzard could smell the gun-oil and powder of their weapons and the musty wool of their clothing but stayed still, breathing tidally, quietly. '*Eh tiens, vous salaud—*' *Hey there, you bastard*. A rough hand grabbed his collar, but he hung limp, letting them do the hard work of getting him up. He spun, seeing their surprise at the scimitar, and it flashed round in an arc, the residual image bright red – a throat, cutting the other across the chest – and they gasped and fell to the floor.

The Lorenzoni useless, soaking wet, Hazzard snatched up the pistol one of them had dropped and pulled himself to one knee, then collapsed – *Christ* – and staggered to his feet, banging into the overturned desk with its shining gilt lozenges and cracked black lacquer, one shaking hand feeling for the pendant drawer-pull. He yanked it open: *empty*.

The ship rocked from beam to beam and he could feel a second turn, this time to port, the great ship lashing its tail like a fish to outfox the gunnery of *Success* and line up a broadside. He fell against the broken bulwark, and saw daylight to his right: an open door to a service area and the captain's private toilet, the quarter galleries. Standing, transfixed, was the figure of a seaman. With a start, Hazzard levelled the pistol – then lowered it as the frozen face flinched, eyes clenched shut, tears streaming: a terrified sailor, possibly the captain's servant – gaunt, frightened, in pale striped Breton jersey and long-tailed cap over long lank hair. He raised his hands slowly to shield his face. '*M-m-m'sieur…*'

'*Le capitaine. Où est-il?*' demanded Hazzard. *Where is he?*

The man opened his eyes warily and raised a shaking hand to point to a door beside him. Hazzard lunged towards it, the man quailing and diving away, seized the latch and threw it open and charged down the panelled corridor.

A marine burst from one of the cabins by the staircase, shouting, '*Anglais! Anglais à bord—*' He stopped short when he saw Hazzard, and tried to drag his musket from his shoulder but it was too clumsy, just as Wayland had said all those months ago. Hazzard was into him in a moment, the tomahawk smashing his clavicle with an audible snap as he passed, the man folding forward with a cry and hiss of breath, not fatal but enough. *Binnacle, wheel.* The guns fired again and he rocked – *Legs weak, keep going* – emerging in the wheelhouse under the dark varnished beams of the poopdeck above, and he thought of the corridors at the Admiralty buildings that day with Blake – *like a Parisian hotel* – and Sir Rafe Lewis telling him, '*Find them, Captain: stop them, sink them, kill them.*'

He crashed into the three men holding the wheel horns and fell into another as he burst into the light of the quarterdeck. Men cried out, '*Aux armes, ennemi à bord!*' *Enemy aboard.* Marines at the shrouds turned about, shock on their faces, dragging their muskets from their shoulders, one faster than the others – but Hazzard saw the billowing white jibs of HMS *Success* as she raced past the starboard bow, and fired a passing broadside.

Peard's marksmanship was perfect. Clouds of splinters and dust burst around them as the 18-pound rounds hurtled through the ship, 32-pound carronades smashing the weather deck, blowing men from the fo'c'sle foredeck, rounds hurtling along the decks to the command centre of the quarterdeck. Hazzard threw himself flat, pulling a young ensign down with him, the boy crying a terrified prayer, a panel exploding just behind them, a round blasting its way through each cabin wall. The starboard shrouds erupted with splinters and a thunderclap of sound, and a lieutenant flew off his feet, the smell of charred rope and wood dense amid the tang of burning powder. Hazzard held on to the boy tightly, keeping him down, '*Bougez pas, bougez pas, attendez—*' *Don't move, don't move, wait.* He looked about, his ears ringing.

Christ above, Renaudin, where are you?

The dust and ash floating in a fine powder, he saw the lieutenant – a big, red-haired man, his hand bloody, his arm torn, the blue coat shredded on one shoulder. Hazzard undid the black stock from round his own neck and tried to staunch the bleeding. Cries of the wounded echoing from stem to stern, he shouted down at him, '*Restez-là, aurez besoin d'un tourniquet—*' *Stay there, you'll need a tourniquet.* He looked round. '*Assistance ici! Officier!*'

It was Lieutenant Rou. He clamped his hand on the black band of Hazzard's cotton stock as Hazzard tore off his coat and pulled it over Rou's chest, the white lining marked with his own blood. The big Norman looked at Hazzard, his eye noting the Bombay scarlet now keeping him warm, '*M-merci, m'sieur…*' and then sank back, shivering.

Hindered by a clodding deafness, Hazzard looked about, the world shifting and sliding from his vision and he blinked, a trickle of blood on his cheek, *Hit.* He felt his head – *Stay awake* – the hair sticky, and he could feel where he had been struck, nerve lights flashing behind his eyes.

To his left, by the portside shrouds, a number of officers had gathered round a figure on the deck. He saw that it was most likely Perrée, in an admiral's coat, blood pouring from a gash above one eye. They called to strike the colours to save the admiral, '*Sauvons l'amiral, capitulons pour la grâce,*' – *for mercy's sake* – but Perrée waved them off, his voice a croak. '*Ce n'est rien, mes amis… Continuons… nôtre besogne…*' *It is nothing, my friends. Let us continue our work.* He protested as they sat him up, '*Continuons… Continuons…*'

One man broke away, hurling himself forward to the quarterdeck rail, watching *Success* and roaring, '*Tous canons babors! Feu à la fois!*' *Fire all larboard guns.*

The horizon shifted as *Généreux* turned to starboard and bared her port broadside at *Success*, firing her angry retort, the massed thunder of 18s, 24s and 36-pounders bringing clouds of gunsmoke, obscuring the outclassed frigate. There were cheers from aloft of '*Vive l'amiral! Vive l'amiral!*'

HMS *Success* hauled away, but came about once again, her sails bright in the winter sun, Peard not letting go, even with Nelson closing in from the southeast.

A figure rose up from beside Perrée and spun round. '*Take the admiral to my cabin!*'

Hazzard saw the face and knew without doubt: it was Renaudin.

The Second Lieutenant argued with him, 'He must command! Nelson is in range. An admiral must face an admiral.'

Renaudin tugged the pistol from his belt. 'Stand by my orders, you damned aristo fool!'

Hazzard watched, the scimitar in hand, when he heard Rou's husking voice. '*Cap'taine…*'

Renaudin turned, saw him, and rushed over, ignoring Hazzard crouching nearby in shirtsleeves, and knelt at the Norman's side. 'Rou… Adalbert… *ça va…*? You big stupid farmer, *hein*? You took a hit, well done, now you go…' He pulled Hazzard's coat away gingerly to reveal the spreading blood on the deck. Hazzard leaned over and clamped his hand over the wound to the chest and underarm. The praying young ensign joined them.

'Tourniquet,' Hazzard demanded of Renaudin. '*Vite.*' Quickly.

Renaudin undid the sodden black stock from under Rou's trembling fingers, looping it under the arm, tying it off as Hazzard maintained pressure, not taking his eyes off him. Renaudin slid a thick splinter of wood into the knot and twisted the tourniquet tight, and Rou groaned with the pain.

Renaudin looked at Hazzard.

'It is you.'

Hazzard did not move.

'It is.'

Renaudin glanced at the sword in Hazzard's lap, the blood on the blade. 'Milord Mamluk. So. *Mon dieu*. The bomb? The gun-ports?'

Renaudin glanced at the discarded pistol lying just out of reach. Hazzard moved the blade, its tip pointing at him.

'No.'

Renaudin stared at him, the flat battering of guns and waterspouts loud all around them. 'I cannot surrender my ship to you, even if I lose in a duel. I am but flag-captain.'

There came a cry from the portside shrouds. '*Capitaine! Elle se retourne!*' She's coming back.

HMS *Success.*

'My ship,' said Renaudin. 'I must—'

Hazzard grated under his breath, 'Logbook.'

Journal de bord.

Renaudin's face creased into incomprehension. 'The ship's *log*…?'

Hazzard brought the sword forward, Rou's eyes following it, Hazzard's voice a low rasp, his French cutting quick and sharp. 'Did Captain Lejoille attack and sink a twin-masted English lugger or *aviso* after his escape from the Nile?'

Renaudin stared at Hazzard as if he were mad, and threw his arms up in an exasperated shrug. 'How should I know this? They… They capture the *Léandre*…'

Another cry from the men gathered round the admiral. '*Cap'taine!*'

Renaudin kept his eyes on Hazzard and shouted over his shoulder, '*Helm one point to larboard! Fire as she comes to bear! Stand by to ram! Engage!*'

'*She is too fast!*'

Hazzard would not let him go. '*Come on, man! Logbook! Le journal de bord! Où est-il!*' *Where is it?*

'*Nom d'un nom, sacre…*' Renaudin looked round again off the midships and saw the approaching English frigate. He threw a vague hand in the direction of the dark passage and his cabin. 'It is there – *there*! I cannot! I must… My ship, *ma foi!*'

Lieutenant Rou coughed, his voice hoarse. 'I remember… *un lougre…*'

A lugger.

Hazzard seized on the news. 'Where? When?'

Rou put a hand to his shoulder. 'Days after… She… She moved fast, *alors*. A clever captain, went to lee… each time we try…' He coughed violently. 'Used the sunset, the mist, every trick… We could not fire a shot. *Capitaine* saw the *Leander* to the north, and we followed…'

They had gone for the *Leander* instead of Tomlinson and the *Valiant.*

Hazzard looked at Renaudin, but the Frenchman had lost his patience. 'Pah! *Mon dieu, putain alors!*' He jumped back and reached for the pistol just as HMS *Success* came in for her final pass and the quarterdeck exploded with fire.

Hazzard rolled away as the rails flew to pieces, the portside shrouds blowing apart, a ball crashing through the chainwale, blocks and lines flying in all directions, the officers around Perrée thrown back by the bursts – Peard had struck the heart of the ship. Hazzard crawled under the fire and flying splinters and langrage-shot towards Renaudin. He was still standing by the mainmast, and Hazzard called to him, '*Get down, you fool!*' but the captain kept shouting, *Fire, fire!* At last, Renaudin took a hit and his leg buckled, one knee going down, and he cried out, collapsing.

Success ran with the wind towards the rest of the blockade fleet, signals rippling up the mast of the *Foudroyant*: *Success to disengage.* But it was too late for Peard. *Généreux* fired a massed broadside as she turned to port. The roar deafening, thudding through his chest, Hazzard gasped with the shock, pulling Renaudin down, someone shouting somewhere, '*L'amiral, l'amiral!*'

Hazzard looked out through the maze of netting and severed lines hanging from the rigging as *Success* seemed to break up, her rails bursting with the heavy impacts, mainmast cracking and tilting, foremast going, the sails holed and flapping, the little ship listing away to port as she drifted, the crew of *Généreux* cheering.

On the quarterdeck of *Généreux* there was a thick silence as they gathered about Perrée once again – no longer propped on his chair, but lying on the deck. Hazzard lurched with a terrible memory of the Nile, of Admiral Brueys on the *Orient*, torn nearly in half – and here too was Perrée, a round having carried away a leg at the hip, leaving him broken and bloody. Renaudin pulled himself up, repeating, *I said, did I not, Admiral?* but Hazzard could barely hear.

Perrée cleared his choking throat and gasped, '*Capitaine*... it is your ship once again... Nelson is at our door.'

Renaudin clasped Perrée's hand, shaking with anger. 'It will cost him dear—'

'No, no,' said Perrée. 'You must get the men through... to Kléber... to Egypt... Marsa Sirocco...'

Renaudin shook his head. 'Malta is impossible, *mon amiral. C'est fini.*' It is over.

Hazzard found himself there at his side, on one wounded knee, one hand in the spreading blood of the French admiral before him, the only other who had been at Shubra Khit. '*Il a raison, Amiral.*' He is right, Admiral.

Perrée blinked at him, with the faintest light of recognition. 'You, *m'sieur.* I know you...'

Hazzard nodded as the other officers looked at him, his torn and bloodied shirt, his French bearing the educated roll of Grenoble. 'Admiral, I saw you command *Le Cerf* on the Nile, supporting the squares on shore.'

Perrée coughed, and blood spilled from his lips, one man whispering, '*Mon dieu, il meurt.*' *He is dying.*

'And you... saved the *savants*... Slew M-Mamluks to do so...' He looked away in sudden pain. 'Is your honour saved, *m'sieur*...?'

Hazzard looked to Renaudin's scarred face. 'It is, sir, as is yours. Like Nelson, you, too, are a victor of the Nile.'

Perrée blinked again, as if unable to see. 'A s-strange people... *cap'taine*... but you are kind. Y-you see...?'

Slowly, Perrée sagged, but his chest rose and fell as he breathed on, unconscious. Renaudin let go of his hand and glared at Hazzard. 'We shall fight your Nelson – fight them all, I *swear it.*'

The officers looked at him, at the admiral, his servant from below come with water, the surgeon leaning over him. It was clear Renaudin would fight Nelson alone if he could.

'Strike your colours,' said Hazzard quietly. 'You are outgunned.'

Renaudin was livid, trembling with rage. 'You mock! We do not... We *cannot*—' He broke off and let out a trembling breath.

'You have no idea,' said Hazzard, 'in what esteem you are both held by the Royal Navy.' He looked at the crew. 'Let them live.'

Nelson, however, was in no mood for parleys. A voice cried down from the tops, '*Enemy sail off larboard bow,*' but it came too late: the *Foudroyant* fired a brace of shot and chain. All on the quarterdeck threw themselves flat, covering Perrée as Nelson blew away the tops with a single salvo, the maintopmast shattering at the crosstree, the bo'sun calling, '*All hands, look out below!*' The rigging tore and lashed out, the back- and forestays keeping the broken topmasts in stricken posture, leaning, sagging, the rigging hands struggling to clear the lines, the bo'sun bellowing, '*Take your lines! Take your lines and braces, damn you!*' But to little avail, as the crew above rescued their fellows, descending the rigging for fear of another shot.

Renaudin turned about, enraged, and saw Hazzard backing away into the passage to the Great Cabin, his bloodied red coat in hand, moving past the binnacle and wheel, Pettifer, Cook and Kite in their undress shirts, like every other sailor aboard, holding the helmsmen and quartermasters at gunpoint. Hesse and Tariq appeared above, at the poopdeck steps, followed by Warnock still in his warpaint, his musket ported at ease, but ready. '*Knock-knock*, eh?'

Foudroyant approached at the port bow, *Northumberland* and *Audacious* nearing the starboard, both ready to rake the *Généreux* if need be. Renaudin looked at Perrée, at Rou. The lieutenant gave him a nod. '*Cap'taine… à la maison…*' *Let's go home.*

Renaudin watched Hazzard and lowered his head, eased the lock on his pistol, and dropped it to the deck. '*Enseigne en bas…*'

Lower the colours.

Kite took Hazzard as he staggered into one of the shattered cabin walls. 'Easy, sir. You call for a cab?'

'Jolly good,' muttered Hazzard. 'Nine Company, to the boats.'

They heard the bells clanging on *Foudroyant*, *Audacious* and *Northumberland*, boats from *Audacious* already rowing out to *Success*. The *Alexander* waited a mile off to the southeast, the *Ville de Marseille* and the other transports under her watchful eye. The *Badine*, *Fauvette* and *Sans Pareille* had run with the wind, scattering far and wide, *Badine* the last visible in the distance, battered and bruised far off to the south.

Within five minutes, Hazzard and the marines were climbing down the lines hung from the Great Cabin, De Lisle, Napier and Cochrane in the remaining boat below. '*We lost the ovver one, sir!*' called Napier apologetically, hoping to explain. 'They shot lots o' 'oles in it.'

Cook and Pettifer manhandled Hazzard through the water and into the boat, heaving him over the gunwale. 'Careful, mind – covered in ruddy splinters an' muck…'

'Just yer reg'lar sort o'Tuesday, eh, sir,' cried Cochrane with unusual cheer.

Cook dragged a pair of boat-cloaks off the bench and draped one round Hazzard, one round his own shoulders. Warnock splashed into the water nearby, jumping from his line from the poopdeck far above. The *Généreux* sat waiting, the waves slapping at her scarred flanks, the debris of her broken tops hanging outboard, rigging hands trying to stabilise the damage, as boats from *Foudroyant* filled with marines headed to the boarding steps.

'I saw 'im,' said Warnock, climbing in. 'Nellie, watchin' on the *Fooder*. Not bad, eh? First *Orient*, and now *Generoox*. We been some places.'

De Lisle took the tiller. 'Eyes in the boat – paddles to fall. Making starboard aye, dig cheerily.'

The marines began to paddle, Pettifer on the forward bench with Warnock, Cochrane and Napier behind Hesse and Tariq, Kite and Underhill to the stern. In the centre, Hazzard sat slumped under the boat-cloak beside Cook, his eyes closed in blessed relief.

Eventually he looked out at the great ships, the sun brightening, burning off the frosted clouds, the Maltese day growing warmer, the sea bluer, the grey ebbing from his mind. The rigging hands on *Foudroyant* had formed up on the ratlines for an impromptu admiral salute. Perhaps it was for Nelson; or perhaps it was for Perrée. Hazzard thought of Shubra Khit, the cut-throat mercenaries, the gun boats – and Perrée. A boat was rowing across from *Généreux* to the *Foudroyant*, an officer in the stern – possibly Renaudin – a sword held rigid in his hand before him. Hazzard would have let him keep it. But not Nelson. Not for the one that got away.

Shortly he became aware of a great mass drawing slowly alongside: the wooden wall of the *Volpone*. The boat began to bob on her wake. Shouts of Spanish met his ear, lines were thrown down, and Pettifer caught them and tied off the painter, hauling them in from the prow, Underhill and De Lisle from the stern.

Hazzard seemed to sag and said softly, '*Jory...*' He exhaled with a sigh, '*She made it. She got home.*'

Sarah.

Tomlinson.

Cook gathered two of their tarred sawn-off Charlevilles, still wrapped in their oilcloth. 'Knew it, sir. Felt it in me bones. She were a determined lass.'

Hazzard remembered his last vision of her in the bloody surf of Acre, the musket-balls fizzing about him, and she faded away, now gone, on her way. Now, she was gone again, truly safe, thanks to Tomlinson, that dour, humourless lugger captain, and the only man he would trust at the helm for such a task. He had chosen well.

Once at the portside rail of *Volpone*, De la Vega embraced him. 'So,' he said, frowning at him thoughtfully. 'The ghosts? Do they sleep?'

Hazzard nodded. 'They sleep.'

Wayland shook their hands, a grim tint to his features: they had yet to speak of the loss of Madeleine, of her true loyalties, of her conflicts. Seabirds wheeled, screeching overhead, the sun flashing from behind the yards high above as the crew reefed the sails, Handley the only unmoving figure, a slowly waving arm – the ginger scarecrow was still there.

The Catalans and Spaniards were still making good the damage done by the *Badine* and *Sans Pareille;* it was minimal, but enough. Porter emerged from the stern hatch, his medical bag in hand, and Hazzard was pleased to see him. Wayland approached him with papers: a messenger had arrived from the *Foudroyant*, waiting on the far side of the quarterdeck.

'Something to read, sir.' He handed over the pages to Hazzard. The first was a scrawled note in an uncertain hand:

> My dear Major Hazzard,
>> That the King's Men were aboard afore the fleets could bring their guns to bear is fine testimony to your efforts and endurance. My congratulations, for you have fed my tigers once again. I shall count the Oddfellows and the new Commendatore Knight of Palermo in shares as just reward.
>> Behold, enclosed the uncivil tone of Grand Admiral his lordship. I pray it will not be too late to spare yet more bloodshed – convey as you wish with all haste to Sir Sidney. I know you will, as ever, take the best course.
>> In victory, and with gratitude to good sound men,
>> Nelson

Hazzard thought of Emma at the Villa Palagonia, her pain at Nelson's departure, and thanked God reason had prevailed.

Wayland waited, then handed over another. 'From the *Queen Charlotte*, sir, about the peace that was signed at El-'Arish last month.'

Hazzard was still in a fog, from the action, and from the tinctures given to him by Porter, and fought to understand. 'But... *why* did Desaix sign if this damned convoy could have reinforced them...?'

Wayland said nothing, but looked down.

'It makes no—' Hazzard put a hand to the gash on his forehead. It had started bleeding afresh. Then he saw it. '*Christ...*'

They had not known it was coming.

His heart sank at the prospect, as if he could feel their helplessness.

'They knew *something* had been promised,' said Wayland. 'Petrides made sure of that. And Madeleine...' He told Hazzard of the midnight rendezvous off the Sinai coast. The marines in earshot lowered their heads out of respect. 'Madeleine...' he said. 'She... that is, *we* managed to convince them the convoy was bound for Malta.' He sounded ashamed at his part in such a deception, but his voice hardened in conclusion. 'And that they had been abandoned. It proved... useful.'

De la Vega asked, 'How many *soldados* did they find?'

'Three thousand, sir. Heavy infantry and *chasseurs à pied*. The best.' Wayland looked at the Spanish crew and translated for them. 'We stopped them all.'

Hazzard looked at the letter. 'Was the peace ratified?'

The marines shifted about, and De Lisle asked, 'Is it all over, sir?'

'No, Lil,' replied Wayland. 'Far from it. Lord Keith received Cabinet refusal, but Lord Melville's men at the War House made them see sense to get the French out – and they rescinded the order. But too late.' He nodded at Keith's letter. 'Lord Keith knew only of their refusal.'

Hazzard glanced over it. 'Good Christ...'

'It was all so... *botched*, badly done, sir, each out of time with the other...' He indicated the page with an angry finger. 'So Lord Keith sent *this* to one of the finest generals of the French army.'

Hazzard read the note, '*Sir, I write to inform you that...*' the careful sloping hand of Admiral Lord Keith blurring under his eye as he read the insult that had been handed to Kléber: '*...His Majesty cannot consent to any capitulation on any terms save total unconditional surrender. Therefore you will...*' He read on, Keith's acid tone and frustration, not with Kléber, but with others, with Smith, with Nelson, demanding now that Kléber's army lay down their arms in abject surrender.

Hazzard thought of the beneficent old man behind the desk, and his general goodwill, but recalled his furious temper. 'Every French soldier will now be with Kléber.' He remembered the army that had sacked Jaffa, and churned the mud of Acre for months. He handed the letter to Cook.

Cook took it and they gathered round, reading. 'The Frogs'll be out for blood,' he said.

Hazzard glanced at the marines, exhausted, wounded. 'Cesár, get me back there. I'll go alone, for a parley. White flag, Sir Sidney's man, and make Kléber understand – make him see that London is behind the peace accord.'

Cook stared at him, his brick-red forehead thunderous. 'A white flag'd count for nuppence if they got a grudge on—'

Underhill was right behind him. 'Cookie's right, sir. White flag won't 'elp if'n we went back on our word.'

'Where you goes, we goes,' said Kite, then more quietly, 'Sir. Beggin' yer pardon...'

'Aye,' affirmed Warnock.

Hazzard looked at them all, as determined as he. Underhill nodded in his best parade-ground, 'Kite's right, sir. Boat goes with its cap'n.'

Pettifer led them in a chorus of *ayes* and *'ear 'ear*.

Tariq spoke quietly. '*Sawf yaqtul Yusuf al-jamiah*...'

Hazzard looked round at the little Bedouin. 'Tariq? *Qu'est-ce qui est?*' What is it?

The Bedouin looked at him over his bristling moustaches. He shook his head, staring into distant memory. 'Yussuf... he kill everyone.'

De la Vega cursed under his breath. '*Madre*...' He smacked the rail with the flat of his hand. 'Aya! *When*,' he said, 'will it be *enough* for you, *amigo*?'

After a moment, Carlos came forward. He knew his captain. '*Listos, Capitán.*'

Ready.

Hazzard looked to De la Vega for the final word. 'We've got to try, Cesár,' he said. 'It's what we do.'

310

Sun god

The marble and gilt palace of Muhammad Bey al-Elfi had changed since the sudden departure of Napoleon Bonaparte six months earlier. *Général en chef* Jean-Baptiste Kléber sat in a simple chair behind a plain Roentgen table, presently covered in army paperwork and dossiers, orders, requests and troop dispositions. But he stared, incredulous, at the letter in his hands.

'What in the name of God's *hell* is *this*?' he roared, getting to his feet. He looked over the letter in his hands once again. '*Ma foi!* This is outrageous!'

Citizen Peraud of the *Bureau d'information* flicked a glance past Kléber at the terrace and rooftops, shining dully beneath the cloudy March skies of Cairo, already at 26 degrees. 'I fear, *Général*, that this is what comes of treating with the Eng—'

'Unconditional surrender... Army of the East will lay down its arms...' He turned the letter over in his hands with incredulity. 'Who, by *God*, is... is this... this *putain de merde Lord Keith*?' He looked at them accusingly. 'We have been dealing with the *Chevalier* Smith, not this damned Keith! Desaix acted in good faith – good *faith. Sacre collisse...!* This bloody *swine!*'

Other guests sitting on the far side of the room watched without comment: the recovered Mustafa Pasha, in elegant Ottoman winter robes and turban, his wounded hand bound in specially made straps of soft leather bands; beside him, two Egyptian attendants, one wearing the fez, the other a *taqeyyah* cap, looking somewhat alarmed.

Kléber glared at Peraud again. 'And now I hear there truly *was* a relief convoy coming? With *Perrée*?' He stared hard at Peraud. '*Well, damn you! Answer me!*'

Peraud bowed, an act of obeisance, and kept his voice low to placate the wrath of the lion before him. 'Once again, *mon général*, one cannot trust the English. Perhaps the First Consul—'

Kléber exploded into an altogether new rage. 'First Consul! The *great* First Consul! *Bon dieu*,' he rasped, putting a hand to his forehead in disbelief. 'That *arrogant* little...' The news of the coup had reached Egypt only a month or so before, and it had been received with the same mixture of celebration and resentment as Bonaparte's midnight departure.

The man beside Peraud seemed quite at ease, if not smug, evidently pleased with Peraud's procession across the glowing coals. Citizen Dideron, the entire right side of his face pocked and distorted by great scars, added fuel to this very useful fire. 'The First Consul is most aggrieved, General. Admiral Perrée is lost, they say, killed in battle, the three thousand line-troops bound for Egypt now captured...' He bowed theatrically to highlight his wounds. 'As I saw with my own eyes.'

'Aggrieved? He damn well makes himself king while we die in the desert? *Damn him!* He does not warn me to expect reinforcements, for he *sent* none! Desaix said so! They were bound for that bloody brute Vaubois on Malta.' He looked round again. 'Well? Were they or not?'

The molten skin on Dideron's face, forehead, neck and shoulders had been saved by the experienced old captain of the Corsican trawler, who had once served under the great Admiral Pierre de Suffren, and seen plenty of men suffer in flames. After weeks wrapped tight in the fish skins and bandage, he had acquiesced to Dideron's demands and found Perrée's flotilla just off the coast of Sardinia, and got him aboard the 26-gun escort frigate *Badine*. Once she had run with the wind as *Généreux* had struck her colours, she set Dideron ashore at Marabout and scooted away before the English blockade could spot her.

'Alas,' said Dideron, 'enemies in Paris prevented the First Consul from removing Admiral Ganteaume, and he sent this flotilla as some small succour, letting the English believe it was bound only for Malta, when in his heart he meant it to come to you here. I discovered only too late that *Contre-amiral* Perrée had the consul's discretion to make this fateful choice as he saw fit. But it was all too late.' He took a breath, playing the moment of foiled heroism astutely. He paused and looked round at Peraud. 'Of course,' he added, 'you had the English spy Petrides in your hands, Citizen, yet discovered nothing.'

Peraud turned on him. 'Then what should I have done? Waded out to sea and drawn the very ships in by the rope? I can no more command ships to come than I can command the tides!'

Dideron almost smiled, his twisted lips rising on the left. 'So you did nothing.'

'*Salaud de merde...*' hissed Peraud, clutching at the pistol in his coat pocket. He complained to Kléber, 'This man has no authority from Paris, no standing, no—'

Dideron coughed lightly. 'The general has seen my orders, signed by the First Consul, Citizen.' He smiled again, the light picking out the horrific scar tissue down the side of his face, the molten ear. 'And Controller Vermond.'

Peraud swallowed. '*Non. Pas possible...*' Not possible.

He flapped open a folded letter from his pocket and held it out, mocking him. 'In this place, Citizen, I *am* Paris.'

Peraud took a stumbling step back when he heard the voice of Derrien, the long-dead Citizen *Croquemort*. '*Mon dieu...* Yussuf must withdraw.' Peraud went red. 'I can parley with him...'

But Mustafa rose from his seat to address Kléber. 'I can speak with him. *Parlementaire, comme vous dites,*' he offered in his rough French. 'I have helped compose your letters to him. I could show him to see wisdom. How you say...? See sense.'

Kléber shouted, 'Colonel Joffrais!'

A tough, weather-beaten adjutant appeared at the door, his heels clicking on the marble floor as he ascended the few steps beside Peraud. Kléber thrust the letter into his hands. 'Undefeated, yet *this* is how this bewigged *fool* treats us! Copies to be nailed up at all depots and garrisons. Louis, I want every French soldier to read this and see how they are so insulted by their enemies.'

Joffrais looked up from the page. 'This will stir the men more than even Bonaparte could.'

'So it should.' Kléber threw down his pen. 'Strength of Yussuf's army?'

Dideron was ready. 'They claim eighty thousand, but the figure will be nearer forty or sixty.' He looked round and bowed to Mustafa. 'I think our friend here will agree.'

Peraud spluttered, 'B-but...'

Yet Mustafa nodded and the interpreter translated. 'It is true, Excellence. Forty thousand fighting men, the rest supporters and followers.'

'And they advance through Belbeis,' replied the adjutant, 'heading for Al Khankah, *Général*, drawing near to Heliopolis, those ruins, a short march from Cairo.'

It was the last straw. Kléber shook with fury. 'He dares? Betrays his own peace accord? Muster the army – every man, walking wounded, reserve, support troops, *all*.'

Joffrais glanced at the letter. 'A reply to this, General?'

'Yes! Add this,' continued Kléber. '*Soldiers! There can be only one answer to such insolence – prepare for battle.*'

Joffrais cracked his heels together. 'May God defend the Turk on this day, General.'

'The Mamluk of Murad Bey are with you,' said Mustafa, moving to the arched doorway, waiting for him. 'They ride from Giza. So said the Lady Nafisa. Though you must not rely upon his number.'

'I shall not!' Kléber buckled on his white sword belt and hanger, the bright steel scabbard of the Solingen dragoon sabre clattering against the desk, 'I want Friant and Reynier to form the divisions with Lagrange and Donzelot, break down the mobile units into two demi-brigades each –' He tugged open his desk drawer and withdrew a gold-mounted Boutet pistol, checked the pan, clapped it shut and pushed it into his belt. '– and they are to find every damned field-gun we've got, from gunboats, forts, I care not a damn.'

Joffrais sounded dubious. 'We have *chasseurs* in the field on reconnaissance, and the 9th, 25th, 85th and 75th Invicibles are ready in camp. If we call in reserves we can field possibly nine or ten thousand men at most.'

'Under your command it should be sufficient, *mon général*,' said Dideron with a bow.

'But Yussuf has so many...' said Peraud, blanching. 'You're not going to *engage* them...?'

'No, Citizen Peraud,' roared Kléber, marching down the steps and shouldering past him. 'I am going to blast them clear back to bloody Syria—' He paused with Joffrais and Mustafa at the doorway. 'And in the process, damn that little *shit* in Paris he was not here to share in it.'

–

It had taken nearly two weeks to reach the Egyptian coast, weather forcing them to divert northeast towards Crete, storms throwing them back out to sea, Hazzard convinced they would be too late, always just too late. He had ridden the bows yet again, gripping the stays in the blowing spray, the sodden jibs cracking like whips overhead. He thought of Muhammad Bey al-Elfi: his placid acceptance in the face of Bonaparte's descent upon Cairo. '*It is written. This thing the French work against Egypt, Captain, it is not your burden.*'

But it is.

When at last they saw the lights of Alexandria and Rosetta, they had taken the *Volpone*'s cutter, De la Vega's disapproval heavy in the cool night air. The Spaniard knew him too well to argue. '*Do not fight the winds, amigo, if they blow you down.*'

After their first messages sent ashore with Hesse and Tariq, Sheikh al-Mansur of the Beni Qassim and two Tarabin scouts were waiting with horses for all in the dead of night, the moon shining bright, as it could only in Egypt.

'*Marhaba*, Hazar Pasha,' said Al-Mansur in welcome, in dark blue robes and *maghrib* turban against the cool air, bowing and taking his hand. It was good to see a familiar face, but Hazzard felt harried, and mounted quickly.

'What news?' he asked in French. 'Shajar al-Durr? Has she come?'

Al-Mansur mounted his dappled grey Arabian and replied, 'Amir Shajar awaits us on the plain by Sais, Hazar, with her troop.'

Their horses eager, the Tarabin kicked their heels in first and the dust flew, the marines following hard, Hazzard and Cook at the front, Wayland and Porter behind with the others, Underhill and Pettifer bringing up the rear. They had returned happily to their desert kit of undress uniform under their Bedouin robes – *shemagh*, *gelabayyah* and *binish* – each man with his scimitar, *jambiya* or *khanjar* dagger and leather bandeau of patent buck-and-ball .65 calibre French cartridges slung across his chest. None would notice them among the sands, assured Al-Mansur.

'The Osmanlis come to ancient Al Khankah, greater in number than the stars in the sky.' He took a breath, the pounding of the hoofbeats loud, his voice almost lost in the winds, 'The French, they evacuate all from Damietta to Belbeis, near to Cairo, the whole Delta frontier. Many of the Mamluk of Murad have promised to fight with Kléber, to keep out the sultan. And Yussuf Pasha, his army rests four hours' march northwest of the capital, just beyond the ruins of the city of the sun. They are many, Hazar.'

Heliopolis.

Where Herodotus once spoke to priests, where Amun-Ra once reigned supreme.

'Some stars fall, Sheikh.'

Al-Mansur chuckled. 'It is good to hear you laugh once again at a fate writ by God.'

'Not by God,' corrected Hazzard, thinking of Lord Keith's letter. 'I know who wrote this fate. And he cared nothing of its consequence.'

Within half an hour they were at full gallop through the ruins of Sais under a cold sky, and on the long Delta road heading for Cairo – Hazzard hoping beyond hope he could bring the armies back from the brink, for it would be a battle, he suspected, none could stop.

They galloped past straggling columns of French infantry and cavalry hauling their dread 4- and 8-pounder field-guns, Al-Mansur raising his arm in salute – '*Allahu akbar! Vive le Kléber!*' And the soldiers waved back – '*Vive les Mamaluques!*' – believing them to be Murad's horsemen, now allies against this new Ottoman invasion.

A canal to the Nile opened up in the distance, gleaming in the dark, a mirror to the heavens, lights of barges and *feluccas* twinkling on its distant surface, trees stark and black against the night sky, winter fields laid out before them. Just outside the glowing white adobe houses of Menouf, they slowed: there were several horses at the side of the track.

'Mamluk...?' whispered Al-Mansur.

'No,' said Hazzard. He recognised the figure of Masoud, one arm waving, holding a horse by the halter, in the saddle a woman in the eerie half-light of the stars. But not Shajar. It was Delphine. A giant rose out of the scrub beyond, and three figures stepped out slowly. There could be no doubt. They slowed to a trot and walk, Wayland producing his fob watch, reading by the glow of the moon.

'Half past three, sir.'

Slowly they approached the silhouetted figures and Masoud stepped forward. He took Hazzard's hand. 'Hazar... once again you come back.'

'Masoud, *sadiqi al'azizi.*' *My good friend.*

'Delphine,' he said, and she reached across and embraced him.

'*William...*' Her arms were tight about him and he could hear her weeping. '*Jamais... Jamais.* Never have I needed you so much as these past months...'

'We are here,' he said in French.

She looked exhausted, perhaps thinner than he remembered, but still the beauty who had saved him at Acre, pulled him from the bloody surf – saved them all.

The other figures moved from behind Masoud, muskets held at lazy angles: three soldiers and a giant, in that motley combination of French, Austrian and Swiss equipment, Bedouin boots and Turkish trousers – the *Alpha-Oméga*.

'*M'sieur l'anglais*,' hailed *Sergent-chef-major* Achille Caron. 'Milord Mamluk.'

'*Stand easy*,' rumbled Cook over his shoulder, and the marines put up their weapons, easing the ratchets on their firelocks, but they knew them as well.

'*Chef*,' said Hazzard in privileged short-form. He dismounted and they shook hands in true Gallic style. They were all there: Rossy, St Michel and young Antonnais, two of whom he had personally wounded at Acre – and Pigalle, looking up at Cook, sizing up the marines behind, giving a respectful nod of appreciation. Kite chucked him a salute, '*Wotcher*, cock.'

Pigalle grunted back, '*Ça va, anglais*.'

Hazzard looked them over. 'Kléber? *Rien de neuf?*' Anything new?

'It is bad, *mon brave*,' said Caron. He spat, and unscrewed the top of a water bottle, handing it to Hazzard first. Hazzard drank and handed it back, Caron taking a swig. 'The army... it was to leave Cairo at three hours this morning.'

'The letter from the admiral?'

Caron nodded. 'Milord Keith. It is nailed on every barrack room wall from Alex to Aswan.'

Hazzard felt a weight pull him down.

My Lord Keith. What have you done.

'I tell them as you said, that the *chevalier anglais*, *le capitaine* Smith, he stands by the convention and has the proof of it...' He sighed. '*Trop tard, mon ami. Trop tard.*'

Too late.

One of the horses pricked up its ears, and each man looked out to the southwest. The Tarabin scouts rode out into the scrub, stopped, then turned to Al-Mansur, pointing to the southwest. '*Mudafieun*.'

Wayland said it first. 'Guns.'

It was the flat, dead thud of field-guns, and each man knew the sound.

'*Douzes*,' said St Michel, as analytical as Wayland. *Twelve-pounders*.

Hazzard faced Caron. 'We can stop this.'

'*Non*. No man can stop this. Our general, he will destroy the pasha.'

Al-Mansur walked his horse closer. 'But how can this be?' he asked in French. 'Yussuf has seven, eight times the number of men.'

Rossy shook his head. 'He has too many, *m'sieur le sheikh*.'

'A new *diable* is come from Paris,' reported Caron, 'a new *Croquemort*. Peraud, he is disgraced, and the new man steps forward, burned, mauled, they say.' He looked at Hazzard and the marines, his toughened face lost in the deep shadow of the night. 'Attacked in Sicily by a gang of *anglais*?' He shrugged. 'So they say.'

Dideron.

'There was an incident.'

Caron smiled. '*Putain*. He must have deserved this incident.' He raised the water bottle in salute. Pigalle grunted.

Rossy stopped pacing and faced Caron and Hazzard. 'So, what now, *Chef*? You promised me once we would never fight for honour. It is too dangerous.'

Wayland translated for the marines, and there was amusement from Underhill. Pettifer and Warnock stationed themselves at the rear, looking out, keeping watch.

'Fear not, *mon garcon*,' reassured Caron. 'Honour, she is not here. Only us.'

'The generals, they are split,' said Masoud, coming forward. 'I have seen the orders. Some delay, others are quick to condemn General Kléber. There is much danger for all.'

'Reynier follows Kléber, and Lagrange and Belliard, all agree – and Desaix has been called to France. But *le con* Menou, and they say Marmont, scribble letters to each other like tittle-tattling women, waiting to see who wins.'

Hazzard looked at Delphine. She had been right. A civil war could erupt among the French without Yussuf's interference. She gathered her rein and trotted forward. 'I must go to the field hospital. It marches behind the army.'

'We shall escort you, *mon ange*.' Caron drank, then sighed. 'We must report enemy movements to the general.' He looked out at the darkness. 'Their advance guard gathers by the salt marsh.'

'The Lake of Pilgrims?' said Hazzard, glancing at Al-Mansur.

Caron nodded. '*Exactement*. By Matariyyah, near ruins, the *Héli-opolis*.'

Hazzard looked at the old sergeant. He was tired, tramping about with the Alphas, driven by God knew what ghosts. 'We will get you all out if we can.'

Caron looked at him. 'I know, I know, but—' He gave a shrug, some strange decision made within, then straightened. '*Salut*. Do not seek us on the field – we might be lost to all finding.' His tone darkened, urgent, as if he feared a premonition. 'Leave it for the day, *mon ami*. To see what God decides.' Hazzard could see his dark eyes blink, then look down sadly. 'Then someone of us all will live, and tell that here, we and old *Tartuf* tried to do the good thing.'

'I will try to stop it,' said Hazzard. 'I will.'

'Then,' said Caron, 'you are truly the *magicien*.'

'Hey up,' hissed Pettifer from the back, trotting forward, the blunderbuss muzzle-upwards, ready. 'Horse to the east. The Beds.'

Antonnais looked out and cocked his Charleville. Rossy nodded. '*Bédoux*.'

They listened, and the two Tarabin scouts with Masoud spoke to him quickly and he said, 'She has come.'

Possibly twenty horse came at a gallop through the scrub beyond the track. Though the moon was bright, the air was hazy with the desert dust and it took a moment for them to appear. At their head was Shajar al-Durr, behind, her women sharpshooters. Hazzard recognised the aged Zeinab, who had helped Porter sear and stitch Wayland's severed wrist – but his eyes found only Shajar. The horses clattered to a stop, Shajar riding forward, out of breath. She tore the dark *shemagh* from her face, and he saw her in the wash of moonlight. There seemed little time for greetings.

'*Marhaban, Hazar Pasha*.' *Welcome*. 'Battle comes. We must hurry.'

'Are we too late?'

'Perhaps.'

The sound of the guns growing louder, a crane cried out and flapped up from the marshes of the Nile, rising into the night sky. It headed south, over the canal, towards the camp of Yussuf Pasha and the Imperial Ottoman army.

–

Within three hours they made the outskirts of the moonlit army camp, torches dotted everywhere, marking lanes, tracks, its spreading boundaries greater than any Delta town – a blanket of campfires flickering over the low hillsides, tents in bare fields stripped by foraging, the villages around dwarfed in comparison: a new city come to their midst, a vast many-headed creature of one warlike mind.

At the northeastern tip of the camp lay the village of Al Khankah, four hours' march from the capital. The caravan of Yussuf Pasha had staked its claim to this much of Egypt, fifty miles from the Sinai, over two hundred miles from the armistice – and well beyond the reach of peace.

So this is Philippi, thought Hazzard.

Napoleon Bonaparte had reached out from across the sea, as Caesar from the grave, and wrought destruction at every turn. His escape to Paris, thought Hazzard, had brought all this upon them. But Hazzard saw no Caesar, no ghosts. He saw only Lord Keith, writing his pompous letter that would cost the lives of thousands.

They followed Shajar's Tarabin, the marines keeping up, now well used to the Bedouin mounts. '*On me*,' he ordered, and they kicked their heels in. Distant horsemen thundered round the outskirts in squadrons and troops, moonlit plumes of dust bursting in their wake.

They charged down the slope towards the edge of the town, Hazzard keeping frantic pace with Shajar and Al-Mansur, heading straight for the central gate in the main corral, his head down, the Lorenzoni heavy across his shoulder, the scimitar bouncing against his hip, the horse lengthening its stride. *Time, time, time – have we time? Yussuf, what will you do, what will you do?*

A troop of horse peeled off from the tail of the squadron patrol and charged them, lances held high. '*Dur! Kim var orada?*' Who goes there? Al-Mansur raised an arm and called in Turkish, '*Yussuf Pasha ichin bilgi getiriyoruz!*' We bring news for the pasha.

The leader hauled over his rein, lowered his lance and charged ahead of them, his embroidered coat flapping open to reveal a breastplate, pistols and sword. '*Takip edin! Chabuk!*' *Follow.* The rest fell in beside as an arresting escort, leading them towards a pavilion of scouts and guardsmen, their tall spears fluttering with the horsetail banner of the sultan, touched by the first glimmers of dawn.

Guns boomed behind them, but the troop leader ignored them and snapped a command; the broad rudimentary gates of lashed poles were pulled aside and he kicked his horse up the slight slope of sand, Hazzard tight behind. '*Jory! Mind the men! Ease your locks! No man makes a move!*'

'*Clear aye!*'

They galloped up the incline, Hazzard detecting the fragrances of the thousands upon thousands of cooking fires, the odours of the livestock, horses and pack animals, their number as great as that of men. The tail of the troop leader's Turkoman mount thrashed as he spun about, his men levelling their lances, and shouted a sharp command at them, his hand out. '*Kim? Kim? Chabuk!*' *Who? Quickly!*

Shajar pulled in the rein beside Hazzard and snapped back. 'Shajar al-Durr,' she announced curtly, '*al-Amir al-Tarabina.*' She handed over a note bearing a seal. '*Duggala Pasha'yı shimdi göreceyiz.*' *We will see Douglas Pasha now.* She thrust out a sealed passport given her at El-'Arish by Reiz. It was not a request.

The troop leader rode over, Shajar's Arabian snorting, raising its head as if to bite. He took the stiff letter and saw the seal. He looked at Hazzard. '*Kim?*' *Who?*

Hazzard tore off his *shemagh* and threw back his *binish* to display his Bombay scarlet; its orders and braid, tattered and dusty as it was, it was enough to mark him as an Englishman with Douglas. ''*Ana Hazar Pasha! Al-Aafrit al-ahmar, ben kirmizi sheytan! Ingiliz subayimi!*' *The Red Devil, English officer.*

The troop leader stared, his troopers gawking behind, the lances rising, the cavalrymen whispering, '*Kirmizi sheytan,*' his dark eyes wide, one hand rising to brush down his moustaches, his voice low with awe. '*Kirmizi sheytan… evet… evet, binbashi.*' *Yes, yes, sir.* He turned about and roared, '*Kenarde bekle! Kapilari achin!*' *Stand aside! Open the gates!*

A battery of torches flickered in the wind, casting their orange glow on darkened faces, turbans, and *maghrib* desert headdresses as the men leapt to their task. They rode through the inner gate, past tents ranged in circular formations, men and women clustered about fires – and all eyes turned.

'*By all that's holy in Bristol…*' mumbled Cook behind him. '*It goes for ruddy miles.*'

'*Yuzbashi,*' called Hazzard. 'We must hurry, Captain – *acete etmeliyiz.*'

The cavalry troop leader waved a hand at them. '*Sadece memurlar. Erkekler burada kalsın.*'

'What did he say?' demanded Hazzard.

'Officers only,' said Shajar. 'The others must stay behind.'

Hazzard turned. 'Mr Wayland, Jory, to me.' He caught Underhill's eye. 'Stay with the Tarabin. Nothing precipitate. Anyone cuts up rough, follow Zeinab, get out, and meet at the rendezvous.'

Underhill smiled his hideous smile. 'We'll watch 'em, no fear sir – eh, Pet?'

'Clear aye, Sarge…' Pettifer hefted his blunderbuss, the giant barrel pointing up into the dark sky.

The central track was blocked by troops and camp followers, all looking up at them as they rode by, some calling, some shouting out, hands pointing at Cook – and Wayland in particular, his blond hair visible even under his headdress. The cavalry captain cleared the onlookers away. But a voice went up from the back of the growing crowd.

'*Kuq Chavush! Kuq guchlu!*' *Sergeant Cook, mighty Cook.* '*Embabeh'in Kuq guchluu!*' *Mighty Cook of Embabeh.*

The crowd began to cheer – '*Kuq guchlu!*' – a voice calling high over them all, '*Hazar bash…!*'

The skirmishers roared, '*Kuq guchlu, Kuq guchlu, Hazar, Hazar, Hazar!*'

The sky lightening by the moment, the cavalry captain led them down the steadily clearing track, hands coming up to greet them, Hazzard shaking them – *Hazar Hazar Hazar!* – his eye catching a flash of red. The crowd parted before the red-coated *Nizam-i Djedid*, a *Muladzim* Lieutenant with drawn sword at the fore. Behind came Captain Shafik Reiz, as impassive and calm as he had been while leading Hazzard and the marines to the shores of Jaffa, a further cry rising up, '*Reiz Reiz Reiz!*'

Reiz cried an order and the *Nizami* formed ranks, parting the mob like a wave. In a moment, the track through the camp was clear. The young moustachioed captain threw a punctilious salute to Hazzard. '*Binbashi.*' *Major.*

Hazzard returned it, aware of all eyes upon them. '*Yuzbashi* Reiz.' He looked into the dark eyes. 'We have little time.'

'Kléber refused the offer of surrender this morning.'

Hazzard had expected no less. 'We have to hurry.'

Reiz and the *Nizami* marched alongside him into the heart of the camp, the skies brightening with the dawn all about them, long shadows confusing the eye, stretching across the pounded scrub and desert.

At last Hazzard saw a large central tent, a reception courtyard before it. But the walkway of some twenty-five yards leading to it was lined with pikes – each studded with a severed French head.

He felt Shajar take a long, hissing breath beside him, and Wayland muttered under his breath, '*My good God…*'

Hazzard brought his horse to an abrupt halt. He heard Reiz beside him.

'*Binbashi*, be wise...'

Shajar flicked a quick glance at him, one eye ever on the crowd. '*Ne dis rien, Guillaume. Ne fais rien.*' *Say nothing, William. Do nothing.*

Behind them, Cook mumbled, '*God save us...*'

Hazzard felt himself sag in the saddle. He had come to prevent a slaughter – of French, of Turks, of everyone – and here he felt the impossibility of the task, of fighting the winds, as De la Vega always said. His outrage was overcome by a wave of bitter sadness.

'Seen worse, sir,' said Cook.

They had. They had seen far worse.

'Yes.'

'It is not Yussuf Pasha,' said Reiz. 'He appeases the peasants here, lest they desert.' He looked up at Hazzard. '*Binbashi* – it is Jaffa.'

Jaffa. The magic spell that excused all atrocity. He nodded.

Intikam.

Revenge.

The tent opened and a coterie of senior Ottoman staff emerged, waiting at the end of the avenue of heads. At the front was Yussuf Pasha, surrounded by his advisers and secretaries, some wearing the fez of the official. Behind them came several officers in scarlet, at their head, Major Douglas, and behind him, Ibrahim Bey, erstwhile comrade of Murad and self-proclaimed ruler of Egypt in exile.

'*Look at that fat shite,*' murmured Cook.

Shajar muttered a stream of oaths and curses as she stared at his plump, self-satisfied countenance. His hand tightening on the grip of his broad-bladed *kilij* sword, Reiz moved forward to escort them. '*Binbashi.*'

Reluctantly Hazzard dismounted. Escorted by Reiz, they walked the gauntlet of sightless eyes, the stench intolerable, Cook mumbling, '*By all that's holy in Bristol...*'

'*We must not comment,*' warned Wayland.

Hazzard grated from between tight lips, '*One word wrong, and by Christ I shall damn them to hell, and let Kléber do his worst.*'

Douglas met them halfway, the black eyes of the dead staring, the putrescent skins glistening and buzzing with flies. Awkward among the sight, Douglas bowed to Shajar. 'Madam. Hazzard,' he said, keeping his voice low and fast, 'I could ask what in hell you're doing here, but will you answer, I wonder.'

Hazzard replied, 'Message deciphered, French convoy intercepted by Nelson, *Généreux* and troop reinforcements captured, Malta blockaded.'

Douglas nodded briefly. 'Understood.'

Hazzard nearly spat his words with anger. '*Why* has Yussuf broken the armistice?'

Douglas, too, flicked a glance behind at Ibrahim Bey and the other amirs. 'It was all we could do to make them stop *here*.'

'All he had to do was *wait*, for God's sake, and we would have marched Kléber out within the month.'

Douglas looked at him, his face expressionless. 'Did you truly believe you could do better?'

'Lord Keith set a match to a powder-keg with his damnèd letter to Kléber. Every French soldier is ready to tear these Turks limb from limb with his bare hands. Don't you *see* that?'

'You have *no idea* what is going on,' Douglas hissed at him.

'*Then bloody well enlighten me, dammit. I have Sir Sidney's letter contradicting Keith, proving the Cabinet is behind the damned convention!*'

Douglas went pale. 'Good God,' he whispered. Then he gave the confession. 'It is too late, sir,' he said, himself appalled with the realisation of it. 'I am sorry.'

Hazzard stared at him. '*Nothing* is ever too late.'

They reached the small clearing before the command tent, an amir of some standing coming forward to greet Hazzard with an assessing look. He was younger than the others, wearing dark robes, a warrior's turban and mail hanging either side of his beard, much as Ali Qarim and the Egyptian Mamluks. Reiz interpreted for him. 'His Excellence Osman *Ferik*, he says, I have heard tales of you, *effendi*.'

Hazzard nodded tersely. A *ferik* was the equivalent of a general or brigadier. His spurs suggested cavalry. 'Did you fight Kléber at Mount Tabor, *Ferik*?'

Osman put out his chest, as if it were a challenge. 'I was not there.'

'You will have your chance now. Good luck with it.'

They reached the command tent and Douglas beckoned Hazzard to Yussuf. The Grand Vizier's eyes crinkled against the lightening of the sky, his face looking haggard. It had been a long journey from El-'Arish. 'Yussuf Pasha,' Douglas said in Turkish, 'may I introduce Major Hazzard of His Majesty's Marine Forces.'

'Ah,' said Yussuf nodding vigorously, '*Hazar Pasha*. The devil in red,' he added, 'who strikes Banaparteh Sultan at his heart.'

Hazzard looked him over. This was no Al-Djezzar. Yussuf was no maniac. But there was something strange about him he could not place: a dislocation, or disorientation – as if he were not really there. 'My lord Pasha,' said Hazzard, and bowed his head. '*Selam sizeh.*' *Peace be upon you.*

'Ah so, peace, yes, yes. Blessed unto God,' he said, nodding constantly, face wrinkled into inscrutable smiles, 'but not blessed unto men.' He lit up when he saw Shajar. 'Ah, too, the gem of all, the Tree of Pearl, become the goddess of battle,' he said, waving his hands as if in prayer. 'The Mamluk queen.'

'Pasha,' she replied guardedly, and bowed.

Reiz clutched at Hazzard's arm. 'Do not displease him, Hazar... *je vous en prie.*'

Yussuf turned from Shajar and said to Hazzard brightly, 'Have you seen my duck pond...?' He indicated with an inviting hand. Behind them in the courtyard area, just in front of the tent, was indeed a little stone-built pond, possibly two yards across. In it floated a small painted wooden duck.

Hazzard looked at Douglas. The other officers made hasty moves to intercede, but Douglas cut in. 'Perhaps, my lord, that can wait for now. Major Hazzard brings news.'

'Ah. So.' Yussuf seemed disappointed, but attentive.

'The Royal Navy will guarantee the peace, Pasha, and remove the French.'

'Ah yes?'

'But your forces must hold here, my lord. Or at least pull back to Belbeis. My lordships make this request.' He wondered how Keith would react to that.

Reiz translated, his expression impassive, but his hand trembling on his sword. But Douglas was not so reticent. '*Hazzard, what are you doing*—'

'Your proximity to Cairo will bring the French to battle – surely you have been advised of this. We hear their ranging guns.'

They moved past the pond to the command tent, the heat rising, the pressure of the sun growing minute by minute. Hazzard calculated it was half past five. Kléber would have arranged his men into squares and be advancing. Yussuf gazed at him for a moment, his eyes smiling.

'You are quick, a true *Aafrit*, fast, zip zip, not the heavy *shaytan*, yes, I know too many of those...' He paused, scratching at his cheek beneath his dead eye. 'If I can see my little friend there, floating in his water, at peace... it stills my mind. And I might think better of men.' He smiled, and Hazzard could see the blinded eye. 'And the world.'

Hazzard felt Osman move in to join them, and turned, confronting the pair together. 'Pasha, *Ferik*, you *must* withdraw, some distance, any distance, to show faith. It is the wise choice—'

Douglas rumbled behind him, '*Hazzard... you do not have the authority.*'

Hazzard faced him. 'Major Douglas, this army is in chaos. Kléber will cut through it like a knife through butter. Tell me I am wrong.'

Douglas was livid, his voice a harsh whisper. 'What in *hell* do you do here, Major? Months I've been with the Pasha's command, and now you try to make them break and run? Like *this*?'

'Blame Lord Keith and Sir Rafe *bloody* Lewis for demanding their unconditional surrender. Everything was set, until Keith blew it apart. They've been *offended*, Major.'

'*Damn you, sir!*' hissed Douglas between his teeth. 'You put fright into the commander of near *sixty thousand men* and demand *peace* in the face of the enemy? I could have you marched out!'

'I would demand peace if I had led men to die for nothing!'

But Yussuf clenched his fists, shaking his head, and hissed back, 'Gentlemen, I cannot! I *cannot*.' He waved a hand out at the crowd beyond. 'If they do not like my orders, they *shoot at my tent*. See the holes!'

'We are too many, Hazar Pasha,' said Osman, 'for such movements now. We are not all *Nizami*, but the levy. The army cannot move but forward.'

The voice that replied came with the whiplash of the past, from the *diwan* in Cairo, the arch-enemy of Murad: it was Ibrahim Bey. 'We shall crush him, England!' he called from some yards away. All stopped talking, turned, and watched. 'You speak false again! As you did at Embabeh, when Banaparteh Sultan took Cairo.' Older and fatter, he was still the viper Hazzard remembered. 'Once again England shall prove the great liar.'

But Hazzard did not back down. 'Were they lies before? Were they, lord Bey?' Hazzard felt Reiz tense beside him: *Binbashi, do not reply.*

'When the Janissaries defended the guns and an army safe behind them *ran for its life?*'

'You dare!'

A cheer rose up again within the spectators: '*Hazar Pasha, Kuq guchlu!*' The chanting began once again: '*Kuq guchlu! Kuq guchlu!*'

Wayland saw Shajar's hand resting on the pommel of the *khanjar* dagger at her front. Osman turned to her. 'Will the Tarabin fight with us, Tree of Pearl?'

Shajar shook her head once. *No.* 'Not with Ibrahim Bey.' Ibrahim scoffed and turned away. 'If we join the field, we shall strike him from the earth.'

'Then *go*, woman,' shouted Ibrahim, 'back to your loom!'

'And you go back to your cushions in Acre and Sidon while your men face French cannon.'

Out of sight of the troops, Yussuf sat hunched among his thick padded robes, his great turban toppling slightly to one side. 'They refused my emissaries. So. What must I do? I *cannot stop* it, you see? Do you?' He looked away. 'This is no army...' He glanced at Osman. 'It is the *mountain* come to war.'

Reiz and Osman watched him, then looked to Hazzard. 'Hazar, what must we do...?'

'Withdraw. It is your only hope.'

Yussuf bunched his hands into fists. 'But we have *more men* than they!' He fell abruptly silent. 'The guns...' He got up, infuriated, frustrated. 'I have no *information*.'

Hazzard heard cannons again. 'Whose guns, General?'

Osman took a moment. 'Nassif Pasha,' he said. 'He has taken the vanguard and marched on towards Matariyyah, near the Lake of Pilgrims.'

North of Heliopolis.

Hazzard felt a cold hand shiver at his heart. 'How many? How long ago?'

Osman could see no harm in it and was almost affronted, frowning at Reiz as he translated. 'Before dawn, to meet the French. Near six thousand Janissaries, foot and horse.'

Hazzard stared back at him, incredulous.

Six thousand. Against Kléber.

'You have split your forces...' Hazzard looked at Reiz, unrelenting: the camp was now a death-trap. 'Reiz, get the *Nizam-i Djedid* out. We must go – *fast*.'

Reiz's perspiring face registered little alarm, the eyes quick, calculating. 'Is Nassif Pasha in peril?'

Hazzard kept his voice low. 'Nassif and his forces might well be lost and the French already en route.'

A horn blew in the distance, and for a moment silence fell over the host of thousands. All heads turned, men looking to one another, uncertain if what they heard was true, until the echoing command soared over the camp.

Savasha hazirlanin…!

Prepare for battle.

Ibrahim Bey took his moment, stepped out, and raised his arms gloriously, a messiah returned to Egypt. '*Intikam…!*'

There came an answering roar unlike anything Hazzard had ever heard – not in Egypt, not in India. The mob turned as one being, racing from the command tent back to their arms, to their pack mules, to their horses, orders raging from all corners, in utter pandemonium.

Kléber.

Hazzard glimpsed scarlet among the mob and shouted, '*Douglas!*'

They were knocked and buffeted from all sides as the senior officers scattered to their commands: '*Evet, albey! Kaymakam! Kaymakam!*' Reiz pulled Hazzard in towards Osman and Yussuf at the corner of the command tent, sheltering by the overhanging flap of thick *kelim* matting. Horses galloped past on the track beyond, the rising shouts of the tens of thousands deafening to the ear. *Intikam! Intikam!*

Revenge.

Douglas roared over it all, '*Hazzard! Get back to your men! Now! I will meet you beyond!*'

'*Binbashi, follow!*' Reiz took Hazzard's arm and called to Wayland and Cook, peasant levy conscripts clustering round the big sergeant, *Kuq guchlu! Kuq guchlu!* They made their way through the crush of bodies, pikemen, Mamluks, squires with clutches of javelins, muskets and bucklers. Wayland called to Hazzard's back as they fought through the crowd.

'*Get 'em outta here, Cap'n Reiz!*' bawled Cook. '*They've gone blood-mad!*'

'*This way!*' shouted Douglas, leading Reiz to the horses down the avenue of severed heads.

'*Sir! We cannot,*' Wayland called, reaching out for Hazzard. '*Sir!*'

Hazzard fought his way through behind Shajar and Reiz. '*What is it, Mr Wayland?*'

'*Orders from the War Office, sir! We cannot… We must not…*'

Hazzard whipped round to look at him. '*Orders? Which orders?*'

The platoon of iron-faced *Nizami* had formed a protective ring of bayonets round the horses, two dead infantrymen at their feet, throats opened, blood in the sand, their wide-eyed fellows rushing past in a confused stream. When he saw Reiz approach, the *Mulazim* Lieutenant stepped out and fired a shot in the air. Men darted away, taking up their chant once again – *Intikam!* – as Shajar, Cook and Hazzard reached them. Douglas and Shajar mounted, the severed heads swept away in the tornado of activity, kicked or trampled underfoot. Wayland stumbled on one of them and cursed, then continued to Hazzard as he climbed into the saddle. '*Lord Elgin was ordered to accept the convention by the Cabinet! That's why Sir Sidney gave us that letter, sir!*'

'*That is why we're here, dammit!*' shouted Hazzard back to him.

'*Mount your horses or be done for!*' ordered Douglas from the track.

But Wayland had the answer for him. '*Because Lord Keith's refusal could lead to a new Franco-Turkish alliance against us! Sir Sidney had to prove to them that we ratified the treaty!*'

Hazzard put a foot in the stirrup. At last it became clear. 'Is that what was behind Keith's damnable letter? *Did the Admiralty do this deliberately?*'

Wayland looked back at him, one hand on the pommel of his saddle, Hazzard black with anger.

'*Thomas! Yes or no, dammit?*'

'I… *No!*' the young man replied. '*Surely*, sir…!'

'Oh good *God!*' Hazzard swung himself up onto his horse. 'Damn them! Bloody *damn them again!*' He felt the long reach of Sir Rafe Lewis, the Admiralty puppeteers' strings reaching even unto the desert and the Nile Delta. 'They *wanted* Keith to foul the convention! *Because we weren't bloody ready with an army to move in!* Good Christ above!'

Cook climbed up to his heavy Turkoman and called, 'So we *want* the ruddy Frenchies to win?'

'Of course not!' called Douglas. 'But they must not negotiate without us!'

Hazzard jerked his mount round, looked at the mob ranting around them – *Intikam! Intikam!* – and remembered Douglas's words: *I've been with them for months.* 'Douglas! This will be a bloody slaughter!'

Major John Douglas looked at him hard. 'I know.'

Hazzard shouted back to Cook and Wayland, 'We *wanted* them to break the armistice themselves! *Wanted* them to, dammit! Because we're not *ready*!' He looked at Wayland, at Douglas, outraged. 'That's it, isn't it? Sir Sidney was too damn *quick*, and we wouldn't get a piece of the spoils!'

'*Flamin' Jaysus*,' called Cook, trying to control his horse. '*Look at this lot! You'd sooner stop a typhoon!*'

Douglas shouted back, 'Our treaty is not to re-establish the Ottomans, sir! *It is to re-establish the Mamluks!*'

Hazzard finally understood.

Ibrahim Bey.

'Good bloody *God*, man!' said Hazzard. 'You *want* that murderous swine to control Egypt? *Are you mad?*'

A group of Turkish cavalrymen battered their way through to ride beside them, General Osman harnessed for war in spiked helm and turban, a white robe over his light armour and gold-mounted *kilij* at his hip. He looked to Reiz and Hazzard. '*Chabuk, effendi, ne yapabiliriz?*' *Quickly, effendi, what can we do?*

Hazzard shouted, '*Withdraw*, General! Withdraw! The French come with fortress formation, as at Shubra Khit, as at Embabeh. *Do not charge the squares with your horse, use only artillery. Do you hear?*' Osman waited for Reiz's interpretation, and the pasha looked at Hazzard.

He pulled his mount away, then looked back. '*Allaha ısmarladık.*' *God be with you.* He turned to his entourage and waved a mailed fist. '*Yolu achin!*' *Clear the way!*

Intikam! Intikam!

Reiz ran beside him at a steady trot, and Hazzard leaned down and spoke in French. 'Keep to the rear, or at least to the north of the field,' he said, 'then reach the coast if there is a full retreat!'

'But what would I be,' asked Reiz, 'if I did not do my duty in this place?'

Hazzard had no answer for him, and knew he had lost.

Reiz threw him a salute. '*Binbashi*,' he said, 'my honour is to have served at your side. The *Nizam-i Djedid* must protect the Grand Vizier.'

The *Nizami* ported their muskets in escort as the crowd pulled at the fence posts blocking their path – *Intikam intikam intikam!* Reiz moved ahead and fired his pistol in the air, the report almost lost on the wind and the howl of the army. '*Kapıları açın! Kenarda bekle!*' *Open the gates! Stand aside!*

There was a roar from the multitude as the gates and fencing collapsed, pushed flat by the urgent press of men and whinnying horses, the dust billowing as the Ottoman cavalry leapt the rails, stray men of the levy trampled, mules braying and camels giving their guttural roars.

The Tarabin and marines had already withdrawn to the right, as the army poured down the hillside of scrub, a river bursting its banks. A long, piercing whistle caught their ear and Cook pointed and called out, '*O'er there, sir!*'

Douglas kicked into a gallop and they darted to the right – then Hazzard saw them, a wave of relief sweeping over him: the Tarabin, the marines, already riding to intercept them, Underhill leading them as they fell in alongside. '*Frenchies by the 'undred, lads, for the use of. Marks yer man and takes yer shot!*'

'*Thank Gawd for that,*' called Kite. '*Can't feel me arse no more anyways!*'

Douglas and Shajar led the way to higher ground, the headlong thunder of hooves and the barking field-guns shaking the ground: it was Shubra Khit once again, following Murad in the attack as they charged Bonaparte's squares.

Not again... Never again, surely.

The rising sun revealed the plain and the whitewashed towns to the southwest, the bending serpentine Nile, and the distant minarets and golden domes of Cairo. A mile off lay Matariyyah, and beyond it, the remains of ancient Heliopolis. An obelisk of red granite pierced the brightening sky, and beyond lay the great temple of Amun-Ra, its broad slab steps rising to broken columns, fallen Hellenic capitals of Corinthian acanthus, tumbled along with the gods who had once held up the heavens, for as long as Memnon evoked the dawn with his song.

Clouds billowed, rising from the south, the broadening Nile shining alongside as the morning sparkled from the massed formations of the *Armée d'Orient*. Hazzard watched, seeing the hand of Bonaparte as the squares advanced. Even at that distance he could detect their speed; they wanted to close with the enemy. Caron too, had failed – they all had. After all Hazzard's hubris, his vain belief that he could defy fate – it had been written after all.

Kléber had come.

Heliopolis

Kléber's army advanced in tight battle formation of five squares of heavy line-infantry, light cavalry in the centre, mobile field artillery at every corner, heavy cavalry guarding the flanks. Battalion commanders despatched companies to the left and right, men forming up, colliding shoulder to shoulder, and the resulting roar as the square slammed shut:

Hwa!

The massed drumbeat and basso chant boomed, '*Un deux, un deux, un deux,*' with greater speed than at Shubra Khit or the Pyramids, the squares rolling over obstacles, unstoppable, then wheeling with precision, three ranks deep, each square a diamond moving forward, undaunted by the numbers opposing them.

'Jaysus shite, they're fast...' gasped Cook.

The Ottoman vanguard under Nassif Pasha had gathered to the south of the dried saltbeds of the *Berket el-Hajji*, the Lake of Pilgrims, forced into blocks, the elite Janissary infantry raked by French artillery, grape scything them down by the dozen, bodies flying from the ranks as the ground burst with *obusier* howitzer shells. The remaining Ottoman army poured down from behind the ruins, a flood of men and horse, the dust rising in clouds to obscure the sight of the full horde to come. Muskets popped prematurely, levy conscripts with spear and sword rushing forward as the Ottoman horse thundered round the flatlands to the north of the town – among them was the troop leader who had challenged them earlier.

Hazzard saw the long-tailed fez and crimson *Nizami* coat charging through the scene on a Turkoman horse, men leaping aside. He knew it was Reiz, and wanted to shout to him, to stop him, but knew there was no point. The *Nizami* rode to the front of the mass of footmen to their pasha, the Ottoman cavalry galloping out across the field, doing precisely what Hazzard had advised against: they charged the squares.

Armoured like medieval Saracens, heavy *kaftan* robes flapping behind, they arced across the open ground towards the first square

on the right. Hazzard saw the French muskets rise all along the lines
– two hundred of them, each rank another two hundred.

Première rang! Feu!
Deuxième rang! Feu!
Troisième rang! Feu!
Fire.

Within the space of ten seconds, six hundred .65 calibre musket-
balls shredded the Ottoman cavalry charge. Horses crashed on stricken
forelegs; riders were plucked from their saddles, tumbling, flailing,
some leaping the fallen, some not, and the roar of the demi-brigades
over it all: '*Fire, Fire, Fire!*'

Hazzard spurred his horse, then hauled back on the rein,
maddened. *Keith, damn you…! May God damn you!* There was nothing
he could do. Nothing.

Down the slope to their right, Hazzard saw a plume of dust rise,
and Kite came riding back from his sentry post fifty yards off. '*Hey up!*
Customers!' A moment later Hazzard saw the troop of French horse
approaching.

A white flag fluttered above one of the riders, a kerchief tied to an
upheld sabre. Two French cavalry officers and two troopers behind,
almost white with dust, their braided Hussars' coats slung over one
shoulder, plumed shakos down over their eyes, fierce men of purpose.

The leading officer galloped round to the front, picking out
Hazzard, Douglas, Shajar and Al-Mansur, the sand kicking up in
luminous clouds as he snapped his mount to an abrupt halt with the
skill of a Mamluk. Lengths of gold braid hung from his epaulettes,
looped to tassels pinned to his breast, braided lengths of hair framing
pointed and ferocious moustaches. He looked at Douglas, then at
Hazzard, and threw Hazzard a sharp salute.

'*Capitaine De l'Eisenau du Bayence, 7ème Hussards.*' He gave a slow
nod. 'Milord Mamluk. I greet you in honour,' he called in educated
French. 'Colonel Cavalier and I saw you ride the field at *l'Embabeh*,
and vowed that, one day, we too should have such valour.'

Hazzard returned the salute. Colonel Cavalier: the man who gave
him water in the heat of Lacroix's prison camp. *Suis désolé, mon vieux.*
Forgive me, my friend.

Du Bayence bowed. 'The compliments of the *Général en chef*
Kléber. You are declared *officiers parlementaires*, and by request of *Chef-*
major Caron of the 75th Invincibles you will not join battle in this place.

There shall be no negotiation further with the *Osmanlis*. These Turks on the field this day are marked to die. They break their bond, break the armistice of honourable men. We now shall break them.'

Cook murmured beside him, '*Jaysus shite…*'

Du Bayence concluded his message. 'The best of the day to you, *messieurs*. My general thanks you for your concern and gives you safe passage.' He threw another salute to Hazzard and wheeled his horse about.

'Where is *Chef* Caron?' demanded Hazzard. '*Où est-il?*' *Where is he?*

'He leads the column of the 75th Invincibles, *m'sieur!* With the *général en chef* who even now advances upon the enemy!'

As he spoke, a charging wing of Ottoman cavalry adjusted their curve, dodging away from the endless volley fire. From Reynier's square they could see a field-gun tip forward, muzzle into the dirt, falling from its mounting. A single soldier stepped out to right it, picking up the gun with a roar, setting it in its carriage to cheers from the ranks — '*Vive le Pig! Vive le Pig!*' — and raising his arms in triumph. The marines all knew who it was.

Pigalle.

From the corner streamed a column of men making a sally from the square into the field, the artillery crumping into the Janissary formations not fifty yards off. Hazzard watched as skirmishers took the vanguard, dashing into the field, kneeling, firing, running — *chasseurs à pied.*

The Alpha-Oméga.

'That is *Chef* Caron, *m'sieur*,' said Du Bayence proudly, 'where he shall ever be, in battle!'

Hazzard saw him, a stout sword-bayonet in hand, striding beside a colonel, a colour guard bearing aloft the banners of the demi-brigades. He could not bear it: *Achille Caron, 75th Invincibles* — the man who had come to save Hazzard in the dead of night out of conscience, tended his wounds, defended him against Colonel Lacroix, who had worked with them to save innocents from the blood of Acre.

Down there.

The square wheeled about once again to cover the sally, two volleys of fire into the disorientated Janissaries — and the Ottoman cavalry swept in an arc to return.

But Hazzard called after him, 'Du Bayence! You would leave him there! You would leave *Chef* Caron as fodder for cannon!'

The Frenchman turned about, the horse rearing. *'It is not my affair, m'sieur!'*

'He has more honour than these two armies combined!'

Du Bayence looked down at the battle, then back to Hazzard. *'I can do nothing, m'sieur! I have a duty to support the General Donzelot!'*

The Ottoman artillery began to respond, fountains of earth rising, stray shots far from the squares – but enough to slow the running column, until it happened: a shell struck one of the corner field-guns and the explosion knocked men flat, one of them, Caron. The marines edged forward as they saw the figure drag himself to his feet, pulling another with him. For Hazzard, it was enough.

'Then you shall watch,' he raged at Du Bayence, *'as others carry your honour for you!'*

He kicked his heels in, and the Arabian whinnied and broke forward.

Shajar called out, *'William!* This is not your fight! *William! Je vous en prie!'*

'Mr Hazzard!' snapped Douglas. 'As you were! *That is an order!'*

Hazzard spun about. *'Damn* you, Douglas! You could have stopped this at Belbeis or Katia! But you let it happen!'

'How *dare* you, sir?' Outraged, Douglas tugged a pistol from its holster and raised it. 'You will mind your place, as I command!'

There was a rattle of locks from behind Douglas as the marines levelled their weapons, and he and his three officers turned in their saddles. Underhill looked down the barrel of his Charleville, and in his best parade-ground voice declared brightly, 'Major Douglas! As agents of the Royal Peculiar Sir Sidney Smith, and under the aegis of the War Office, Lord Melville and Mr William Wickham, I do fail to recognise your authority on this field, sir!'

'What? *Are you mad?'*

'But, sir, be in no doubt,' he grated, aiming carefully as Pettifer levelled his blunderbuss, the others following suit. 'If you don't drop that rabbit-gun o'yours,' he promised in a deathly whisper, 'you're a bloody dead man.'

Douglas stared. 'Damn it, man! I'm...' He turned. 'Hazzard, he...'

But Hazzard had gone.

Du Bayence tugged his mount round. '*Merde alors…*' He drew his sword. '*Hussards à moi! En avant!*' *Hussars to me, forward*.

Cook's horse spun about. '*Christ jaysus…* 'Miah!'

Al-Mansur shouted after him, '*Hazar Pasha!*'

Hazzard galloped down the slope, dust and stone flying from the blur of flailing hooves, pursued by Du Bayence and the Hussars – but they were not stopping him: they were riding in close escort.

Wayland charged forward at Douglas. 'Damn you, Major, indeed! You *knew* Elgin rescinded Keith's orders! Sar'nt Cook! On me!'

The big man red-faced with frustration, Cook jolted forward on his Turkoman, the horse fighting the snaffle-bit, black mane flashing, forelegs prancing. '*Come on, damn ye, beast!*'

Al-Mansur reached out a hand and took his rein. 'No, my friend.' He looked to Wayland. 'Wayalandeh *effendi*, no.'

Wayland raised his prosthetic hand and cursed himself, furious. 'By *God* above…'

Al-Mansur drew his scimitar. 'I go, for he who would come for us.' He looked to Shajar. '*Rabbena ma'ak.*' *God be with you.*

He set off, his white *keffiyah* headdress flying, his blue *binish* robe becoming wings as he charged down the incline, his scimitar held high.

Shajar snapped a command and ten of the Tarabin burst forward, the sand blowing into clouds as they galloped after him. Hazzard and the Hussars had come within a hundred yards of the first square. Time had run out. Cook cursed in outrage.

'God's *bloody truth*, 'Miah!' He turned to Douglas. 'You 'ear me now, *sir*! If Mr 'Azzard don't come alive from this field, I will leave you *dead* on the spot!'

Douglas turned about, pistol in hand. '*You'll watch your damned tongue*—' and flinched from a thunderous boom as Pettifer fired his blunderbuss just over his head, loose shot striking him, blood drawn from his temple.

Douglas stared, eyes wide, his voice a whisper. '*By God, I'll see you hang for that…*'

Pettifer shook his head. 'No, sir,' he said, 'you won't.' He sat back, easy in the saddle, and reloaded, every marine musket pointing at Douglas. 'Covering fire,' he said to Underhill. 'Mobile arrow, Sarge?'

'Aye,' said Underhill. 'Any bugger gets in our major's way, friend or foe, he goes down. On me an' Cookie, marchin' advance.'

The marines of 9 Company formed up behind Cook and Under-hill, and began to trot down the incline, slipped into a canter, and then galloped after Sheikh al-Mansur and the Tarabin towards the French and the Mamluks, their only guide a trail of dust left by Hazzard and the Hussars.

–

From the far side of the field, a wing of General Friant's cavalry hurtled round the rear of the Janissary ranks, his square spinning slowly, maintaining formation, artillery barking at the Ottomans, vulnerable in their open order. From the squares the forward batteries flashed every fifteen seconds, a gun hauled back on squeaking carriage-wheels to reload, then rolled into a new position to fire. Caron's column rallied, but the Ottoman cavalry had seen them and come back: the square moved forward to support them, but the line of men were exposed. Within minutes the volleys erupted again and the Turkish cavalry flew to pieces, its remnants descending on the column.

There had been no question for Hazzard, no solution, merely the certainty that he could not rest, could not leave Caron there – *never, not like that* – but by the time he tried to establish in his own mind what he intended, he was at full gallop, the wind and dust in his face, his *shemagh* covering his mouth and nose tight, constricting, the world shuddering to the ceaseless repetitive thud of the horse's hooves. He streaked down the incline, sliding partially from the saddle and leaning to the left side of the horse's neck, as he had learned from the Beni Qassim. Du Bayence and the Hussars were determined to keep up with him just behind, their honour at stake – '*Milord Mamluk en avant.*' The temple of Amun-Ra rose in the distance. *Gods, be ye alive or be ye dead, guide me.* He was lost in the avenue of severed heads and their staring eyes, in the roar of '*Intikam, intikam,*' the arrogance of Ibrahim, the weary reluctance of Yussuf, General Osman's eyes quick, intelligent, aware of the forces reigning over him.

God, *God, God*.

The Turkish cavalry was among the French column now, razor-edged *kilij* and *yataghan* swords slashing through them, the colours nowhere to be seen, Reynier's square almost on top of them – *Avancez! Un deux, un, deux* – firing, no man breaking ranks. Caron was in the centre of the column, standing over a fallen officer, the *sergent-chef-major* with two pistols, firing one, then the other, a Turkish rider falling. Hazzard righted himself in the saddle, the scimitar in his hand, the blade at the trail, low in his extended grip, the flying tassels knocking against his wrist as the thunder of the horse numbed his legs, his chest pounding.

Reynier's cavalry came in to support, sweeping round the Janissary ranks now in confusion, and tearing through the Ottoman ranks. Mamluks off to Hazzard's left swam into sight – *Ibrahim's men* – white robes floating, curved blades high. A field-gun boomed close by and a cry rang out, '*I am Pigalle! And where I plant my boot, there shall I not be moved,*' and the answering call, *Vive le Pig! Vive le Pig!*

Hazzard charged through Reynier's horsemen and out the other side, Du Bayence in escort. '*Hussards, hussards!*' A cluster of Ottomans appeared ahead, riding in circles around the column; a shout from behind him, and a clash, the flash of a sword-blade, a Mamluk falling. *Du Bayence.* A Mamluk reared, his horse spinning on its hind legs, Caron below, thrusting with a discarded pike among dead horses, his officer on one knee, sword high.

At full gallop, Hazzard pulled the reins of the Arabian and brought its neck round low – *Not too sharp, not too sharp.* It whinnied and slid to the ground, its hooves clawing at the earth and the air, smashing into the Mamluk horsemen with the force of a half-ton carronade, knocking them in all directions, Du Bayence's men behind – '*Hussards!*' – the blades slicing down, Du Bayence rallying Renyier's light horse to circle the Mamluks.

Hazzard crashed into the wounded French, a whirlwind of images: Rossy's face – *Chef!* Hazzard was up – '*Caron!*', his own voice among them all, the stocky sergeant-major heavier than he'd thought as he hefted him, one arm across his shoulders, dragging him – *Where, where?* – and he saw the steps of the temple. *Amun-Ra, thank you.* '*Achille! Venez! Chef Caron!*' he was shouting Caron's name as he pulled him along, the sergeant-major's feet dragging, the steps so far, *soo very far.* There was a loud bang next to him: Rossy firing his Charleville – '*Allez vite anglais!*' *Go, quick.* A bearded Mamluk now before him, face suddenly bright, enraged, sword raised, and Hazzard fired the Lorenzoni, the face vanishing in a cloud of gunsmoke. A horse leaping, a scimitar sweeping, and the Mamluk's head vanishing. '*Hazar-bash*'…!' *Al-Mansur.*

Charleville in hand, Rossy battered a path through the running pikemen of the Janissaries as they broke ranks. '*Anglais! Suivez-moi!*' *Follow me.*

The squares marched towards them at the double, diamond points driving into the fleeing ranks of Albanians, Levantines and Turks, caught on their exposed flank. Caron was a dead weight on his shoulder and Hazzard fell to one knee, trying to pull him, the Lorenzoni out, but he could not reload. '*Anglais! Anglais!*' Rossy beside him, firing, drawing a pistol, aiming, firing. The thud of hooves behind and a voice calling over it all, '*Outta me way ye dam' mollies!*' It was Cook.

'*Jory*—' He saw them, the marines in their *shemaghs* and *binish*, firing in staggered ranks as Wayland had taught, a hand pointing to them: '*O'er 'ere! I got 'im!*' Thunder clapped and Hazzard rolled as shrapnel struck nearby – *Pettifer's blunderbuss*. An Albanian Janissary falling dead behind him, dropping, eyes wide. '*Sir, sir, this way!*'

Hazzard staggered, his eye seeing the sharp edge of masonry.

Steps.

Temple.

He fell against it as the square swarmed round them, a gun-carriage exploding, its field-gun twisting. He lost the marines, his voice hoarse, '*Jory!*' Rossy jostled him, shouting but he could not hear, Antonnais, St Michel, firing from the shoulder, Caron down but behind him as Hazzard fell, tumbling down the steps, looking for them among the running shapes. '*Jory!*' Rossy called out, but Hazzard did not hear, needing to find them. '*Anglais! Anglais restez ici!*' Stay here. Hazzard saw an arm held low from a horse, as if he were reaching down to offer help.

Mamluk.

Club.

The blow came, a shell bursting, a horse screaming, and the rider fell, arms, legs thrashing beside him. Hazzard was flung to the ground, pistol in hand, Caron reaching, clutching at his jacket to pull him into the shelter of a temple column.

'*Caron…*'

'*Anglais.*'

Satisfactory.

The day turned to night and blessed silence – deep, deep silence.

–

Faites attention, le général a dit.

    L'honneur de l'armée. Incroyable.

Oui hein. La coeur de lion, ce-ci. Faites attention…

A solemn tone, with reverence, but he could not understand the French, see nothing, the light too bright – then night again.

A deep voice and weightlessness.

'*Il n'est pas lourd.*'

Pigalle, carrying me. Must be. I'm not heavy.

Nelson arose before him: *a good man.*

A voice, demanding, a voice of authority – '*Where is he? Oú est-il alors?*' – and soon Delphine looked down, her face smudged with smoke and blood, her cool hand touching his cheek, her fingers gently prising open his eyes, leaning over him to peer into his mind.

A man beside her, looking down, long hair, bloodied shirtsleeves. '*Ceinture. Oui.*' He noticed Hazzard's eyes were open and tried English. 'The bones… the… ehh, ribs, yes? They have broken, but we fix them, hm?' He smiled. '*Je suis Larrey, chirurgien.*' He was a surgeon, called Larrey.

A camel grunted outside somewhere and Hazzard remembered the smell – a flying ambulance they called it: *ambulance volante.* Tightness round his chest. 'Can't move,' he said, but few words came out, his jaw numb, mouth swollen. '*Ca*'… '*oof…*'

Delphine nodded. 'Rest please, William.'

Shouts outside: *Jory?*

'*We can take 'im to our ship—*'

'*His back, le dos, compris, m'sieur? He cannot be moved. We have best chir'geons in the world, m'sieur. Can your ship docteur do this? Can he? No.*'

Then the deep French voice again. '*Eh, Jean Bull, we make him safe.*'

Pigalle.

Delphine's voice outside, low and quick, reassuring.

Hours passed in moments. The clanking of equipment – *medical instruments,* he wondered. Then soon after, a rattling scabbard, boots, a voice. '*Comment fait-il? Survivrai?*'

How is he? Will he survive?

And a rapid, garbled response. '*Oui, oui, mon général, on a besoin seulement de temps.*'

We need only time.

He understood. Delphine leaned over again, her hand stroking his face, his hair, something numb – *bandage.* 'A message to Sir Sidney,' she said, but in French, and he had understood that as well. 'And your Sergeant Cook, and the others, all well, released by General Kléber…'

She looked up at some disturbance and moved away, in deference to someone else. Into his vision came another: a wild shock of greying hair atop a strong face, broad whiskers to his jaw, high collar, dust on the gold epaulettes and a sash over his blue coat, a sense of power, the smell of horses, bun oil and powder, blood on his cuffs.

Kléber.

'They tell me you will live,' he said, and Hazzard blinked in reply. 'Perhaps walk again. They tell me you tried to prevent the battle, met Yussuf. They tell me you disobeyed your orders, to save my greatest *chef-major*. His men sit outside, to keep you safe.' He shook his head, not in the slightest conflicted or confused. 'I give you the highest commendation. But that is higher still.'

With that, he looked to the surgeon, Larrey, and rose with his gloves and orders and dust and blood on his cuffs, and went out, the boots clumping, the spurs clanking. The tent darkened as a flap was lowered, and Hazzard slept amid dreams of thunder.

—

With the new morning had come the warmth of early summer. Hazzard had spent weeks in a benign open arrest in Kléber's residence, the palace of the former Mamluk statesman Alfi Bikah Bey. Kléber had taken what he needed from Bonaparte's abandoned house of Muhammad Bey al-Elfi's, and moved to more discreet quarters in a quieter district of the city.

With the advent of summer, blossom had burst everywhere, his world now scented by orange, lemon, jacaranda and tamarind, the waving fronds calming in the northerly breeze form the Nile nearby. Caron walked with him most days, the older man now in a state of semi-retirement, each enjoying the quietude of a peculiar private peace.

The Battle of Heliopolis, or El Matariyyah as many called it, had not lasted much longer after Hazzard's fall beneath the charging Mamluk: the Janissaries, leaderless, routed and cut off, had scattered into the main bulk of the army, equally unprepared to face the French artillery, breaking their ranks, the vast majority of the conscripted levy running, leaving the field to the Ottoman elite with no support. The *Nizam-i Djedid* had closed round Osman and Nassif, and withdrawn to protect Yussuf Pasha on the retreat and fight a rearguard action – but they had heard nothing of Reiz. Kléber had been true to his word: he had sent Yussuf's army nearly as far as Syria. France, he had told them some time later over dinner, had lost six hundred men – Yussuf, six thousand.

After the explosion of the gun-carriage, Cook and the marines had been cut off from Hazzard and the temple steps, fighting off stray Ottoman Bashi-Bazouk skirmish troops and Mamluks with the Tarabin, until French dragoons challenged them: the marines were taken to the field hospital as prisoners, Delphine acting as guarantor. Few escaped without wounds: Tariq, Napier and Cochrane had taken sword-strokes and broken bones, but Pettifer and Warnock had taken the worst hits to the back and shoulders, and been put into surgery under Larrey before release. When Hazzard was brought in by the Alphas with Caron, the story became clear to Generals Friant and Kléber. When the surgeon explained that Hazzard could not be moved for days, perhaps weeks, Kléber did not hesitate to ensure his recovery and guarantee his safety. Satisfied, albeit reluctantly, Cook took the news back to Sir Sidney Smith on the *Tigre* with the remainder of 9 Company.

Cairo had risen in revolt, stirred by the proximity of Yussuf Pasha's forces, the mob running riot, led by Yussuf's son Nassif Pasha, and a handful of Ottoman officers who had entered the city during the battle. Strapped to a plank of wood to stabilise his back for hours a day for the first weeks of his hospitalisation, Hazzard heard the cannon booming as the city was bombarded. Resistance had broken after a month, and Hazzard had taken on the Mamluk fatalism of those around him – of one who recognised what he could change, and what he could not.

Insha'allah.

God willing.

Larrey had later applied gentle traction to Hazzard's legs and got him moving once again; soon he was standing with braces to his lower back until these, too, were discarded. Hazzard had leaned on a single crutch padded under his left arm, spending his days of recuperation in the gardens, in a strange haze of mild opiate and Egyptian *hashish*.

He had healed, eventually needing only a walking-stick, his broken ribs knitted, his knee still strapped tight for support, and his face stitched neatly from the hairline to the jaw – by Delphine, as it happened, who tended him every few days, Larrey and Desgenettes personally marking his progress.

It was with a numb irony that he learned Lord Keith had recanted, insisting he now would uphold the Convention of El-'Arish, and move to evacuate French forces from Egypt. Hazzard had acted as liaison between Kléber's staff and Smith's visiting naval envoys from the blockade – but still reported what he could: French troop dispositions, strengths at coastal forts, anything and everything he could pick up to assist the plans to evacuate the French forces. Hazzard also conveyed the delightful news that Dideron and Peraud had been sent out to administer Upper Egypt together, with Kléber's hopes that neither would return. The naval envoys informed him likewise that Cook and 9 Company were enjoying much-deserved recuperation on Cyprus, at Sir Sidney's expense. There abounded a springtime freshening after a long, drawn-out winter. The two-year desert war, for what it had been, seemed at last to be over.

On that day in June, he and Caron had stopped for a drink in the gardens in their usual spot, beneath the long drooping leaves of a giant strelitzia, brought from the Cape of Good Hope. The old sergeant-major looked better than Hazzard could remember, but still worn, the eyes longing for home. 'What awaits you at Aix?' Hazzard asked him.

'Ah,' said Caron, waggling his hand. 'The stable, perhaps, some horses, perhaps, hm? We know nothing of what is still there, any of us.' He shrugged. 'So we never talk of it, do we?'

'No.' Hazzard thought of St Jude's, his uncle, the Reverend Thomas Hazzard. According to a letter from Clarke, Hazzard's friend at Jesus College, Cambridge, the old curate was on a slow decline, often found wandering among the gardens, lost, or hoping to find Sarah and Hazzard in the wood, or by the river, thinking they had married after all. The tenants affectionately nicknamed him Old King Georgie, and were 'keeping the increasingly popular mad-doctors away'. Caron was right: he had no idea of what might await him, and no, they never did speak of such things: it betokened hope and its sad counterpart.

They heard voices along the colonnaded path that ran beside the gardens. Hazzard knew it was Kléber. The general had just lunched with Damas, his Chief of Staff, and Hazzard had now met them all, the meetings as curious as that aboard Bonaparte's flagship when he had encountered the *savants* for the first time. It seemed that, with the renewed negotiations, Hazzard was not seen as an enemy.

Kléber appeared from behind a tamarind, in shirtsleeves on the warm day, as many of them were, relaxed and at ease in the gardens.

With Kléber was Protain, a bespectacled architect and *littéraire* of Bonaparte's *Institut d'Égypte*, and Kléber's very good friend, walking-stick in hand, often seen in his company. Hazzard assumed they spoke of the new construction works they had begun, a subject close to Kléber's heart – other than the ribald caricatures he drew of Bonaparte at boisterous dinners.

'Trouble,' murmured Caron, 'she has found us again.' And they chuckled.

Trouble seemed far away. The sound of clicking heels brought Hazzard to attention, and he saw Delphine, not in her gown or apron, but in a fine pale cotton dress, flowered and decorated in the Turkish style. He had come to rely upon her kindness, more than perhaps he should, he knew, for one day it must end – but this fact only heightened the intensity of his feelings. He got to his feet, even the walking-stick now a memory.

'*Messieurs*,' she said sternly, 'what do you think you are doing in the heat of the afternoon?'

'Having chilled Meursault on a fine day,' replied Caron rebelliously.

Hazzard kissed her hand. '*Madame*.'

She smiled and Caron got to his feet. 'I shall leave you both, for now I must rest—'

But his words were cut off as they saw Kléber and Protain enter the gardens. Both Caron and Hazzard watched them as an Egyptian merchant or labourer, threadbare with poverty, possibly one of the construction workers, moved towards them in supplication. Protain tried to shoo him away back to his work, but when he failed, turned about to get a guard. The man knelt to Kléber, to take his hand and kiss it.

There was a sudden shout from Protain as the man sprang at Kléber, stabbing him again and again in the chest, the face, the abdomen. Protain beat at him with his stick, crying out, '*Au secours! Au secours! Le général!*' Help, help.

Staring, incredulous, Hazzard tried to run to them, his legs heavy as concrete, as if in a nightmare, unable to move any faster – Caron ran ahead, dragoons rushing in, boots crunching on the gravel and sand on the paving stones, as Kléber fell into Protain's arms.

Hazzard reached them, the assailant gone, Caron dropping to support Kléber. 'That way!' gasped Protain, and Hazzard followed the dragoon troopers down the path. Somewhere a woman cried out, and Hazzard saw her, on a flat rooftop nearby, pointing, the dragoons shouting, following her lead. Hazzard stumbled after them as fast as he could, and they found the man, sheltering under the shrubs. *'Par ici! Je lui tiens!'* I have him.

He was shaking, the maddened face staring into his, a young face. *The brother with the gold*, he thought as the dragoons hauled him upright, pinning his arms, the bloody knife clattering to his feet. Hazzard shook him, *'Kim? Kim?'* Who are you?

'Sultan…' gasped the man, his head lolling, *'K-kebr…'*

The dragoons dragged the assailant to the scene of the crime, and Hazzard found Caron cradling Kléber's bloody head, a deep gash in his face, one cheek torn open, his shirt cut to pieces by the attack, his throat choked with blood, eyes wide. Delphine tried to stem the flow from his chest-wound, shouting something – but he gasped, went rigid, then sagged in Protain's and Caron's arms.

Without knowing it Hazzard had seized the young man and was shaking him, his fists bunched in his stinking *kaftan*, *'Who are you? Who sent you?'*

'Go,' said Caron brusquely. 'Go, *mon vieux*. You have safe passage under his name, but if command goes to the wrong man, and an *anglais* was here…'

Hazzard knew he was right, and let go. He could smell *hashish* on the man's clothes, on his breath. Delphine looked at him over Kléber's bloodied body. 'William… hurry.'

Hazzard looked at the dragoon troopers and they nodded – *'Vite, m'sieur d'Azzard.'* The guard captain was marching towards them, and Hazzard went down the track taken by the assassin and found his Bombay Marine coat, left on the stone seat where he had, for a time, enjoyed peace. He pulled it on over his stiffened limbs and headed for the stables, where Walid knew him, and would prepare a horse.

He thought of Smith and the *Tigre*, Cook, and the waiting sea, and their old oath: *Get us safe to sea.* He thought of those last weeks with Masoud and his agents: of Kléber in Cairo, the search for Faiza and the young girl, Nefer, and the brother with the gold. When the weeks had passed, and Kléber had survived worse than any single assassin could bring, they had all put it from their minds – but he knew now that this, too, had been written.

As he climbed stiffly into the saddle and made his way to the gate, the world behind him began to burn once again, as enraged men shouted, troops running, their boots churning the timeless dust once again into war.

Historical Note

When General Jean-Baptiste Kléber galloped at full speed from Damietta to garrison HQ in Rosetta, expecting to meet Napoleon Bonaparte on an 'urgent matter', he found only a dossier and a letter of instruction awaiting him – in an empty office. Reading the letter, observers say, he gasped, incredulous at its contents: he was now the new *général en chef* of the *Armée d'Orient*. Bonaparte had already sailed from Alexandria, thirty kilometres away.

Some have suggested Bonaparte was afraid of Kléber, and had carefully arranged this deception to avoid a confrontation – with good reason: the leonine Kléber was absolutely furious. His loathing for Bonaparte would know no bounds, and his outrage comes verbatim from fellow officers: 'That *bugger* leaves us with his breeches full of *shit*. We shall go back to Europe and rub them in his face!'

The army was split between hopeful faith at Bonaparte's departure (to send reinforcements) and mutinous revolution. The army was bankrupt, exhausted, in rags, riddled with sickness and now abandoned. Kléber wanted nothing more than to get his boys back home. An honourable peace was the only course, and by no means unreasonable; despite the retreat from Acre, the *Armée d'Orient* remained undefeated in the field. The one man on the scene who could fix this for them all was William Sidney Smith.

For Sir Sidney the key was to broker the deal with the Ottomans personally. No independent peace could be permitted between the French and Ottoman Empire alone – Britain would have been left out of the spoils and, worse, could possibly have faced a newly allied enemy. He hoped that by extracting the French from Egypt virtually without British bloodshed he would not only earn glory for himself, but also ensure Britain's place in the proceedings. General Desaix and Citizen Poussielgue were invited to discuss terms aboard HMS *Tigre* at the end of 1799. The wheels of diplomacy began to turn.

But Troubridge was right: Kléber needed time. Yussuf Pasha had passed Gaza and now reached the border fortress of El-'Arish, with an army of sixty to eighty thousand (and, according to eyewitness accounts, a small duck pond). An officer was sent out from the fort to parley: this is the second time history encounters Lt Pierre François Xavier Bouchard. He was the engineer *savant* and aeronaut who had discovered the Rosetta Stone in July that year.

The value of this discovery cannot be overstated. This broken stele eventually provided the key to the history of Egypt and its treasures. Bouchard found it in the foundation ditch of the old fortress tower at Rosetta – after a brief analysis of its value with other local *savants*, he sailed in triumph up the Nile with the stone to the Institute in Cairo in August 1799, where the academics rushed to gather round it.

It was over a metre high, 76 cm wide, a massive 28 cm thick, and weighed three-quarters of a ton. Across its face were three bands of script, Greek at the bottom, cursive demotic Egyptian across the middle and, at the top, fourteen broken lines of incomprehensible hieroglyphs. No one had been able to read these secret signs since the last days of the priesthood under Rome. The *savants* calculated that if they could correlate the Greek script (which they could read) to the hieroglyphs at the top, they might solve the 2000-year mystery. Eventually, Jean-François Champollion cracked the code twenty-three years later. 'Egyptology' was born.

It was this same celebrated Bouchard who rode out to face the one-eyed Yussuf Pasha. But mutiny broke out in the fort, the men sacked the liquor stores and, incredibly, threw ropes over the walls to help the Ottomans climb in. Yussuf's army did just that. Bouchard was arrested, possibly for his own safety, but Yussuf and Major John Douglas (who was there as liaison officer) were too late to stop the massacre to come.

In the interests of peace, Kléber waived his right to vengeance for the slaughtered garrison – it was incomparable to the scale of French atrocities at Jaffa. Smith soon had his wish, and the three parties signed their Convention of El-'Arish on 24 January 1800. Smith duly sent a copy to London for ratification. He would be surprised at the response.

After reading an intercepted letter by Kléber to the Directory, complaining of the miserable and penniless position in Egypt, the British Cabinet refused the treaty, feeling the weakened enemy was ready to crumble. This initial refusal was despatched to Admiral Lord Keith as Commander of the Mediterranean Fleet. But after various appeals from Smith, London reconsidered, and eventually agreed. However, news of this about-face did not reach Keith in time. A fuse had been laid to a diplomatic powder-keg.

-

Napoleon Bonaparte's seizure of power was a seamless coup within a coup, the fruits of careful calculation by Bonaparte and his brother Lucien, and their supporters in Paris. The unfortunate Citizen Sieyès had no idea of the nature of the man he had chosen to tag along behind him. In the tumult of the assembly, Bonaparte did indeed cry out to the deputies, '*The revolution is over!*' There was a scuffle, and Bonaparte emerged from the mob bloodied on one cheek – the grenadiers set about the 'rebel' deputies, clearing the orangery of Château St-Cloud. The Republic was quite suddenly dead. The French Revolution had lasted some ten years.

Once in power, Bonaparte claimed that he wanted to rescue the army in Egypt but also that Kléber had more than enough men to protect the colony. His true intentions are unclear, but he would not have wanted Kléber to return and reveal how the hero of France had abandoned his army. The new 'First Consul' was damned either way. His delegation of the problem to Perrée might well have been his temporary solution.

-

The tale of HMS *Leander*, as told by Shepherd, is drawn from Admiralty records and the London *Gazette*. The 50-gun *Leander* under Captain Thompson outsailed and outgunned the 74-gun *Généreux* for several hours before eventually being dismasted and overcome by fire. The battle had cost the *Généreux* some 288 men, (100 killed and 188 wounded) compared to *Leander*'s 25 (some records raise this to 35 and 57 wounded).

Their small boats destroyed by gunfire, Captain Lejoille's prize crew had to swim to *Leander* to take command. They began to loot the personal possessions of their prisoners. When Lejoille at last arrived he did not stop it. 'It angers me,' he said, 'but the fact is we French are good at plundering.' The British and French press made full use of this propaganda.

Desperate for men at Corfu, Lejoille later demanded that *Leander* prisoners sign on in the French navy. Maintopman George Bannister is credited with the response from the rigging: 'No, you damned French rascal! Give us back our little ship, and we'll fight you again until we sink!' Shepherd's accounts of beatings could quite possibly be accurate, though likely later exaggerated. Yet the ship's carpenter was detained in Corfu for refusing to reveal the specifications of *Leander*'s mainmast.

Captains Thompson and Berry were acquitted with honour at the court-martial enquiry at Sheerness, and were rowed ashore to the sound of rousing cheers from the gathered fleet. The enquiry had been held aboard HMS *America*, Hazzard's old ship at the Cape in 1795.

Captain Lejoille did paint *Généreux*'s sails black and slipped through the Russian blockade at night; he was later killed off the Italian coast in an attack on Brindisi. The *Généreux* limped home and passed to a new captain: Cyprien Renaudin. Hazzard's assessment of his cool command was accurate. As a junior officer Renaudin had famously stayed aboard the sinking *Vengeur du Peuple*, trying to save the crew, just as Hazzard had remembered.

–

At the crossroads of East and West, Constantinople at this time was like Len Deighton's Cold War Berlin: a city of spies. Not surprising then that young Wayland was sent by Sir Sidney to keep his ear to the ground, and liaise with the talented Mr Stanford. Lord Elgin (of his infamous Marbles) was a dashing, educated Scots nobleman and former army officer, and a respected host at Timoni House. Intelligence archives make no mention of the unique Small Library, and operations were later moved to the new embassy built in gratitude by the sultan for Nelson's victory at the Nile.

The ambiguous nature of Madeleine was the curse of the French émigré at the time: was she friend or foe? Royalist French operatives, though sheltering in Britain, would still have had their own intelligence agenda, as Madeleine had. However, Madeleine's bona fides from the French Committee were real – the Home Office created this secret think-tank of exiled French officials and ministers to analyse the actions of the Revolutionary government in Paris. They filed their reports to Sir William Wickham, head of the bureau which would later become MI5 and MI6.

After the first battle with the *Généreux*, when Hazzard and the *Volpone* headed round the northwest of Sicily to the ancient capital of Palermo, they discovered the decaying state of the kingdom of Naples, which ruled the south of Italy and Sicily. Palermo was much as described, beset by privation, filled with refugees fled from Naples after the French-backed revolution.

This is a dark time in Nelson's career, and many historians have wrestled with its disturbing facts. Once the revolutionaries surrendered in Naples, Nelson had sailed his battle-fleet into the bay and counter-manded a British captain's agreement with the rebels, and forced them to remain in sweltering transports with little food or water.

For interfering in the affairs of a foreign power Nelson fell foul of the Admiralty and baffled his captains, who wanted to send their captives back to France as was honourably agreed. But Nelson's apparent cruelty was born partly by his affection and dedication to the royal court and his adherence to protocol: the King of Naples had not assented to the release of captives, therefore they were not released. One of the rebels, Francesco Caracciolo, Duke di Brenza was given over to a summary court by Nelson on his flagship and hanged like a common criminal from the yardarm. The Royal Navy was shocked.

Nelson had suffered a head wound at the Nile, and some have suggested a form of concussion as an explanation, that 'he was not in his right mind', and struggled with a continual malaise, consistent with such injuries. Considering the consternation among his colleagues who knew him so well, this could be an explanation. But there was something else: after the Nile Nelson had been idolised by the Neapolitans, feasted, celebrated, worshipped, and raised to the title of Duke of Bronte. The king and court of Naples had shown him far more affection than the Royal Navy had, which had passed him over for promotion twice, to Sir Sidney in the Levant and to Lord Keith as Fleet Commander.

Chief among his worshippers in Palermo was the very attractive Lady Hamilton. Wounded, Nelson then stayed in Palermo for convalescence, and flatly refused to go on blockade duty off Malta under Keith. He lived with the Hamiltons throughout – and enjoyed a long affair with Emma Hamilton, while her cuckolded husband Sir William ignored it.

The Royal Navy blamed Emma alone for keeping Nelson ashore. One evening at a court dinner, British officers watched in disgust as a Turkish general drew his sword to display the dried blood of French prisoners – Emma Hamilton allegedly thrilled at this, kissing the bloodied steel lasciviously, as the appalled officers cried 'shame, shame!'

Hazzard's experience at this same dinner gives us an alternative interpretation, that perhaps she was keeping the peace at a difficult diplomatic moment, the tale embellished to her detriment. She held a high position in court as adviser to the queen and nurse to the young prince. Ousted with Sir William from their luxurious properties in Naples, she was also as vehement an anti-revolutionary as any courtier. It seems Nelson was, as well.

—

Admiral Perrée's convoy from Toulon was shadowed by the 38-gun frigate HMS *Success*, under Captain Shuldham Peard. When the convoy passed Sicily, the news went to Lord Keith and he made his plans accordingly (without Nelson). But someone, at some point, took the news to Nelson in Palermo. Perhaps it really had been Hazzard; unlike Keith, he knew that Nelson would want the *Généreux* above all others, as 'the one that got away'.

The admiral's flag was raised on HMS *Foudroyant* for the first time in months. With *Audacious* and *Northumberland*, they gave chase. When they sighted the distant enemy off Malta, his agitation was evident: Berry really did warn his lieutenant that Nelson was 'working his fin', (flapping his arm amputated at the elbow) and Nelson's aggressive shouts dramatised here come from verbatim accounts: according to Midshipman Parsons, he did threaten to knock the QM at the wheel 'off his perch' and declared that the *Généreux* must surrender to him alone – he was particularly concerned that the *Northumberland* would get there first.

Flying downwind at Perrée as Nelson's ships fought their way to windward, HMS *Success* took her chance and engaged the French flotilla single-handed. She charged at the heavy *Généreux*, the escorting frigates and transports scattering. They had seen Nelson and his ships approaching from ahead, but perhaps they had taken fire from the *Volpone* from astern.

The raking broadsides by HMS *Success* ravaged the quarterdeck, splinters blinding Perrée. He called out, 'It is nothing my friends! Let us continue with our work!' But the second broadside tore his leg off at the hip. In the confusion, the officers managed to return fire on *Success*, and disabled her, but too late. *Généreux* was dismasted by Nelson himself in the *Foudroyant*, closing fast. For Nelson, honour was satisfied. Keith had missed the battle.

Some in the Navy were appalled that Perrée had broken his parole, (he had been captured by a Captain Markham, whose less able younger cousin had crossed swords with Hazzard in *Napoleon's Run*) – but that, in dying, he had 'regained some of his honour'. Those who had seen Perrée in action in Egypt, as Hazzard and Cook had done, would have been kinder to such a fearless and dutiful officer.

It has puzzled commentators of the Battle of the Malta Convoy why the French would resupply their besieged garrison in Valletta and then give them another three thousand mouths to feed. The solution could be just as Hazzard had guessed and Bonaparte had hoped: that the convoy had two purposes, to resupply Valletta and to transport the men onwards to Egypt. If those three thousand had reached Kléber, it could later have tipped the scales against the British.

–

It was roughly at this time that matters with Yussuf and his army came to a head. Keith received Smith's first version of the Convention of El-'Arish and the Cabinet refusal. Incensed by Smith's proposal to feed and clothe the enemy and convey them comfortably homeward in British ships, Keith sent an offensive rant direct to Kléber, demanding in the most insulting language that his troops lay down their arms and surrender unconditionally. At the same time, the host of Yussuf Pasha reached the outskirts of Cairo. The powder-keg exploded.

Historian Nicholas the Turk claims when Kléber read Keith's letter he let out a roar 'like an infuriated camel'. Kléber's roar would have shivered the Nile. Within forty-eight hours he cancelled all measures taken for the evacuation, notified Yussuf that the treaty was now terminated, and mobilised the remnants of the outraged French army and marched them north to meet the Ottomans before dawn.

Nearly all commentators agree that Admiral Lord Keith and Yussuf Pasha cost Egypt, Britain, Turkey and France a reasonable peace, and the lives of thousands in bloody battles. Yet, what of the machinations of the Admiralty? After the Texel campaign, Britain had no fresh taskforce to send to Egypt. They really were unready for a sudden peace. Perhaps Blake and others had taken a hand in the delay of communications to Keith, leaving the dour admiral to ensure France and the Ottomans would never become allies. If so, the plan worked.

Kléber vented his fury on the army of Yussuf Pasha at Heliopolis. Barely nine thousand French crashed into Yussuf's unwieldy army of between forty and sixty thousand, and threw them clear across the Sinai Peninsula to the Syrian border, in arguably the greatest victory of the campaign. Kléber then put down a new revolt in Cairo, incited by Nassif Pasha. Peace took another two months to fall upon the capital.

What is described next is how Solimann al-Halabi (of Aleppo) brought down General Jean-Baptiste Kléber. This young Syrian student, some say attending the Al-Azhar in Cairo, had tailed Kléber throughout the day, even to lunch with General Damas. He followed him to the palace of Elfi Bey, where he was mistaken at first for a labourer among the construction works, going unseen and unchecked. Kléber appeared, discussing the new works with friend and architect Jean Constantin Protain. Solimann approached them, his hand out. Deciding he was a beggar, Protain turned to find a sentry to get rid of him.

It is generally considered that the assassin was hired by Al-Djezzar, the Butcher of Acre, but this is unclear; though Nefer from Faiza's brothel might well have existed, we have no evidence. What is certain is that when Solimann knelt to take Kléber's hand, he pounced with a dagger, stabbing Kléber violently in the chest, abdomen, arm and face. Protain ran back to them and beat at Solimann with his stick, until Solimann ran off. There were no guards nearby and help arrived too late – in our case in the shape of Caron, Hazzard and Delphine. Soldiers were alerted by drums and the manhunt was on. Solimann was spotted hiding in the bushes of the gardens by a woman on a nearby rooftop, and he was arrested. But Kléber was dead.

As a bizarre footnote to Kléber's story, on the same day in Italy, his greatest friend and colleague, General Louis Antoine Desaix, was killed by a stray musket-ball at his moment of victory at the Battle of Marengo. The names of Kléber and Desaix live on in Paris and elsewhere to this day.

The strange peace between the British and French, who were soon to be carried home, was shattered. The new *général en chef* to follow was not a Bonaparte, or a Desaix or Kléber. Instead, he was an inexperienced, blustering oaf, despised by both colleagues and the rank and file: *Général de division* Jacques 'Abdallah' Menou would take the reins of the fragile colony – and thousands would pay the price.

Jonathan Spencer, 2024

Acknowledgements

I would like to thank the esteemed Professor Carlo Knight of Naples for his insights into Nelson's time during the Neapolitan revolution of 1799; Grace Sprocket for her technical knowledge; Alistair France for research memoranda; interpreters and transliterators Muhammad Wafa, Essam Edgard Samné, and former Naval Intelligence officer Hassan Eltaher; and my editor at Canelo, Craig Lye.

Jonathan Spencer, 2024